THE WAY OF LIGHT

Storm Constantine

THE WAY OF LIGHT

GOLLANCZ
London

Copyright © Storm Constantine 2001

The right of Storm Constantine to be identified as the author
of this work has been asserted by her in accordance with
the Copyright, Designs and Patents Act 1988.

This edition published in Great Britain in 2001 by

Gollancz
An imprint of the Orion Publishing Group
Orion House, 5 Upper St Martin's Lane, London WC2H 9EA

A CIP catalogue record for this book is available
from the British Library

Typeset at The Spartan Press Ltd,
Lymington, Hants

Printed in Great Britain by
Clays Ltd, St Ives plc

ACKNOWLEDGEMENTS

As usual, there are many people I'd like to thank, who supported me through writing this book and who have helped in different ways. Thanks to my husband, Jim Hibbert, for announcing, apropos of nothing, a twist for the end of this book; to Deb Benstead and Eloise Coquio for late-night workshops and world-building visions; to Andy Collins, Graham Phillips and Paul Weston, for their knowledge and willingness to share it; to my editor, Jo Fletcher, for her continuing thorough and inspired appraisal of my work and her ability to pull my writing back from a rarefied universe and pick up inappropriate use of the word 'seem'; to my agent, Robert Kirby, for all that he has done and continues to do in representing my work; to Yvan Cartwright for his web-mastery and the time he denotes to it while working hard on his PhD; to Claire Cartwright, for promoting my work, but also for her brilliant sense of humour; to Caroline Wise and all at Atlantis Book Shop for their staunch support; to Vikki Lee France and Steve Jeffery of my information service, Inception, for their friendship and continued good work. Finally, I'd like to thank all those who have listened patiently when they haven't had a clue what I've been talking about, and to those who've offered advice when they have, to my close friends and family (who haven't yet been mentioned), one and all fab dudes: John Bristow, Norma Bristow, Steve Chilton, Mark Hewkin, Dot and Harold Hibbert, Deb Howlett, Paul Kesterton, Steve Nash, Tigger Nelson, Linda Price, Bettina Rhodes, Jon Sessions, Ash Smith, Karen Townsend, Paula Wakefield, Freda Warrington and Steve Wilson.

Storm Constantine's official web site:

  http://www.stormconstantine.com

Inception
The Storm Constantine Information Service
  c/o Vikki Lee France and Steve Jeffery
  44 White Way
  Kidlington
  Oxon OX5 2XA

Email: Peverel@aol.com

This book is dedicated to Graham Phillips,
who first led us on the quest and
revealed to us the secret territories.

CHAPTER ONE

The Prisoner of Cawmonel

Rain whipped down like furious tears upon a landscape of bleak curving moors, where spines of rock humped out of the earth resembling, through the deluge, enormous petrified reptiles. Winter. Darkness. Arthritic trees bent away from the wind. Along the wide flat road a horse came: galloping, galloping. The rider's coat flew out sodden behind him. His hair was a drenched rag. The horse's nostrils flared wide, as if struggling to gasp the last of its breath. Its neck worked madly, the legs a blur, throwing up a glutinous spray of mud. And ahead, the great cyclopean edifice reared like a giant's curse against the darkness: too dense a black, too severe.

There were lights in the fortress, dim pale gleams barely seen through the rain. The windows were narrow, high up, and there were few of them. The only entrance was via a moat and a looming portcullis, held up on gargantuan chains, from which hoary beards of lichen hung down. The rider brought his exhausted mount to a halt before it. The animal pranced and reared, slipped. Its limbs shuddered.

'Aye!' called the rider. 'Guardsmen, open the gates!'

He was not sure his voice could be heard through the tumult, but he felt eyes upon him. They would not recognise him, not yet. A face appeared at a window, which was pushed out against the elements.

'Who hails?'

'General Palindrake, Dragon Lord of the Splendifers. Give me entrance. I have the emperor's seal.'

There was a pause, as if a host of watchers clustered at the narrow pane, looking down. What would Lord Valraven Palindrake want here in this wilderness?

There was no spoken response but presently the chains began to scream and slowly the drawbridge rose and the portcullis descended. Below it, spears of rain stabbed the black water of the moat. A stench of bogs arose from it, perhaps tainted by waste from the fortress.

Valraven rode over the soaked boards of the bridge. His horse's head hung low now, for his hands were slack upon the reins. He passed beneath the entrance arch and was then enfolded by the fortress. Rain came down into the yard beyond, but somehow less fiercely. Men rushed about, wearing waterproof capes and enveloping hats. Some ran forward. Valraven dismounted and handed his mount into their care.

A captain hurried down the steps on the inside of the wall from the guardhouse above the gate. His coat was dry, indicating he had only recently put it on. He looked flustered and his formal bow was jerky. 'Lord Palindrake, you were not expected.'

'No,' said Valraven. 'Take me inside.'

'At once,' said the captain. 'Welcome to Cawmonel, my lord.'

They crossed the yard and entered the main building opposite. Cawmonel Castle had once been the seat of a now extinct Magravandian ducal family. It had become something else. Not a prison, exactly, because there were no dank cells, no dungeons that were used. It was termed a secure house. Luxurious, perhaps, in comparison to the Skiterings, the imperial gaol in Magrast, but it was a prison nonetheless. Troublesome people were put there – people who had done nothing wrong, particularly, but who might do. People who, for various reasons (amongst them royal connections), could not be thrown into the Skiterings. Cawmonel was not that far from civilisation: Magrast was only a few hours' ride away. Yet standing in that courtyard, Valraven felt as if he'd left the world he knew behind and had come to a barbaric corner of the country; perhaps this was because there were no towns nearby, and the only other inhabitants of the landscape were tough little sheep and the small, dark people who tended them.

Inside the black walls, a semblance of noble life remained. There were tapestries upon the walls, dark red rugs underfoot. A fire burned in the hallway, in a hearth that stretched fifteen feet up the wall. Heat blasted out of it. Valraven took off his coat and handed it to the servant who had materialised at his side. His long black hair stuck to his face, his shoulders.

The captain bowed again. 'I'm Sanchis, my lord, overseer of this establishment. How may I help you?'

What he really wanted to ask was: what in Madragore's name are you doing here? But that would have been impolite.

'I am here to interview one of your guests,' said Valraven.

2

The captain looked puzzled, but nodded. 'Of course.' A pause. 'Might I ask who?'

'Tayven Hirantel,' said Valraven. 'He *is* here, isn't he?'

Sanchis appeared embarrassed now. No one was supposed to know Hirantel was there, not even the Dragon Lord. Eventually he said, 'Yes. Would you care for a hot meal or a bath before you interview him?'

'Take me to him at once. You can have your people bring food to me there.'

'Very well, my lord. This way.'

Sanchis led Valraven up the wide stone stairway and along a maze of corridors. The walls were raw black stone and looked as if they should have been studded with reeking torches, but instead, oil lamps flickered mildly against the stone. There were many closed doors, once family bedrooms perhaps, but now ornate cells. Valraven had no idea who else might be secreted behind them. People often disappeared from court.

Sanchis jogged up another flight of stairs and turned into a passage at the top. Here a pair of guards were stationed before a heavy wooden door. They spotted Sanchis and stood hurriedly to attention, staring straight ahead. 'Unlock the door,' Sanchis said to them. The guards glanced at Valraven curiously, then one of them took a key from a jangling bunch at his belt and applied it to the lock. The door creaked open, just a small way. The guard held his arm across it, as if some maddened beast inside might try to make a run for it.

'You may leave me now,' said Valraven. 'I would like a dinner of roasted fowl, with vegetables. A flagon of wine, and some cake.'

Sanchis looked uncertain, perhaps thinking Valraven was mocking him. The Dragon Lord wanted cake? He ducked his head. 'It will be attended to, my lord.'

'Excuse me,' Valraven said politely to the guards, who stood to the side. He walked between them and pushed the door wide.

There was a flurry of movement as a gang of pages fled from the threshold. Valraven stepped over it. The room beyond was large, sumptuous, if rather archaic in its décor. It was lit by the glow of a fire and two mellow oil lamps. A man in his late twenties stood stooped beside a table, as if frozen in the act of rising from his seat. He was dressed in loose-fitting tunic and trousers of soft grey wool – plain, but not homely. His long pale hair was confined at his neck, tendrils of it falling free to frame his face. That face had beguiled princes and kings. It was older now and had lost the soft prettiness of youth, but Tayven Hirantel was still beautiful, his eyes almond-shaped and dark, his cheekbones high. He had the look of a cornered animal. 'Good evening, Tayven,' Valraven said. 'I trust you are well.'

3

Tayven said nothing, perhaps silenced by shock.

Valraven closed the door behind him. He glanced at the wide-eyed young servants, crouched like kittens, half terrified, half fascinated, against the furniture. 'Shoo!' he said to them, and they ran.

Tayven straightened up. 'Are you here to kill me?' he asked.

Valraven sauntered forward. 'Why would you think that?'

'Who sent you?'

'Does someone have to send me here?'

Tayven frowned. 'No, but . . . '

'No one sent me,' Valraven said. 'I'm here of my own volition. The empress has taken great pains to conceal you, but my intelligence network is second to none. I'm here to learn why you are here.'

Tayven sat down. 'I'm a prisoner, that's all there is to it. I presume my family has paid dearly to keep me alive.'

'I don't think so. No one is supposed to know you are here. How did you get here?'

'Under armed guard.'

'You'll have to be more specific. Who took you into custody? Where did it happen?'

Tayven did not answer. Valraven could tell he was wondering how much he should say and how truthful he should be.

Valraven sat down at the table opposite him. 'Very well. I will make an offering first. Merlan Leckery sent word to me from Mewt that you had failed to keep an appointment with him and Lord Maycarpe. When, after a few days, they realised you had really gone missing, Maycarpe started asking questions, backed by coin.'

Tayven uttered a caustic laugh. 'Is that so? I'd believed Maycarpe was involved in it.'

'That's doubtful,' Valraven said. 'Maycarpe and Merlan managed to discover you'd been taken against your will by unidentified men. More than that was impossible to learn. All avenues of enquiry dried up, but somewhere along the way, the name of the Empress Tatrini was whispered. Merlan wasn't sure about this connection, but asked me to help look for you. It has taken me valuable time to do so, and has cost me dear. Mouths were tightly shut, almost beyond price. Eventually, my enquiries became enough of an irritant for Tatrini to tell me personally of your whereabouts. She gave me a feasible reason for your arrest. Unfortunately, because of the clandestine nature of your work in Cos some years ago for Prince Almorante, you are still under suspicion of the attempted assassination of Prince Bayard. Tatrini could give me no reason for the secrecy, though, or why she hasn't sent you to trial. I guessed she believed she could benefit from having you in her clutches, and she virtually confirmed as much, without actually saying so. You must know something of use to her. Emperor Leonid is dying, and this is a sensitive time in Magrast. No one knows what will happen when he goes.'

'His sons will fight for the crown,' Tayven said. 'That is what will happen and everyone knows it.'

'Where do your allegiances lie nowadays?'

Tayven pulled a sour face. 'With none of them. When I was younger, I was naïve enough to go along with Almorante's schemes. After I was left for dead in Cos, I abandoned my Magravandian heritage. Leonid is not my emperor, nor will any of his sons ever be.'

'Then what does Tatrini want with you?' Valraven put his head to one side. 'You are here for a reason, Tayven. Never think otherwise.'

Tayven gestured with one hand. 'Perhaps they think I am still part of the game. But I'm not.'

'Aren't you?'

Tayven glanced at Valraven furtively, an expression he quickly smothered.

Yes, Valraven thought, *wonder now just how much Merlan has told me.*

'You obviously think I'm still a player,' Tayven said, 'otherwise you wouldn't be here. I don't believe you looked for me simply to oblige Merlan Leckery.'

'Why not? Lord Maycarpe, as Magravandian governor in Mewt, is a man of great status. Merlan is his esteemed assistant. Perhaps they have good reason to fear you being a captive of the empress. You have powerful friends, Tayven, like it or not. I know you've been an agent of Maycarpe's for some years now. He found you in Cos when Almorante's people failed. I think he must have offered you the chance of revenge against those of the royal family for whom you bear grudges. Am I right?'

'Maycarpe is always careful with words. He would never promise such a thing. How could he, anyway? He will ally with whichever prince wins the crown. As will you.'

Valraven laughed. 'Tayven, you do me an injustice. I am sworn to Prince Gastern, the rightful inheritor.'

'Then you are a fool, Lord Palindrake.' Tayven got up, shoving his chair aside. He went to the fire, held out his hands to it. 'There will be no winners, only survivors. I opted out of the game, but they've dragged me back. Why? I'm not that important. I was Almorante's spy, sent to warm the beds of those who might let interesting words drop from lust-slackened lips. That was many years ago.'

'And since, you have been close to the exiled Cossic king and his sister, Princess Helayna. The Malagashes would dearly like to get their paws on Helayna.'

'Why would they bother? She barely has any troops since her brother accepted Tatrini's bait and went as her lap dog to reclaim his throne in Tarnax. Reclaim! What a joke. He is Tatrini's creature now. Cos is hers.'

Valraven stroked his chin thoughtfully. 'If this infighting you predicted occurs, Helayna might have more room for manoeuvre. Her support would still be valued by any of the young Malagash wolves. Should King Ashalan get a reasonable chance to fight for Cos's independence, I'm sure he'd still be prepared to try for it. He's not that tamed, Tayven. He's merely waiting, as are many.'

'Not me.'

'But you are in Maycarpe's employ. That's hardly not being involved.'

Valraven could tell Tayven felt as if he was being backed into a corner. How much would it take to get him to talk? 'What was the nature of your employment? What intelligence did you supply to Darris Maycarpe?'

'I was in Cos, part of the resistance, close to Ashalan and Helayna. Maycarpe wanted to keep abreast of what was going on.'

'He hardly needed you for that. Ashalan was desperate for allies. He knew Maycarpe was a slippery fish, but he'd have still welcomed the alliance. I think you were rather more than a go-between. You did other work, didn't you? I think it involved talents other than those of a courtesan. Almorante knew of those talents, didn't he?'

'You have a fertile imagination,' Tayven said, his back still turned. 'I had my skills, which I learned from Almorante in Magrast and had to turn to good use to keep myself alive. Maycarpe paid well.'

'You didn't need his money. You were sheltered by the Cossics, clearly held dear by Ashalan and Helayna. You can't fool me.'

A knock came at the door and servants entered, bearing a meal for the Dragon Lord. Valraven was silent as the servants puffed a sail of ice-white cloth over the table and laid out the cutlery, arranging it carefully to please him. He was impressed the meal had arrived so quickly. The best restaurants in Magrast were not as prompt. Covered dishes were opened with reverence to reveal their treasures. Valraven's mouth watered as the savoury scent of succulent roast fowl slathered in clove and ginger sauce wafted to his nose. Once the servants had bowed and departed, Valraven applied himself to his meal. 'They keep you fed well,' he said, in between mouthfuls. 'I must dine here more often.'

Tayven was watching him from beside the fire. 'I would rather eat frugally, in possession of my freedom. What do you want from me?'

Valraven took a sip of deep red wine, holding it in his mouth, enjoying the bouquet. Sanchis had a good kitchen, no doubt of that. How fortunate to arrive in time for dinner. He swallowed. 'I want the truth from you.'

'There are many truths.'

Valraven put down his goblet, turned it slowly upon the tablecloth. 'Indeed, indeed. The one I'm interested in is what you really did for Darris Maycarpe, because I am convinced the reason why Tatrini brought you here lies in that truth. I tried to help you once before, Tayven. Merlan told you of that, didn't he? But I was too late. Circumstances differ now, and I am a different man, thanks partly to Merlan Leckery. I know he'll have made you aware of what happened to me in Caradore some years ago. See sense. You have only to gain from trusting me a little. We spoke briefly in Cos, remember? I have never doubted your importance.'

Tayven said nothing for some time. Valraven ignored him and continued to eat. He let the silence drag on, sensed the gradual change in its mood. As he was wiping his mouth with a napkin, his plate wiped clean of sauce, Tayven came to sit opposite him again.

'The only currency I have is information,' he said. 'What exactly will I gain from speaking to you? Can I leave here with you?'

Valraven put down his napkin. 'Unwise,' he said. 'You must be patient.'

'Then what?'

Valraven picked up a plate bearing a thick slab of yellow cake. Its vanilla scent reached towards him provocatively. How much Tayven had been like good food: a delight to the senses. People had wanted to gorge on him and they had. But the flavours, eventually, had become bitter. 'Tatrini won't kill you. She'd have already done so if that was her plan. Has she spoken to you, or sent anyone else to do so?'

'No,' Tayven replied. 'I've seen no one, and have been given no reason for my imprisonment. I don't think the people here know anything.' He glanced around the room. 'I suspect that is the case with most of the *guests* in this place.'

'Have you any suspicions as to the empress's true reason for bringing you here?'

The crackling of the fire was the only sound. Tayven stared at the table, his arms folded, pressed tightly against his chest. 'I have been here for four weeks and three days. I believe that Tatrini will play me, in whatever manner she deems fit, once Leonid dies. She could use me to discredit Almorante, bring up the alleged assassination attempt on Prince Bayard again. She might even use me against Bayard, or

7

Maycarpe. I don't know. I think I'm hanging on a fine thread, and my security is precarious at best. I don't want to be part of this. It doesn't concern me any more.'

Valraven reached out and took Tayven's chin in his hand, lifted his face. 'Is it possible Tatrini knows what you did for Maycarpe?'

Tayven jerked away. 'I have no idea. He may have told her himself for all I know.'

'It would help you considerably if you'd confide in me.'

'I have no proof of that. Tatrini might have sent you here. I'm not that stupid.'

Valraven raised an eyebrow.

Tayven rested his chin on a bunched fist. 'Very well. You might not like the answer, but Maycarpe employed me to find Khaster Leckery, Merlan's brother. He did not die in Cos as everyone believes.'

Valraven kept his expression bland, but his mouth was dry as he spoke. 'What interest did Maycarpe have in Khaster?'

'I cannot tell you that,' Tayven said.

'Were you successful?' Valraven enquired.

Tayven stared at him for a few moments. 'Yes,' he said at last.

'Where is Khaster?'

'In Cos. Like me, he has cut himself off from the past. We have no contact, in case you were wondering.'

'So, if he didn't die in battle as Bayard claims, what happened to him? Was he with you in Cos, with Ashalan?'

'No. He fled to Breeland and became a hermit. What more is there to say?'

'Quite a lot, I imagine. You found him in Breeland? Yet now he's in Cos? No longer a hermit, then?'

'I found him in Breeland, yes. And I imagine he went to Cos to hide himself again. He is not the man you once knew. He hates you, Lord Palindrake, with every fibre of strength he possesses.'

An idea was forming in Valraven's mind. Khaster, his own brother-in-law, hated him. To someone who wanted to curb the Dragon Lord's actions, an enemy of that intensity might be of use. Was this Tatrini's game? Khaster had fled his life, but Valraven knew him too well, despite what Tayven implied Khaster had become. Khaster would still yearn to return home to Caradore. That would be the bait Tatrini would offer, Valraven was sure of it. That, and his own destruction, along with that of his sister, Pharinet, Khaster's wife, who'd been estranged from him long before his reported death. Valraven wondered whether he should warn Pharinet about this. 'Do you think Tatrini could be in contact with Khaster?'

Tayven laughed loudly. 'What? I hardly think so. Khaster detests the Malagashes more than I do.'

'More than he hates me?'

Tayven was still grinning. 'In about equal measure, I think. Don't worry. He won't ally with the empress to attack you. I told you, he's like me. He wants no part of the game. He certainly refused to play it Maycarpe's way. He's no use to any of the players, believe me.'

It appeared feasible, yet Valraven detected an urgency beneath Tayven's practised tone. It suggested Khaster was more useful to some people than Tayven was prepared to say. Tayven and Khaster had been lovers once. How much of what Valraven had heard tonight was true?

'So what will you give me?' Tayven said. 'What are your plans for the future?'

'I have no doubt there will be unpleasant consequences to Leonid's death,' Valraven replied evenly. 'I support Prince Gastern, because of all Leonid's sons, he is the least sly, self-serving or debauched. I cannot take you with me now, because I need to see how the land lies back in Magrast. You are safe for the moment, probably in the safest place there is. You must wait. I give you my word I will do what I can to aid you when the sword falls. But you have to realise I may find myself in conflict with the empress. You must be aware that she does not favour Gastern, but wants her beloved Bayard on the throne.' Valraven could not speak of his private contingency plans. If all went bad, and Gastern fell, he intended to return to Caradore, taking as many of his men who were loyal as possible. He would try to hold Caradore against whichever of the princes won the crown. He had asked Tayven to trust him, but he could not bring himself to do likewise in return. 'I will send some of my best men for you if things look tight,' he said.

'That's not assurance enough,' Tayven said. 'You know it's not.'

'It's all I can give you.'

'Then you've lied to me, Lord Palindrake. I've gained nothing from our conversation.' He sighed heavily through his nose, and when he spoke, his words were slow, laden with hidden meaning. 'You have no idea how much that disappoints me, no idea at all.'

Valraven guessed then that Tayven had more to say. 'Have you been testing me in some way?'

Tayven fixed him with a wide-eyed gaze. 'I cannot speak,' he said. 'Not yet. If I were close to you – always – it would be of benefit to you, as then you would be near when the time was right. But I cannot speak yet.'

'You're making no sense,' Valraven said, making an effort to stem the irritation in his voice. 'It's not enough to sway me. It sounds as if you're merely trying to fool me into getting you out of here.'

9

Tayven blinked, considering, debating with himself. 'It is said there is a true king, a divine king, waiting to shine upon the world,' he said. 'And he is not of the Malagash dynasty. You know my talents, Lord Palindrake. I have the far sight, the wyrding way. I know things that others do not.'

Valraven held his breath for a moment. Here it was. He must play the moment right. He'd suspected this, of course. The instability that was sure to follow Leonid's death meant that factions other than the royal sons might fancy their chances at seizing control. Was Maycarpe part of a coup conspiracy? Could the Mewtish governor possibly view Tayven as a potential king, a beautiful figurehead for a clandestine movement of mages? He did not believe for one moment that Tayven had received some kind of divine message about the future. This was all a game, and its board was very much in the here and now.

Tayven obviously mistook Valraven's silence for disapproval. 'I've shocked you,' he said. 'But can you honestly say you hadn't considered the matter yourself? Empires have risen and fallen throughout history. The Malagashes are weak now, because they are divided. They are corrupt. Gastern isn't a fine upright young prince, he's a neurotic ascetic, who'd be as bad an emperor as rakehellion Bayard. It is time for a change, don't you think? There – how is that for shocking?'

Valraven wasn't shocked at all. 'I think only of my family's safety,' he answered, somewhat stiffly, 'and do what is best for them. I support Prince Gastern as the rightful heir.'

'Rightful heir to what, though?' Tayven's voice took on a sly note. 'The empire that wrested your family's power from them? Remember what Caradore once was.'

Valraven smiled. 'Ah, Tayven, we are not in bed together and I am not swooning in your embrace, ready to spill all. I see through your wiles.' He stood up and bowed his head in mock respect. 'I appreciate your candid words, and will do as I promised.'

'Now you will run away from me, because I have touched a nerve,' Tayven said. 'You asked me to trust you. Why should I do that if you won't trust me in return?'

'Tell me who you believe the true king to be, then, and also who else shares your politics.'

'I told you – I can't speak yet,' Tayven replied. 'And I certainly cannot confide in you until you trust me.'

'We live in a cruel world,' Valraven said, 'and trust is a commodity that comes dear, because it is so rare.'

'You know enough now to have me hanged,' Tayven said. 'I've trusted you more than a little.'

'I am quite sure you could have been hanged five times over for other reasons,' Valraven said. 'You've told me nothing I hadn't guessed.'

'Even about Khaster? You haven't asked me much about him. I thought it would interest you more. He is your brother-in-law, after all, and was once your closest friend. Will the Lady Pharinet be pleased to discover he still lives, do you suppose?'

Valraven realised these provocative words were because Tayven wanted to keep him there, but he'd heard enough for now. It wouldn't do any harm to leave Tayven hungry and curious. Cawmonel was only a few hours' ride from Magrast; Valraven could return there any time. He would stay for the night, because the weather was so bad, but decided not to let Tayven know that. 'I have urgent business in the city,' he said. 'I must leave now.'

'You're easily offended,' Tayven said.

'Not at all. Good night to you.' He could feel Tayven's eyes on his back all the way to the door.

CHAPTER TWO

A Fear of Wolves

In the morning Valraven rode back to Magrast in weather equally as dismal as that of the night before. As he approached the north gate of the city, the battlements of the high walls were almost invisible in the downpour. Dark, bloated clouds hung low in the sky and the wide, paved Emperor's Road was slick with mud. The rain had seeped through the Dragon Lord's thick coat. He felt chilled to the bone.

Even before his horse trod the cobbles beneath the arch, the sergeant of the guard ran out of the gatehouse and grabbed hold of the horse's reins. He jerked hard upon the bit, for the animal squealed and jumped to the side. The sergeant's face was pale, the eyes wild. 'My lord!' he cried, before Valraven could remonstrate at his somewhat importunate behaviour. 'The emperor is dead!'

Valraven didn't wait to hear more, but ripped the reins from the sergeant's hold and urged his horse into a gallop. He hadn't expected this so soon. He should have been there.

It was clear that the news had already flooded the city. The hour was early, but people were already out on the streets. They looked up as Valraven's horse clattered past them. He saw their white faces as blurs. What would happen now? Fear and anxiety hung in the very air. As Valraven careered through Northgate Market, he saw a man in ragged clothes standing on a crate, shouting at the crowds that had gathered around him. Once past them, he heard the roar of voices raised in unison. It had begun.

The atmosphere in the imperial palace shivered with tension. Still wearing his sodden coat, Valraven marched straight to the emperor's apartments. All the corridors were full of nobles, councillors, mages and servants. Did they mourn for Leonid, the mild and intelligent emperor, who was perhaps untypical of the Malagash line? Probably not. What they mourned was the last stable influence in their lives. Now the wolves would prowl.

Valraven presented himself at the great double doors that led to Leonid's private rooms. He was familiar with the two guards on duty; they had been in Leonid's service for many years. The emperor had liked and trusted the men, granted them privileges. Gorlaste, the elder of the two, looked stricken. He would grieve for Leonid more than the emperor's own family would. 'Lord Senefex has been looking for you all night,' he said, as he opened the door.

Valraven nodded abruptly. 'I am sorry I was not here. I had pressing business to attend to. When did it happen?'

Gorlaste accompanied Valraven into the reception hall, where senior servants sat around in high-backed chairs against the walls, murmuring softly together. 'After his mightiness took his dinner last night, he began to go into decline,' Gorlaste whispered. 'By midnight, the physicians were called. He died at three o'clock.'

'He has been ill for some time,' Valraven said. 'His passing was not totally unexpected.'

'Aye.' Gorlaste sighed heavily. 'But it still comes as a shock.'

They had reached the door to the room Leonid had used as an office. It was a vast chamber, lined with floor-to-ceiling bookcases, but its atmosphere was not that of a library. In this room, some of the most crucial decisions of government had been made.

Lord Senefex of Sark, Leonid's vizier and chairman of the Fire Chamber, sat behind an ocean of polished desk. Around it stood other members of the Chamber, as well as Mordryn, Archimage of the Church of Madragore, and Prince Gastern, who looked as if he was about to be sent to the gallows. Three mages stood in a protective group behind the prince, grim and pale. One of them was Alguin, a pinch-faced man, who had fought his way up through the church to become Mordryn's Grand Mage, his second-in-command. Alguin had a gloating expression on his face. The scene looked frozen, each figure as motionless as those in a picture. A fire burned in the great hearth, but it could not dispel an atmosphere of chill that was conjured by the cold light coming in through the long arched windows.

'Palindrake!' Senefex said, getting to his feet. 'Where were you? We've been looking for you all night.'

Valraven took off his coat and peeled his soaked gloves from his hands. A servant came forward silently to take them from him. Valraven didn't give the man a glance. 'My apologies,' he said. 'I was out of the city.' He could not see Senefex's face clearly because the light was behind him. 'If I'd had any idea Leonid's condition had become so grave, I would have made sure I was here.'

Senefex nodded and came out from behind the desk. He was a tall, thin man, and young for the position. His dark hair was plaited severely down his back and he was dressed in a dark indigo velvet suit of mourning. Senefex always looked starved, but today the ashen hollows in his cheeks looked particularly deep and his large dark eyes were ringed in purple, the flesh puffy beneath them. He had clearly been up all night. Poor Senefex. He would need all of his wily wits to keep his head on his shoulders now. 'Gastern must be crowned as soon as the funeral has taken place,' he said.

Archimage Mordryn made a soft sound of assent. He was a massive man, broad of shoulder, built more like a warrior than a priest. His face was kind and avuncular, his voice always gentle. Valraven considered him to be one of the most dangerous men in the empire. 'The church is already attending to the arrangements,' he said. No one wanted Gastern on the throne more than Mordryn.

Valraven glanced at Gastern, whose face was curiously impassive. He was like a caricature of his father, possessing similar features of face and body, but somehow the components were askew. How could the same nose, mouth and eyes appear handsome in one man, merely plain in another? Where Leonid's hair had been a luxurious leonine mane, Gastern's was hacked short. The emperor had moved with grace, while Gastern always appeared slightly awkward. Leonid's expressions had been wry and mobile; Gastern's were stiff and repressed. He did not have an ounce of his father's presence. Looking upon him, Valraven's heart sank. He doubted Gastern was strong enough to hold off his hungry brothers. 'My condolences, your highness,' he said. 'This is a difficult time for you.'

Gastern uttered a sound of derision. 'There is blood in the water,' he said, 'and soon the feeding frenzy will begin. Madragore help us all.' He made a sacred sign across his brow. Gastern was very religious, held in the grip of the fire priests, Alguin in particular. Perhaps he had turned to religion seeking something solid in his life, but it had ruined him, made of him a stern, ascetic and intolerant man. Almorante or Bayard would not bow their necks so willingly to the church. Mordryn knew this. He would put the full might of Madragore behind the Crown Prince.

'Order must not be allowed to descend into chaos,' Mordryn said mildly. 'The funeral must take place as soon as is feasible.'

'I have already sent messengers to all the provinces,' Senefex said. 'Leonid must have a full state funeral, for to conduct a smaller one in haste would impart an undesirable message to Gastern's brothers. We do not want them to misinterpret any of our actions. They must not perceive weakness.'

'How long will it take to arrange?' Valraven asked.

'At the least, three weeks,' Senefex replied. 'If any foreign dignitaries find that too short a time to prepare themselves and make the journey, we can do nothing about it. In essence, we predict that rulers from our most influential provinces, Mewt, Elatine and Cos, will be represented. The King of Jessapur could attend, if he leaves Madramurta as soon as he receives the news. I have, of course, sent word to Princess Varencienne in Caradore.'

'Thank you,' Valraven said. He glanced at Mordryn. 'I would like to view the body.'

The Archimage inclined his head. 'Of course. I will accompany you.'

The imperial bedchamber lay at the end of a long corridor with many doors leading off to either side. The firedrake crest of the Malagashes hung over the entrance, an imposing carving in marble. As they approached it, Mordryn sighed deeply. 'This day was inevitable, but now I fear we must steel ourselves for the consequences.'

'Perhaps they will not be as bad as we think,' Valraven said. 'For years, Almorante and Bayard have speculated about the outcome of their father's death. Now it has happened, they might not be as inclined to act as rashly as they'd anticipated. Gastern has your support, which is not to be taken lightly.'

'And yours, of course,' Mordryn said. 'The mages are mine, but the military is yours. Senefex has a firm control of the Chamber.'

'So between us, it appears we have things to our liking.'

Mordryn smiled wryly, said nothing. Valraven knew the man was not afraid for the future. His comment had been a test. All it would take was one weak leak in the trinity of state, church and military for one of the younger princes to take advantage.

A servant got up from a chair beside the bedroom door and opened it for the visitors. Valraven crossed the threshold first. The curtains were drawn across the day and the air full of the sweet scent of incense. Two oil lamps burned dimly on tables either side of the bed. And there lay Leonid. Valraven stood over him. The royal embalmers had already been at work. The emperor looked asleep, restful, a slight smile on his lips. Perhaps he was glad to leave this world. Valraven shivered, unable to dispel the image of his ancestor, Valraven I, whose life had been changed for ever by Leonid's forebears. In his mind, he saw that boy kneeling at the water's edge at Old Caradore, forced to speak an oath in the name of Madragore, binding his domain to the Malagashes for eternity. Now a son of Caradore stood over the dead emperor, and the empire was in flux. Tayven's words seeped into his head. Was this the time to reclaim his ancestral power? No, don't even think it. He could not put his family at risk. Valraven did not have Mordryn's certainty. The world was far bigger than Magrast, and Almorante and Bayard had cultivated strategic friendships in all the provinces.

Mordryn glided up behind him. 'He is at peace.'

Valraven nodded curtly. 'It would appear so.' He turned to face the Archimage. 'What have the physicians said?'

Mordryn recoiled a little. 'What do you mean, Palindrake?'

'I think you know.'

Mordryn's gaze did not flinch from Valraven's own. 'Senefex has taken every precaution over the emperor's health. He had food tasters and trained Mewtish assassins disguised as servants forever round him. I don't think we need worry he died of unnatural causes.'

'Leonid was a hale man,' Valraven said. 'His health declined alarmingly over the last few years. I am not the only one to question that, as I know you are aware.'

'We took every precaution,' Mordryn said. 'I doubt someone was cunning enough to get round them.'

'Has the empress visited these chambers?'

'She was with Leonid when he died. She held his hand.' Mordryn's mouth curled into a small smile. 'She is a grieving widow, Palindrake, have no doubt of that.'

'That is what we will see,' Valraven said.

'Quite,' Mordryn agreed. 'If everyone keeps calm now, all should proceed without problem.'

Valraven glanced back at the body. He remembered Leonid when he'd visited Caradore, his wild laugh echoing through the castle walls. Leonid had come directly to the Palindrakes when Valraven's mother had died. He had been a family friend and a father-in-law. Do I owe you anything? Valraven wondered. Or is the lament of old blood a stronger pull? He leaned down and kissed the cold, marmoreal brow of the body in the bed. 'Goodbye, old friend,' he murmured.

CHAPTER THREE

Divination and Memory

Three Weeks Later

Varencienne had not set foot in the imperial palace since the day after she'd been given in marriage to Valraven Palindrake. On that day she'd left her childhood behind, riding in a carriage to far Caradore with only her servant, Oltefney, for company. It was strange to be back. So much had happened in the intervening years, and now she had no father.

Had she changed so much or did the palace feel different? Was it really empty, devoid of her father's huge presence? But the women's quarters she'd lived in had been far from where the men of the empire planned their futures. Men, including her father, had played little part in her childhood. She'd felt enclosed in womanliness, even though her mother had never been maternal exactly. Varencienne hadn't been aware of when her father had been at home or away. Perhaps the way she felt now was something to do with the fact that she hadn't been given her old rooms, but a suite in the guest wing of the palace. The children, Ellony and Valraven junior, had been swept off by servants to a nursery, some corridors away from her, tended by royal nurses. She felt like an outsider and wondered whether that was the desired effect.

Her mother, Tatrini, had not yet visited her. Her brothers – some of them – had sent her flowers and messages, perhaps dictated to secretaries in haste. Bayard would not come. He'd sent her a bouquet of perfect purple roses that filled the dark room with their hothouse scent, but he'd shy away from facing her alone. Even now. She had been given to Valraven as little more than a child. Tatrini had believed her to be a pawn, to be used when the time was right. But Varencienne had

17

found herself in Caradore; its beautiful wild landscape had woken her, given her strength. If she did not love Valraven Palindrake in the way a wife was supposed to, she was fiercely loyal to his clan. Her children would not be playthings for the Malagashes as Valraven's ancestors had been. This savage independence had not been anticipated by Tatrini. No doubt it had upset some of her plans.

Like a dark omen, a letter had been waiting for Varencienne from Merlan Leckery. It had arrived in Magrast virtually at the same time she had, which meant Merlan must have written it as soon as he'd heard the news of the emperor's death. Varencienne and Merlan had seen each other occasionally, when he'd visited Caradore on leave, but had never spent any private time together. Not since the affair. She was half afraid to open his letter, for she suspected what would be implied in its contents. Leonid's death had been a trigger. She remembered the conversation they'd had about what would happen when her father died. *If there must be an emperor, it should be someone in whose blood magic runs strong.* Dangerous words. Did he still believe them? They'd not spoken of it since. Their secret had remained buried for all these years. What did he want with her now?

Oltefney, unhappy to be back in Magrast, came bustling into the room laden with gowns which trailed from her arms and tangled round her feet. She was a large woman in her forties, who looked far more comfortable as a woman of Caradore in functional soft clothes than she had as a lady of Magrast, bound into stiff corsets and immovable costumes. 'Ren, my dear, I thought the green for tonight. What do you think?' Oltefney attempted to wrest the arm of the dark green gown from her bundle for inspection. It was made of the finest wool, barely weighing anything, yet designed to keep out the cold. Its elegant lines flattered Varencienne's slim figure. She would wear it in defiance of Magrast's pretentious, over-ornate fashions.

Varencienne nodded. 'Whatever you think best, Teffy.' The last time she'd been here, Oltefney had curtsied to her, called her 'your highness'. Varencienne smiled to recall how Oltefney had been disgusted when her young charge, relieved to be free of Magrast, had discarded city finery in favour of Caradorean comfort. In those days, Oltefney would have curled her lip at the green woollen gown. Caradore had changed them both. Oltefney had been more of a mother to Varencienne than Tatrini ever had. She'd held Varencienne's hands as the twins were being born. She'd shared celebrations and sadness and loved Caradore as much as her mistress did. She was part of the family.

Oltefney laid down the gowns on a couch and stood, hands on hips, to survey the room. 'My, it feels odd to be back, doesn't it? You know,

I'd forgotten what it was like. Dark and huge.' She mimed a shiver. 'I'll be glad to get home, won't you?'

Varencienne smiled sadly. 'I wouldn't be here at all if we didn't have to cremate my father.'

Oltefney's face crumpled and she hurried to take Varencienne in her arms. 'Oh, of course. Forgive me. I shouldn't have said that.'

'But I agree with what you said,' Varencienne said. She was far taller than Oltefney and could virtually rest her chin on the woman's head 'Neither of us wants to be here, but we are.' She sighed. 'I come to cremate a man I never knew. I have no feelings for him. The emperor lies in state in the great hall, but what is that to me?'

Oltefney drew away. 'No fault of yours,' she said. 'You know who your real family are.'

Pharinet and Everna, Valraven's sisters, had been worried about her coming to Magrast. It was as if they feared she would never return to them. Everna, particularly, had been furious that the empress had asked for the twins to accompany their mother to the city. Everna was by nature suspicious, but though Varencienne had attempted to calm her fears, in her heart she couldn't help wondering what plans Tatrini had. Her mother would never do anything out of love or compassion. Varencienne was already steeling herself for a fight of some kind.

While Oltefney finished the unpacking, Varencienne picked up the letter from Merlan which lay on a table by the heavily draped window. She put the thick envelope to her nose. It smelled of Mewt, or how she imagined Mewt: a hint of incense and the burned aroma of the desert. She broke the envelope's seal and took out the single sheet of thick paper from within. It was printed at the top with the address of the Magravandian governmental offices in Akahana. She imagined Merlan, dressed in flowing native garb, sitting in a shady room, taking out this sheet of paper, wetting his pen with ink, pausing before he began to write. She sensed he'd wanted to write to her many times. Sometimes, in dreams, she had felt him near. He addressed her as 'My Lady Palindrake', no doubt in fear that others might see the letter. He wrote to express sympathy for her father's demise. He understood that she would soon be visiting the Magravandian capital for the funeral. There was no mention of why he hadn't written to her at home. Merlan knew something. He'd known Leonid was about to die. That was no doubt the influence of his mentor, Lord Maycarpe. It was said Maycarpe was a great magus. Or perhaps the information had come from a more mundane source: the intelligence network Maycarpe was said to employ throughout the empire. Merlan went on to enquire as to the health of Varencienne and her family and then mentioned he'd been travelling a great deal, 'seeking out curios of antiquity, which in their essence have great bearing upon present concerns'.

'When we look into the past,' he wrote, 'we see a window into the present and all the great kings of legend are walking upon a road towards us.'

Varencienne smiled to herself. The letter seemingly made no sense, sounding like the ramblings of a romantic drunk. She tapped the paper against her lips, staring down from the window into the courtyard below where a troop of soldiers was marching past, decked in the indigo livery of mourning. No king to lead them. Not yet. She glanced back at the letter. What *had* Merlan picked up on his travels?

After a few more anecdotes of life in Mewt, Merlan finished the letter by saying he hoped he would see the Palindrake family again in the near future.

He will arrive here soon, Varencienne thought. After years of silence and repressed emotion, Merlan had decided to wake old ghosts. At Maycarpe's directive? Varencienne was not gullible. She would wait and see, although she was aware of a slight tremor of excitement at the prospect of seeing Merlan again. It would be different this time. She knew that one of them would make sure they found time alone together.

A formal invitation arrived from the empress as Varencienne was putting on her gown for the evening. Tatrini requested her daughter's presence for dinner, along with the grandchildren. This was unusual, for children rarely ate with adults in the palace.

As Oltefney fussed with Varencienne's long, dark-gold hair, fashioning it into a semblance of a Magrastian coiffure, Valraven came to his wife's door. Oltefney, always thrown into a panic by the sight of the Dragon Lord, curtsied and bowed away from him as he came into the room.

Varencienne held a mirror in one hand. She looked at her husband in it, touched her hair. His dark beauty, as always, unsettled her, mainly because she could not allow it to affect her. Every time she saw him after a long break, she experienced a slight shock, as if seeing him for the first time. They'd not seen each other for months, but there would be no fond reunion. That wasn't part of their relationship. 'Good day to you, my husband,' she said. 'Are you here to escort me to dinner?'

She noticed, in the mirror, that Valraven looked slightly worried, which probably meant he was extremely distressed. He rarely displayed any feelings. She turned in her seat, one hand draped over the back of the overstuffed chair. 'What is it?'

Valraven came and kissed the top of her head formally. 'The palace is like a nest of hornets about to be poked. Surely you feel it?'

'I can't feel anything,' Varencienne said. 'Mother has shut me away in a cupboard. What's going on?'

'Your father's vizier wants Gastern crowned with indecent haste. Thunder clouds are gathering.'

Varencienne looked back into her mirror. 'I can't help thinking that, despite their loud voices, my brothers are really too cowardly to do anything . . . *desperate*. Surely Gastern will be crowned. Senefex is wise to expedite the coronation. It will end all the speculation, anxiety and fear.'

'So speaks a Malagash, in simple terms,' Valraven said, but his voice was light.

'I'm a Palindrake,' Varencienne said. 'Your sea wife. I've earned that. Don't push me back into the enemy camp.'

Valraven sat down on a sofa. 'It was merely a joke.'

Before Varencienne could comment on his poor humour, Oltefney came in, saying, 'Oh, this is annoying. We can't make tea. I'd forgotten you have to order servants to bring you even the most meagre of refreshments here. You can't make your own. I'm used to Caradorean ways.' She appraised the Dragon Lord. 'I'm sorry I can't offer anything, my lord. Shall I send for something?'

'Order a tray,' Varencienne said. 'But bearing something rather stronger than tea. I need fortification to meet the beast in her lair.'

Valraven laughed. 'You have swum with Foy, queen of the sea dragons. You have controlled the dragon daughters. Yet you still fear your mother?'

'It's not fear,' Varencienne said, 'but weariness. I can't be bothered with the subtle knifing.'

'I'll order a tray,' said Oltefney, sharing a conspiratorial glance with Varencienne.

Oltefney left a silence behind her. Varencienne sensed there was more on her husband's mind than concern about royal inheritance. 'Something has happened, hasn't it,' she said.

Valraven stared at her unblinking for a few moments. 'Yes.'

'Will you speak to me about it or leave me to interpret the flavour of your silence?'

'You are always so adept at guessing, Ren. I'd like to hear your thoughts.'

Varencienne appraised him for a while. 'You had better tell me. I'm in no mood for games.'

'Then you're hardly ready to meet your mother.'

'Val!'

He raised his hands. 'You are waspish today, my dear. Very well. The empress has taken Tayven Hirantel into custody.'

Varencienne frowned. 'That name – I've heard it before. But it means nothing to me now.'

'Hardly surprising. He was thought dead for a long time.'

Varencienne felt a wave of cold plunge through her. Now she remembered. 'Khaster,' she said. It brought back to her the night Valraven had told her why Khaster could never forgive him. He could have saved Tayven's life, saved him from Bayard, but he hadn't. Apparently, it hadn't been necessary.

'You've gone quite pale, Ren. Have you guessed the rest?'

Varencienne glanced sharply at her husband, felt her colour rise once more. He could not possibly know how many times she had lingered before the portrait of Khaster Leckery at his family home, Norgance. For a while she had been infatuated with a dead man – until his brother Merlan had come into her life.

'Khaster is alive,' Valraven said. 'Hirantel told me so himself. They worked a fine disappearing act on us. Khaster did not fall in battle, as his family fondly believes. He's been living in Cos, presumably with the Cossic rebels.'

Varencienne turned away, sure her face must betray her feelings. 'This is . . . astounding news.'

'What's wrong? Are you worried for Pharinet? Why? She is hardly the grieving widow.' How much awareness was there in his voice? She could not tell whether he suspected the truth or not.

'It is a shock,' Varencienne said, forcing herself to face him once more. 'You know your family – and the Leckerys – are my own now. This has great implications. The Leckerys believe Khaster died nobly in battle, despite the rumours of cowardice that Bayard put about. What will you tell Saska?'

'It is not yet time for Khaster's mother to receive this news,' Valraven said. 'I need to discover more, Khaster's exact whereabouts, for example. I can't go to Saska with this information. She'll be distraught that Khaster sent her no word he was safe.'

'Has Hirantel been with him all this time?'

'Apparently not. Tayven was apprehended by Tatrini's agents in Mewt. He's been in Darris Maycarpe's service for some years. Merlan knows him. We can only presume Merlan has known quite a lot he's kept to himself.'

'I can't believe he'd keep this from his family. He knows the way they feel about Khaster.'

'And that is undoubtedly why he's kept silent. Saska has enshrined Khaster. The truth might damage her. She's not even aware of Khaster's relationship with Hirantel.'

'Merlan said there was no proof of that. They were only friends.'

Valraven gave her a meaningful glance. 'If Merlan spoke to you of this matter when your mother came to Caradore, I can only say he's learned a lot since then.'

'I see,' said Varencienne.

'What we have to ask ourselves,' Valraven said, 'is what your mother wants with Tayven now. Is she interested in him because he works for Maycarpe, or because she's heard a whisper about Khaster? We should be careful at this time. Tatrini knows I do not support her desire for Bayard to become emperor. She will want to put a curb on Bayard's enemies.'

'She does not yet know where my loyalties lie,' Varencienne said. 'Perhaps I should steel myself for a grilling.'

'And where do they lie?' Valraven asked.

'With you,' Varencienne answered.

Valraven laughed quietly. 'Thank you for the show of support, but you know what I mean.'

'I do.' Varencienne stood up. 'Are you coming with me to dinner?'

Valraven was staring at her speculatively, clearly mulling over what she'd said to him. 'What? Oh, I'm not invited. Tatrini wants a motherly private meal with you. I thought I'd let you know what I'd learned so you could undertake some careful investigation.'

'Nothing gets past my mother's guard, you should know that.'

'Perhaps if she believes she has an ally in you . . . '

Varencienne raised her eyebrows. 'Are you suggesting I lie to the empress?'

'I don't know. You haven't revealed your private thoughts to me. For all I know, you may support your favourite brother.'

'Val, I support what is right for my children. They are my prime concern. I do not want Rav to follow the life you've had to lead, forced to become a general in the imperial army. Who do you suppose I should support to achieve that aim?'

'None of your family would allow the Dragon Heir to avoid the customary role. It's a tradition rooted mainly in superstition and fear, and therefore rigid.'

'It would appear that way.'

'What are you saying, then?'

Varencienne stared at him, unsure of whether she should speak her mind or not. She hadn't had to think about this matter since her mother had visited Caradore four years earlier and she'd enjoyed her brief but intense affair with Merlan. She'd learned much then of the Dragon Heir and what he symbolised. She'd helped her husband partly reclaim his heritage and had thought this event would have at least inspired discussion, if not action. But from the day after the ritual on the beach at Old Caradore, Valraven had made it clear he did not wish to take the matter further. As far as he was concerned, he'd laid Foy to rest, and a cycle in his family's history had come to a close. Had he thought of it since? She'd always known that one day this would become the focus of their lives. Valraven could not hide from what he truly was. He'd defied the empire's decree and had renewed his family's contact with the sea dragons. He was awake in the world, as generations of Dragon Heirs had not been. The Palindrakes were held in high esteem by the empire that had conquered them. Varencienne knew her father had trusted Valraven and his father implicitly. The Dragon Heirs had bowed to the yoke of Madragore because, hundreds of years before, a Palindrake son had submitted to the will of Magravandian fire mages, unable to do otherwise. His home had been ransacked, his father killed. Perhaps the spirit of Palindrake had been broken then, but in Valraven it could flare anew. Leonid's death heralded a time for great change, and the Palindrakes should be part of that. Merlan Leckery knew it. Valraven's sisters knew it, and so did the Sisterhood of the Dragon, the secret organisation to which they belonged. Even Darris Maycarpe, Magravandian governor of Mewt, knew it. Only Valraven didn't seem to know, or perhaps he didn't want to admit to it. Had he ever desired to be king?

'Speak,' said Valraven. 'We must close ranks at this time.'

'Years ago, when my mother came to Caradore, and together we performed the ritual to the sea dragons, there was talk of you being given power again in Caradore. You know what my mother promised you. Are you sure you should go against her now?'

'I'm not sure I regard her promises as lasting,' Valraven said.

'I will find out what I can,' Varencienne said. 'Come to me for breakfast.'

Valraven stood up. 'I shall look forward to it.'

Some distance from Varencienne's chambers, in a dank store room far below the women's apartments, the empress Tatrini spoke with her augur, Lady Grisette Pimalder. The Pimalder family had served the imperial line for many generations. Their women were gifted with the faculty of second sight, while their menfolk were skilled in the art of perfumery. Lady Grisette's own husband created the sensual aromas with which Tatrini dabbed her wrists and neck. Now the two women were intent on a business of a less delicate nature.

'Tell me what you see,' said Tatrini.

Grisette stood over a table, her hands daubed to the wrists in blood.

Before her lay the corpse of a beautiful young man, whose belly had been opened, flaps of skin held to either side with silver pins. His guts lay on the table beside him, a complicated story of twists and turns. Gore-spotted cutting instruments were arranged upon a silver dish beside the body's head. Lady Pimalder wore a veil of shimmering silver voile over her head, tied at the neck to enclose her entire face. She glanced up at her mistress, who stood some feet away by the wall, a handkerchief held to her nose. Wan sunlight came in through the webby panes of the small window high overhead, for the rain had passed. The air smelled of earth and rot and it was very cold. Grisette's breath steamed before her. 'There is much to see,' she said. 'Nothing is certain.'

'This much I know. Speak to me, woman. Tell me what lies there.'

Grisette poked the entrails with a tortoiseshell pointer. 'Prince Gastern will become emperor.'

Tatrini lowered her handkerchief and approached the table. 'Is that all?'

Grisette shook her head. 'Indeed not, your majesty. Beneath your hand lie ingots of gold, of different value. You must choose. Royal blood will be spilled into the great rivers of Magravandias. The four shall become one and the elemental beasts reunite. Madragore may be consumed by the very beasts he put in chains to serve him. The fire drakes writhe in their nests of flame and call to their brethren of the earth, sea and sky. The blood of ancient pacts seeps from the mountains and the heir to Caradore is in threat of bondage.'

'What is this? What do you mean? Do you refer to my grandson?'

'He is in danger,' said Grisette. 'It will come down from the mountains.'

'Can it be stopped?'

'Do not let him into the mountains. Keep him low.'

'What mountains?'

'Those of his home.'

'Are you saying I must not let Rav return to Caradore?'

'If you do, you will lose him.'

Tatrini turned away. Varencienne would never countenance that. Was it possible to keep both her and the children here at Magrast? It would not be easy. Varencienne had become a true woman of Caradore, as was right and needful, but she was a spirited young woman. She liked to believe she had autonomy. 'You must tell me more of this danger,' Tatrini said. 'Look deeper, Grisette. Who threatens the Dragon Heir?'

'Shrouded,' replied Lady Pimalder. 'Whoever it is hides themselves well. It is no one of your clan, nor are they affiliated to Madragore. It is an outside influence, slippery and swift.'

25

'Then you must do more to strip them of their disguise.'

'I will apply myself to it, but it cannot be read from the entrails.'

'Make haste.' Tatrini took a purse from her belt and held it out to the augur. 'Take this for Lord Pimalder, Grisette. My late husband found great comfort in the sweet perfume that was made for him.'

Grisette bobbed a curtsey and took the purse with a bloody hand. 'We are your servants, your majesty,' she said. 'Our hearts are with you in your grief.'

'Responsibility is a great burden,' Tatrini said. 'I am hagridden by needful actions that hang heavily upon the heart.' She glided past the augur and spoke to a man clad in black who stood just beyond the door. 'Dispose of the remains, Master Dark.'

The man came into the room, sweeping a bow. He did not speak, but then, he rarely did. He was like a shadow creature of earth, mould clinging to his clothes.

'Wait!' Grisette said. She poked about in the pile of guts once more. 'The crown has been found.'

Tatrini paused at the threshold. 'What crown?'

'I don't know. The splay of the viscera suggests a crown, that's all. A hidden crown. I can tell you no more at present.'

Tatrini sighed impatiently. Sometimes, the augur's predictions created more confusion than they cleared. 'If it is of importance to us, then discover more,' Tatrini said. 'I must go now. My daughter has arrived in Magrast.'

Lady Pimalder nodded and unwrapped the veil from her face, then cast the shimmering fabric over the opened belly of the body on the table. She went to a water pipe sticking out from the wall to wash her hands. Business was concluded.

CHAPTER FOUR

Funeral Games

On the day of the funeral, at ten o'clock in the morning, a dozen fire mages went in procession to the roof of the palace, where the flags of many nations flapped heavily in the soaked air. Far below, in the wide rectangle of the Imperial Parade Ground, thousands of mourners had gathered, all of them titled or noble, huddled together in the fine rain that fell from a colourless sky. Awnings had been set up for the benefit of foreign visitors, to many of whom the cold late winter of Magravandias was anathema, if not life-threatening. Amongst them were Queen Neferishu of Mewt and King Ashalan of Cos, perhaps the two most intriguing of the dignitaries.

The fire mages spoke prayers which were carried away soundlessly on the wind. Their ceremonial robes of black and purple were blown about their gaunt bodies, their tall conical caps in danger of being taken captive by the elements. From wicker cages they released a host of black doves, which, despite the weather, fluttered up with spirit into the sky.

Varencienne, standing with her family upon the Balcony of Viewing, thought the wings of the doves sounded mechanical, like clockwork. Surely she was not really here, but at home in Caradore, dreaming? Valraven was not beside her, because presently he would lead the Splendifers, the Holy Knights of Madragore, out of the palace with the emperor's body, but at least her children were with her. At one time, they would not have been allowed to attend any state events, not even weddings, but Tatrini had done much to change this custom. Varencienne's son, Rav, was straining against the balcony, trying to peer over the balustrade, full of curiosity. Ellony, his sister, shrank against the front of her mother's stiff black coat. Varencienne knew the child would be discomforted by the conflicting emotions raging about her. She was named for Khaster and Merlan's dead sister, who had been Valraven's first wife. Varencienne had chosen the name herself, perhaps rather an odd choice for a second wife to make, but she felt that Ellony and Rav were, in some ways, the children Val's first wife had never had. Her daughter was not related in blood to Ellony Leckery, yet she'd somehow managed to inherit her namesake's rather fey nature. Pharinet, Valraven's sister, insisted young Ellony was far stronger, braver and more robust than the original, but there was no doubt she was highly sensitive, and sometimes this affected her badly. Varencienne squeezed the girl's shoulder lightly with a gloved hand. Ellony glanced round at her, eyes full of messages. Varencienne blinked mildly at her: a signal. *Be patient. We'll soon be indoors again.*

All the royal princes were present, standing in a line behind their mother, the empress. Gastern's wife, Rinata, stood at his shoulder, with their sulky-faced son, Linnard, beside her. Rinata and Gastern might have been cut from the same bolt of cloth. Varencienne could not image how two such rigid, prudish creatures had steeled themselves for the act that had produced Linnard. Perhaps the child's dour nature reflected the lack of pleasure involved. Two of the lesser princes, Pormitre and Celetian, also had wives; polite little countesses who stood dutifully behind their husbands. Almorante had never taken a wife but had two high-ranking mistresses, neither of whom Tatrini would allow upon the balcony. Bayard's mistresses and male lovers were all too disreputable even to be mentioned in polite company. Bayard and Almorante stood at either end of the line of brothers, unable to produce a façade of fraternal affection even at their father's funeral. Between them, with the others, were Eremore, Roarke and Wymer, and also the younger brothers, who were little more than children: Leonid, Parrish and Osmar. But for Almorante, who was untypically dark-haired, all the princes shared the same fair Malagash appearance. Many people called them the Lions of Magrast, but Varencienne had heard her husband refer to them as wolves, and this description seemed more apt: pale wolves, with gemstone eyes, tongues lolling in the dark, panting, waiting, claws clicking along the bare passages of the palace.

Who are these people? Varencienne wondered. The only brother she'd ever really known was Bayard, and she'd discovered so many unpleasant things about him since she'd left home, she'd had to conclude her previous knowledge of his character had been misguided. During her childhood, she'd never been truly close to any of her family. Only Caradore had given her a feeling of belonging. She was anxious to return there. She wouldn't feel safe until Magrast was behind her. *But what are you afraid of? To your brothers, you're 'only a woman'. You have nothing to fear from them. But your mother . . .* The inner voice faded. Tatrini was interested in Valraven. She would soon remind him of the service she had done him four years before and demand he help her now. What would Valraven do then? Varencienne had not seen the empress since she'd dined with her mother, two days before. The dinner itself had been frighteningly devoid of tense moments. Tatrini had acted well the role of doting grandmother, asking only about domestic life at Caradore. Varencienne had been suspicious, taut as steel, waiting for the blades to emerge. But Tatrini had played with her, chatting mildly about the foreign visitors filling the palace and even stooping to reminiscences about her late husband, which, considering the lack of closeness in their marriage, had seemed indelicate at best. Tatrini had deliberately kept away from tender topics. But it would come eventually, Varencienne had no doubt of that.

Varencienne shivered and pulled the neck of her coat closer to her throat. Closing her eyes, she uttered a prayer to Madragore in her mind, a god to whom she had never paid fealty. But this was his territory, his responsibility. *Make Gastern emperor, mighty lord. Keep him safe.* It was the least of many evils.

At each end of the balcony a flight of steps led down to the Parade Ground below. Between the sweep of these steps, at ground level, a stand had been erected, where members of the Fire Chamber and various other Magravandian dignitaries were arranged. Varencienne wondered whether Merlan Leckery was there. She had heard from the ladies-in-waiting who had been appointed to her that officials from the governmental office in Mewt were expected, but had felt it imprudent to make direct enquiries. Surely if Merlan was in Magrast, he'd have attempted to contact her.

The main doors to the palace opened and a company of Splendifers came slowly through, carrying the glossy black sarcophagus which was draped with flags and official sashes. Valraven walked behind them, dressed like they were, in a black ceremonial tunic emblazoned with the crimson dragon of Madragore, and a fine chain mail that glistened like oil in the rain. His hair was plaited tightly, tucked into the hood of mail that lay in a supple pool over his shoulders. The imperial band began to play a dirge and the mourners on the Parade Ground all bowed their heads. Varencienne stared down at them. The rain had gathered on her lashes, so that when she blinked it was as if she were weeping. Some of the duchesses and countesses down there were openly shedding tears. Leonid had been held in affection. Perhaps some of those women had been his mistresses.

An open hearse drawn by black horses powdered with ash stood ready

29

to receive the sarcophagus. The Splendifers moved carefully with their great burden, manoeuvring it slowly onto the carriage. Valraven stood to attention, his eyes gazing out above the heads of the mourners. He barked a command and the Splendifers dropped to one knee, their arms crossed over their chests. Archimage Mordryn emerged from another doorway in the palace wall, leading a company of fire mages and their young novices. The novices sang an obsequy, voices sweet and melancholy. Thick clouds of incense drifted down from the great golden censers in their hands. Mordryn reached the hearse, and the novices fell silent. The Archimage spoke a prayer and then the Splendifers rose to their feet, each standing beside one of the six horses yoked to the hearse. Valraven called out another order and the Splendifers turned to face the Balcony of Viewing. Prince Gastern inclined his head to them and began to lead his family down a flight of steps to the Parade Ground, where they were joined by Senefex and the Fire Chamber. Varencienne glanced around herself discreetly and was sure she caught sight of Lord Maycarpe in the crowd behind her, but it was impossible to see whether Merlan was with him.

The Army in Residence filed out from an adjoining yard: first the cavalry and the rest of the Splendifers, their horses' hooves muffled by socks of purple linen, and then the infantry, followed by the cannon. Valraven raised one arm and cried out another almost wordless order. The procession began to move, heading for the ceremonial arch that led to the cathedral and the pyre that had been built in the ambustiary behind it. The hearse went first, followed by Valraven, on foot, and the royal family. Then came the mages, the Fire Council and the army. Other mourners fell in behind them. All the mages raised their voices in a hymn, deep baritones mingling with the higher tones of the novices. Beyond the ceremonial arch, servants and officials lined the main driveway. As the hearse passed them, they cast branches of evergreen onto it, which were presently ground up beneath the feet of the procession, releasing a strong tart scent.

Out in the city proper, the streets were thronged with citizens. Funerals and weddings were the only time they could catch a glimpse of royalty at such close quarters. Prudently, the mounted personal guard of the family had moved forward to form a barrier between them and the crowds, while other divisions of the army provided protection for the foreign dignitaries. Many women called out to the empress, 'Bless me, my lady', because she had done much to improve the female role in Magravandian society over the past couple of years. From being invisible, a voiceless presence at the emperor's side at state functions, Tatrini had manoeuvred herself into prominence with a loud voice of her own. Leonid had supported her, his liberality perhaps the result of encroaching sickness and death, which had mellowed him. It was as if Tatrini had been waiting for the right moment to show her claws, her image to the people now part of a carefully contrived plan. 'My lady' was hardly an appropriate title for an empress, but entirely so for a saint or a goddess. The implications of this were not lost on Varencienne. Surrounded by people, she felt slightly faint. She could not help but be reminded of the last time she'd visited the cathedral: the day of her wedding, when she'd sat beside her father in an open carriage. Life moved so quickly. You didn't realise it until you paused to reflect.

Ellony kept close to her mother, discreetly holding her hand, while Rav marched slightly ahead of them, head high. It was clear he was conscious of his elevated status amongst the population of Magrast. A pang of anxiety stabbed through Varencienne's heart. She didn't want her son to like Magrast, or the life there, too much.

It took nearly an hour to reach the cathedral and, once there, half an hour more for everyone to be seated in the stands around the ambustiary. Varencienne took her seat, with her children to either side of her. It was then that she saw Merlan Leckery sitting in the stand opposite. For a second, she could not breathe. He did not appear to have noticed her, but was conversing with Lord Maycarpe, who was seated beside him. It was difficult to believe she had once been intimate with Merlan. The face was familiar, but the memories of him no longer felt real. Her old fantasies of Khaster had more substance. Where Valraven's male beauty was direct, even aggressive, Merlan's was subtler. He had the soft brown Leckery hair, so similar to Khaster's in the portraits Varencienne had seen, and the artfully sculpted face, devoid of the dashing planes and angles of the typical Palindrake countenance. He did not raise his eyes or glance around the crowd, which to Varencienne seemed unnatural. Could he be avoiding her eye? Perhaps he regretted sending the letter and had thought better of re-establishing contact. Telling herself it was for the best, Varencienne sought to ignore the pang of disappointment.

The army fired their cannons, the Archimage spoke prayers and the mourners sang hymns. Members of the Fire Chamber and foreign rulers ascended a podium to deliver speeches. Varencienne watched Ashalan and Neferishu closely. The Mewtish queen knew Merlan Leckery well and now it appeared that Ashalan might know Khaster. Ashalan looked tired, the ghost of a once-handsome man, and his speech lacked feeling, but Neferishu spoke warmly, the force of her character bringing a spark of interest to otherwise dour proceedings. Then the talking was all over and the fire mages had formed a circle around the pyre. Cathedral officials stepped forward with ceremonial brands, and presently flames began to lick round the tinder.

I don't want to smell it, Varencienne thought. Must we sit here until he's ash?

But it appeared the mourners' sensibilities were catered for, because soon the Archimage was leading everyone back into the cathedral itself, while lesser priests burned bushes of rosemary in braziers to mask the stink of burning flesh. Inside the cathedral, a few more hymns were sung and prayers intoned before the grimacing countenance of Madragore's idol. After that, the assembly filed out to the waiting carriages and was conveyed back to the palace for the wake. As if the elements themselves were relieved the ceremony was over, the sun had begun to shine wanly through a gap in the clouds.

'Mama, those ladies are staring at us,' Ellony whispered to her mother. They had taken plates of food from the buffet and now sat on the outskirts of the empress's entourage in the Great Hall of the palace. Varencienne had been hoping for an introduction to Queen Neferishu, but so far Gastern and Rinata had monopolised the Mewt's attention. Merlan had kept his distance. Varencienne hadn't even caught sight of him since they entered the hall. Now she looked up from her plate and for a moment held her breath. The ladies in question were her two childhood friends, Carmia and Mavenna, familiar, yet strangers. She waved to them, inviting them to approach. The two women exchanged a glance and then sailed over. Mavenna had put on a lot of weight, while Carmia had lost it. Strangely, they looked like caricatures of their younger selves.

'What is wrong with you?' Varencienne asked in what she hoped sounded like a light tone. 'Are we now strangers that you avoid me?'

'Oh, Ren,' Mavenna said, bending low to embrace her, 'not at all. We felt it best to wait for your signal.'

Varencienne returned the embrace. 'You should have come to visit me. I've been here several days.'

'Well, when we had no word from you . . . '

'Then we are all at fault. Please, sit down. Tell me your news. Both married now, I presume?'

Mavenna nodded. 'Yes. I to Duke Ivan Thornamonte, Carmia here to Sir Geraint Mantipore, who is a Master of the Splendifers.'

'You have married well, then.' Looking at Carmia's drawn face, Varencienne privately wondered about that.

'Life has treated me – us – well,' said Mavenna, directing her piercing gaze upon Ellony. 'My, your children are lovely.'

Ellony was still pressed close to her mother, glaring at the women in distrust, but Rav was nowhere to be seen. 'Thank you. This is Ellony. Her brother Valraven is no doubt off exploring.'

Mavenna sat down and indicated for the silent Carmia to do likewise. 'Well, my little rascal is probably with him. It's good that children are welcome at these events nowadays. Your mother is responsible for many changes in the way women are viewed in Magrast.'

Varencienne smiled tightly. 'I hope all her other changes are as pleasing.'

Mavenna gave her a shrewd glance, which she smothered quickly with a wide smile, patting down the foaming folds of her mourning gown. 'So, how is life married to the Dragon Lord – forgive my importunity!'

Varencienne smiled. Mavenna hadn't changed. 'Caradore is more than I could have dared hope for. I'm very happy there.'

'We should have written to one another,' Mavenna said. 'We must make sure we do so in future.'

'Of course.' Varencienne doubted that would happen. Her life in Caradore was another world to that of Magrast. She didn't want any crossovers. She leaned forward to peer round Mavenna. 'How are you, Carmia? Have you any children?'

Carmia shook her head. 'No, Madragore has not yet blessed us.'

'Not for want of trying, though, is it, my dear?' Mavenna said gently and then in a confidential tone to Varencienne, 'Poor Carmia. Two stillbirths.'

'How dreadful. I'm so sorry.'

Carmia shrugged thin shoulders. She looked as if she wasn't really there.

Varencienne's spine tingled unaccountably and she turned quickly to discover the attention of her mother upon her. The empress turned in her chair and the ladies seated around her seemed to fade into the background. 'Duchess Thornamonte, Lady Mantipore, how wonderful you've found your old friend again! Knowing Ren, she probably didn't send word to you that she was home.'

'Mother, I . . . ' Varencienne began, but the empress drowned out her words with her commanding voice.

'We must have a get together in my chambers in the next day or so. I'll have my secretary arrange a date.'

'That would be lovely, of course,' Varencienne said, 'but I intend to go home as soon as . . . '

'Ren, I haven't seen you or the children for four years. I simply will not countenance you fleeing back to the country yet. You know, ladies, I believe she has quite forgotten what it's like to be in genteel company.'

'I assure you I haven't,' Varencienne said.

'How can you neglect your old friends? You grew up together.'

'We haven't seen you since your wedding day,' Mavenna said. 'Come now, Ren, you should spend a little more time here. I'd adore to take you visiting. So many people would love to see you.'

'Well . . . '

'Childhood friends are very important,' Tatrini said. 'Do Rav and Ellony have many friends?'

Varencienne thought it best not to mention that the twins spent most of their time with the servants' children, running around the draughty corridors of Caradore, or out riding on the moors beyond the castle. 'Of course they do.'

'But the noble families all live so far apart, don't they? It must be difficult for the children to see any other youngsters regularly.'

'They're quite content,' Varencienne said, and then, putting a hand on her daughter's head, 'aren't you, Ellie?'

Ellony nodded. 'I miss home. I miss my pony, my kittens, my dog and Aunt Everna.'

'How charming!' cooed Mavenna and then, with a fawning glance at the empress, 'But only animals for friends, it seems!'

'Quite,' said Tatrini. 'For a girl, that is not too bad, for her mother and aunts can be excellent company, but for a boy . . . ' She shook her head. 'You should be thinking about Rav's future now, Ren. He's seven years old.'

'What? Are you suggesting he should enlist already?'

Tatrini laughed tightly. 'Indeed not, as you know very well. But I have been giving the matter some thought. Rav is your beloved son, whom you want near you, but he is also Valraven VI, the heir to Palindrake and, like it or not, destined to become part of Magravandian life. Surely it would make sense for him to spend more time with his father, and to cultivate friends of his own age and status?'

'Mother, what is this?' Varencienne asked darkly.

Tatrini shrugged elegantly. 'Well, Valraven will be stationed here in Magrast for the foreseeable future, won't he? Why not let Rav stay here with him? You needn't feel as if you're losing him. You too could spend more time here. This is your home, after all, and conditions are changing. I've made sure that women have more freedom in the palace, and intend to expand upon this new circumstance.'

'You are an inspiration to all of us,' said Mavenna.

'I'm not leaving Rav here,' Varencienne said. 'His home is in

Caradore, with his sister, his aunts and myself. Valraven was torn from his home and I do not intend to let that happen to his son.'

'You make it sound as if life in Magrast is a torment,' Tatrini said, 'yet the evidence is clear that your husband thinks anything but that. At least speak to him about this.'

'Valraven will be in accord with me over this matter.'

'I hardly think so.'

'You don't know him.'

'I know him enough.'

Mavenna made a sound of discomfort. 'I would be happy to bring my own son to the palace to play with Rav.'

Varencienne sighed. She knew there was no point in continuing this argument. 'It's a matter for thought,' she said, as if relenting.

'I only have Rav's best interests at heart,' Tatrini said.

'I know, mother.'

'He could receive a proper education here, like your brothers did. The university now boasts tutors from Jessapur and Mewt, the greatest of thinkers and scholars. Some of Rav's uncles are close to his own age. How can you deny him his rights to have friends, family and education?'

'I will consider it,' Varencienne said. 'In fact, I ought to look for Rav. It's been a tiring day.'

'Ren! Really! He's in the palace. What harm can come to him? Let him enjoy himself.'

That's the last thing I want him to do, Varencienne thought.

Unaware of the discussion of his fate, Valraven Palindrake VI was sitting beneath one of the long trestle tables, hidden by the tablecloth, in thrall to his uncle Leonid. Leo had sought him out soon after everyone had arrived back at the palace. He was four years older than Rav, a worldly, knowledgeable boy. Rav had some older friends amongst the Caradorean servants – boys of ten or twelve years old – but he thought Leo talked like an adult, and was awed by it. The prince had led Rav beneath the tables, telling him it was the best way to eavesdrop on adult conversations. Rav wasn't sure why they should want to do that, but complied, glamorised by Leo's startling pale Malagash beauty and knowing eyes. The tables formed a maze of tunnels around the room. Voices above sounded remote and echoing. Rav had watched Leo all day, thinking of his own friends at home, who now appeared coarse and immature in comparison. Rav had dared to fantasise what it would be like to have friends like Prince Leo, and perhaps even become a little like that himself. But he had been surprised rather than delighted when the prince had left his group of friends, all grown-up and sophisticated, in order to introduce himself to his nephew. 'Mother will summon us both to her chambers very soon,' he said, 'but I want to make your acquaintance first, without her.'

Why? wondered Rav. He grinned shyly and couldn't think of anything to say.

'You'll meet Osmar and Parrish as well,' Leo continued in a supercilious voice, 'but they're too much like Gastern. Boring. I am a true Malagash, like Almorante and Bayard. If you've got any sense, you'll get me on your side. You will need powerful friends in Magrast, as your father did. Your future lies here, Valraven.'

These comments confused Rav. He could talk about the countryside and horses and also the sea, but this was alien territory to him.

Leo sighed at the lack of response. 'Clearly you need an education. You'll get nowhere staying dumb.' He laughed. 'In both senses.'

It had quickly become obvious that Rav had no idea that one day he would be expected to move to Magrast. In their hiding place, Leo had told him all about it. 'Mother wants you here soon. She's told me so. She thinks you should be educated here and be closer to your father. What do you think about that?'

Rav thought of the pomp and ceremony of the funeral, the noble Splendifers, the magnificent horses, the immense buildings, the important people. It was like something out of a storybook. He thought also of his father, whom he adored above all other people. 'I want to come,' he said. Why hadn't his mother told him about this?

'Thought you would,' Leo said. 'Nobody wants to stay at home with the womenfolk. It's no life for a man.'

Rav didn't really know what Leo meant by that. He was rarely unhappy at home, and enjoyed the company of his friends and family, but here – this was something entirely different. If he'd been older, he'd have considered that a love of city life ran in his blood. He would feel as if he'd come home at last. But he was only a boy, who'd lived rather a wild, ungoverned and untutored life so far. He just wanted to be like Leo. All the Palindrakes were dark-haired and olive-skinned, but for him. Even Ellony, his twin, didn't share his pale complexion. People were always commenting on it, which he found embarrassing. His Aunt Pharinet had once said to his mother, laughing, that if he and Ellie weren't twins, she'd suspect Valraven wasn't his father. His mother had laughed in return, while punching Pharinet lightheartedly on the arm, but the comment had hurt Rav deeply. Did it mean his father wouldn't be pleased with him? He had tried to darken his face and hair with mud, but this act had not been met with approval by anyone. Here in Magrast, the royal family looked like him. He was one of them.

'Does mama know about this?' he asked.

'Varencienne?' Leo pulled a scornful face. 'She knows, but she'll fight it. Mothers always want to cling onto their sons. Bayard told me that. You'll have to tell your father what you want. He'll understand.'

Rav could not imagine doing such a thing. The only time he saw his father was when Valraven came home on leave. Then they would go out riding together and visit ancient sites. Valraven would also take him to the homes of other noble families, where Rav was proud to be his son, feeling less like a child than on other occasions. He was always treated differently when he visited the same families with his mother. But it might be ages before the Dragon Lord came home again. He sighed deeply.

'What's the matter?' Leo asked.

'I don't know when I'll get to see papa on his own.'

Leo blinked in apparent perplexity. 'But he's here, isn't he?'

'Well, yes.'

'Then go and speak to him now.'

Rav thought of the important people who would no doubt be clustered around his father at this very moment. He knew it was bad manners to interrupt adults when they were talking.

Leo seemed to know what he was thinking. 'You are the heir to Palindrake,' he said. 'Start acting like it.' He crawled out from beneath the tablecloth and Rav followed.

The Dragon Lord stood nearby with a group of people: Prince Gastern, his mean-faced wife, and a large dark-skinned woman, from whom Rav couldn't take his gaze. She was dressed in some shiny stuff of dark green, like serpent skin, and her hair hung in dozens of plaits to her waist. When she laughed, it was as if you could feel it in your stomach.

'That's Queen Neferishu of Mewt,' Leo said, noticing Rav's rapt attention. 'Bayard said she's the only weighty woman he'd ever consider taking to his bed.'

Again this remark was lost on Rav, but he paid it no attention anyway. They were close to the group now, who were all looking at them. Perhaps it was because of Leo's commanding presence.

'Ah, this is one of my younger brothers, Prince Leonid,' Gastern said to the foreign queen. 'We call him Leo.'

'Lion,' said the queen, smiling. 'Yes, he has the Malagash leonine look. The hair.' She looked back to Gastern. 'You shouldn't hack yours off like that, you know. It's such a waste.'

Gastern reddened, which made Rav smile. The crown prince uttered a few anguished and annoyed sounds, then wrenched at his collar. 'I am not one for vanity.'

'Indeed not,' brayed his nasal-voiced wife.

Valraven too was smiling. He gestured towards his son. 'This is Rav,' he said to Neferishu, 'my son and heir.'

'Oh, he has your eyes,' Neferishu said, 'and his Malagash grandfather's mouth and hair. Truly a potentially deadly combination.'

Rav now worshipped Neferishu: she had likened him to his father, the only person ever to have done that.

'Hello, Rav,' said Neferishu. 'When is your divine father going to bring you to Mewt then, eh?'

'He's only seven,' Valraven said, then pondered for a moment, 'but yes, in a few years, perhaps I could bring the whole family to Akahana. Varencienne has never seen it.'

'You imply my beloved country is dangerous to young children,' Neferishu said, although her voice was still full of smiles. 'I should be insulted.'

'I did not mean to imply that,' Valraven said. 'It's just that I wasn't sure whether the children would be able to appreciate it properly yet.'

Neferishu rolled her eyes. 'Then you know little of children. Anyway, even if that is the case, they can come again. I would like to meet Princess Varencienne.'

'We will speak of this,' Valraven said.

Leo, meanwhile, was nudging Rav painfully in the side with an elbow. For a moment, the adults were silent. Desperate to keep Leo's respect, Rav squeaked, 'Leo said I could come to Magrast.'

'Well, of course,' Valraven said. 'You may come more frequently when you're older.'

Leo clearly realised Rav wasn't up to the task. 'Mother says he should come to school here,' he said.

'I'd really like to,' Rav added hurriedly.

Valraven glanced at his companions and Neferishu said, 'Here's a young man who's had fun at a funeral! Do you like Magrast, Rav?'

Rav nodded. 'Yes. Very much.'

'Perhaps you should consider it, Val,' said Prince Gastern. 'Your countryman, Merlan Leckery, came to be educated here at a very young age, and look where he is now. If Maycarpe ever retires, he'll be governor of Mewt. A Caradorean has never held that post, but it's no secret the Fire Chamber holds Leckery in high regard.'

'As does the subjugated queen of Mewt,' drawled Neferishu. 'Merlan has provided me with many happy hours of entertainment.'

Rav could see that his father was uncomfortable, and didn't know why. He wondered what he should say to help the situation.

'I shall discuss it with my wife,' Valraven said, in a tone that meant the subject should be dropped.

'Run along, Leo,' said Prince Gastern. 'Why don't you go and find Linnard? I don't suppose Rav's met him yet.'

Leo took hold of Rav's arm and dragged him away. Rav felt disappointed. He wasn't sure whether he'd gained anything or not.

'The last thing I'll do is introduce you to Gasburn's putrid son!' Leo said, suddenly sounding much more like Rav's friends at home. 'Lindy's a pile of sick! I'm always telling him so, just so he won't forget.' He let go of Rav's arm and began to run. 'Come on, let's go. I'll show you where they used to hang criminals on the wall outside.'

CHAPTER FIVE

The Fruit of the Quest

Varencienne retired to her chambers with a headache. The empress had monopolised her attention all afternoon, and it looked like a plot was being engineered by the ladies of the court to keep Varencienne in Magrast. She could not decline the numerous invitations without sounding ungracious or critical, and, if she were honest, there really was no valid reason to go scurrying back to Caradore at once. There was so much she could show the children here, and she did quite like the idea of renewing old acquaintances, just to see how childhood friends had turned out, but still she had a compelling urge to flee. Ellony had tried to help in her quiet way, talking always of home and how she missed it, but then Rav had bounced up, full of stories about Leo. When the empress had asked him if he wanted to stay on for a while, he'd reacted with delight.

As Varencienne sat before the mirror in her dressing room, rubbing the back of her neck, she acknowledged a painful truth: Rav loved Magrast. Sighing, she applied some lemon cream to her hands. She felt defeated, caught up in a process over which she had no control. Tatrini clearly adored Rav, and it was the natural instinct of any caring grandmother to want to do more for her grandchildren, but the empress had made no effort to do so before. Why now? Varencienne couldn't help feeling there was something more than Rav's education at stake.

Varencienne turned on her seat as Oltefney came into the room. The woman's expression was a curious mixture of disapproval and excitement. 'You have a visitor, Ren,' she said.

Varencienne instinctively knew who it was, but still asked, 'Who is it?'

'Merlan Leckery,' said Oltefney.

Varencienne turned to face the mirror once more, aware her face and neck were flushed. She hoped Oltefney wouldn't notice, but that was perhaps a vain hope. 'I will see him in the drawing room,' she said. 'Perhaps you could ask the servants to bring us refreshments.'

Oltefney went out without another word, which was unusual behaviour for her. Varencienne examined herself in the mirror, wound a few stray hairs into place. So, he had made contact. Varencienne sat up straight, attempting to slow her racing heart. She should not feel guilty about Merlan coming here. He was, after all, virtually a relative.

She heard his laughter before she entered the room. When she opened the door, she saw Oltefney, blushing and giggling, sitting in a chair opposite Merlan's own. He had been at work exercising his charm, it appeared. As she crossed the room, he stood up and swept a bow. 'Varencienne, you look marvellous.'

'Thank you,' she said. 'You are well, I trust? How is Mewt?'

'I am very well, and Mewt continues to delight me. Have you met Neferishu? She told me she would very much like to make your acquaintance.'

'Not yet. My mother chained me to my seat this afternoon.'

'I noticed.' Merlan glanced at Oltefney, his meaning clear.

Taking the cue, Varencienne said, 'Did you order a tray, Teffy?'

Oltefney, who was astute, narrowed her eyes slightly. She rose from her seat, 'I was just going to see to it.'

'Thank you.' Varencienne waited until Oltefney had left the room, before saying, 'I did wonder whether you'd come to see me or not. I received your letter, by the way.'

'Hmm.' Merlan had dropped his expression of flirtatious levity. 'That is partly why I am here now.'

Varencienne sat down in the chair Oltefney had vacated. 'Only partly?'

'I know what you are thinking – I didn't write or visit. I couldn't, Ren. You must know that. We were both aware of what we were doing and how ephemeral it must be.'

'I wasn't thinking that at all, actually. Don't believe I think you're here because you can't resist laying eyes on me once more. I just want to know the real reason.'

'We are conspirators,' Merlan said. 'I hope you haven't forgotten.'

'I never forget anything.' Not least his warm eyes, his resemblance to his brother. How could she broach that subject? It pressed upon her like a hot iron. 'Val and I have come to the conclusion you are quite a conspirator in many ways. Have you adopted the Mewtish way of being secretive?'

41

Merlan's face remained expressionless. 'What led you to this conclusion?'

I have currency, Varencienne thought. I know things that he does not. 'Val interviewed someone who is a prisoner in Cawmonel, who is known to you. He had quite a lot of interesting things to say.'

Merlan's face changed now. It became animated with hope and surprise. 'Tayven! Val found him?'

'Yes.' Disappointing he had guessed so quickly. 'He told Val about Khaster, Merlan. Val knows everything.'

'Oh.' Merlan dropped his eyes. 'I would have told him myself, but I couldn't. I was sworn not to – not yet.'

'But now he knows anyway.'

'Is he angry I didn't inform him?'

'No. But I expect he will want to speak to you about it, don't you?'

'What else did Tayven say?'

Varencienne shrugged a little. 'Val and I have had little time to talk privately since I came here, but I think that was all Tayven *would* say. You are all ones for secrets, I think.'

Merlan stood up and came to stand over Varencienne. She made herself remain still. She would not flinch from the fire in his eyes. 'Ren, there is good reason for it!' Merlan snapped. 'I am here now because there are things you should know. But you must swear to me on your children's lives you will not pass any of what I say on to Val.'

'You have no right to demand such of me!'

'Do you want to know or not?' Merlan said. 'I seem to recall you had quite a fondness for my brother – a man you have never met.'

'Naturally, I want to know,' Varencienne said coolly, 'but aren't you curious about Tayven?'

Merlan went back to his seat. 'I know already that Tatrini had him taken into custody, because Maycarpe has made enquiries of his own. It makes sense she'd put Tayven in Cawmonel. She no doubt intends to use him in some way to further one of her pet causes.'

'Aren't you concerned about him? Don't you want to get him out?'

'That would be impossible,' Merlan said. 'Tayven is no fool. He can look after himself. He's shown that beyond question.' He paused, then said, 'Will you give me your word I can speak in confidence?'

Varencienne inclined her head. 'Very well. I refuse to swear on my children's lives, but I will give you my word. That must be enough. But you'll have to convince me why Val must not know.'

'I will try.' He drew in a deep breath, then said, 'Last year, I went on a journey with Tayven and Khaster and a young man named Shan, who is

Khaster's apprentice. We went on a quest, which I believe has direct bearing on your husband's future, therefore your own.'

Varencienne frowned. 'Then why can't you speak to him about it?'

'Because people involved – very knowledgeable people – do not think the time is yet right. We need to see how things go here first. If things get out too soon, it might ruin the delicate web that could lead to changes we both dearly want.'

'Tell me about it,' Varencienne said.

She listened without commenting as Merlan told her how he met Shan in Akahana and learned that his brother was still alive. 'It sounded incredible, but apparently Khaster had become a kind of host to the intelligence of a powerful magus. He calls himself Taropat now.' Merlan told how Khaster had fled the battlefield in Cos, believing that Tayven was dead and wanting only to die, but that he'd been led instead to Taropat, who was dying himself and wanted to pass on his knowledge. Khaster, in effect, *became* Taropat, through a process Merlan could not describe in rational terms. Eventually the rejuvenated Taropat had taken an apprentice: Shan.

'When Shan came to Mewt to train under General Tuya in the martial arts, he set a chain of events in motion. He brought with him an artefact, which a sorceress had helped him acquire. It was the Dragon's Claw.' Merlan then related how Maycarpe knew of this artefact, and of others, all connected with the fate of the True King. And who was the True King? Maycarpe and Merlan believed him to be Valraven. 'Maycarpe possessed another artefact himself, the Dragon's Eye. He said that, along with the lost Dragon's Breath, these items were the totems of the brotherhood who had once surrounded the True King – the bard, the mystic and the warrior. He wanted us to quest for the third artefact, and also a fourth, which in some ways represented the sum total of the other three. It is known as the Crown of Silence. Only the True King may wear it, a man of magic, wisdom and courage. Who else but Val in this world do we know who fits that description?'

Merlan spoke of how Shan had initially been suspicious of Maycarpe as Taropat had indoctrinated him thoroughly against anything Magravandian, but eventually Maycarpe had won Shan over. He brought Tayven to Mewt, who then travelled to the Forest of Bree to find Taropat and persuaded him to join the quest. 'Khaster, or Taropat, was very important to Maycarpe. He believes him to be the incarnation of the mystic of the True King, as Shan is the warrior and Tayven the bard. The trouble is we had to keep Taropat in the dark about our beliefs, because he has a fanatical loathing of Val now. Tayven, reluctantly, had come to concur with Maycarpe and myself. I joined them on the quest, as my official status would help them cross sensitive boundaries. We were ever an uneasy company, but we reached Recolletine, the Seven Lakes, north of here, in the summer of last year.'

At this point in his narrative, Oltefney reappeared with two servants bearing trays. Varencienne waited impatiently while they set out the refreshments with infuriating slowness. Eventually she ordered them to hurry up and leave the room. Oltefney gave her a pointed glance as she left.

'Did you retrieve the artefacts?' Varencienne asked the moment the door was closed.

Merlan nodded. 'Yes. We fought like wolves, fell out, made up, starved ourselves, nearly died, but we were ultimately successful.' He described the events of the quest in detail, everything that had happened to them at the lakes. It stretched Varencienne's credulity beyond measure, despite the strange events she had lived through herself. She might not have been there to witness the quest first-hand, but there was no doubting the passion and conviction in Merlan's voice. Mystical events may have happened there, or they may not, but it was certain Merlan believed they had. 'The brotherhood surrendered the three Dragon artefacts at the seventh lake, Pancanara, and the Crown was given to us there. We returned with it to Bree and gave it to the sorceress, Sinaclara, who had been instrumental in Shan's training, and who had helped him attain the Claw. We'd agreed the Crown would be safe in Sinaclara's keeping until it was needed. Unfortunately, that was when things fell apart. Sinaclara revealed that she believed the Crown belonged to Val, and Taropat was furious. It ended up with him going off with Shan to Cos, no longer speaking to Tayven or me. He vowed to fight any attempt to make Valraven king, which is presumably why he sought out Princess Helayna of Cos.'

'That is an incredible story,' Varencienne said. 'I feel quite breathless!'

'I know how it sounds,' Merlan said, 'but I was there. I saw what happened. I experienced it. It changed us all.'

'But possessing an artefact, no matter how impregnated with symbolism it is, will not change things here,' Varencienne said. 'Valraven would not want to replace my father. The empire should be broken up, its subjugated nations emancipated. If we want a new world, we should seek unity through co-operation, not force.'

'I agree. There's no way we want to make a new emperor in the Malagash vein, if you'll forgive my aspersions upon your blood. But it is folly to believe that weak people make good rulers, and even more stupid to believe that humans can govern themselves without strong leaders. We need Val's strength. We must put him upon the throne of Magravandias, and then seek to make changes further afield.'

Varencienne uttered an outraged snort. 'You can't *make* Val anything! Your arrogance astounds me. He should be informed of your ideas and beliefs and be instrumental in whatever plans you have. It sounds to me as if you and Maycarpe and Foy knows who else want to use Val as some kind of figurehead, but that the real power behind the throne will be hidden. He's no puppet, Merlan.' She shook her head in agitation. 'This puts me in a very difficult position. I won't do anything behind Val's back.'

'You must not tell him, Ren. You promised. I know how it sounds, but you have to trust me on this.'

'Trust you?' Varencienne laughed coldly. 'I would as soon trust a shadow on the wind. Anyway, haven't you forgotten certain things, namely my family? You might recall that Bayard and Almorante also have aspirations to the throne. Gastern has the support of just about everyone here in Magrast. I cannot see Val agreeing to be part of a coup, I really can't.'

'Precisely. He won't go along with us – yet. This is why you must keep silent.'

'So what do you intend to do?'

'We have allies. Ashalan and Neferishu. Caution forbids either Maycarpe or me confiding in them fully, but enough guarded allusions have been made to suggest they will stand beside us should the need arise. It's obvious the entire Magravandian nation is extremely anxious about what will happen following your father's death. The army is ostensibly loyal to Gastern, but I believe that if it came to it, they'd support Val. They know, trust and love him. Gastern they are suspicious of, for obvious reasons.'

'Almorante has strong support,' Varencienne said. 'All Mordryn and Senefex care about is their own skins. At the moment, they're loyal to Gastern, because they believe Almorante or Bayard would take their power from them. They'd certainly lose power if the empire crumbled. The last time I spoke to my mother, her aims were similar to ours in many respects, except that she wants Bayard as king. A sun king, who will unify the disgruntled realms through the power of the spirit.'

'Whatever she says, she wants to maintain the empire,' Merlan said. 'I want Caradore to be free. Val has a valid claim to the Magravandian throne, because he is your husband.'

'We are talking in circles,' Varencienne said. 'Tell me straight. What do you and Maycarpe intend to do practically?'

Merlan hesitated, looking Varencienne directly in the eye. Then he said, 'The Malagash princes must die.'

He said it so baldly, so calmly, Varencienne was filled with horror. It was real. She saw it in her mind: the shadowy assassins, the glinting blades, the cups of poison, the blood and death. This man, whom she had once loved, who had ignited her body with feeling, was capable of ordering it done. It was expedient, necessary. She saw a pile of lifeless bodies with clouded eyes, flies buzzing over them. 'No,' she said.

'What do you mean, "no"?' Merlan said. 'Have you no stomach for it? It is the only way. You must see that, no matter how distasteful it seems.'

'They are my brothers. *Distasteful?* How dare you!'

'Oh, don't speak so morally to me, Ren! How do you think it must happen? Do you really see us all sitting around a table, chatting amicably, and your brothers agreeing that, yes, Val would really make a better king then they would? For Foy's sake, wake up!'

'They could be taken prisoner, exiled . . .'

'You know them better than that. You have no true feelings for them. You once told me that. They despise your womanhood and, if you got in their way, would think nothing of killing *you*. The Malagash ethic is conquer or be conquered, kill or be killed. You are nothing to them, you are Val's brood mare. You should care only about your own future and that of your children. Change is needed, Ren, but we won't achieve it with clean hands. That is the great responsibility, and it *is* distasteful. You must harden yourself. I know you can. I've seen what you are, your strength, your dignity, your wisdom. You are completely Val's comple-ment and for his sake, you must come into your own, take up the power of your blood. For, of all of them, you are the only one fit to wield it.'

Varencienne pressed her fingers against her eyes. She felt as if she was caught in a dark whirlpool. How easy it had been to talk of potential futures in Caradore with Merlan, four years ago. The future, then, had seemed so far away, her father immortal. Now, it had become real, urgent and unavoidable. People like Merlan were courageous enough to take desperate measures to achieve change. Was she like them? Surely not. She could neither countenance nor condone murder. But she must be alone in that. Even her mother could not believe she could get Bayard on the throne without spilling blood. Gastern was the rightful heir. The only way he wouldn't become emperor would be if he were dead. Varencienne's only instinct now was to get out of Magrast, take Rav and Ellony with her, return to Caradore where it was safe. She lowered her hands. 'Merlan, at this moment, I feel I want no part in this.'

His expression was almost contemptuous. 'So you are happy to let things continue as they are, for Foy to remain a slumbering, decaying

46

goddess beneath the sea, her true power – and yours – denied, for
Rav one day to take Val's place as the Dragon Lord of the imperial
army?'

Varencienne banged closed fists against the arms of her chair. 'No, I
am not happy with it, but I can't help feeling the odds are stacked in
Gastern's favour, or even in Bayard's or Almorante's. It's too much of a
risk, and I don't want to put my children, or anyone in Caradore, in
danger.'

'That attitude has helped perpetuate empires throughout history.'

'It is easy for you to say, Merlan. You are a free agent, unmarried and
childless.'

'If I had a wife or children, I would want liberty for them. In my view,
it is worth the risks. But why do I bother even saying that? I think your
views are similar to mine, but you just can't face the unpleasant prospect of disposing of your brothers.'

'Maybe I'm not as hard and driven as you want me to be. Yes, the
thought of killing my brothers repulses me. What kind of creature
would I be if it did not? Surely not one fit to rule others! I could not
stand before any of my kin and plunge a dagger into their heart, and if I
haven't the guts or will to do it myself, there's no way I should send
another to do it!'

'You're a hypocrite,' Merlan said. 'If someone you'd never met
threatened you, your family or Caradore, you'd have them killed
without a thought, in order to defend what's dear to you. If anyone
went for Ellie or Rav with a knife, you'd plunge that dagger into their
hearts.'

'This is not the same. My brothers are not a direct threat to me.'

'Not to you, maybe, no. But we're not seeking change simply to please
ourselves, are we? What about those children who *are* threatened? Shan
was one of them. Magravandian soldiers razed his village and raped him
when he was only a child. That is what you will allow to continue with
your pious morals! They are the morals of a woman in a high ivory
tower, who cannot even see the world through the clouds.'

'If I am in an ivory tower, it is that of my family and my blood. I do
not believe that atrocities will cease with the end of the Malagash
dynasty. Humans will always be cruel to one another. You are using
emotive propaganda to sway me, but I can see through it. It does not
change my view.'

Merlan gestured languidly with both hands. 'So, we reach an impasse.
You will put up with the way things are, and any foul developments that
might occur under Gastern's rule. However, I can't help feeling that
should any rebellious faction achieve success without your aid, you'll be

only too eager to partake of the rewards. Happily, under those circumstances, you will not have blood on *your* hands.'

Varencienne was silent for a moment. 'I would like you to leave now, Merlan. I've heard quite enough for one day.'

He stood up. 'Close your ears to it, Ren. That's the best way, isn't it? Be a good little woman of the empire, as women always have been. Great Foy, even your mother does more for your gender's cause than you do.'

'This is nothing to do with my gender,' Varencienne said. 'It is to do with my ethics. Good day to you, Merlan.'

'We must talk again.'

'No. Talk to Val, not me.'

He hesitated. 'I can't believe you're behaving like this. You're not the Varencienne I knew in Caradore.'

'And you're not the Merlan I knew either.'

'No, I'm not,' Merlan said bitterly. 'The quest for the Crown changed me. I told you it did. But it is an essential, needful change. You would be wise to emulate it.'

She wouldn't snap at his bait any further. 'Good day to you, Merlan.'

After he had gone, Varencienne put her face in her hands. Merlan had spoken of the great responsibility of her position, or her potential position, and in her heart she saw the sense of it: for the greatest good a few might have to be sacrificed. If she believed in that, what difference did it make if those few were her brothers?

Oltefney came back into the room and uttered a sympathetic sound when she saw Varencienne's agonised face. 'What is it, my pet?' she cried, hurrying over to Varencienne's chair. 'What did he say to you?'

Varencienne pressed her face against Oltefney's belly, sank into the older woman's embrace. 'He spoke of the future, Teffy, and it is terrible.'

'We should go home.'

'Yes,' Varencienne agreed, 'we should.'

That night, writhing restlessly in her bed, Varencienne awoke from a nightmare. At first she couldn't remember where she was, and the unfamiliar shapes around her in the room were threatening and unrecognisable. She called out the name of a nurse who had died when she was six years old. Then, as her eyes adjusted to the dim light, she remembered she was in Magrast. The bed was cold and wide around her like an ice flat. The only time she had not slept alone, in all her life, was during her brief affair with Merlan. Valraven had never spent a whole night with her.

The dream must have been brought on by the events of the day and

48

the fears that had quickened within her. It had to be. She couldn't bear to contemplate an alternative.

She had been standing on the cliffs above Caradore, a fierce wind blowing her hair into her eyes, so that she'd had to hold it back with both hands to see around her. Below, on the beach, two shadowy figures had been wrestling with a struggling burden. She thought they had an animal and were trying to sacrifice it to the sea. Then she had seen it was her own son in their grasp, his mouth wide as if in a scream, but all she could hear was the spiteful lament of the wind. She had called his name, but the sound had been snatched from her lips, carried back towards the castle in the hurrying air. Her feet had been mired in mud, which had also sucked at her skirts. She could not move. Rav's voice had begun to echo in her mind: 'Mama! Mama!' She could do nothing, only watch helplessly as Rav was taken away from her, offered to the sea.

She had thought there was someone standing behind her, for her spine had tensed. She had turned and there was Khaster Leckery sneering down at her from a great height. Was he really that tall? His hair billowed around his face, somehow more than hair. 'Help me!' she'd cried. 'Help my son.' But it was as if Khaster were nothing more than a statue of bitterness. She had admired this man for so long, and in the dream she'd been sure he'd known that, but all there was in his eyes was contempt and loathing. He'd sprung forward suddenly, his lips stretched into an ugly snarl. He'd raised his arm to strike her, the fingers closed into a fist. Then she'd woken up.

It had been years since she'd had a dream so real it had felt like she'd been awake. In her early years in Caradore, when the magic of the sea dragons had made itself felt in her blood, strange events and dreams had occurred regularly, but since Val had performed the ritual at Old Caradore four years before, they had tailed off. Varencienne had believed a job had been done, and she'd played her part in it. The rest would be up to Val. But now old feelings came crashing back. It was no use trying to convince herself otherwise: the dream had been a warning. But of what, of who? She couldn't understand why Caradore should be shown to her as a place of danger.

Varencienne sat in the bed, hugging her knees, resting her cheek upon them. She shivered, feeling sick with a strange longing and a terror of the future.

49

CHAPTER SIX

Mother Love

'Are we going to let this happen, mother? Are we?'

Prince Bayard stood before the empress's chair in her morning room, his face contused with frustrated anger.

Tatrini, the fingertips of her left hand plunged into a bowl of rose water while her deaf-mute manicurist worked diligently on her right hand, expressed a faint sigh. 'Bayard, we will gain nothing from impatience.'

'But Senefex and Mordryn will have Gastern crowned within the week.'

'Yes. That is because they want to keep hold of our foreign guests in order for Gastern's inauguration to be blessed and witnessed by all.'

'No. It is because they are afraid. Of us.'

The news had been released that morning. Of course, it would be inconvenient for people like Neferishu and Ashalan to return to their realms and then come back to Magrast for a coronation only weeks in the future. It made sense for Gastern to be crowned immediately. This did not worry Tatrini. She intended to move slowly and carefully.

'One has to take care in times of fear,' she said. 'A sudden move and those who feel threatened will strike out in panic. Let their feathers become smooth.'

'And what of Almorante? Will he wait before he acts?'

'Almorante, I am quite sure, intends to let fate do its work. After a short time of Gastern's rule, which I am sure will be remembered for its many instances of religious persecution, Almorante will simply become the voice of the people and slide into his disgraced brother's place. I believe Mordryn thinks he can control Gastern, that he is a pious and

50

loyal Madragorean, but the Archimage will have a rude awakening. Suddenly Almorante will be a much more attractive prospect.'

'Precisely!' Bayard cried, gesturing abruptly with his arms. 'Where will we stand then?'

'Exactly where we do now,' Tatrini said softly. She lifted her hand from the bowl, examined her fingernails. 'Remember, my son, where we began. Gastern is the devoted follower of Madragore, Almorante fancies himself a magus, but we know the truth. Only through the dragons will you acquire the throne. The elements must combine to create a greater whole. You are fire, Bayard, and the fire drakes will bow to you, but we need others.'

'If you're talking of Valraven Palindrake, forget it,' Bayard said. 'That is a pipe dream. He'll never support me.'

'I accept you are right,' Tatrini said mildly, 'and have amended my views.'

Bayard frowned at her. 'But he was your water man, wasn't he? The Dragon Heir, avatar of the sea dragons?'

'He is that,' Tatrini said, 'but then, so is his son.'

'Ah,' said Bayard, beginning to smile.

'Indeed. Earth is a problematical element, but I have made a decision. Leo must be our basilisk.'

'My brother Leo?' Bayard pulled a disagreeable face. 'He's just a boy.'

'As is Rav. That doesn't matter.'

'And air? Have you someone lined up for that? Another of my puling siblings, perhaps?'

Tatrini winced as her manicurist dug too deep into a cuticle. 'Ah, how appropriate,' she murmured. 'A thorn.'

'Mother?'

'Yes, I have an avatar of air waiting in the wings.'

'You have not said a name. This disquiets me.'

'As well it should. Sometimes the past comes back with the force of an apocalyptic storm. But you must face it, Bayard, as a divine king would face it, with dignity and equanimity.'

Bayard said nothing, staring at her with wide eyes, his handsome face as white as bone.

Tatrini made him wait for a while, then said, 'Bayard, you must listen to me now. I have not told you why I feel you, above all others, should take Gastern's place. Never think I do not know what you are, what you have been. But despite your less prudent excesses, which I trust age and experience will temper, you are still nobility. You, as your ancestors did, will rule through a superior strength. Empires have risen and fallen throughout history, but they all suffered the same fate before they fell:

51

they became sickly. This need not happen to Magravandias. We, the true Malagashes, hold our feelings of power in esteem. We do not curb or repress them. As nobility, we believe we have a right to give free vent to our instincts, whether they are animosity, compassion, cruelty, love, raiding, changing or destroying. Unlike your brothers, who feel they have to justify these instincts or indeed suppress them, as in Gastern's case, you, my son, know as I do that what is good is what is useful. Those who seek to overthrow our rule – in essence Mordryn and his minions – are riddled with pathetic ascetic beliefs in piety, rectitude and right-eousness – a disease of the psyche! They have no nobility. They have risen from the ranks of those who resent our power and therefore seek to destroy it. Only the weak make of their weakness a virtue. The Malagash dynasty, through the Madragorean priests, has been infected by the sickness of moral virtue. It is in danger of becoming like those we are supposed to rule, full of fear. Under your father's rule, the empire expanded, yes, but where was he? Sitting here amongst his advisors, doing what the priests told him to do. We should not be subservient to them, terrified of their god, who is but a distorted image of the elemental fire drakes. Neither should we put our feelings of power onto entities outside ourselves. We are power too, like and equal to them. Life is nothing other than the will to conquer, and we must affirm this. If you doubt my words, look only upon the battlefield, with which you are already intimately familiar. You are a hedonist, but your will is great. You have fought alongside your men in battle. You are an elemental force, primal in your being, an authentic man. Not everything about you is admirable, but what you represent is nobility's highest aspira-tion.'

Bayard stared at her in silence after this speech; the only sound in the room was the scrape of a sandboard against the empress's fingernails. Then Bayard said, 'Who is air, mother?'

'Tayven Hirantel,' Tatrini answered. 'You might remember him.'

Bayard's poise was remarkable. 'A whore,' he said in a flat voice.

'A dead whore, if you could have had anything to do with it,' Tatrini said. 'But still, he lives. Yes, I know about what you did, Bayard. You acted through fear, which I hope you regret.'

'Why him?' Bayard said. 'I should imagine he regards me as fondly as Palindrake does.'

'Hirantel is a rare creature,' Tatrini said. 'And very similar to you, although I'm sure he'd be most affronted by such an idea. I have him in custody, in a safe place. He is a survivor, who has held onto life and power with matchless tenacity. For this reason, he will eventually see reason. I've kept him waiting. By now, he will be in a frenzy of anxiety

52

and curiosity, wondering what I have in store for him. When he finds out, it will come as a relief.'

Bayard smirked. 'Your faith is as great and optimistic as that of Mordryn.'

'It is not faith,' Tatrini said. Her manicurist had now finished her job and gathered up her tools. Tatrini nodded thanks to her, momentarily dismissing Bayard from her attention.

He, meanwhile, paced her chamber, apparently so full of words he couldn't decide which to spit out first.

'Varencienne will be here soon,' Tatrini said. 'You'd better go.'

'She is my sister, and I've not yet seen her,' Bayard snapped. 'Has Palindrake turned her against me?'

'Varencienne is a moderate,' Tatrini replied. 'Now she is adult, she deplores certain of your behaviours.'

'What? Are mine any worse than Palindrake's?'

'If you are present, she will not speak freely.'

Bayard's face had gone quite white again. He was learning to contain his anger, gradually. 'How under your thumb is she, mother? Will she surrender her son to you?'

'I enjoyed our chat, Bay. We will speak again soon.' She knew he detested being dismissed, but respected her enough not to argue.

He bowed curtly. 'I hope your chat with Ren goes as favourably as the one we've just had.'

Tatrini smiled mildly. 'Goodbye, Bay.'

The empress, in fact, felt slightly anxious about seeing her daughter, but knew she only had herself to blame. Over the last ten years, when she could have been cultivating Varencienne's friendship, she had left her to her own devices. What an oversight not to realise the quiet little teenager would turn into a stubborn and independent woman. Varencienne had been a nobody here in Magrast, hidden in the shadow of her brothers. In Caradore, she'd found status and power, things that any Malagash craved, although Varencienne herself would be the last to admit that.

Only minutes after Bayard had left, Varencienne came marching into her mother's chamber, her face set rigidly for a fight. Tatrini sighed inwardly. She saw her younger self in the challenging expression before her. It was the one she had used to persuade her mother-in-law she was ready for the knowledge guarded by the Malagash queens.

'Ren,' she said, 'you appear most defensive. Sit down and relax.'

'I don't intend staying for long,' Varencienne replied. 'I'm taking the children home tonight.'

'Oh, a change of plan? Yesterday you seemed quite taken with the idea of spending a little time with your friends here. And there is Gastern's coronation, of course.'

Varencienne folded her arms. 'Stop toying with me. I don't belong here any more. I won't be part of your schemes, or anyone else's. Neither will my children. As for seeing Gastern crowned, I couldn't stoop to it. I sincerely doubt he'll live to enjoy his new position for long.'

'I'm sure it won't come to that,' Tatrini said. 'You're aware I don't want Gastern on the throne, and for very good reasons, but there are ways to change the situation politically.'

'It won't happen,' Varencienne said. 'If you truly think otherwise, you are not the woman I believe you to be.'

This was going to be more difficult than Tatrini had thought. She could see the resentment and fear in her daughter's eyes. 'Why are you so afraid?' she asked.

'You expect me to dispute that, don't you? Well, I won't. I *am* afraid. It is because I believe you and my brothers to be capable of anything. I am afraid of what you will do. Why can't you accept I'm not like you? You can't keep me here, and you can't have Rav, and that's the end of it.'

'Have Rav?' Tatrini enquired delicately. 'What do you mean by that?'

'You know very well. You've never shown an interest in him before, so I can only assume you've decided he could be useful to you in some way.'

'You are harsh,' said Tatrini. 'I know I've not been a good mother to you, Ren, and have been neglectful of my duties as a grandparent. You must appreciate it has been difficult for me to keep hold of the reins I have snatched for myself here. I have had little time for the gentler aspects of womanhood. But that will change. When you look into the future of Magrast, you see blood, smoke and fire, but I see only light.'

'Stop it now,' Varencienne said. 'You will not convince me.'

Apparently not, Tatrini thought. She heard doors opening close by and knew that reinforcements were nigh. She had sent for Rav from the nursery, aware how her grandson's feelings were running. Leo was a good boy, with the potential to be greater than Bayard, if his older brothers didn't corrupt him along the way. He did as she asked and reported back to her in detail. She knew every word of the conversation Leo had had with Rav the previous day. *Every* word – even those inspired by what Bayard had said to his younger brother.

One of Tatrini's ladies came into the room, ushering Rav before her. Tatrini did not look at her or the child, but watched Varencienne's face.

She saw dismay and despair. Varencienne too knew how Rav felt. 'This is low, mother,' she said softly, shaking her head.

'I've asked Rav to join us so that he may be given a voice,' Tatrini said. 'We are discussing his future after all, and he *is* the Dragon Heir.'

Rav looked embarrassed, clearly uncomfortable with the rancour hanging in the air between the adults.

'You set Leo to work on him, didn't you?' Varencienne said.

'Rav,' said the empress, 'how would you feel about coming to school here in Magrast and spending more time with your father?'

Rav glanced sheepishly at Varencienne. He was half Palindrake and therefore the instinct to have his own way was not quite as strong as it was in his uncles. 'I don't know,' he said, obviously worried about offending his mother.

'You can speak freely,' Tatrini said. 'Your mother wants to know how you feel as much as I do.'

'He is too young to make such a decision,' Varencienne said. 'This is ridiculous.' She went to her son and took his hand. 'Come along, Rav, we're leaving.'

Tatrini rose from her chair. 'Ren, you are making a grave mistake.'

Varencienne would not answer, put her hand upon the door knob.

'Rav is in danger,' Tatrini said. 'It has been foretold. He must remain here in Magrast for his own safety.'

She saw her daughter pause, her spine stiffen. There was no other response for a moment, and in that brief time, Tatrini realised she had unwittingly hit the right mark. 'You *know*, don't you,' she murmured, the surprise in her voice genuine.

Varencienne turned round. 'Tell me what you mean,' she said. 'Tell me!'

'My augur, Lady Pimalder, has warned me that Rav should not return to Caradore, because he would be threatened.'

'In what way?'

Varencienne wasn't arguing. She wasn't retaliating in any way. What could this mean? 'Whoever threatens him is powerful, because Grisette could not see through their defences. This is a real danger, Ren. I did not want to speak of it, but it is clear I must.'

'Mama?' Rav said fearfully.

'I had a dream last night,' Varencienne said. 'Someone was trying to throw Rav into the sea . . . ' She glanced down at her son, who was now clinging to her skirts.

'Caradore is out in the middle of nowhere,' Tatrini said quickly. 'Here in Magrast, Rav would be surrounded by the Magravandian army and his father would be close.'

'But who would want to harm him?'

Tatrini went to her daughter, put an arm about her. 'I do not yet know, but I will. You must realise that the Palindrakes are an important family to the Malagashes. Enemies could seek to use Rav against us.'

'But who? One of my brothers?'

'No,' said Tatrini. 'That much is definite. Someone else.' She examined her daughter's face and could tell that Varencienne had ideas of her own, but that she would not speak. It didn't matter. 'I know you are afraid that Magrast will soon be thrown into civil turmoil and that Rav's life could be at risk. But the change, when it happens, will not occur that way. I promise you this, Ren, upon my life. May the fire drakes strike me dead if I lie.'

For the briefest moment, Varencienne leaned against her mother. 'He should not have heard this,' she murmured. 'He is so young.' She pressed Rav against her.

Tatrini squeezed Varencienne's shoulders and crouched down beside the boy. 'There's nothing to fear, Rav. I will keep you safe, and so will your father. You are a very important person and as you grow older, will have to become used to the fact that in some ways this makes you vulnerable. Here in Magrast you can learn how to be strong, like your father is. You'd like that, wouldn't you?'

Rav nodded, his face dark with fear, streaked with tears. 'Mama,' he said again and put his face back against Varencienne's gown. Now it came to it, he was afraid of being separated from her.

Tatrini stood up. 'You could remain here with him, Ren.'

Varencienne stared at her mother, and Tatrini had the distinct impression that the very fact of Rav's endangerment in Caradore meant her daughter would have to return there. It was to do with her suspicions of who was involved. She straightened up, recovered her poise. 'I'm not saying I will let Rav stay here for ever, mother,' she said, 'but until I know the nature of this danger, I consent to him remaining here under Val's care. Rav must live in his father's apartments, and suitable guardians must be found for him. If Val is agreeable to this I will make no further objection. But you must swear to me that Rav will be well guarded at all times. There must be no gadding about with Leo, no being left to his own devices with other children, even within the palace or the homes of courtiers. Will you promise me that?'

'I swear it,' Tatrini said. Privately, she was surprised at this capitulation. She'd thought she'd have to use far more persuasion. The dream must have been very real. 'We must work together to learn about this threat,' she said.

'*I* will uncover it,' Varencienne said. She lifted Rav's chin in her hand.

'You can stay here for a while, my love, but never forget where your home is. Do you understand?'

The boy nodded, his lower lip trembling.

'Ren,' said Tatrini, 'if you insist on going home, you might well be in danger yourself. You should reconsider.'

'I am not afraid,' Varencienne replied. 'I will meet whatever awaits me with courage and fire. I will know the truth.'

CHAPTER SEVEN

The Power of Princesses

So, Shan thought, here is Caradore. They had climbed up from the beach, twelve men fighting against the wind that had transformed the dune grasses into a whispering, rippling ocean, blown flat yet undulating in the spectral light. Clouds, big as heavenly galleons, surged across the sky, skirting the uncanny blue halo around the moon. Shan was first to reach the top of the cliffs and here he paused. A landscape of rock and wild grass and twisted trees stretched away from him. Great white owls drifted like flotsam on the night wind. In the distance, lights upon hills: the castles and manses of the noble families of Caradore. The night was *alive* around him, as if spirits streamed through his body and plucked with invisible fingers at his hair. This was indeed a magical land.

Taropat came up beside Shan, breathing heavily, which Shan thought was nothing to do with the exertion of the climb, for Taropat was extremely fit.

'You are home,' said Shan.

Taropat said nothing. Shan wondered what the man was thinking. Only a few miles away, his wife lay sleeping in Caradore Castle, unaware of his presence on this soil. Did Taropat want to see her again? Was he remembering her rich dark hair, her wild laugh? Did he want to love her or kill her? Pharinet Palindrake believed he was dead. He could rise up like a ghost beside her bed, fill her with fear, condemn her for her treachery. Perhaps her heart would stop. But Taropat had no intention of going to Caradore.

The ship had waited offshore from Cos for a week before beginning the journey west. Seven days of tension. Taropat had insisted he would know the right moment to lift anchor. They had ten Cossic warriors with them, men who were ill-used to sea travel and restless with the delay. In Cos Taropat had hired a large fishing vessel, so as not to arouse the suspicion of any imperial patrols. They must be in and out of Caradore quickly. Timing was crucial.

Taropat signalled to the Cossics behind them and walked silently into the band of trees that skirted the coast road. Shan followed with the others. They were here because of a vision which was driven by Taropat's obsessions. Shan was still not entirely convinced they were doing the right thing.

Soon after they'd fled Breeland, following the Seven Lakes quest, Taropat had begun to dream of Valraven Palindrake. To him, the dreams were hideous nightmares. He came out of them disorientated and sometimes raving. He said the Dragon Heir would come to wear the Crown of Silence. There was nothing they could do.

'Can we not change fate?' Shan had said, trying to inspire hope within his mentor. 'Haven't we proved that?'

'I don't know,' Taropat had answered, and those were words that rarely passed his lips.

In Cos it had taken them months to find Princess Helayna. Taropat had the power of the Dragon's Eye within him, and most of their map derived from impressions in his mind. It was as if the land didn't exist until he'd invented it in front of them. A tree with a bent limb. A crossroads marked by scorched earth. A pool surrounded by willows. That is the way.

They could not speak of what had happened at Sinaclara's house, because even to think of it filled them with a fury it was impossible to dispel. They would kill each other if they broached the subject, inspired only to violence, to hate. It seemed Magravandias only had one enemy: Helayna, exiled princess of Cos. She had become a saint in their hearts, the one true royal soul left alive. They must find her. Shan thought that Taropat would want Helayna to help him steal the Crown from Sinaclara and once had even suggested so in covert terms. But Taropat had shaken his head. It took Shan a while to realise why. Taropat, though a powerful magus, was afraid of Sinaclara, perhaps afraid of the Crown itself. It had become evil in his eyes.

Taropat wanted to know Helayna's plans. He intended to offer her his aid rather than the other way around. Both he and Shan had been changed by their quest in Magravandias. Shan was the Avatar of the Dragon's Claw, potentially a great warrior. Taropat was the Magus of the Dragon's Eye, his powers intensified and honed. They lacked the Bard of the Dragon's Breath, of course, because that was Tayven. And they did not have a True King to serve, but perhaps they could make a True Queen and find themselves another Bard.

As winter took a grip on the gaunt crags of the Rhyye, the mountain range that bisected the country, Cossic warriors had taken them prisoner. Since her brother's capitulation to empress Tatrini, Helayna had become doubly suspicious and paranoid. They were lucky not to have been killed outright, which was the usual fate of strangers who strayed into the princess's territory. For a while, she refused to see them. Apart from their clothes, all their possessions were taken from them, and for a week they lived in a wooden cage dusted with snow, exposed to the elements, fed with mush that appeared to be fodder for pigs. They spent all their time huddled together, seeking warmth. The guards could not be bribed, for there was nothing to bribe them with. The Cossics either couldn't speak Magravandian or Breenish, or pretended they couldn't. All the prisoners could do was repeat Helayna's name and try to draw pictures in the air to show they were not enemies.

One night, Taropat lost his temper. His fingers had become numb and he was afraid he would lose them to the cold. Without warning, he leapt to his feet, knocking Shan aside. He roared in rage, flinging back his ragged brown cloak. He raised his arms high, his blue fingers splayed above his head. Stamping his feet, he called out in a tongue Shan did not know, perhaps Caradorean. After a few minutes, some of the Cossics came out of their makeshift dwellings, no doubt wondering what the noise was. Taropat snarled at them, his hair wild around his head and shoulders, his teeth gleaming whitely through his thin beard.

'Taropat, no!' Shan hissed, afraid they would be beaten or killed.

Taropat's body suddenly jerked and then a spear of light shot down from the heavens. It struck the frozen soil outside the cage, sending up a spray of pebbles and ice. Taropat gripped the bars of the cage, shook them so that snow thunked down from the slatted roof. He gestured madly with his arms and more lights came whizzing out of the frost-rimed trees, earthlights that bobbed and swerved around the astonished people.

'Helayna!' Taropat had yelled, and she had come then.

The princess could speak Magravandian. She stood before their prison, a tall woman in a warrior's garb, swathed in a thick wolfskin cloak. Her face, though handsome, was hardened by bitterness and grief. She said, 'Speak.'

She had been keeping them waiting on purpose. The Cossic resistance did not generally keep prisoners. He and Taropat should have guessed this. They were the only ones.

So Helayna had heard a brief version of their story. At first she did not believe it or pretended not to. She said, 'You lie!' and then to her guards, 'Kill them.'

'Your people have seen what I can do,' Taropat said calmly. 'It will take many of your men to kill us, and you will lose most of them in the process. Can you afford that?' He was bluffing, of course, and perhaps Helayna knew that. Desperation had temporarily heightened Taropat's magical ability. Shan did not believe the man could kill others with it.

Helayna turned back to him. 'You have not used your powers to escape,' she said contemptuously.

'That is because I have come to the Rhyye seeking you,' Taropat replied. 'I am a patient man, and appreciate your reserve concerning strangers, but I do not want to lose my hands to frostbite before you grant us an audience.'

'Let them out,' the princess said.

She was a cornered woman, driven into the most inhospitable terrain of Cos by Palindrake's patrols. Like a hunted animal, she was afraid and unpredictable, but masked it with a cold savagery. Taropat had at first addressed her as 'your majesty', but she'd turned on him in fury.

'I have no majesty!' she spat. 'I am a warrior, at one with my people, without whom I would be dead. That term offends me now. It speaks of all I have come to despise.'

Namely, Shan reckoned, her brother Ashalan.

But perhaps Helayna was not as hard and ruthless as she liked to appear. She took them to her dwelling, which was a large cave she shared with the most trusted of her people, both male and female. Here she let Taropat and Shan bathe and shave. Clean clothes of thick wool were given to them. Now Helayna wanted to hear their story in more detail, even though it was the middle of the night. A man had built up the fire and they sat around it, talking, until way past dawn. Taropat did not hide his origins, and spoke at length about the Dragon heritage of the house of Palindrake and his dead sister's unwitting part in it. This surprised Shan. He'd always thought Taropat was ashamed of having once been Khaster. Helayna had heard of him. The story of Khaster Leckery had become a legend, because in some ways he was a martyr, destroyed by Magravandias. Tayven had also spoken of Khaster to Ashalan and Helayna when he'd lived with the resistance.

Helayna interrupted the narrative only once, and that was when Taropat spoke of Tayven's betrayal. It was clear Helayna was fond of him. 'You are wrong about him,' she said. 'He would never serve the Dragon Lord.'

Taropat hesitated, then said, 'Perhaps.'

'You once loved each other. He told us. You have no proof he supports Palindrake. You ran from that woman Sinaclara's house too quickly.'

'Well . . . ' Taropat clearly struggled for words. 'I can only tell you what happened. Draw your own conclusions.'

After that, Shan noticed Taropat did not mention Tayven again, obviously aware he should not offend the princess or alienate her before he'd won her over.

After the story was out, Helayna leaned back upon a pile of furs, taking swigs from a skin of crude wine. 'Only a fool would believe you,' she said. 'You've told me a fairytale.'

'Yes,' Taropat said. 'I have. But it is still true.'

'Palindrake could have sent you here. Perhaps Khaster Leckery is still dead and you are a lie.'

'I would think that,' Taropat said. 'But surely the utter outrageousness of our tale belies its truth? No sane spy would rely upon such a pre-posterous story.'

Helayna nodded. 'True.' She handed Taropat the skin, from which he drank.

'We are here to offer you our services,' he said. 'We are the Magus and the Warrior of the True King. Those we trusted want Palindrake as king. It is a terrible falsehood. We cannot countenance it.' He handed the wine to Shan. 'Is it possible we could find a True Queen?'

Helayna laughed at that. 'Queen? Me? I am nothing now, merely a fugitive, hiding from Palindrake's men. He has vowed to track me down, you know. It galls him I would not succumb to his glamour and Tatrini's empty gestures, like my rat of a brother did.'

Shan thought Helayna was probably slightly wrong in her assump-tions. Glancing around himself, he knew she was indeed nothing, certainly not a threat to the Dragon Lord. He'd probably forgotten about her. Imperial patrols in the Rhyye would be on the lookout for bandits and smugglers. Helayna would come into that category now. She had lost everything else. What are we doing here? Shan wondered. Not for the first time, he wondered whether Taropat's hatred of Palindrake was based upon jealousy because he wanted to be the True King himself.

'I think you would be a splendid queen,' Taropat said.

Helayna's smile faded a little. Shan saw that, for a moment, she dared to believe someone had come to her who could restore her power. She wanted so desperately for that to be true. 'How I long to rid Tarnax of vermin,' she said softly, her eyes glinting in the firelight. 'My family ruled there for eight generations. Our blood goes back to Great King Alofel. Ashalan has betrayed it. Alofel must writhe in his grave. In his day, Cos bowed to no one.'

'Indeed,' Taropat said.

'How can you help me?' Helayna asked sharply. 'The task is too big and we are too few.'

Taropat contemplated her for a moment, his fingers steepled against his mouth. 'I do not yet know,' he said at last. 'I need to know you, become familiar with your ways. I need the time and space to look into the aethers, discern what is happening in other places. I could find allies for you, other magi who travel the astral realm. You can be sure the world is full of men and women who secretly detest the empire and would give their loyalty to a woman intent on toppling it.'

'This is a dream,' Helayna said. 'A wonderful dream, but like snow beneath the sun.'

'Look at me,' Taropat said. 'I am living evidence that miracles can happen.'

Helayna's smile returned. 'Whatever happens, you have entertained me. You may stay with us.'

Over the next few months, Shan came to realise that Helayna very much liked having a personal vizier like Taropat. There had once been a wise woman with the resistance, named Old Mag, but she had died during the summer. Shan was wary of becoming known as Helayna's champion warrior, because it would only cause resentment in people who'd fought at her side for years. He maintained a low profile, bore the jokes and tricks of those around him, and gradually made friends. But occasionally he caught Helayna watching him, a speculative expression on her face. Shan was unsure what lay behind it: suspicion, awareness or mistrust? While Taropat spent most days talking with Helayna and teaching her the rudiments of the magical craft, Shan went out hunting with his comrades, tended the meagre crops they had, repaired the dwellings or cared for the animals. It was a simple life, similar in many respects to the one he'd had and lost in childhood. Perhaps this was how it would be now: a return to humble roots. He'd had his moment of glory on the quest for the Crown, but it was over. He'd played his part and the light of the gods must now shine upon others. He did not think Taropat could help Helayna. As she'd accurately pointed out, the resistance was too small to affect the might of the empire. It had just been a dream. Ultimately the quest had been, for him at least, concerned only with personal growth, not with changes to the world.

Then Taropat had the vision. As he'd promised Helayna, he spent many private hours in meditation, his spirit winging through the astral realm, seeking allies. No one he'd yet encountered had been persuaded to back Helayna. The magi of the world thought it a fruitless and pointless endeavour. But one day, close to sundown, Taropat came staggering blindly from the cave where he meditated. Shan, who was grooming a horse nearby, dropped his tools and ran forward to his mentor.

'Taropat, what is it?' The man had been blinded on the quest at Lake Pancanara, but his sight had been restored to him. Had it now been taken again?

Taropat put his hands against his eyes and sank to the ground. His whole body was shuddering. By this time, others had gathered around him, asking questions. Shan held Taropat close, his head whirling. 'Stand back,' he said. 'Fetch Helayna.'

The princess came quickly and once she was before him, Taropat pulled away from Shan and got to his feet. Now he appeared perfectly all right. 'I know what we must do,' he said.

'What?' Helayna demanded.

'I have the power of the Eye within me, and my vision travels far. The emperor is not long for this world. I have seen him dying. I went into his mind and for some time had to fight to escape it.'

Helayna uttered a choked laugh, almost of incredulity. 'If Leonid dies, Magrast will be unstable. His sons will fight for succession.'

'But perhaps not in any way we could imagine,' Taropat said. 'I have seen many times that the Dragon Heir will wear the Crown. But until today one crucial thing escaped me. It seems so obvious now.' He paused.

'What? What?' Helayna demanded.

'Who is the Dragon Heir?' Taropat said.

Helayna screwed up her face in vexation. 'Palindrake, of course. What do you mean by this?'

'Precisely,' Taropat said softly. 'Valraven Palindrake. The heir to Caradore, whose father serves the empire.'

There was a silence, then Shan said, 'The Dragon Lord's son.'

'I saw a child as king,' Taropat said, 'but a child who aged before my eyes and turned into Valraven Palindrake. The message is obvious. We must go to Caradore.' Pushing people aside, he marched towards the dwelling he shared with Shan.

'He means to kill the child?' Helayna said to Shan.

Shan shrugged. 'I have no idea.' He hurried after Taropat.

In their shared dwelling he found his mentor gathering up some of his possessions. He was fevered, his movements jerky. Without looking up at Shan, who was standing helplessly in the doorway, Taropat said, 'Palindrake knows it's too late for him in this life. He'll invest all his energy into his son.'

Shan came into the room. 'You want to kill this child?'

Taropat looked up then. 'Kill him? Well, actually, I hadn't thought of that. It seems clear to me we must take the boy for ourselves.'

64

'Why?'

'If he is indeed the True King, then we must ensure he becomes one. Close to his family, which is loathsome on both sides, he will eventually become tainted. He must be taken from them.'

Shan stared at Taropat in dumb disbelief for some moments. So, he failed with me, he thought. And now he seeks a new apprentice, someone worthy, a child to mould. 'Just how do suppose you might accomplish that?' he asked in a cold voice.

'Fate is on our side. Once Leonid dies, Palindrake's family is bound to go to Magrast for the funeral. The wife is the emperor's daughter, after all. The children might travel with their mother, or they might not. I will continue to quest for information in the aethers. If the boy leaves Caradore, we will snatch him on the road. If not, we will take him from the castle. Palindrake won't be there, just the domestic guard. I know that place inside out. It won't be that difficult.'

'You are insane,' Shan said. 'It can't possibly be that easy.'

Taropat threw a bundle of clothes angrily onto the floor. 'Since we left Breeland, my dreams have been plagued with images of Palindrake as king,' he said. 'It was as if my own mind was tormenting me. But all along, it was trying to show me the truth. I am now completely sure what must be done. It is meant to be.'

'You can't make a king out here,' Shan said. 'If you think you can, the future is condemned to remain in the realm of dreams. Palindrake will come looking for the boy. He has access to magi too, doesn't he?'

'You are too comfortable here,' Taropat said with a sneer. 'Remember the quest, what we learned upon it, how we felt. It cannot have been for nothing. Pancanara surrendered the Crown to us. We were deemed worthy. Therefore I believe we can do whatever we set our minds to, as long as we follow the destiny of the Crown. Do not waste the power of the Claw, Shan. Remember who you are.'

I do, Shan thought, but perhaps you have forgotten.

Helayna supported Taropat's idea, probably because she had come to have faith in him, and also because she wanted, once more, to have an effect upon the world. She offered ten of her best warriors as escort, men skilled at moving invisibly in the landscape.

But perhaps Helayna was not quite confident in Taropat. Before he and Shan left for the coast, Helayna contrived to speak with Shan alone, approaching while he was cleaning the stables and asking him to accompany her to her dwelling, which during the day was generally deserted. Once there, she confronted him with a direct question. 'Do you think this child is the True King?'

'No,' Shan answered honestly. 'And neither does Taropat, in his heart. He is driven by his visions and his fears.'

'This act will inflame Palindrake.'

'Of course.'

'Hmm.' Helayna folded her arms, gazed past Shan's shoulder for a moment, then her eyes swivelled back towards him. 'I know you fear Palindrake will come looking for the boy here, but does he really have any idea that Khaster Leckery might return from the dead to steal his son, and that he would bring him to Cos?'

'I think Palindrake knows Khaster isn't dead by now,' Shan said, 'and there are few enemies to the empire left who have the will to act against the Dragon Lord. You will fall under suspicion, I'm sure.'

Helayna nodded slowly. She appraised Shan. 'I'm surprised Taropat hasn't tried to make a king out of you.'

'Why?' Shan felt his face flush.

'I have been watching you,' she said. 'I've seen the way you are with people. You have grace, Shan, an inner quiet, but it is also very clear how strong you are, how purposeful. You would make a king whose people would love him. Taropat must have seen this.' She paused. 'I can't help thinking your apprenticeship began along different lines to what it has become.'

'I no longer look upon myself as Taropat's apprentice,' Shan said. 'Perhaps I am not the person he thought I would grow into.'

Helayna said nothing for a moment, a silence that filled Shan with discomfort. What was she trying to say to him? Eventually, she said, 'The child must be removed from his family, if there is any chance Taropat's vision might be correct. But I'm not sure we should make a king of him.'

'Then you would kill him?'

She glanced at him sharply. 'I did not say that.' A pause. 'You do not have noble blood, do you?'

'I would think that was quite obvious.'

Again she looked thoughtful. 'A champion may be given title by a queen.'

'My lady . . .'

'What?'

He shook his head. 'I am unsure of what you mean by this conversation.'

'Then think on it,' she said.

Troubled, Shan left her and went to make the final preparations for their journey. Had Helayna implied she would consider making him her consort if she became queen of Cos? Without allies, she could never accomplish that. She was as full of dreams as Taropat was.

Now Shan and Taropat were in Caradore, following a vision. Taropat had assured his company that Leonid was dead and that Varencienne Palindrake had travelled to Magrast with her children and a small escort. Taropat knew the Caradorean terrain well and had selected an area where the kidnap would be attempted: a narrow pass in the mountains that led to Caradore Castle. It was far from any settlements or noble estates. Shan still felt uneasy. Palindrake was not stupid. Given the instability of the empire and the fact that he was ostensibly a supporter of Prince Gastern, he'd surely realise his son should be placed under extra guard. It was unlikely the Dragon Lord would be able to return with his family to Caradore at this time, but it was not impossible. What would I do in his place? Shan wondered. Keep the family in Magrast perhaps. We might be wasting our time here.

The company camped in the mountains for several nights and the only people who passed beneath their hidden base were a few farmers, merchants and travellers. Even the Cossics were becoming sceptical that Princess Varencienne would return upon this road, at least in the near future. But Taropat remained convinced that she would. Shan wondered how long Taropat would keep this up. Any day now, a member of the Leckery household might pass beneath them, servants whom Taropat would recognise, or perhaps even one of his family. Did he feel nothing being so close to his old home? Didn't he yearn to see it once more? He'd always spoken of it with such affection. But no mention was made of Norgance, the Leckery domain, and Shan didn't have the will or the desire to mention it himself. Taropat was a hard, self-obsessed man. But he hadn't always been that way. During those few days of waiting, as the early spring rain relentlessly soaked the mountains, Shan reminisced wistfully about his early days in the Forest of Bree, when Taropat had been like an uncle to him. He had pulled Shan from the dark pit of despair that had followed the destruction of his village, Holme, by the Magravandian army and the hideous violation that had been perpetrated upon him. In the wake of recovery, Taropat had taught him so many wondrous things. Shan remembered summer evenings outside the tall narrow house beside the mill pool, when he and Taropat had talked into the night over good food and wine. He remembered Nip, Master Thremius's apprentice, who had become his best friend. Had she forgotten him now? And Sinaclara, who had taught him how to love a woman, and who had ultimately betrayed him.

In the late afternoon, sitting on a rocky ledge high above the road, Shan tortured himself with morbid thoughts. I have been torn from every place I ever loved. Holme was destroyed, my relatives killed. The Forest of Bree, where I found solace and friends, is denied me. And now I am removed from Cos, where perhaps I might have had a simple but fulfilling life. Am I weak and foolish to follow this distempered man so loyally?

He picked up a small rock, intent on throwing it across the pass, but a sound from below stilled his hand. Horses. The rumble of a carriage. At once Shan's mind cleared and became alert. The sun had not yet set behind the peaks, but already the road below was in twilight. He crouched on the rock peering down. A chittering animal call from the rocks opposite advised him that Cossic scouts posted there were also alert and ready.

Then Taropat was beside him, hunched down, energy thrumming from his body like a physical force. Shan glanced at him and realised that for the first time in months Taropat looked handsome, as a Caradorean knight should appear. Perhaps you are not quite dead yet, Khaster, Shan thought.

The horses came into view first, six of them: dark glossy bays ridden by armoured men wearing the Palindrake livery. The carriage came behind, black and polished, with high wheels, its sides adorned with the sea dragon crest. In that carriage Varencienne Palindrake travelled, no doubt tired and longing for home, oblivious to the danger that lurked so close. Shan almost felt sorry for her, but then he reminded himself she was a Malagash, undoubtedly a spoiled and vicious creature.

'Move,' Taropat hissed at him.

Six Cossics, all trained archers, would remain on the high ledges, while the rest of them would attack the escort from below. Even as Shan hurried noiselessly down the steep narrow path that led to the road, he heard the hiss and thunk of arrows, the hoarse calls of the Palindrake guard.

By the time he and Taropat reached the scene, the Cossics had already engaged the remaining guards. There were twelve of them altogether, but four had been taken by arrows. The power of the Dragon's Claw rose in Shan's blood. He drew his sword, emitting a mighty yell. The sound of it caused some of the Caradoreans to freeze, but not for long. They were skilled fighters, no doubt the best of Palindrake's domestic guard. Shan had never seen Taropat in combat and only afterwards would he recall the ferocity of his mentor's attack. He struck at his countrymen as if they were Magravandians, until the last guard was left standing, defending the door to the carriage, his weapon knocked from his grasp.

Taropat lunged forward, sword raised, but before he could strike, the guard cried, 'My Lord Khaster!', his tone that of utter disbelief and shock.

Taropat paused. For a moment, Shan thought he would recover himself and finish the guard off, but then Taropat lowered his weapon.

Around them, men lay on the road, motionless and silent or groaning, four of their own as well as eleven Caradoreans. From within the carriage came the sound of a child whimpering.

'Hamsin,' said Taropat. 'I will spare your life. You will tell Palindrake who did this to him.'

The surviving guard was an older man, perhaps in his late fifties. He had probably known Khaster as a boy. 'My Lord Khaster,' he said again, as if trying to convince himself of what he saw before him.

The door to the carriage opened. From it stepped a woman, clad in a dark cloak for travelling. Shan would never forget that moment. Her hair was gold and in the twilight it seemed to glow. Her face: it too was glowing. She was smiling as if she had just seen an angel. Shan had never beheld such a beautiful creature. Her every movement was filled with grace. 'Khaster,' she said and sank down onto the road in a billow of fabric. At first, Shan thought she had fainted, but then he realised she was actually bowing to Taropat. Why? Perhaps this was not Palindrake's wife, but one of the Leckery women.

Taropat did not move. He stared at the woman in some perplexity. 'You are Varencienne Malagash?' he snapped, but his voice lacked its usual hard edge.

'I am Varencienne Palindrake,' said the woman, rising, her chin held high. 'I had wondered who it would be, and now I know it is you.'

'Your words mean nothing to me,' Taropat said. 'Bring forth your children, my lady.'

Varencienne smiled and Shan was awed by her calm courage. If she'd turned her gaze upon him, he would have bowed before her. 'You will not have him, Khaster. Rav is in Magrast.' Her voice was clear and carried far. She was a princess through and through, more so, Shan could not help thinking, than Helayna. 'We knew there would be an attempt on his life, and were prepared for it.'

'Not that prepared,' Taropat said. 'Consider yourself in my custody.' He turned away from her and spoke to Shan. 'Examine the interior of the carriage.'

Varencienne did not even look at Shan as he edged past her. She continued to gaze at Taropat's back. Within the carriage, Shan found a woman he assumed to be a lady-in-waiting, who was clutching a dark-haired girl child to her body. 'We will not harm you,' he said. 'Please get out of the carriage.'

The woman spat at him and the child uttered a cry of terror.

'Get out of the carriage,' Shan repeated. 'I do not wish to remove you forcibly.'

'Teffy,' said Varencienne Palindrake behind him. 'Do as he says.'

Glaring, the woman did so, holding the little girl by the hand. On the road, Varencienne pulled the child against her. 'What do you intend to do with us, Khaster, as Rav is not with us?'

This was a question prominent in Shan's mind also. He supposed Taropat did not know the answer.

'You are a captive,' Taropat said.

'For what ends?'

Taropat ignored the question. He addressed the leader of the Cossics. 'How many of your men are dead?'

'Two, sir. Of the others, it would be better if one were dead. He is gravely injured and will not be able to travel.'

'Release us and we will take your wounded to Caradore,' Varencienne said.

Taropat still ignored her. 'We must manage as best we can. The able-bodied must support the wounded. Unharness the horses from the carriage. We have enough mounts for everyone.'

'Aye, sir.'

'Be quick.'

While this was being attended to and the injured men given what treatment was possible, Varencienne attempted to calm her daughter. Hamsin, the Palindrake guard, addressed Taropat. 'Your mother will almost certainly die from the news she must receive.'

'Then don't tell her,' Taropat said harshly. 'Hamsin, I do this because of the great wrongs the Palindrakes have wrought against my people. You knew me. I hope you remember enough to realise that there is a purpose to my actions.'

'The Khaster Leckery I knew would never have done this.'

'Valraven Palindrake has made me what I am,' said Taropat. 'I cannot leave you a horse, for which I am sorry, but I cannot risk you finding reinforcements in time to intercept our escape. You should reach the nearest village before dawn.'

'And what am I to say to Lord Palindrake? Will Lady Varencienne be held to ransom?'

'You need say only what happened and who did it. Give Pharinet my regards. I am sure she still grieves for me.'

Hamsin pursed his lips, his expression full of disgust.

'Khaster,' said Varencienne Palindrake, 'let Ellony return to Caradore with Oltefney. She is only a child. I will remain as your hostage.'

Shan knew the name Ellony was that of Taropat's dead sister and considered it rather morbid that Valraven and Varencienne had named their daughter for her.

Taropat turned on the woman slowly. Shan had never seen such an expression of fury of anyone's face before. 'What kind of sick creature are you?' Taropat said in a low voice.

'There is nothing sick about considering the welfare of a child,' Varencienne replied.

'You named her, presumably?'

'I did. It was a mark of respect. We cannot erase the past, but we can atone for it.'

Shan glanced at Taropat. Would he soften to her now?

'My lady, you have no concept of reality,' Taropat said. 'Your woman may go with Hamsin, but you and the child remain with me.'

'Mama?' murmured the girl. 'I must stay with you.'

At first Shan thought the child was complaining, but then he realised she was agreeing with Taropat's suggestion. Like mother, like daughter, perhaps. Shan took hold of the reins of one of the horses and led it to Varencienne's side. He bowed.

Barely glancing at him, Varencienne took the reins from his hold and swung herself up onto the horse's back. Then she looked down at him. 'Pass Elly to me, please.'

Shan lifted the girl in his arms. For a moment she held onto him tightly, until he passed her to her mother.

'Do not give her the reins,' Taropat said to Shan. 'Lead the animal.'

'Where are you taking us?' Varencienne asked.

Taropat did not answer. He mounted his horse and the Cossics did likewise. They took their dead with them, and also the wounded, one of whom would certainly die within the next hour. The dead would be buried at sea. Behind them, Shan heard the diminishing wails of Lady Palindrake's servant.

Varencienne held the child Ellony before her on the saddle. She looked straight ahead up the road, apparently without fear.

'You will not be harmed,' Shan said.

She glanced at him haughtily. She did not expect to be harmed.

CHAPTER EIGHT

A Day of Destiny

It had taken longer to organise than the Magravandian officials had expected. Archimage Mordryn insisted that various high-ranking priests and magi be recalled from the provinces to help officiate the momentous occasion. The Fire Chamber wanted as many foreign rulers as possible to be present, as a display of loyalty to Gastern. An international holiday was declared, so that the common people could celebrate the event in the streets. Feasts were planned, and dramatic displays. None of it could be put together overnight, or even within a week. But even so, it was conducted in haste.

Valraven Palindrake had no time to himself during these frantic weeks. The Splendifers would play a great part in the coronation ceremony itself, and there was much to organise. Valraven, too, would be responsible for security throughout the day, not just for Gastern, but for every other person of importance.

Rav had been given rooms within Valraven's private apartments and a personal tutor, Master Garante, had been appointed to remain by his side. Garante came from the ranks of the Cathedral Guard and was both a scholar and a fighter. Valraven had chosen the man himself. Garante, of all the applicants, had been the least dour and ascetic. Valraven did not want Rav to be bored or intimidated by his companion guard, but his security was paramount. Once the coronation had taken place, Valraven hoped to spend more time with his son. He remained unconvinced of the nebulous threat his wife and her mother claimed hung over the boy. In such claims, he perceived Tatrini's manipulative paws, and he was surprised Varencienne had agreed to leave Rav in Magrast.

On the morning of the coronation, which was due to take place at midday, Valraven was in the cathedral, supervising the final security arrangements. He had made sure that Splendifer guards could observe every inch of the building, and the ceremonial way that led to it. These were his best men, trained to react independently and decisively should the need arise. One of Khaster's old friends, Rufus Lorca, had recently been initiated into the Splendifer order, proposed by the Dragon Lord himself. Lorca was a Magrastian, born and raised in the city. Valraven was always on the alert for promising men, and now Lorca was his personal aide. As they checked the array of security mirrors placed discreetly around the high altar, Valraven said to Lorca, 'All these flowers – the perfume of them. It reminds me of when Ren and I were married here.'

'I remember,' Rufus said. 'In those days, of course, I was in the crowd outside.' He pulled a wry face. 'My parents were given good seats in the main stand, but even so, our family was not considered noble enough to enter the cathedral.'

Valraven smiled. 'No longer, though – at least for you.'

'And that is down to you, my lord.'

'You had some small part in it,' Valraven said. He looked around. 'Well, all is in order. If we are lucky, we'll have time for breakfast before we have to present ourselves at Gastern's chambers.'

The two men began to walk down the wide central aisle. To either side, cleaners were putting the final polishing gloss to the pews and arranging the abundance of flowers. Ushers with intent faces were scanning their seating lists. Perhaps it was possible the day would progress without major problems. Valraven could not imagine Almorante or Bayard doing anything rash in public. The time of danger would come afterwards.

Before they reached the immense doors to the cathedral, a Splendifer marched hurriedly towards them. He bowed. 'My lord, there is someone to see you on an urgent matter.'

'Who?' Valraven enquired.

'A man named Hamsin, of your guard in Caradore. He insists on speaking to you. I believe he wishes to report on a domestic matter.'

'Where is he?'

'At the door, my lord.'

Valraven said nothing more but walked quickly to the entrance. His heart had become cold. Outside, he saw Hamsin, surrounded by suspicious Splendifers. The man was unshaven. He looked wretched. Valraven pushed through the guard and took Hamsin by the arm, dragging him away. People looked at them with curiosity. Valraven forced a smile. 'It is good to see you, Hamsin. I am in a hurry, so please accompany me to my chambers. We may speak along the way.'

Hamsin said nothing but followed Valraven to one of the carriages that had been laid on for the convenience of the coronation staff. Once the door was closed upon them, Valraven said, 'Speak concisely. Tell me all.'

Hamsin squirmed, swallowed convulsively then said, 'Khaster Leckery has kidnapped Lady Varencienne and Lady Ellony.' His voice was cool, but his mouth worked nervously. Valraven could tell he expected to be blamed for this.

'How and where?'

'On the road to Caradore. We were taken by surprise. Leckery had a company of men with him. They looked like outlaws, although they were clearly men of Cos. They killed all of the escort but for me. Leckery spared me to bring you this news. My Lord, I cannot tell you how sorry . . . '

'Silence,' said Valraven. 'Did Leckery give any reason for this affront?'

'We suspect he hoped to snatch Lord Rav, but in the event could not go away empty-handed.'

'What are his demands?'

'None,' Hamsin replied. 'Neither did he give any indication of where he intended to take Lady Varencienne. We fought as best we could.'

'I have no doubt of that,' Valraven said. 'When you return to Caradore, the families of those who died must be given compensation. What action have you taken to rescue Varencienne?'

'I went to Caradore directly, without horse, for Leckery took them all. I could not go quickly for I had to escort Lady Varencienne's companion home, who had difficulty with the journey on foot. At Caradore, I mobilised the guard immediately. The castle is on alert. I sent a division to the scene of the kidnap, while I rode on here to you. Our men are scouring the area for clues to attempt to track Leckery's company.'

Valraven nodded. 'You acted well.'

'Will you come to Caradore, my lord?'

'As soon as I am able. Unfortunately, it is impossible for me to leave Magrast today, but even so, I shall make some enquiries that may help us.'

Hamsin rubbed a hand down his face. 'We were lax. We should have been more prepared. I will accept any penalty you deem fit to exact.'

'It is I who was lax,' Valraven said. 'My wife was aware of danger, and for this reason Rav remained here in Magrast. I should have sent some of my men with you to Caradore. Still, what is done is done. Flogging ourselves for mistakes will not help Varencienne and Ellony. Tomorrow I will send a company of Splendifers to Caradore with you, as well as Mewtish trackers. It may be they'll have to go on to Cos. If Khaster's men were Cossics, it's likely he has made contact with Helayna there. She is probably behind the kidnap.'

Hamsin hesitated. 'You *knew* Khaster Leckery was still alive, my lord?'

'Only recently. He will not get away with this, I assure you. He and Helayna will pay the penalty, not you. I do not blame you for what happened. Do not blame yourself, either. Concentrate fully on avenging this outrage.'

Hamsin ducked his head. 'I will, my lord.'

'One more thing,' Valraven said. 'Have you told anyone in Caradore who accosted you on the road?' He fully expected Hamsin to have revealed all to Everna at least, but the man shook his head.

'No, my lord. Oltefney and I discussed it on the road home and decided that this was something you should tell the Leckerys and your sisters yourself. It is momentous news and I am unsure how Lady Saska will react.'

'Good man,' Valraven said. 'I hope, however, that my inquisitive sisters haven't bullied Oltefney into telling all. Pharinet will smell a rat, I'm sure. She will know something is being kept from her.'

'I impressed upon Mistress Oltefney that you would regard any revelations from her in a harsh light,' Hamsin said.

Valraven smiled grimly. 'Then let us hope she is fearful of that threat.'

The Dragon Lord took Hamsin to Rav's chambers, where he told Garante to make sure he was given a meal and allowed to rest. Later Garante would accompany Rav, with the royal family, to the cathedral.

'There has been trouble at home,' Valraven told Garante. 'Rav's mother and sister have been kidnapped. I do not want you to tell the boy this, or indeed anyone else, but be extra alert today.'

'You may count on me, my lord,' Garante said.

Valraven could tell from the expression on Garante's face that he was surprised his employer could remain so cool after receiving this news. But what point was there in panicking, even reacting with anger? Everything must be made neat, Valraven thought as he marched from his son's chambers. Everything must be in order. He felt devoid of emotion, but needed to act decisively, efficiently. He went directly to Merlan Leckery's rooms in the guest wing of the palace.

Valraven had not spoken to Merlan privately since he'd arrived in Magrast, and had sent only a message to inform Merlan that he'd learned of Tayven's whereabouts. He'd received a short, formal reply. At the time, he'd suspected Merlan already knew where Tayven was. How penetrating *was* Merlan's intelligence network? Valraven liked Merlan, and looked upon him as a younger brother, but he could never completely trust him. Darris Maycarpe had infected him with a propensity for cunning.

Valraven strode into Merlan's chambers without knocking. Merlan stood in the centre of the main room, being dressed in splendid robes by a couple of valets. He and Maycarpe had obviously shared breakfast, for Maycarpe still sat at a crockery-strewn table beneath the window, scanning a city news-sheet. When Merlan caught sight of Valraven, he froze, and dismissed his servants immediately. Valraven could see at once that Merlan knew *something*. He looked slightly guilty. 'I would speak to you alone,' Valraven said.

Maycarpe looked up from his paper. 'Is everything all right, Val?'

Valraven glanced at him. 'It is a personal matter.'

'We can talk in the bedchamber,' Merlan said. His face was white.

Once the door was closed behind them, Merlan laughed nervously. 'You look grim. What is it?'

'I have good news for you,' Valraven said.

'Good news?'

'Your brother Khaster is alive.'

'Oh,' said Merlan. His face began to colour and he dropped his eyes from Valraven's stare.

'A fact of which you are patently already aware,' Valraven said coldly. 'Did you also know of his plan to kidnap Varencienne and the children?'

'What?' Merlan sat down heavily on the window seat.

'He has taken Ren and Elly. It happened on the road to Caradore.'

'No!' Merlan displayed his hands as if to demonstrate his honesty. 'Val, this is not how it seems.'

'Well, as I am totally perplexed, I have no assumptions whatsoever. I don't know *how it seems*. You are his brother, Merlan. If you know anything at all, you must tell me.'

Merlan almost writhed upon his seat. 'I saw Khaster in Akahana last year,' he said. 'I learned he had survived, but also that he had taken up the life of a scholar and mystic.' He pressed his fingers briefly against his eyes. 'By Foy, this is going too far. I had no idea . . . '

'I think that you did,' Valraven said. 'How would Khaster know Ren would be on that road at that time?'

Merlan looked up at him beseechingly. 'I know nothing of this. Khaster and I parted badly last year. We had a disagreement. I was aware he harboured a hatred for you, but that was a legacy of the past. There was no indication he'd take action like this.'

'Why did you not inform me of what you knew? You could have sent word.'

'I could not,' Merlan said.

Valraven uttered a sound of irritated disbelief. 'Merlan, you are a fool. You're well thought of by the Fire Chamber. You are risking everything.'

'I know that,' Merlan said, 'and I hope you know me well enough to appreciate I would not do so without good reason.'

'Until you reveal your reason to me, I cannot say. What do you know of Khaster's links with Cos?'

'I knew he had gone there.'

'Did this not strike you as important enough to tell me? You know Helayna is still at large in Cos.'

'I did not believe her to be a threat. She has no army left.'

'No, she hasn't. But like all accomplished terrorists, she can still cause immeasurable harm without one. Why would Khaster want my family?'

'I don't know. To hold to ransom, perhaps? To draw you out?'

'Does he want to kill me?'

'How can I say?' Merlan replied awkwardly. 'I know I should have told you he was alive, but I couldn't. I was sworn to secrecy, for your sake more than anyone's.'

'Your logic is surreal,' Valraven said. 'Please explain how your silence was for my own good. It has undoubtedly resulted in the kidnap of my wife and daughter.'

The door opened behind him. Valraven turned to see Maycarpe at the threshold, who had clearly been eavesdropping. 'He can't explain, Val. It was I who persuaded him to silence.'

'Why?' Valraven demanded. 'What in Madragore's name is going on? Explain now or, Mewtish governor or not, I'll have you thrown into the Skiterings. Let the torturers convince you to speak.'

Maycarpe sighed long and deep through his nose. 'I understand your anger, Val. This is most difficult for us. It concerns your heritage.'

'What has that to do with you?'

'Quite a lot. The Dragon Heir will be of great significance in the near future. Know only that you have my loyal support, and that of Merlan. Last year, we worked with Khaster Leckery, who now calls himself Taropat, to try and help you. Both of us underestimated Taropat's antagonism towards you and your family.'

'I can't believe Khaster would do anything for my benefit. What exactly do you mean?'

'We kept Taropat in ignorance of our true aims,' Maycarpe said. 'When he discovered them, he fled in fury.'

'Aims? What are they?'

'To restore your power in Caradore,' Merlan said. 'To restore the power of the Sea Dragon Heir. When the Malagash princes begin to fight, we believe Caradore can break free of the empire.'

Valraven stared at both men in disbelief. 'I'm flattered you are so concerned for my future,' he said, 'but still mystified as to why you decided to act in this way without telling me. It makes no sense. None of this makes sense. It sounds like a fantasy.'

Merlan and Maycarpe stared at one another for a moment, then Maycarpe said, 'Last year, we recovered an ancient artefact with unusual properties. Taropat's skills helped us locate it.'

'An artefact,' Valraven said flatly. 'What is it, a magical sword, a flying carpet, a speaking mirror?'

'Nothing like that,' said Merlan.

'I'm relieved to hear it. In fact, I don't care what it is.'

'Well, you should,' Maycarpe said. 'It is the Crown of Silence and can be worn only by the True King.'

Valraven turned on Maycarpe. 'Darris, enough of this rubbish. You are Magravandian, a high-ranking figure in the political arena. Why should you care about my country's emancipation? There must be more to this than you are telling me.'

'There is,' Maycarpe agreed. He took a breath. 'It is our belief that *you* are the True King.'

Valraven uttered a short shocked laugh, without humour. 'I am *what*?'

'You heard,' Merlan said.

'Now I know you are both completely deluded!' Valraven said. 'Why, in Madragore's name, have you picked me to hang your dreams on?'

'Make your judgements once you are aware of all the facts,' Maycarpe said. 'I care about the world, Val. If you like, I am a traitor to my emperor. And I am not alone. Others share my beliefs, throughout the empire. Over the years, as Leonid failed and his sons grew to power, all eyes turned inexorably towards you as the only fit person to succeed him. Does this explanation satisfy you?'

'Completely,' Valraven said sarcastically. 'You have a kingdom in your minds without a king and seek desperately to make one. You would have been wise to inform me of your ambitions earlier. I will not risk my family's safety by becoming a traitor myself. It is a futile venture and would end only with the execution of all the conspirators. What is wrong with you? Are you blind to reality?'

'Not at all,' Maycarpe responded coolly. 'If anyone is blind, it is not us.'

Valraven ignored the implication in his words. 'Your delusions are interesting,' he said, 'as manifestations of the fear and uncertainty that grips every Magravandian citizen. Unfortunately, I have no time to discuss it.' He turned to Merlan. 'I want you to help retrieve Ren and Elly. Now. I'm sending a company of Splendifers to Caradore tomorrow and trust that Lord Maycarpe, seeing as he's such a champion of Caradore, will give you leave to go with them. If you have any idea where your insane brother might go, follow him. Cos, presumably. Do not make contact with my family or your own. I don't want to see your face again until you stand before me with Ren. If you fail, I will kill you. Do you understand this?'

Merlan replied stonily, 'Yes.'

'You are both fools,' Valraven said. 'I do not need your help, nor will I become part of some mystical fairytale you're obsessed with. You people should come out of your smoke-filled wizards' towers and face reality occasionally.'

'You raised Foy, the Sea Dragon Queen!' Merlan cried. 'How can you call that a fairytale?'

'I did not raise Foy,' Valraven replied. 'I laid her to rest. The time of dragons is done. This is the time of humanity, and we must solve our own dilemmas.' He bowed curtly. 'Good day to you, gentlemen. I hope you enjoy the coronation.'

Gastern's high-ceilinged rooms were filled with courtiers, all talking at once and dithering around. Pieces of extravagant costumes were draped over nearly every surface, along with ceremonial weapons. A group of musicians played a merry tune in the corner of the room, the sound virtually drowned out by the babble of excited voices. Valraven attempted to compose himself at the threshold, feeling dazed. Rufus Lorca was already present and came over directly when he saw his commanding officer. His face showed concern. 'Is everything all right, sir?'

Valraven nodded shortly, forcefully dispelling the frown he could feel pulling at his brow. 'It will be dealt with.' He smiled, hoping it would not appear a rictus. Suddenly he felt overwhelmingly tired. This day was always going to be stressful enough, without the news of Ren and Elly's kidnap and the revelations about Maycarpe and Merlan's clandestine schemes. None of it had really sunk in. He could not think about it.

'Valraven,' called Prince Gastern, arms outstretched as a bevy of tailors sewed him into his ceremonial robes, 'is everything prepared to your satisfaction?'

'Yes, your mightiness,' he replied. 'You may feel safe in the arms of the Splendifers.'

Gastern jerked his neck, as if his collar was too tight. 'I hope you're right.' He gestured imperiously to his valet, who came forward with a goblet. It would not contain wine, but a herbal aperitif. Gastern did not consume liquor.

Shortly before eleven o'clock, Tatrini made a grand entrance into her son's chambers, accompanied by Princess Rinata and Prince Linnard. This was a departure from tradition, as women and children generally kept to their own apartments. Tatrini had made many changes in the palace. Grudgingly Valraven had to admit this was an improvement, but he was never convinced Tatrini acted through altruism or the desire to improve the lot of all females. Still, on this occasion, Valraven was relieved to see her. After she'd greeted her son and upbraided his dressers on minor matters, Valraven signalled he wished to speak to her. They would have only a few moments to themselves before the entourage began its ceremonial trek to the cathedral.

Tatrini came to the refreshments table, where the remains of a sumptuous breakfast lay scattered over the cloth. Valraven concentrated on pouring her a hot drink spiced with merlac. He smiled at her in a manner that would suggest they were merely exchanging small talk. 'There has been a development,' he said through his smile. 'It seems you and Ren were correct in your fears. Today I received news from home that Ren and Elly have been kidnapped.'

Tatrini blinked, blank-faced, and then expelled a trilling laugh, touching Valraven's arm as if he'd just made a witty remark. 'This is terrible,' she said, although grinning convincingly. 'Do you know by whom?'

'Unfortunately, yes. A countryman of mine, Khaster Leckery. Merlan's brother.'

'Why?'

'We must assume he was after Rav. Khaster is disaffected with both your dynasty and mine. I'm sure it's a personal matter and nothing to do with national security.'

'Perhaps so, but Rav's personal security must be increased to ensure his safety.'

'I have seen to it, although Khaster must be on his way to Cos by now.'

'Cos?'

'There are indications Ashalan's sister is involved.'

Tatrini rolled her eyes. 'That woman is a menace. She lacks the poise of true breeding. Sometimes I suspect King Gorlache was not her father. What action have you taken?'

'Tomorrow I will send Splendifers to Caradore, and trust they can track Khaster to Cos.'

'Ashalan will help. You must speak to him.'

Valraven hesitated. 'I prefer to keep this matter as private as possible.'

'I'm sure you can rely on his discretion.' Tatrini took a sip of her drink. 'Allow me to inform him.'

Tatrini believed Ashalan was utterly her creature. Valraven wasn't convinced of this, but was sure the man feared the empress enough not to risk upsetting her. She had helped him regain his throne, albeit under the banner of Magravandias, but he would be aware that privilege could easily be withdrawn.

'Mother!' Gastern called. 'I am ready.'

Tatrini turned languidly from the table. 'Good. I see we are running a little late.' She glanced back at Valraven. 'We will speak later.'

'Madam . . . '

'What is it, Val?'

'Tayven Hirantel. He may be able to assist us.'

Tatrini gave Valraven a hard stare. 'A dubious assistance, I feel, but do what you must.'

'I would like to take him with me to Caradore.'

'Impossible,' said Tatrini. 'You must interview him at his residence.' She put down her cup. 'Hirantel is a terrorist himself. He cannot be allowed his freedom. I have the welfare of the new emperor at heart.'

Lies, thought Valraven, falsehood and half-truths. Did anyone in this city ever speak the truth?

The short trip to the cathedral was naturally a far more joyous occasion than the last journey of Leonid a few weeks before. Also, it was less encumbered by grim ceremonials. The royal company assembled on the Parade Ground, but this was no regimented affair with dolorous prayers and slow, silent movements. In fact, it was virtually chaos. When Gastern emerged from the palace onto the balcony and descended the stairs, the gathered courtiers and foreigners surged forward, cheering and throwing flower petals. The air was full of swirling blooms. Today the skies were clear and the sun shone benignly upon the trees, which were gowned in the green mist of new growth and the pink and white confections of blossom. Bells were ringing madly all over Magrast. Valraven felt the hairs on his skin rise. It was impossible not to be affected by the giddy tide of excitement, which was perhaps the city's reaction to the fear, anxiety and uncertainty of the previous weeks. Spring had come. Gastern was not greatly loved in Magrast, but what he represented was welcomed. Later, people might regret their well-wishes, but for today everyone was in an exhilarated and vivacious mood.

There were no fire mages to bring a dour note to the proceedings, as they had already proceeded to the cathedral, and the Splendifers, as well as the regular army, wore their finest, most glittering livery. The Splendifers were truly the most excellent of Magravandias' young bravos, smiles flashing whitely in their handsome faces. Their horses,

which were prancing on nervous hooves, were caparisoned with gar-
lands of flowers and bells. The gilded imperial carriage was festooned
with ribbons and everyone present was dressed in bright, vibrant
colours, rather than the usual dark reds and crimsons of formal
occasions. Gastern, for a change, looked splendid, and the smile on the
face of his wife made her appear more comely than usual. Despite the
gravity of the impending ceremony, both Gastern and Rinata were
relaxed and happy. Valraven reflected that if they were only different
people, if smiles and free movement were an intrinsic part of their
personalities, the future might be very different and there would be no
need for doubt and fear.

At Tatrini's suggestion, the Church had incorporated some new
material into the coronation ceremony, so that Rinata would be
crowned as empress after her husband. Tatrini herself had never been
officially crowned, but as she was so popular with the people, Mordryn
had clearly seen the sense of elevating the emperor's wife's position. It
had not been lost on the Church that Tatrini had swayed public opinion
in moments of crisis, such as when Leonid's campaigns abroad had
brought financial hardship to the populace. Perhaps Rinata, groomed by
experts in etiquette and couture from Jessapur, could become a first lady
to inspire a similar devotion. It was unlikely, however, that she would
be allowed to eclipse Tatrini, who would no longer possess the title
empress, but be known as the Grand Queen Mother. Valraven knew
Tatrini would never really hand over her reins of power.

Gastern and Rinata rode through the city streets in their golden, open
carriage, like a prince and princess from a fairytale. All the guests had
gone before them to take their seats in the cathedral. The streets were
congested with citizens, throwing flowers and singing patriotic songs.
The couple smiled and waved, Rinata weighed down beneath a festoon
of bouquets that spilled over her lap and covered the floor of the
carriage. Prince Linnard rode with his grandmother in a carriage behind
and Valraven, riding just after, noticed how many of the women in the
crowd put their hands together in a gesture of prayer as they gazed upon
the erstwhile empress. She looked beautiful, stately and regal, the
perfect lines of her neck and upper breast displayed by a discreetly low-
necked dark gold gown. Her abundant hair shone like gold itself, and
was wound with strings of pearls and white buds. She must be in her
mid-fifties by now, but appeared far younger. Beside her, Linnard, who
was unable to emulate the happy, carefree mien of his parents, looked
aged in comparison.

Gastern's brothers, along with their wives and children, rode in four
carriages behind Tatrini and the Splendifers. They all looked to be in

good spirits, even though two of them might be gritting their teeth throughout the coronation itself. Again at Tatrini's suggestion, Rav had been allowed to travel with Prince Leo. Garante rode on a magnificent chestnut gelding just behind their carriage.

The bells of the cathedral were a cacophony, so loud Valraven had to shout to make himself heard to his men. People laughed and wept at the roadside. They waved flags and blew kisses with both hands to the emperor-to-be. Gastern alighted from the carriage and held out his arm to his wife. A great cheer went up. Gastern turned to the crowd and waved, clearly affected deeply by their adulation. Valraven thought he might go up to some of the people and address them personally, and was prepared to intervene, but perhaps Rinata tweaked Gastern's elbow, for he turned his face to the cathedral, adopted a more serious expression and began to walk slowly towards the towering entrance.

A new emperor had come, a new sun king. But would his radiance set too soon, by others' designs or his own mistakes?

By the time Valraven could excuse himself from the post-coronation festivities, it was past midnight. He felt as if he were running on pure tension, but still ordered his groom to saddle his horse to make ready for a journey. He wanted to ride to Cawmonel that night; his instinct told him that Tayven Hirantel might well disappear fairly soon. He should not have mentioned his interest in Tayven to Tatrini, for it was clear she had plans for him of her own.

The Grand Queen Mother had lost no time in speaking to King Ashalan. That very afternoon she had summoned Valraven to her side at the feast and told him that Ashalan would send agents of his own into the Rhyye the moment he reached Tarnax. 'He is most embarrassed,' Tatrini said. 'I made sure of that.' She touched Valraven's hands lightly. 'You must not worry, Dragon Lord. I'm sure you won't need to go to Cos yourself. Ren and Elly will be returned to us very soon. Ashalan will make sure of it, for he fears my displeasure.'

Valraven thought that Helayna was quite capable of outwitting her brother or any of his agents, but merely inclined his head. 'Thank you, my lady.'

'By all means, go home and console your sisters,' Tatrini said. 'You've worked hard these last weeks and deserve a rest.'

Properly, it was Gastern's place to give him leave, and no doubt the new emperor would want to have his General-in-Chief close to him over the next few weeks, but Valraven also knew Gastern would not go against his mother's wishes.

'I will order Rufus Lorca, who is a fine Splendifer, to remain at the emperor's side,' Valraven said. 'I will not leave him unprotected.'

'I know you won't,' Tatrini said. 'I had no need to enquire.'

Now, as Valraven's horse galloped through the night, the Dragon Lord wondered what he would do at Cawmonel. If he took Hirantel away with him, Tatrini would know he was responsible, but who else knew the hideouts of the Cossic resistance like Tayven? He could go against the Queen Mother's wishes, of course, then return Hirantel safely to Magrast, thereby proving he was capable of keeping a prisoner. However, he knew Tayven was quite capable of slipping away from him in Cos. Valraven did not underestimate him. But he owed it to Varencienne, who had stood by him loyally, despite the fact there was no passion between them, and Elly, who was as innocent as her namesake had been, to do everything in his power to rescue them. How dare Khaster do this? What did he seek to prove or achieve? Was his hatred of the Malagashes and Palindrakes so strong he would kill or torture to vent his anger? Valraven knew, in his heart, that Khaster would be far from impressed by Ellony's name. The rest of the Leckerys had been flattered by Varencienne's choice, but Khaster would see it as an insult to his sister's memory. It would infuriate him further. There might be little time to save Ren and Elly, if indeed it was not too late.

Tayven was asleep when Valraven was let into his chambers. At once he awoke, crying, 'What has happened?' Perhaps he feared Gastern was dead and that his own demise was imminent.

'The coronation went as planned,' Valraven said. 'Order is ostensibly restored to Magravandias, but the matter I am here to discuss is something else entirely.'

Tayven got out of bed and shrugged himself into a soft dressing-gown of white lamb's wool. His eyes looked puffy from sleep. 'Then tell me of it.'

Valraven did so, as briefly as possible. At the end of the story, he said, 'Do you know where he'd go, Tayven? Can you give me precise directions?'

'Helayna's people move around,' Tayven replied. 'I could probably find them for you, but . . . ' He let the sentence hang, gazed up at Valraven from beneath lowered brows.

'I had thought of this. Unfortunately, Tatrini is reluctant to let me take you from here.'

Tayven expelled a snort of derision. 'What do you expect? Can you not act independently, or is her approbation too important to you? Why did you even ask her? If you hadn't, you could have just come here, ordered Sanchis to let me go with you, and then claimed ignorance of the woman's displeasure.'

'I realise this,' Valraven said dryly. 'Still, it is too late now. However, I have decided not to obey her directive.'

Tayven's face bloomed into a smile. The heaviness of slumber faded from his countenance in an instant. 'I will get dressed,' he said.

Valraven merely nodded, frowning. Would he regret this?

Just as Tayven was pulling on his boots, a knock came at the door. Valraven went to open it and saw Sanchis standing outside, his face set into a fretful expression. Valraven saw loyalty to the Dragon Lord, and that was enough. 'What is it, man?' he snapped.

'The personal guard of the empress is here,' Sanchis said in a low urgent voice. 'They mean to take Hirantel to Magrast.'

'Take care who you call empress,' Valraven said. 'She is only the Queen Mother now. Can you not hold these men off for a while? I mean to take Hirantel myself. There is business between us.'

'What has happened, sir? Why are you all here in the middle of the night for this prisoner?' Sanchis was importunate because he knew he held the keys to this place and that Valraven needed his aid.

Valraven put a hand upon the man's shoulder. 'Nothing has happened that will affect you. This matter is personal. Tatrini fears I will lose Hirantel if I take him. This is not the case. The welfare of my family depends upon Hirantel's co-operation.'

Tayven was now at the door behind him. 'Let's go! Why are you wasting time?'

Valraven heard the sound of boots – many boots – upon the flagstones further down the passage, around a corner. 'Damn!' he hissed.

Sanchis gestured in the opposite direction. 'This way, my lord. Quickly.'

Tayven made to follow, but Sanchis pushed him back into the room and swiftly locked the door. Valraven heard Tayven's outraged cry through the thick wood.

'Sanchis?' he said.

The warden firmed his jaw. 'I'm sorry, my lord. If you'd come earlier, I'd have let you take him, but I will not risk the wrath of the empress. Please understand this. Turn that corner and wait. I will come to you.'

There was no time for further argument. Valraven did not want to be seen by Tatrini's men. He had good reason to be there, of course, as he'd spoken to her earlier about it, but the fact that Tayven was dressed and ready to travel, and the unusual hour of Valraven's visit, would cast suspicion upon him. Tatrini was clearly already suspicious: perhaps she'd had spies waiting to report on his movements. Valraven turned the corner and pressed himself against the wall. Should he care what Tatrini thought? Would her personal guard even prevent him from taking Hirantel if he explained the need? He knew he had the loyalty of all the military, but Tatrini's people would not dare to cross her. You fear her, he thought. Like all of them, you fear her.

CHAPTER NINE

Beyond Old Caradore

Varencienne stood against the side of the ship with her daughter standing on an upturned box in front of her, so that the child might look out towards land. Varencienne's arms gripped Ellony firmly, but the girl wriggled against her, laughing. Her mother had never seen her so happy. Perhaps she loved being out on the ocean. At Caradore, Varencienne had never thought to take her daughter sailing, despite the fact that the sea was such a big part of their lives, always present, filling the air with its noise and scent.

'There, Elly, look! Old Caradore!'

'Where, mama?' Ellony jumped up and down on the box excitedly.

'*There*, my love, round the headland.'

The ship was some miles from the shore, but even so the early morning sun shone off the quartz-veined rock of the castle, which stood proud, if ruined, against the pale sky. Old Caradore Castle, once the seat of the Palindrakes, to where Cassilin Malagash had led his armies and claimed the Dragon Heir for himself. The castle hadn't been lived in since the ransack and, as far as Varencienne knew, had been visited only twice by members of the current Palindrake family. Four years before, Merlan had taken her there, then some months later she had visited it with Tatrini and Valraven and his sisters. At that time, Valraven had been reintroduced to his heritage. He had communed with Foy, the Sea Dragon Queen, and swum with the dragon daughters.

Varencienne had always meant to go back. She'd had plans to renovate the old pile, but somehow she'd never got round to it. The fact that none of her husband's family were keen on the idea hadn't helped. Old Caradore was a symbol of their destruction. But despite these sad associations, Ellony and Rav should have seen it before. Now she found herself wishing Rav was with them. The castle looked so beautiful from the sea.

'Oh, Mama!' Ellony breathed. Her small, yet surprisingly slender hands were pressed against her mouth. 'We should *live* there.'

'I felt that way when I first saw it,' Varencienne said.

'Will we land there? We will, won't we?'

'No, sweetness. Your uncle wants to take us further north, but to a place as beautiful and strange. You'll love it just as much.'

Taropat, naturally, detested being referred to as 'uncle'. Varencienne hadn't suggested it, either. Ellony's initial fear of Taropat had swiftly faded. Unfazed by his continuing hostility, she ignored his cold mien and called him Uncle Taro. She hadn't used the name Khaster, even though she'd been told an expurgated version of his history a long time ago. Varencienne had shown her the best portrait of Khaster at Norgance a couple of years before. 'He's beautiful,' she'd said. She shared her mother's tastes in most things. Now, it seemed, that fascination had developed into a crush. Varencienne told herself she mustn't fall under the same spell. This man, whatever his heritage, had taken them both captive. He was an enemy.

They had been supposed to travel to Cos, but the plan had changed. After a panicked ride back to the coast, during which one of the injured Cossics had died, they'd boarded the waiting fishing vessel and had set sail for the east. During the first night at sea, Taropat had awoken raving from a dream. The cacophony had roused Varencienne from sleep in the small cabin she and Ellony had been allotted as quarters. Pulling on her cloak, she'd ventured onto the deck, where she'd seen two shadowy figures engaged in what appeared at first to be a furious debate. One was Taropat, the other, Shan. The ship clove slowly through a placid sea, beneath the benevolent gaze of a fat moon. The scene was that of utter tranquillity; Taropat's chaotic movements and harsh voice seemed unnatural and out of place. Shan was trying to restrain Taropat, who was waving his arms about, shouting incoherently. As Varencienne stepped forth to investigate, Marius, the captain of the vessel, also appeared. He glanced at Varencienne and said, 'What's all this about?' Captain Marius did not know she was a captive, and so far Varencienne had seen no good reason to tell him. She doubted this information would inspire him to help her.

Varencienne shrugged. 'I've no idea.'

Together they approached the others. Shan shot them a wild glance and said, 'Please, leave us. I can deal with this.'

'Deal with what?' Varencienne said.

'Shut him up,' said the captain. 'This will worry my men.'

The night watch of the vessel had also come to observe. As with all sailors, they were deeply superstitious; any unusual behaviour was considered darkly omenic.

Taropat calmed down abruptly and slapped Shan's hands away. 'It is clear,' he said.

'What is?' Varencienne asked.

As had quickly become usual, Taropat ignored her and addressed Shan. 'A dream came to me. I found myself in a high land, where I could barely breathe. Flags fluttered all around me in a freezing wind, tattered flags of many colours. I saw a temple that covered the side of a mountain and from it flew a man, barely more than a boy. He said to me, "I am the destiny of the Dragon's Crown." He took me by the hand and we flew with the eagles above the high rocks. We came to a volcanic lake, similar to Pancanara, except that its waters were a deep rusty red. In it, I saw Cos overrun with Magravandians. I saw Helayna taken prisoner by Valraven himself. There is no sanctuary for us there. We must go north, to the most ancient part of Caradore, to High Hamagara.'

There was a silence while they digested this information.

Then Captain Marius cleared his throat and said, 'We cannot spend all year on a pleasure cruise. We have our livelihood to think of.'

'You will be recompensed,' Taropat said. 'Take us north.' He swept past the captain and went back into his cabin.

At once the Cossic sailors gathered around the captain and began chattering heatedly. Marius raised his hands as if to fend them off. Varencienne smiled to herself. They would take some convincing.

Shan came to her side. 'I am sorry about this, my lady.'

'Sorry for what?' she enquired icily. His politeness had begun to grate on her nerves. She would have preferred him to be rude and unsympathetic. Then it would be easier to hate him. 'Sorry for this whole outrage or the change of plan? Frankly, your sympathy means little to me in either case.' She was driven to be waspish with him, even though she knew he was uncomfortable with what Taropat had done. He was also shyly awkward in her presence, which she took to mean he liked her, perhaps in the obvious way. Shan was a very attractive man. It was difficult not to feel flattered by his demure admiration.

The captain marched away up the deck, his sailors following him, still gesticulating forcefully and all speaking at once. Shan and Varencienne were left alone. Varencienne was not displeased; she would take sport in tormenting Shan. Deliberately she waited for him to speak first.

'I know you feel there is nothing to be gained from our kidnapping you,' Shan said. 'I want you to know that I counselled Taropat against taking you captive.'

Varencienne went to the side of the ship and leaned upon it. The ocean looked so harmless, as if it couldn't hurt anyone. How it lied to the world. 'You go along with him,' she said, 'so please don't bother me with your objections. I am not the person to whom they should be voiced.'

'You do not understand him,' Shan said. 'Sometimes he seems insane, but ultimately his strange behaviour is for the greater good. I am with him now because I believe that the destiny of the world lies partly in his hands. I have denied this – and him – because I wanted an easy life, but now I am decided. Fate has decreed that your son should not fall into our hands, but instead we have you. I can only believe that is what was meant to happen. If Taropat says we should go to Hamagara, we will find something important there, and you will be part of it. You are the sea-wife, as was Ellony, Taropat's sister, and your daughter bears her name. I think a cycle is being repeated.'

Varencienne stared at him in the moonlight. 'Why tell me this? Do you suppose I care about your beliefs?'

'No, but I hope knowing them might help you understand why and how you are in this circumstance.'

His face was mostly in shadow, but sincerity rang through his words. Varencienne felt a pang of regret for needling him. 'You mean well,' she said in a softer tone, 'but if you really support what is left of Khaster Leckery, you should persuade him to put Ellony and me ashore, so we may find our way home. We are not part of your destiny, whatever you believe it is. Valraven will kill you both for daring to lay hands on me, and despite what you might think, I do not want to see that happen.'

'Taropat is driven by instinct,' Shan said. 'My lady, forgive me for this, but you know so little of the world. I can see good in you; if you saw the whole picture you would sympathise with our aims.'

Varencienne snorted in outrage, immediately wishing she had not shown him a chink of kindness. 'Know so little? How dare you! Do not see good in me, for I assure you, you will be disappointed. Our separate understanding of what is "good" has no correspondence.' She looked at his face and even in the wan moonlight could see the bunched muscles, the words they repressed. He was too polite and considerate to vent his thoughts. She could not help softening towards him again. Her feelings were like the waves around them, too fluid and unpredictable. She knew she should be careful. 'I know of your history, Shan, for Merlan has told me about it. I do not have to tell you this, but I do not condone all that has been done in my family's name. But one thing you should realise is this: whoever is in power, however altruistic the government, human beings will still commit atrocities against one another. Essentially, we are beasts, and apportioning all blame to one faction is naïve.'

Shan expelled a choked sound. For a moment, Varencienne thought he would strike her and instinctively backed away. 'You *do not know*!' he cried. 'You weren't there. You have never been there. You live in a castle, a wife and mother. You have seen nothing and know nothing. Until you have witnessed people die senselessly, seen your children raped by monsters who call themselves men and whole villages wiped out for nothing more than blood lust, you have no right to speak.'

Varencienne was silenced by his passion. She opened her mouth, but no words would come.

Shan shook his head. 'Forgive me. I cannot blame you for what you are. You speak only what you know.' With these words, he walked away from her.

Varencienne watched the space where he had stood for some minutes, feeling as if she'd just come up for air from beneath a tempestuous sea.

As Taropat desired, they had sailed north, following the Caradorean coast, instead of east to Cos. And in the morning following the scene on deck they were passing close to Old Caradore, whose sad ruins lay dreaming of past glories. 'Long ago,' Varencienne said to her daughter, 'the people of the sea would swim to caves beneath the castle and the Palindrakes would commune with them. Stories say that originally the Palindrakes came from the sea.'

'Who are the sea people?' Ellony asked.

'Ustredi,' Varencienne replied.

'Can we see them?' The child squinted at the castle and then at the sea around them.

'No,' Varencienne said, 'they are gone now. The stories are very old.'

'Oh,' said Ellony in disappointment. She squirmed away from her mother and jumped down from the box. 'Can we have breakfast now? I'm hungry.'

It was clear to Varencienne that Ellony was very much enjoying their unexpected excursion. She lived totally in the current moment, and although she had missed home when in Magrast, out here on the ocean she seemed to have forgotten her pony, her pets and her friends. All for the best, Varencienne thought. She could not bear it if Ellony was afraid or suffering. How different her two children were. Ellony was a free spirit, far more at home in the open air than in a city. She'd never been on a ship before, yet had found her sea legs immediately. Rav, on the other hand, had clearly thrived in Magrast and was no doubt enjoying himself there as much as Ellony was now.

Because the weather was fine, the ship's cook had laid out a table on deck for the captain, his first mate and the most august of the passengers. The Cossic sailors and Taropat's men would take their breakfast in the galley. Taropat was absent, although Shan was sitting at the table, looking moody. Varencienne sat down beside him on purpose. It amused her to see his discomfort. As the cook passed round plates of scrambled eggs mixed with rice and smoked fish, she said, in a low voice so that the others might not hear, 'Merlan told me of your quest last summer.' She did not look at Shan, but smiled up at the cook, saying, 'Thank you.' She took a plate for herself and Ellony and began to eat, conscious of Shan's tense scrutiny.

'This is very good,' she said. 'I've heard people say that food tastes better in the open air. It seems they are right.'

Beside her, Ellony was tucking into her breakfast like a famished crow. For such a slender child, she had an enormous appetite.

Shan made a sound in his throat. 'You know of what we found?'

'The Crown?' Varencienne said airily. 'Oh yes. Would you pass me some bread, please.'

Shan did so, saying, 'You know also then of what happened at the end of our quest?'

Varencienne nodded, swallowed, then patted a fragment of egg from her lips with a napkin. 'Yes, that too. There was some dispute over who the Crown belonged to, wasn't there?'

'Merlan and Tayven think it belongs to your husband,' Shan said, in a voice that clearly showed he believed this to be the most farcical suggestion.

'Who do you think it belongs to?' Varencienne enquired. 'Yourself?'

'I am more fit to wear it than Palindrake,' Shan said, 'but no, I do not really think so. I am the Warrior of the True King, but not a potential king myself.'

'Mmm,' Varencienne murmured. 'I heard that also. Well, answer my question.' She adopted a theatrical ringing tone. 'To whom does the Crown belong?'

Captain Marius glanced up briefly from the conversation he was having with his mate, then looked away again.

Shan's reply was almost a whisper. 'Lady Sinaclara, a sorceress of Bree, told us it belongs to the Dragon Heir, but we believe she is wrong, because your husband is tainted by his past. He has forfeited that role. At first, Taropat thought that perhaps Helayna could be queen instead, but he had a prophetic dream in Cos, and now thinks it is in fact your son. That is why we wanted to kidnap him, so that he could be freed from the corrupting influences of the Malagashes.'

'His mother is a Malagash,' Varencienne said, barely containing her annoyance. 'Am I so corrupting an influence?'

'I did not mean you,' Shan said.

'Why not? You do not know me. I could be a necromancer, for all you know.'

'I think I am a good judge of character. I knew, from the first moment I saw you, that you are not tainted.'

'What a relief,' said Varencienne. 'You should be my champion, Shan, and whisper in my ear whenever I meet someone new, just in case they're tainted.'

It was obvious that Shan was unsure whether to laugh at this comment or not. Varencienne was enjoying the conversation immensely, and was therefore disappointed when Taropat appeared from his cabin, his face set into a disagreeable expression. He was heartbreakingly like the portrait of Khaster with which a younger Varencienne had virtually fallen in love, and it seemed almost an inconvenience he didn't have a pleasant character to go with his face. Varencienne could not help feeling he was being wilful and difficult, and that his natural instinct was still to be warm and charming. If this inner personality existed, however, there was little evidence of it today. Taropat came directly to stand behind Shan's seat and said, 'Don't speak to her. She's pumping you for information.'

'Too late,' said Varencienne with more levity than she felt. 'He's already told me everything.'

'You must eat in your cabin, madam,' Taropat said. 'This is not a holiday for you, and none of us are your sport. Shan, use your head and ignore other parts of your body. This woman is a Malagash.'

The captain and the first mate were now looking on in disapproval. Varencienne smiled at them. 'Don't worry about it. I am a captive.'

'A Malagash?' said the captain. 'On my ship?'

'Captive?' said the mate.

'Yes,' said Varencienne. 'But don't worry, I shan't complain of your service. So far, it's been very good.'

Marius glared at Taropat. 'You should have informed me of this. I want no part in it.' He turned to his mate. 'Turn to shore. Our passengers will be disembarking.'

'There is no need to panic,' Taropat said. 'No one knows about this, and they never will.'

'That sounds like a threat,' Varencienne said. 'Do you intend to add murder to kidnap? Your execution should be quite a spectacle.'

'He means no such thing,' Shan said.

'Off my ship!' roared Captain Marius.

Half an hour later, the company was in a small rowing boat, being taken to shore.

The Cossic elected to return to Helayna, with Taropat's blessing. Their leader made a perfunctory show of offering to escort them to Hamagara, but Taropat declined. 'This is my country,' he said, 'the wildest part of it. We will be less conspicuous as a smaller company.'

Privately, remembering what Hamsin had once told her of the wild, nomadic people of northern Caradore, Varencienne hoped that Taropat and Shan were capable of protecting her and her daughter. Still, as she had no influence whatever over this strange man with the unsettlingly familiar face, she held her tongue.

They had no horses, and only the barest of supplies. Taropat was unconcerned, claiming they'd be able to acquire provisions along the way. Varencienne could see that Shan was worried about this and at the first opportunity questioned him about it.

'Taropat hoarded money in Bree,' he said, 'and we brought a sizeable fortune with us, but I don't think much of it is left.'

'I have no money with me,' Varencienne said. 'Only a few bits of jewellery. Are we likely to starve?'

Shan shrugged. 'Taropat is a survivor. You should have seen him on the Crown quest. He will provide for us, I'm sure.'

'Let us hope so.'

They made landfall some miles north of Old Caradore, where thick forests came right down to the shore. Varencienne had to restrain Ellony from haring off into the trees. She ran about so quickly, she was no more than a flashing blur, like a wood sprite. 'Uncle Taro, look, look!' she cried, turning in a mad circle. 'The trees touch the sky.'

Taropat observed the child with an expression of distaste. 'They do not. Nothing can touch the sky.' He glanced at Varencienne. 'Control your child, woman.'

Ellony, unperturbed, only grinned at him.

'Come here,' Varencienne said. 'We don't know what's in the forest, Elly. It might be dangerous.' She wondered whether it had been wise to tell the girl of her tenuous relationship to Taropat. He was still technically married to Pharinet, so was a bona fide uncle, but clearly in name only. Varencienne could tell Ellony was fascinated by Taropat, in the same way she'd always been fascinated by unusual things, an oddly shaped stone or a person with peculiar characteristics. It would take an inhumanly hard man to resist her innocent charm indefinitely.

Shan shouldered most of their luggage, which was scant. Taropat had allowed Varencienne only to bring the clothes she and Ellony were wearing, as well as her jewels, should they need something with which to barter. Varencienne had no intention of surrendering any of her necklaces and rings. Those she had taken to Magrast had been given to her by Valraven, and some were heirlooms.

They climbed a steep dune path, hugged by spiky grasses, and began to follow a narrow track that wound into the trees ahead. The air was fresh, a little chilly, but not too cold. Spring flowers burgeoned on the forest floor and the air was full of birds, their calls and the whirr of wings. Perhaps Ilcretia, Valraven's ancestress, had come to these woods at one time. The menfolk might have hunted here.

'What do you know of this area?' Shan asked her.

'Very little,' she replied. 'I only ever came as far as Old Caradore, but I understand the land beyond is quite wild, its people doubly so. They adhere to a very ancient belief system, which derives from the time of the dragons. They worship the king cockatrice and his horde of demons, although they are known by different names to those used in the south.'

'Paraga, king of the air,' announced Taropat behind them.

Both Varencienne and Shan stopped and turned, so that Taropat caught up.

'As Foy, the sea dragon, represents the element of water, so Paraga represents the element of air,' Taropat said, more human as he talked about a subject that interested him. 'The religion based around the wind spirits is very ancient, and has hardly changed for thousands of years. It, and its devotees, are called Par Sen, and can rival the beliefs of Mewt for its bewildering array of gods and demons.'

'You know a lot about it, then?' said Varencienne. 'That will be useful, I hope.'

Taropat nodded. 'Well, I know a little about many things, but I researched Par Sen while I was in Bree. There is a schism between the north and south of Caradore, because the religion centred around Foy made hostile incursions into Hamagara two thousand years ago. The Hamagarids are the true Caradoreans. They comprise many factions and tribes and have little to do with the south. The southerners derive from ancient clans that moved north from Magravandias. They've steered clear of the northern territories for a long time, apart from the occasional intrepid explorer, or some needy soul seeking enlightenment.'

'This is not exactly talked about at home,' said Varencienne.

Taropat frowned. 'Home? Who in Magrast would care a fish about Hamagara?'

'I meant Caradore,' said Varencienne dryly.

He shrugged. 'That doesn't surprise me. I only learned about it once I'd left Caradore far behind. Anyway, you'd have to travel for several days beyond Old Caradore to reach the border to Hamagara.'

Ellony began to tug on her mother's hand. 'What's that?' She pointed into the forest. Varencienne peered into the dark green gloom and saw a tumble of grey stones covered in moss and lichen.

'Can we go and see?' Ellony was already dragging her mother towards the stones.

'That's an old shrine,' Taropat said. 'This country is full of them.' He began to walk towards it and Ellony pulled free of her mother to follow.

By the time Shan and Varencienne had caught up with them, Taropat was already pointing out moss-filled carvings on the stone to the girl. 'That is a representation of Foy, a marker to represent her territory. At one time, this was probably Hamagarid land.'

Ellony scraped at the moss with her fingers. 'She's snarling at something. It's curled up at her feet.'

'That's probably Paraga,' Taropat said. 'He is shown as a submissive consort, but that was hardly the case. He is as invisible and quick as the wind. His people simply melted away from those who would oppress them. Legends say that Foy banished the cockatrice, but in essence, he just hid from her.'

'Are we going to look for him?' Ellony asked.

'Not exactly.'

'Then why are we here? We are the sea dragon people, but now we have come onto land. We must stop the cockatrice hiding from us.' Her fingers lingered over the stone.

Varencienne noticed Taropat staring at the girl contemplatively. 'What else do you think?' he said. 'What does your mind say to you?'

Ellony stood up straight and gazed around herself. 'The forest is watching us,' she said.

'Which way should we go?'

Ellony pondered for a moment, then pointed towards the northwest. 'There, but that is the way to the mountains anyway. You know that.'

Taropat nearly smiled.

'She's just a child,' Varencienne said. 'She likes stories.'

'A child's mind is free of dogma and restriction,' Taropat answered. He glanced at Shan. 'He used to be like that.'

'I was hardly a child when you found me,' Shan said. 'I was more than twice as old as Elly. If I am full of dogma and restriction now, it is because you put them there.'

'Only a fool does not listen to the wisdom of a child,' Taropat said. He looked down at the girl. 'Come along, use your nose. But don't run off.'

As they headed back to the path, Varencienne felt uneasy about this new development. She didn't want Taropat to dislike her daughter, but neither did she want him to invest her with abilities she didn't possess. He would only be disappointed, and the ensuing rejection would be more hurtful to Ellony than his previous coldness.

CHAPTER TEN

Forced Honesty

The small, dank room lay far beneath the palace, in the warren of passages and chambers known to only a few. The cell was lit by a single candle that guttered on a table; the captive sat upon a chair beside it. Drugged to within an inch of his life, he should have appeared mindless and dull, but his eyes, as their gaze fell upon the Grand Queen Mother, were like windows onto the universe, the pupils too large. Tatrini would not have been surprised to see stars within them. 'Tayven,' she said. 'How glad I am that we meet at last.'

He could not, or would not, answer her. His expression remained a void.

Tatrini rustled closer. 'Can you understand me, Tayven?'

He nodded, very slightly.

'Do you know who I am?'

Again, a nod.

'Good. I am sorry you are in this condition, but the philtre was a necessary precaution. You are a violent young man, which is quite at odds with the more mystical side of your character which I am assured exists.' She paused, but he did not react. 'You must have been wondering what it is I want with you, and why I had you taken into custody in Mewt. I am here to answer your questions.'

Only it appeared he could not ask any. Perhaps this interview was pointless, until the effects of the philtre had worn off a little. He had fought like a wild beast when her men had come for him in Cawmonel the previous night. He had managed to injure two of them with well-aimed high kicks before they overpowered him. What a magnificent creature: a killing machine of great beauty, who had the wyrding way. An alchemist could not have grown a more perfect specimen in a vat.

Tatrini reached out and touched his face. He didn't move, but for a fleeting instant she imagined that he was feigning docility and would, at any moment, rear up and break her neck. She withdrew her hand hastily and took a few steps back.

'The empire is in flux,' she said, 'and everything is unstable. My son Gastern is emperor and I have heard that already he plans to squander a fortune on building new cathedrals to Madragore throughout the land. He speaks of holy wars, of purging the world of gods other than his own. That was never Leonid's way, as you must know. The Malagashes have conquered many nations, but part of the reason the empire remained strong was because it allowed certain freedoms of belief amongst its subjugated realms. Nothing good can come of Gastern's innovations. He will shape a new god, in the image of his own fear, and he will make resentful enemies where before there were only resigned puppets. Do you understand what I am saying?'

Tayven blinked. 'Yes,' he said. His voice was clear, unslurred.

'I intend to prevent this chaos from occurring. I intend to preserve, yet also to expand. You are part of my plans.'

Still he asked no questions.

'The elemental forces must be invoked and combined. Whoever controls this force will have the power to create great change. I have picked four individuals to represent the elements. You personify the element of air, the dragon known as the cockatrice.'

Now Tayven frowned slightly, as if in puzzlement. 'I am the Bard of the True King, who wields the dragon's breath.'

Tatrini stared at him in surprise. The philtre he'd been given was designed not only to subdue but also to invoke truth. Strangely, Tayven's words seemed to be those he might speak *after* taking part in the rituals Tatrini had devised. Perhaps this was a manifestation of his psychism. 'You will be this,' she said.

'I *am* this,' Tayven said. 'I am already this.'

Intrigued, Tatrini sat down upon a plain wooden chair next to the table and pulled it closer to Tayven's seat. 'Explain this to me,' she said. 'Am I more correct than I believed in choosing you to represent air?'

'That was not my site,' Tayven replied. 'Mine was Rubezal, the lake of spirit. It was there that the dragon's breath was bestowed on me and I was initiated into my role as the Bard.'

Tayven's words made little sense to Tatrini, but she knew that name, Rubezal. After a moment, she said, 'Rubezal is one of the lakes in Recolletine, isn't it?'

Tayven nodded. 'The sixth.'

Tatrini knew of the ancient legends associated with Recolletine, and also that her second eldest son, Almorante, had once taken Tayven there to attempt the mystical quest of the lakes. Her spies had reported that nothing of note had occurred. Either the quest was nothing more than a myth or Almorante hadn't performed the correct ritual actions. Tatrini herself had never considered the lakes quest to be that important. She looked upon it as a male ritual, perhaps something that Bayard might attempt in the future, simply to enhance his spiritual awareness, but perhaps she'd overlooked something vital. It could be no coincidence that Tayven talked of it now. It had been many years since he'd visited the place with Almorante. Her spies' report might have been erroneous. 'I understand that you did not reach the seventh lake, so therefore the quest was not completed.'

Tayven smiled. 'Oh, but it was. We reached Pancanara.'

Tatrini drew away, breathing in deeply through her nose. Another thought occurred to her. 'When did this happen?'

'Last year.'

'Was Almorante involved in this?'

'No.'

'Why did you attempt the quest again? It failed the first time.'

'Last year we went to Recolletine in search of the Crown of Silence. That was always the true purpose of the quest. Almorante did not know that, so he failed to reach Pancanara.'

Tatrini's body went cold. 'The Crown . . . ' This must be what her augur's message had referred to before Leonid's funeral. Tatrini had not thought of it since. 'Did you find it?'

'It was given to us.'

'Where is it?'

'It is hidden. Only Sinaclara knows its whereabouts.'

'Who is she?'

'A sorceress of Bree. We took the Crown to her. She is its guardian.'

'What is the Crown, Tayven? Why were you seeking it?'

'It is the symbol of divine kingship that can be worn only by the True King. There is no king yet, but we were the brotherhood who would wait for him and serve him.'

'Who was your brotherhood?'

'Taropat, Shan and myself. Taropat is the Magus and Shan the Warrior.'

'I don't know these people. Who are they?' If she did not know of them, surely they could be of no consequence.

'Taropat is Khaster Leckery. Shan is his apprentice.'

'Leckery!' Tatrini stood up. 'He has taken my daughter and granddaughter captive. Were you supposed to be part of this plan?'

'No. We are no longer associated.'

Tatrini paced up and down, her mind full of rushing thoughts. Leckery had meant to kidnap Rav, that was obvious. The question was: why? He thought he served the True King, but Tayven had said there was no king. Leckery would certainly not think it was any of her sons. He hated Palindrake, but perhaps he had not been seeking Rav merely to exact revenge for ancient hurts. Was it possible he wanted the boy as a possible candidate for kingship, a rebel king to challenge the Malagashes? No matter. He'd failed in his scheme and Rav was safe in Magrast. But there was always the possibility Leckery could find himself another candidate. 'I want this Crown,' said Tatrini. 'Does Leckery have access to it?'

'Unlikely,' Tayven replied. 'He is Sinaclara's enemy now.'

'He seeks a Caradorean king, doesn't he?'

'I don't know his desires. He did not want Palindrake to be king.'

Tatrini expelled a snort of laughter. 'The idea of it! Did you share his sentiments?'

'I was unsure. Merlan Leckery and Maycarpe were the ones who believed in Palindrake.'

'Maycarpe? *Darris* Maycarpe, governor of Mewt?'

'Yes.'

Tatrini sat down again, took Tayven's limp hands in her own, shook them. 'Does Maycarpe conspire against the crown, the Fire Chamber? You *must* tell me, Tayven.'

'I cannot help but tell you. My words belong to you. They are no longer mine. Maycarpe has dreams, but I could not see how they could become reality. He fears Gastern's rule. He wants change. Palindrake has the power of the sea dragons and the might of his heritage behind him. Maycarpe believes him to be a natural king. I do not think Palindrake would agree. He would not talk to me about it.'

'You've seen him recently?' Tatrini asked, letting go of Tayven's hands.

'Yes. He came for me last night, because he needed help to find his wife and daughter. I would have helped him, but then your men came and Sanchis would not let him take me.'

'But you have spoken to him about the concept of the True King?'

'Yes, on a previous visit. He was not interested in knowing about it. He swears allegiance to Gastern, as he and his father swore allegiance to Leonid. The Palindrakes are slaves of the Malagashes. This is why Maycarpe's desire is but a dream.'

Tatrini was relieved Valraven was not involved in any treasonous scheme, but it had not occurred to her that some people might regard him as a possible rival to her sons. It made sense, however. The Palindrakes were a legendary family: suitable, charismatic figureheads for any conspiracy against the empire.

'Who do you serve, Tayven?' Tatrini asked. 'Is there a king of your heart?'

Tayven hesitated and Tatrini saw cunning in his eyes. The philtre's effects must be fading. Now, after revealing so much, he sought to lie.

'Answer me.'

'In this world, there is no king. I do not serve the emperor's line. I serve no one.'

Tatrini examined him for some moments. Perhaps this was exactly the answer she was looking for. She must not make the mistake that others made, of sticking to one course of action. Strength came from flexibility, from creativity. 'But you want change, don't you?'

'I did. Now I wonder whether it is possible.'

'Oh, it is,' Tatrini said softly. 'I shall make it so. Will you work with me willingly to achieve it?'

'Willingly, no, but I have no choice but to work with you. You can fill me with potions that restrict my autonomy. How can I refuse you?'

'You might not believe me, but I would prefer not to do that.'

Tayven shrugged. 'I am here,' he said. 'If you do not drug me, I will attempt to escape. You will have to kill me.'

Tatrini sighed heavily. 'I would so much prefer our relationship to be easy, for we *are* to have a relationship, Tayven. And you must overcome your prejudices. I will tell you now the names of the other three I have chosen: Valraven, who is Palindrake's son, Leo, one of my sons and also Bayard, with whom, of course, you have an unfortunate history.'

'Good,' said Tayven.

Tatrini eyed him suspiciously. 'Good? I do not like this word coming from your mouth. Don't think you'll have the opportunity to avenge yourself on Bayard, Tayven. If necessary, I will poison you to prevent it.'

'As you poisoned your husband?'

Tatrini smiled gently. 'It seems another dose is in order.' She went to the door and called, 'Master Dark!'

Her man was in the passageway outside. He'd been conversing with her personal guards who were stationed beyond the door. 'Dark, administer to my guest a measure of Lord Pimalder's excellent tonic.'

Dark bowed and made to enter the room.

'A moment,' said Tatrini, 'where is Prince Bayard?'

'Awaiting your word nearby, your mightiness.'

'Do your work, then summon him,' said Tatrini.

She watched as Dark forced the philtre between Tayven's lips. There was a struggle, but only a minor one. As Dark flowed out of the room like a column of black mist, Tayven slumped panting in his seat, his pale hair falling in damp rats' tails onto his chest. Tatrini could see why he'd caused so much trouble in his life. She believed that true beauty was essentially fuelled by evil. Almorante had loved him, as had Bayard, in his peculiar way, and also Khaster Leckery. Now, it appeared, Valraven Palindrake had been visiting Tayven in his captivity. Was this another lovelorn victim? If Bayard possessed half of Tayven's essence, he would be an indomitable force, but that perhaps was not a desirable circumstance.

'We are more alike than you think,' she said.

Tayven tried to shake his head, but his muscles would not obey his will. He trembled violently, as if in the throes of a fit. Tatrini watched him, waiting for the sound of footsteps outside the room. She saw him struggle against the effects of the philtre. She saw his fury and frustration, which distorted his face into an ugly mask, proof of the demon that lay within the flesh. Bayard had, in effect, created this visible monster. But for the regrettable incident in Cos, Tayven might still be pretending to be modest and demure. No, surely not. He was wiser than that. In a beautiful boy, those characteristics were charming, but in a man, they would be only foppish and weak. She wondered how Tayven would have reinvented himself, left to his own devices.

Lost in this reverie, Tatrini did not notice that Dark had returned until he stood at the threshold. She turned and saw Bayard standing behind her manservant. 'You look anxious, my son,' she said. 'Please, come in.'

Bayard swallowed convulsively and stepped into the room, while Dark closed the door upon them.

Tatrini realised, with some wonder, that Bayard was afraid. This would be the first time he had laid eyes on Tayven Hirantel since he'd ordered his lackeys to kill him.

'There,' said Tatrini, pointing at Tayven, 'sits your nemesis.'

Bayard uttered an unconvincing, nervous laugh, wiped his fingers over his mouth. 'He looks mindless.'

'Mmm, his condition is for your benefit. He would like to kill you, and I do not blame him. You must make amends, Bayard. Hirantel is important to us.'

Bayard glanced at his mother. 'Amends? How? I doubt he'll allow it.' He stepped closer to Tayven, his movements slow and cautious. His shadow was thrown over the hard narrow bed against the wall. 'I can't believe it's really him, that he survived.' He turned round. 'Mother, what I did was expedient. Hirantel was plotting with Almorante against me. You should not have sympathy with him.'

'Oh, I don't deny he is a snake,' said Tatrini, 'but you made a gross mistake. I sympathise with him because he is stronger and wiser than you are. If you'd had any sense, you'd have cut his throat yourself, and not left your cronies to do it. You were foolish not to realise what Tayven was. He could not be eradicated so easily, which, for my purposes, is a blessing.'

Tentatively, Bayard reached out and grabbed a fistful of Tayven's hair, raised his head. 'The same, yet not,' he said, his voice full of emotion.

'You have never liked being denied,' Tatrini said. 'You always want your own way, and might have had it all those years ago, but for Khaster Leckery. Tayven spurned you, and for that you wanted to kill him.'

'It was not so simple,' Bayard said. He looked shifty, clearly wondering how much his mother knew of what had transpired in the past.

'We will perform the first ritual two nights hence,' Tatrini said. 'You must be ready.'

'I've been ready for a long time.'

'There is a difference between desire and preparation. I will leave you now.'

Bayard stepped towards her. 'I will come with you.'

'No,' said Tatrini. 'Stay here a while. The philtre is potent. You are quite safe.'

Bayard eyed his mother suspiciously. 'What action do you expect of me?'

'That of your nature,' Tatrini replied. 'Slake the thirst that has assailed you for so long. It will be for the best.' With these words she turned away from her son and left the room, closing the door behind her.

Master Dark stood in the shadows of the corridor, alert and waiting. 'Keep your ears open,' Tatrini said to him. 'Although I don't think your interference will be needed.'

Master Dark bowed. 'As you wish, your mightiness.'

Secrets of the Fire Chamber

Rav was uneasy. It had seemed like an adventure at first, when Leo had appeared at his bedside and woken him up. Rav had sat up immediately, wondering why Garante had let his uncle in. Garante slept very lightly, a fact Rav had discovered on the couple of occasions he'd tried to sneak out of their apartments to meet with Leo in the gardens.

Leo had held a finger to his mouth, and merely beckoned for Rav to get up. Making barely a noise, Rav dressed himself, and then Leo led him to the back wall of the room, where a hidden doorway stood ajar. Another palace existed within the one Rav knew. It was disguised by panelling and walls, but present all the time. It might be filled with watchful eyes, looking out into the real world.

Only once they had crossed the threshold into darkness and the door was closed behind them did Leo say, 'Mother told me of this route. She wants us to go to her.' From a sconce in the wall he took down a torch which he'd clearly left there earlier.

'Why?' Rav asked. 'It's the middle of the night.'

'Time to learn things,' Leo replied. 'Come on. Don't dawdle.'

They squeezed along a narrow high corridor, lit only by the guttering flame of Leo's torch. The walls were sometimes of stone and sometimes of wood panelling. Occasionally Rav heard noises beyond them. When they passed between wooden walls, Rav was afraid the flame from Leo's torch would set fire to the dry ancient wood. Leo walked quickly ahead, so Rav could not ask questions. He feared raising his voice.

Eventually Leo paused, allowing Rav to catch up with him. A passage opened up to the right, much wider than the one they had followed from Rav's chamber. Just to the left, a flight of stone steps descended into greater darkness: a black so dense as to be almost alive. Rav shivered. He did not want to go down there. Why would Tatrini want them to come to her at this hour and in this manner? Perhaps Leo was lying and playing a prank, trying to frighten his nephew. It was not beyond him.

'Don't look so scared,' Leo said in a low voice. 'Ghosts can't harm us, and few living people know of these routes.'

Rav had not considered ghosts. He attempted to still his twitching jaw. 'What's this about, Leo? Garante will kill me if he finds me gone.'

'How can he kill you if you're not there?' Leo uttered a snort of derision. 'He's your servant, Rav. Your grandmother wishes to speak with you in private, that's all. It is quite within your rights to slip the leash for a while.'

Rav could not look on Garante as a servant, mainly because his father held the man in such high esteem. Also, Garante had warned Rav subtly about Leo's influence. He could not speak out directly against the Malagashes, but implied that Leo's impulsive character and disregard for authority could lead to nothing but trouble. Again, through careful implication, Garante had explained that Rav was the direct heir to Palindrake, whereas Leo was only a minor prince in the Malagash line. Therefore, like Bayard before him, he sought to find an identity through wayward behaviour. Rav should consider such antics beneath him. In fact, Rav was torn. He could see the sense of what Garante had said, but even so he enjoyed Leo's company. The other boys he'd met in Magrast were dull and lacklustre in comparison.

'Let's go, then,' Rav said.

Leo grinned. 'Delights await you.' He ran down the shallow steps, making the torch flame leap and flare. Grotesque shadows writhed across the wall. The steps were deeply worn in the middle, as if thousands of feet had trodden upon them. Rav almost slipped trying to keep up. He did not want to be left alone in the dark.

At the bottom of the steps was a corridor, lit by torches. Huge arched doorways punctuated the walls, which were of immense stone blocks. 'Are we beneath the palace?' Rav asked.

'Beneath part of it,' Leo replied. 'There are deeper vaults than this.'

Perhaps the immense wooden doors, studded with iron, concealed cells in which the remains of prisoners rotted. Rav was alert for sounds, but heard nothing. The walls seemed to breathe heavily, exuding a damp, noxious breath. This was not a good place.

Leo appeared unaffected by the surroundings and walked jauntily along the corridor, humming softly to himself. He turned a corner, went down another wide flight of shallow steps and led the way into a wider corridor below. Here the ceiling was vaulted with ancient carvings of elemental spirits and the air smelled of burning wax. The floor was swept, as if this was an area used regularly.

'Do you know this place?' Rav asked.

'Not well,' Leo replied, 'but Mother's instructions were clear. These ways have always been used by my family, but few of us are privileged to know them.'

A set of tall double doors lay ahead, unadorned except for forbidding bands of iron. Rav's spine prickled. He felt that once beyond those doors there would be no way back for him, but he lacked the courage to flee.

Leo pushed the doors with both hands and they swung inwards silently on well-oiled hinges. Rav crept up behind him, peering fearfully over his uncle's shoulder. Beyond the doors lay an immense domed chamber. A circular firepit, surrounded by a three-foot wall of stone blocks, dominated the centre of the room. Blue-tinged flames writhed there with unnatural lethargy. Despite the flames, the air was cold and damp. A cloaked figure stood next to the fire with its back to them. Rav knew it must be his grandmother, but even so was afraid that when the figure turned round it would have the face of a demon. The room was lined with columns around which stone dragons coiled. Stylised representations of fire drakes, with wings uplifted, stood between the columns, snarling towards the pit. The atmosphere was oppressive, threatening. Rav shuddered.

The figure by the fire turned as Rav and Leo came through the door. Rav was relieved to see Tatrini wore her usual face. 'Well done,' she said, presumably to Leo.

Tatrini glided forward, throwing back the hood of her cloak. In the strange firelight, her coils of golden hair looked like white metal, immovable and hard. 'Rav, don't be afraid,' she said, smiling. 'This must seem strange to you, I know, but there is nothing to fear.' She put a hand on Rav's shoulder and guided him forwards. 'This is a sacred flame and it comes from deep within the earth. It is the breath of Efrit, the King Drake. We are in the original Fire Chamber, which in ages past was used by the magi of the King of Magravandias. To this day, the government is called the Fire Chamber, but they no longer use this sacred place for their meetings. Few know it exists.'

Intimidated, Rav could say nothing. His heart was beating fast.

'Tonight,' said Tatrini, 'we will work magic together. Rav, what do you know of the sea dragons?'

He knew very little. Sometimes his mother had talked about the dragons when she'd taken Elly and him for walks on the beach. He knew the story of how his family had once been able to talk to the dragons, but he hadn't really thought it was more than a fairytale. Varencienne had made it sound as if it was. He found it hard to believe his grandmother thought the old stories were real. Tatrini was staring at him with unblinking eyes. She was waiting for an answer. 'They are supposed to live under the sea,' he said, hoping that would satisfy her.

Tatrini nodded in encouragement. 'I presume your mother told you this, which is good. Your father's mother did not give him that privilege.'

'She died when he was born,' Rav said.

The Queen Mother's smile had a tight edge. 'Even if she'd lived, she'd have stood by the conventions of your family curse. But circumstances are changing. Now is the time for you to understand the dragons' true nature. The world comprises four subtle elements: fire, water, earth and air. We can see them as water in a lake or fire in the hearth, but we cannot see the energy within them that makes them that way. Water can be the crash of mighty waves or the gentle fall of spring rain. All the elements are emanations of the universal life force, which is a power we cannot see but which gives everything life. It enables your body to breathe, your mind to think. Nature creates and destroys with these four forces. Whoever understands them understands nature, and can create and destroy as it does.'

Rav shifted from foot to foot uncomfortably. He could not fully grasp what his grandmother was saying.

'I know it's a lot to take in,' Tatrini said, 'but I believe one experience is worth a thousand words. You, as your father's son, are heir to the sea dragons' power, because your family has a long association with them. Tonight, we will call upon the elemental forces. It will be an introduction. You will greet the power of water, which is the essence of the sea dragons, and it will greet you.'

'I'm earth,' Leo said proudly. 'I will be the avatar of the basilisks and their queen, Hespereth.'

'That's right,' Tatrini said. 'You have learned well, Leo.' She looked away from the boys towards the shadows at the back of the chamber. 'And there are two more, to represent fire and air.' She made a sound of mild annoyance. 'Where are they?'

Rav stared hard at Leo, seeking reassurance. Leo looked excited, whereas Rav felt only dread. Nothing good could happen to him in a place like this. It didn't feel right at all. Rav knew instinctively that Leo was incapable of sensing the atmosphere properly. Oblivious, the prince concentrated only on his mother's words, because they made him feel important.

Gazing around the room as they waited, Rav noticed that the floor was carved with a circular design marked with the four points of the compass, as well as a lot of peculiar curling symbols in between. At each cardinal point, at the edge of the room, a high-backed throne stood between the columns. Above the chairs, wooden shields hung down from the ceiling. In the west was a design similar to the Palindrake crest: it depicted a dragon of bony coral, with spines erupting from its elegant head, its tail that of a giant fish. Fire, in the south, was represented by the majestic coils of the fire-drake, rising from a nest of embers.

Tatrini noticed Rav's inspection. She touched his shoulder. 'There is Hespereth,' she said, pointing to the shield in the north. The basilisk queen was a serpent with multiple legs that had scimitar-like claws. Her head was crested with a bristling crown of thorny spikes, while three tongues lolled from her mouth like tassels. 'Of all the dragons, Hespereth and Paraga, the lord of air, are the most elusive,' Tatrini said. She indicated the shield in the east. 'Paraga was once the consort of Foy, the sea dragon queen. He hides in the high mountains of the world. He is the wind.'

Paraga was a delicate creature, with an elongated neck and large eyes. Long whiskers drooped from his jaws and enormous batlike wings sprouted from his shoulders. Rav thought he looked the most friendly of the dragons, but it was difficult to tell from a painting.

There was a noise at the back of the chamber and two figures came out of the shadows. One was Prince Bayard; Rav did not know the other, whom Bayard was supporting as if he were drunk.

'Good,' said Tatrini to herself.

Rav was scared of Bayard. He knew his father disliked the prince, but not the reason why. Instinct advised him he should be wary now.

'This is Tayven Hirantel,' Tatrini said to the boys, pointing at the seemingly drunken man. 'Pay no attention to his apparent condition. He is the element of air.' She addressed Bayard. 'Put him in his chair at the appropriate quarter.'

Rav could not imagine how so leaden a person could represent the rarefied free element of air. He had little knowledge of magic and its symbols, but lethargy did not suggest the wind to him. Tayven's limbs lolled like those of a broken doll as Bayard attempted to position him on the throne.

Tatrini placed a palm upon Rav's back and pushed him towards the west, apparently to stop him staring at what was occurring in the east. 'Go and sit in your own chair now, child.' She nodded at Leo. 'You too, my son.'

Rav had to climb onto the throne rather than sit down in it. His feet did not reach the floor once he'd arranged himself upon its hard seat. He put his small hands upon the carved arms of the chair and a shiver coursed through him. He sensed countless others before him doing the very same thing, and could feel their vanished anticipation. Their fingers would have curled over the ancient carvings, their sweat greasing the wood. Rav stared across the Fire Chamber. It looked bigger to him now. In this place, men in dark robes had discussed Caradore and its future. Someone here had given King Cassilin the confirmation he needed that Caradore was too weak to resist him. The fire mages had summoned up the elements and had constrained the power of the sea dragons. Rav's fingers dug into the arms of his chair. How could he know this? He knew the name Cassilin vaguely, but could not remember how. He glanced fearfully at Tatrini, who stood before the fire, her head bowed in concentration. To his right, Leo stared at the flames, dwarfed in his seat. To his left, Bayard sat erect and haughty, as a king might, his eyes closed, his head thrown back. Opposite, Tayven Hirantel slumped on his throne, his hair hanging over his face. A thought came clearly into Rav's mind, as if a voice he did not know had spoken it. 'He's not meant to be like this. She has done something to him.'

Tatrini drew in her breath deeply through her nose, a sibilation that filled the chamber like the hiss of a great serpent. Slowly she raised her arms.

For some minutes the Grand Queen Mother spoke in a language Rav did not understand, but the sound of the alien words raised the hairs along his arms. They were ugly sounds, yet beautiful: guttural hisses and angry clicks engorged with a power that seemed to smoke from Tatrini's mouth. Rav's heart now beat so fast, he was afraid it would explode within him. Spots of light danced before his vision. He felt sick.

For a moment, all went black. He blinked and the room swayed around him. He felt so ill that tears came to his eyes. Then his gaze was drawn to the man sitting opposite him.

Tayven had raised his head and was staring intently across the room. His eyes burned intensely blue, like the flames in the fire pit. They were not the colour of human eyes. Rav could tell Tayven was shaking, for strands of hair writhed over his face. His fingers gripped the arms of the chair, the knuckles white. The intensity of this image pushed the sickness from Rav's mind. He was transfixed by the power of Tayven's eyes.

Tatrini's voice sounded muffled, as if heard through a thick stone wall. The air in the chamber sparkled, even though it was in shadow. The only light emanated from the throne opposite and the man who sat upon it.

How long Rav was transfixed by Tayven's stare, he could not tell, but then, in an instant, time and space seemed to fracture. With a nauseating jolt, Rav felt as if something had sucked him off his seat and hurled him across the room. One moment he was sitting on his throne, the next found him standing next to Tayven. It was like a dream and, with the bizarre logic of dreams, it was natural and right.

Tayven began to convulse, his mouth wide in a rictus of pain. Without thinking, Rav reached out and gripped one of Tayven's taut hands. He could feel the bones grinding beneath his fingers. 'Stop it,' he said, 'stop it.'

He glanced round, seeking Tatrini's help, but the air in the chamber was a whirl of colour, obscuring everything within it. Rav could no longer see any of the others. Why didn't Tatrini do something? Perhaps it was meant to happen.

Tayven uttered a coarse gasp and then fell still and silent. He wasn't breathing. Rav stared into his face, his empty stare, for what felt like long minutes, but which was perhaps only seconds. Then, Tayven's eyes swivelled abruptly towards him. Rav started back, but was unable to move his hands. It was as if he and Tayven were fused together: the bones and fibres of their fingers had become one. Rav did not feel afraid, but was on the verge of fear. He had never felt so strange.

'You,' Tayven said huskily. 'Sinaclara.'

Rav realised that Tayven was no longer looking at him, but beyond him. He turned and caught a fleeting glimpse of a tall column of blue smoke that surged forward. It passed right through Rav's body, bending it like a bow, forcing him onto tiptoe, filling him with both cold and heat. He uttered a choked cry.

A woman dressed in a peacock-blue gown stood before him. Her long red hair fell in a complicated tangle of loops and plaits over her breast and down her back. Her face was pale and sombre and in her hands she held a crown. It looked as if it was made of bone or coral, with tall delicate spines. Some of the spines were broken, and Rav thought that every injury the crown had received told a great story that would take whole days to relate. The woman held the crown out to Tayven, and said, 'Take it, Bard, for you know to whom it belongs.'

Tayven reached out, pulling away from Rav's grip. It felt as if his flesh and bone passed entirely through Rav's own. The crown hung suspended in the air between the woman's hands, surrounded by a soft radiance emanating from her fingers. The moment Tayven touched the crown, Rav was hit by a blast of energy that smacked him up towards the ceiling. His spine collided with the carved vaults: an explosion of pain. It was as if a great metal hook had passed through his body and now he dangled from it, helpless.

111

Panicking, limbs flailing, Rav screamed for help. In terror, he called his mother's name, his father's, even his grandmother's. He could see Tatrini beside the fire pit and her mouth was moving. Rav could not hear her words. Bayard and Leo stared at Tatrini, oblivious of anything else. Tayven, the man of air, still stood before the blue woman. Rav expelled a shrill scream: he couldn't help himself.

Then a deep female voice murmured close to his ear, 'Hush now, child. You must take this for your own.'

He thought at first that someone else was up there with him, but very soon his eyes were drawn to the shield above the water throne. The image of the dragon queen had come alive. She turned her head and now she gazed upon him, her long black tongue flickering out across the vast distance to touch his cheek. She was tasting the salt of his tears. The tongue flicked away again, leaving his skin cold where Foy had kissed it. He looked down, calmer now, and saw that his body still stood beside the throne below. How could he be in two places at once? It was weird, but he was no longer frightened. Neither did his body hurt. There was no hook through his back. He was floating free. Gazing down, he saw the body below begin to change. It grew taller, flickering as it did so. Its hair grew longer, writhing down its back. Rav saw himself become his own father. Valraven stood below him, serene and without expression. Tayven bowed to one knee, holding the crown up before him. Then he rose and placed it upon Valraven's head.

At once Rav was hurled back to the ground. His head collided with the stone floor and darkness consumed him.

With a jolt, he was awake. His body felt strange, all wrong, as if it had been twisted into complicated knots and had only just untangled itself. He realised he was back on the throne in the west quarter. Opposite, Tayven was staring at him through lank strands of hair. There was no blue woman beside him, no Dragon Lord.

Rav uttered a wordless shout and only when his grandmother stopped speaking did he realise she had continued her invocation throughout the entire episode. The part of him that had never moved from the throne had heard it.

'Rav?' Tatrini said.

Rav could not speak now. He was conscious of a shrill, vibrating hum issuing from the walls.

Opposite him, Tayven stood up, his body burning with a peculiar white light. Rav was compelled to point at him with one hand.

In the south, Bayard made an anguished noise and leapt from his seat.

Tayven raised his right hand, pulled it back behind his head. He made a gesture of release, as if he were throwing something. Rav could see neither missile nor bolt of energy, but Bayard was hurled back against his throne. Rav felt the impact in his own bones.

'Tayven!' Tatrini roared. 'Sit down. You cannot do this.'

In a blur, Tayven ran across the room, pushing the Grand Queen Mother from his path. She staggered, her hip crashing into the wall around the fire pit.

Rav shrank back against his chair, sure that Tayven was about to commit murder. He was curious, in a morbid, horrified way, but also repulsed. When Tayven made contact with Bayard's flesh, there would be blood, lots of it.

Bayard cowered back, perhaps unmanned by the strange nature of the attack. Tayven loomed over him, his hair flying up as if it were wound with ribbons of lightning. His hands were hooked claws.

'Tayven!' Tatrini cried. She ran towards her threatened son.

Tayven took hold of Bayard's shoulders and lifted him bodily from the throne. At the same time, Tatrini threw herself upon Tayven's back. With desperate fingers, she reached blindly towards his face, his eyes. Rav could not bear to think of those searing orbs ruined, but Tayven shrugged Tatrini off. The Grand Queen Mother stumbled back, holding her throat as if it pained her.

Now it would happen. The eerie vibration in the room had become a shriek.

Tayven held Bayard up with superhuman strength, as if the prince weighed no more than a child. Bayard's expression was that of stark horror. He was no longer a person to be feared.

Then Tayven laughed. He lowered Bayard back onto the throne and, to Rav's utter astonishment, kissed him briefly on the mouth. Bayard spluttered, rubbed the backs of his hands over his lips as if to wipe away a caustic fluid. The humming sound diminished, although it did not cease.

Dismissing Bayard from his attention, Tayven turned to Tatrini and said, 'There is no power on this earth that shall contain me.' His voice was low, echoing.

'Who are you?' Tatrini cried hoarsely, still gripping her throat. 'Name yourself.'

'Do you not know me, great queen?' Tayven said. 'I am that which you summoned.'

'I saw a woman in my mind, dressed all in blue. Are you her?'

'Sinaclara? No. I am Paraga, power of air. She put the will of the Crown inside me.'

'The Crown is ours,' Tatrini said. '*You* are ours.' She had recovered her composure and stood with straight spine, her hands curled into fists at her sides.

'The Crown of Silence belongs to no one,' Paraga said. 'But the True King belongs to it. If it rests upon the brow of any but the rightful bearer, it will bring chaos and destruction.'

'Did you summon the sorceress Sinaclara to this place? What was the purpose of it?'

'The owner of this body has answered your questions without reserve,' Paraga said, 'for he had no choice, but now no philtre in existence can sway his tongue against his will. I will tell you this: your rite connected the sorceress with all that you do. He, she and I are connected. She is the Guardian of the Crown.'

'Does she still possess it?'

'She does not possess it. She is its Guardian.'

'And she lives in Bree?'

Paraga did not speak for a while, then made Tayven's face smile. 'Great queen, you have already gained this information from him.'

'But where in Bree?'

'You must discover that for yourself.'

'You say the philtres will no longer affect Tayven. It seems we must test your theory.'

Tayven's body shrugged carelessly. 'As you will.' Then he began to shudder violently, and the light went out of him. The strange high-pitched humming in the chamber ceased. For a few moments, Tayven stood swaying on the spot, then he straightened up and rubbed his hands through his hair. He looked weary, dazed. Rav could tell the voice of the cockatrice had left him.

Tatrini reached out and touched Tayven's arm briefly, as if afraid to let her hand linger upon him. 'That was magnificent,' she said. 'More than I could have hoped for.'

Tayven looked at her through his hair, his expression enigmatic.

Tatrini frowned, then said, 'You could have escaped here, but you did not. Why? Why didn't you kill Bayard when you had the chance?'

For the briefest instant, Tayven glanced over at Rav, but Rav was sure Tatrini did not notice. 'The dragons must be summoned, but beware of who you invest with their combined power.'

'You kissed Bayard,' Tatrini said carefully. 'Is this a sign that he is the one?'

'He is fire,' Tayven replied, 'of that there is no doubt.'

'What of your enmity?'

Tayven glanced at Bayard, as someone might glance at the body of a dead foe. 'I know of a man who clung to past grudges,' he said. 'It weakened him. I will not do the same.'

Tatrini narrowed her eyes. Rav could tell that many meanings lurked in Tayven's words. He could not understand them, and neither could his grandmother, he thought.

'So you will work with me?' Tatrini asked. 'With us?'

'You must decide whether you can trust me,' Tayven replied.

Tatrini considered for a moment. 'Your change of heart concerning Bayard is sudden. That, I mistrust.'

Both she and Tayven turned their gaze to Bayard, who still crouched upon his throne, his knees drawn up to his chest. 'Would you trust a demon?' he said in a cracked voice.

'You trusted me enough to paw at me in my cell,' Tayven said in a reasonable voice. 'Did I harm you then?'

'You were drugged,' Bayard said.

Tayven laughed caustically. 'How noble of you to admit that in front of others,' he said. 'The question is: how long did that drug last? I was charitable, prince, not to spit upon your words of love. I indulged your fantasy, and I had no good reason to do that. At one time I would have given my own life to take yours.'

Bayard said nothing. His face was white, even his lips, while his eyes looked too dark and too large.

'You are perverse, Tayven,' Tatrini said. 'Your motives are unclear.'

Tayven merely shrugged. 'If I choose to live in the past, I am still its victim,' he said.

Tatrini narrowed her eyes. 'You would have to be more than a man to own such strength and virtue. Much more than a man.'

'I do not speak from virtue,' Tayven said, 'and I do not forgive. I have merely elected to free myself from needless pain. It does not require strength. It is, in fact, very easy.'

Tatrini did not appear to be convinced, and neither was Rav. He did not know what had happened in the past between Tayven and Prince Bayard, but he sensed that it was terrible. He did not think that Tayven was lying now, but playing with words. It was the first time Rav realised how powerful words could be.

'There is something you want from this situation,' Tatrini said. 'What other reason would you have to comply with us?'

'None,' Tayven said, 'but that does not mean you can't benefit. For now, I am in accord with your aims.'

'Did the cockatrice reveal something to you? Or did the sorceress give you information?'

'I know only that what proceeds here is part of a pattern, and that I am part of it.'

Tatrini released her breath, as if she'd been holding it for some time. 'Then, with wariness, but also satisfaction, I will recognise our alliance.' She turned and gestured to both Leo and Rav. 'Come here.'

Rav slid down from his throne. His uncle appeared to be frozen in shock. Rav went over to him and took his hand. The flesh was icy cold. Leo breathed quick and shallow, the pupils of his eyes very large. 'It's all right,' Rav murmured. 'Come.'

Leo directed a mad-eyed glance at Rav and swallowed convulsively, as if it hurt to do so.

'It's over,' Rav said.

Reluctantly, Leo slid out down from the throne and allowed Rav to lead him across the chamber. Rav felt as if he held the hand of a much younger child and recognised the glow of pride in his heart. He had done better than Leo this night.

Tatrini thought so too. She smiled upon her grandson and said, 'You are a strong little man, aren't you? When you first came here, you were afraid, while Leo was not. Now, after all you have seen, it is you who is the most fearless.'

The Grand Queen Mother's words warmed Rav, but in some ways he wished she hadn't said them, because Leo wouldn't like it. 'I *was* afraid,' he said, 'through all of it. I was afraid of the blue woman.'

Tatrini leaned down. 'You saw her?'

Rav nodded, looking at Tayven. 'She walked through me.'

Tatrini took hold of Rav's shoulder. 'You had a vision,' she said excitedly. 'What happened?'

Again Rav glanced at Tayven, whose expression was bland, but he sensed an order deep within Tayven's eyes. There was no reason why he should obey it, but instinctively Rav opted for offering only part of the story. 'I thought I was standing next to Tayven's throne, then a blue woman appeared. I was thrown up into the air, and when I came down again, I was back on my throne.'

'This is marvellous,' Tatrini said. 'What about you, Leo? What did you see?'

'Everything went blurred,' Leo said in a low, miserable voice. 'I saw a mass of colours and the air became . . . *hard*. I could barely breathe.'

Tatrini turned round. 'Bayard?'

The prince uncurled himself slowly. It was clearly difficult for him to muster much dignity, given what had just occurred. '*Something* happened,' he said, in what Rav took to be a falsely haughty tone. 'I sensed movement, but saw little. A power came and took me by the throat. Like Leo, I could barely breathe.'

'But neither of you sensed the power of the element you represent?'

'The whole ritual seemed concentrated on Tayven,' Bayard said dryly, 'but that is hardly surprising.'

'What about you, Rav?' Tatrini asked. 'Did you feel the presence of the sea dragons?'

'I'm not sure,' Rav answered.

'Perhaps it will take time to invoke all the elements,' Tatrini said. 'Tonight, we had success with air. That is a satisfactory first step.' She clasped her hands together and smiled upon Rav and Leo. 'Well, both you young men had better get back to bed. You might have some interesting dreams, in which case, make sure you remember them. It would be best to note them down. I'll see you tomorrow.'

She turned to her elder son. 'Bayard, I will instruct Master Dark to escort Tayven back to his quarters. You may return separately to yours.'

Rav thought the forced smile on Bayard's face was full of cracks. 'You had better know what you are doing, Mother,' he said.

Rav crept back to his bed, wishing that Leo could stay with him. Alone in the dark, he was both wide awake and exhausted. He didn't want to think about what had happened that night, because it made the dark come alive with unseen spirits, but thoughts and images filled his mind. Foy had been an almost comforting presence in the Fire Chamber, but now the idea of her was terrifying. She could be hiding in any shadow, her great eyes fixed upon him. Rav burrowed beneath the bedclothes, where the sound of his own breathing was too loud. He was cold, yet his body was sweating as he mulled over the confusing events of the evening. Gastern was emperor, so what was all this talk of new kings? It looked like Tayven wanted to crown Valraven as king, but he was pretending to support Bayard. It made no sense whatsoever. Why couldn't people tell the truth?

When at last Rav did fall asleep, he was assailed by a strange dream of enormous creatures flying around the moon. He stood upon a cliff-top near his old home, watching a ghostly ship sail down a road of moonlight towards him. He knew that the ship carried someone who was dangerous and frightening. He called out to the spectral shapes in the sky. They must be sea dragons and therefore they must help him. But they continued to spiral lazily around each other and now they had transformed into gigantic women with wings that looked like fins of fishes.

A voice murmured in Rav's head. 'Think carefully before you call upon my daughters for aid, Dragon Heir. They are the dragon daughters and few may command them.'

At once the women in the sky turned towards him. They swam through the air, their limbs parting the vapour that surrounded them. They were laughing.

Now the ship and whoever travelled in it seemed far less of a threat. Rav realised he should not have attracted the attention of the dragon daughters, because it meant they knew him and would recognise him again.

'Go away!' he cried, waving his arms at them.

The dragon daughters, smaller now, circled round him. Their laughter was cruel and he could tell they delighted in torment. One after another, they rushed at him, causing him to cringe away, but they did not touch him. Their faces were both beautiful and hideous. He could see that the insides of their mouths were black and their teeth were pointed.

'I am Misk,' said one. 'Speak my name, little man.'

'And I am Jia,' said another. 'Let me hear it on your lips.

'And I am Thrope,' said the third. 'Sing my name to me.'

Rav knew that the last thing he should do was speak the names of these demonesses. In desperation, he spluttered, 'Get the ship! Get the ship!'

The dragon daughters did not even glance towards the sea. 'Do not fear it,' Jia said.

'It will never reach you,' said Thrope.

'Give us something better to do,' said Misk. 'I am she who once lived within your father, but he cast me out at the old domain. I miss him so badly. I miss the warmth of flesh. Let me in, Dragon Heir. Let me lie comfortably in your skin. I can show you such delights.'

'We are your slaves,' said Jia. 'Can't you see how we adore you?'

Rav was not comforted by these words; they might be true, but the love of the dragon daughters was a very dangerous thing. They were circling closer now, reaching out to brush his body with their clawed fingertips. He was surrounded by them.

Then the sea erupted beneath the cliff and an immense dragon of coral and weed and broken ships lifted from the threshing maelstrom of water. She spread her ragged wings against the sky and moonlight shone through their rents and tears.

'Great mother! Mighty Foy!' cried Misk and backed away from Rav, followed by her sisters.

The dragon queen swept towards the cliff-top and hung in the sky on slowly beating wings. 'I begin to wake!' she roared. 'Someone wakes me! Who defiles my endless sleep?'

At once Rav was awake in his own bed, sitting upright. His panting breath steamed on the cold air. His ears echoed with Foy's booming voice. The light in the room was a grey twilight, for dawn was soon to break.

Rav put his face into his hands and wept. *He* had woken Foy. Because his grandmother had made him do it. Now the dragon queen was angry. She might come for him. He couldn't control her: he didn't know how. Should he speak to his father about this? Surely Valraven would laugh at him and say it was only a dream. Rav certainly couldn't talk about what he'd witnessed in the old Fire Chamber. Tatrini would be furious. Glumly, Rav wiped his face and waited for the sun to rise. He had never felt so alone.

A Voice from the Aethyrs

Sinaclara woke abruptly in the early dawn. Outside, a storm raged against the house and an open window had slammed against its casement. Sinaclara rose from her bed and went to close it. She felt disorientated, slightly threatened. It was as if the storm had evoked a nightmare that she had already forgotten. Strange, the weather had been so mild when she'd gone to bed. Now it was as if winter had come again. Shivering, she put on a woollen robe over her nightgown. She would go down to the kitchens and warm herself some milk, perhaps fortified by a measure of good Jessapurian liqueur.

Beyond her room, the house was in utter darkness. All the oil lamps had been turned off, which was unusual because Nana, Sinaclara's assistant and housekeeper, generally kept the lights burning low throughout the night. In a house of magic, a Jessapurian such as Nana would leave no shadowed corner where a demon, fetch or djinn might hide. Sinaclara had no means of lighting the lamps with her, so had to feel her way down the stairs. She hoped there was nothing wrong. Her honed senses detected no untoward atmosphere, yet it was odd that the lamps were out.

At the bottom of the stairs, she noticed that the door to her sitting room was ajar, and that light showed beyond it. Nana could be in there, but it was rare for her to be up so late. Sinaclara went to the door and pushed it wide. A fire was lit in the hearth, and ranks of candles burned around the room on every available surface. Someone was sitting in the armchair beside the hearth.

'Nana?' Sinaclara said. It could be any one of her Jessapurian staff, but this was not usual behaviour for them. The figure was shadowy.

She could discern no recognisable features, but neither was there any chill or peculiarity in the atmosphere that might suggest a supernatural visitor.

Cautiously, Sinaclara ventured forward. In her mind, she conjured a caul of protective white light around her. Only when she faced the chair could she see who sat upon it: a man with long pale hair.

'Tayven!' she cried. 'What are you doing here?'

Tayven looked up at her with a severe expression. 'They will come for you, Clara. You must take care of the Crown. It is vital.'

'Who will come for me? What do you mean?' Sinaclara scraped her sleep-mussed hair back from her face. She was always alert for threats in the aether and had felt nothing unusual recently, but now Tayven had come to her from Mewt. It was a long journey. He would not undertake it without good reason. Maycarpe should have sent a psychic message to her.

'Tatrini, who was empress,' Tayven said. 'She knows of the Crown and will come for it.'

'How does she know of it?' Sinaclara demanded. 'What has happened?'

'She has taken me captive,' Tayven said. 'I have only a short time here.'

'What do you mean?' Sinaclara reached out impulsively to touch Tayven, but at the moment before her fingers made contact, she drew back. This was not a creature of flesh and blood. She could see it now: the translucence to the skin, the faint glow around the whole figure.

'Leave this place,' Tayven said. 'Hide the Crown. Protect yourself.'

'Tayven,' Sinaclara said, 'you must tell me more.'

At that moment, every door and window in the house opened and slammed shut simultaneously. The room filled with a cold, noxious wind. Sinaclara's hair was blown into her eyes. She struggled to push it back, her body buffeted by hectic air. Then everything became abruptly still.

Panting, Sinaclara peered at the chair. The candles and the fire had blown out, but even in the meagre blue-light of predawn, she could see there was no one sitting there.

A noise behind her made her jump. Instinctively, she drew a symbol of protection on the air, but when she turned, it was to see Nana's tall dark figure in the doorway.

The Jessapurian held a lamp. She looked perplexed. 'My lady, what is going on?'

'Someone was here,' said Sinaclara, belting her robe more tightly.

'Tayven Hirantel. A fetch of him. The room was ablaze with candlelight. There was a fire.'

'Yes,' said Nana. 'I had lit them myself. I intended to perform a short rite to Tali-ma, goddess of storms, for the gale last night had spirits within it. There is something afoot.'

Sinaclara felt suddenly chilled. 'We must check the Crown,' she said and, almost pushing Nana aside, hurried from the room.

She and the Jessapurian went down to the lower basement far beneath the house. Here, behind seven locked doors, was a strong-room, within it a safe bound by physical locks as well as magical charms. Filled with dread, Sinaclara deactivated all the protective locks. She held her breath as she opened the heavy door. The only object inside was wrapped in a dark blue cloth. Carefully, she removed it and held it out to Nana, who undid the wrappings. Within, lay the coralline Crown of Silence.

Sinaclara exhaled deeply and bowed her head in relief. 'Tayven warned me that the empress has discovered the existence of the Crown. She must also know I am associated with it. The artefact must be taken to safety without delay.'

'Jessapur,' said Nana. 'You know I have contacts at the king's court. You will be safe there.'

'No,' Sinaclara said. 'I must go to Mewt. Maycarpe may not know that Tayven is held by Tatrini. The Mewtish priests can protect me as well as the Jessapurian magi.'

Nana nodded shortly. 'That is true, but Mewt is more accessible to Magravandias than Jessapur. I would feel happier knowing you were under my people's protection.'

'So would I,' said Sinaclara, 'but I am sure I must go to Mewt, even if it is more dangerous. Mewt is the heart of the world. If events are beginning to unfold concerning the destiny of the Crown, it must be taken to the Womb of Power.'

'I will accompany you,' said Nana.

Sinaclara smiled ruefully. 'I should say I must go alone, but your company would be most welcome, Nana.'

'If forces of the empire come to the house, the rest of the staff will be in danger.'

'Then we must close it up,' Sinaclara said. She looked around the little room. 'My house will be violated, but we must let it happen. The rest of the staff must return to Jessapur for a time.'

'This house is eternal,' Nana said. 'You need not worry. All will be restored one day.'

Sinaclara sighed heavily. 'But perhaps not in my lifetime.' She mustered her strength. 'Still, there's no point in being sentimental. We must begin preparations at once.'

CHAPTER THIRTEEN

The Magic of High Hamagara

It was clear to Varencienne that Taropat had thought very little about the practicalities of living rough with a woman and child, especially those who were used to comfortable living. Ellony did not complain, and didn't appear to feel the cold, but Varencienne was far from pleased about having to sleep in thickets, caves or ruins. She hated not being able to bathe properly, loathed the food and her clothes were soon filthy and torn. Taropat was driven, allowing them the minimum of rest.

'He was like this on the lakes quest,' Shan said. 'Once he's got a goal in mind, he's unstoppable.'

Varencienne considered whether she should attempt to escape. The further they travelled from Caradore, the more difficult this would become. But she did not know the route home, other than to travel south, and the way would be fraught with obstacles and dangers. Was it best for Ellony if they remained passively with their captors, or was she deceiving herself and just opting for the easiest course? While Shan was obviously concerned for her welfare, he did not react favourably to her suggestion that he should escort them home and receive a reward for his endeavour. He was astounded that Varencienne was not as excited and intrigued about their journey to High Hamagara as he and Taropat were.

Ellony did not share her mother's doubts. It made Varencienne's heart clench to see how the child was so grateful for any attention Taropat would give her. And he, this enigma of a man: what were his true feelings? Why was it so difficult for her to believe in his prickly and pompous exterior? Shan was happy to answer Varencienne's questions and told her everything he knew about Khaster's strange transformation into the magus Taropat. If it were true, then Taropat had effectively stolen only Khaster's face. The man who lived within the flesh was someone completely different. But sometimes a ghost seemed to stand in his place.

One evening, as Shan built a camp fire, Varencienne had watched Taropat climb a nearby spur of rock to scan their surroundings. As he stood tall against the sky, one hand shading his eyes while his hair blew free in long strands from the cord at his neck, she thought she caught a glimpse of the person Pharinet had married. Here was the man who had existed before Magrast had crushed his spirit, who should have gone on to become a wealthy landowner, caring for his land and the people under his protection. Khaster must have been weak to have been beaten and destroyed so easily. Other men, such as Valraven himself, underwent terrible trauma, wrestling with the darker side of themselves as with a demon, but they emerged from their experiences cleansed and renewed: better people. In comparison, Khaster had gone rotten: resentful, peevish and vengeful. It was ridiculous that he could call himself a great magus.

The further north they travelled, they outran spring, which dawdled behind them. The air became colder and the land was shrouded in a seething mist that rarely dissipated, even when the sun shone. The path headed ever upwards, towards mountains that were hidden by fog, but whose oppressive eternal presence nevertheless dominated the landscape. A forest closed in upon the path. To Varencienne, the primordial trees were like an army of gargantuan, implacable warriors. Sometimes, when she and the others made camp, they would hear great boughs crashing down nearby, as if the forest were advising them how easily it could crush them, should it desire to do so.

Varencienne was always cold, and feared they must die of exposure if they continued to travel with so few supplies. Shan and Taropat hunted small animals for food, and taught Ellony and her mother which plants and berries were edible. Ellony, impatient with this women's work, persuaded Shan to teach her how to hunt. Varencienne did not enjoy the unbridled bloodlust on her daughter's face when she brought her first rabbit for inspection. She was like a cat bringing a dead rat to the hearth, expecting praise, but Varencienne felt like a disgusted cat owner: she could have cheerfully pushed Ellony away with a broom.

The land was sparsely inhabited. Occasionally they would come across a farm, if you could so dignify the mean thatched hovels they encountered. The farms were really small villages, built either in cleared areas of forest or else on the occasional sweep of valley meadow that occasionally opened up amongst the trees. The people were surly, dark-skinned and closed-faced, but generally offered a frugal meal and overnight accommodation in the meagre lean-tos where their goats and hens spent the night. By this point, Varencienne would eagerly have traded all her jewellery for a clean, warm room, but the Low Hamagarid farmers had no interest in jewels. They would accept a payment of labour, which meant Shan had to work for them. Taropat rarely got his fingers dirty, but his charisma ensured that the superstitious Hamaragids believed him to be a foreign magician. Sometimes he would work protective magic to purge demons from their houses and land, but only sometimes. When Varencienne questioned him about this, he explained that they might need his reputation later, and that as news would travel fast through the countryside, it would not do if he was seen as too accommodating. His magic would be regarded as stronger if he was selective about where he worked it.

The most astonishing thing to Varencienne was that they managed to communicate their needs to the Hamagarids without the use of spoken language. It was all done with gestures and simple tone of voice. When a smile appeared on a dour Hamagarid face, it was a reward equal to a bowl of goat's milk or a hunk of sour cheese.

Only two weeks after their journey had begun, her previous life was a dream, that she had once lived in a castle, with servants and every comfort her husband's wealth could buy. Her beautiful hands were ruined, the nails ragged and dirty. She had no make-up, so she knew she must look hideous. Her hair was always filthy, so she wore it wound up on her head. She had to squat in the forest to relieve herself like an animal. The onset of a menstrual period was a nightmare. She had to make herself pads from leaves, which she tore up and wadded together to create a little absorbency. Surely the men could *smell* her, though. It was disgusting. Life became a minute-by-minute struggle for survival. Comfort derived from the smallest thing, like finding a wild plum tree still hung with some of last year's fruits, sweetened and softened by winter's claw. Insects had been at the plums, and birds, but as the sweet gritty pulp exploded with flavour in Varencienne's mouth, she did not care. If she found a wind-break den of rhododendron for the night, it was the most exciting news she could give her travelling companions. A dead rabbit became not an object of disgust, but a mouth-watering welcome sight. Surely she should hate Shan and Taropat for what they'd done to her? But as the days went by, they melded into a surrogate family and she had to remind herself forcibly that she was not on this journey by choice and that the men who'd abducted her were nothing more than criminals. She wondered if Valraven would ever find her. She might vanish into the wilderness of Hamagara and never be seen again.

At first Varencienne had refused to work at the settlements they visited, but circumstances eventually changed her mind. Desperate to stop feeling so cold, she learned how to milk goats and repair garments, so that the stout, silent Hamagarid women would pay her in clothing. Now she was dressed in a thick homespun tunic and voluminous skirt in dark greens and browns, over which she wore a bulky woollen coat. It was hardly attractive garb, but it kept out the cold and was effective camouflage in the wild. Varencienne never took these garments off. Bathing was a sweet memory. She could not bear to think of undressing herself in the chill air to bathe in the icy streams and lakes of Hamagara.

Ellony also worked readily. She would chatter to the farm children, even though they could not understand a word she said, nor she them. However, after only a short time, she had learned a few Hamagarid phrases, which she taught to her mother. The Hamagarid children liked to stroke Ellony's face, where the skin was so much lighter than their own. They thought it must feel different too. Ellony would chuckle with pleasure at this attention. She was changing into someone else, someone more confident and outgoing.

One afternoon, after their work was done, Varencienne, Ellony and Shan went for a walk together down a steep hillside below the farm where they were staying. Only a short time ago Varencienne would have refused Shan's company on principle, but now he was the nearest she had to a friend. They sat down on the sweet meadow grass while Ellony scampered around them, lost in her private make-believe. Varencienne gazed at the landscape, its soaring heights and shadowed depths. The colours were so pure, the air like an essence of magic. Hamagara could be the otherworld reflection of Caradore, if that were possible. It shared the same topography, but here everything was more extreme. For just a moment, Varencienne sensed a purpose to everything – why she was there, what she would learn from it – and the feeling unnerved her.

'Why are we doing this?' she said abruptly. 'Where are we going? What's the point?'

Shan looked up at her lazily, as if emerging from a dream. 'We are going to High Hamagara,' he replied, 'and there we will discover something important.'

'I don't believe it,' Varencienne said. 'I have lost myself.' She gestured angrily at her clothes. 'Look at me. I am destroyed. Is this Taropat's revenge?'

'You are not destroyed,' Shan said, 'you are very beautiful, more so than you were when I first saw you.'

'You're perverse,' Varencienne said. 'I look like a bog-grubber.'

Shan snorted in laughter. 'I don't believe you've ever even seen a "bog-grubber"! I prefer a woman who looks and smells like a woman, rather than some powered, primped and corseted doll.'

127

The reference to smell made Varencienne blush. 'I was asking neither for your opinion nor approval,' she said, looking away from him. 'It's how I feel about myself that matters.'

'This is real life,' Shan said. 'How most people live. How you used to live, how you looked, isn't real.'

'I will ascribe to my own version of reality, thank you,' Varencienne said stiffly. 'Why should your peasant existence become mine?' As soon as she uttered the words, she realised how rude and arrogant they sounded. Shan had shown her kindness, whereas Taropat, who came from noble stock, treated her with contempt.

Shan did not respond to her remark, but his silence was eloquent.

'I'm sorry,' Varencienne said. 'That sounded like a true Malagash.'

Shan stared at her darkly, refusing to be wooed by her lighter tone.

'I didn't choose this for myself,' she said. 'Can you blame me for resenting it? And don't say this is a salient lesson in harsh reality, from which I shall march forth enlightened and changed.'

'I wouldn't say that,' Shan said. 'I don't resent you for the privileges you had, and I don't blame you for missing them.' He grinned fiercely. 'You see, I am a noble savage! I lived at Queen Neferishu's court in Mewt, so I've had a taste of that life. I looked upon Neferishu as a friend. Given the choice, I would probably be back there now.'

Varencienne rolled onto her stomach and rested her chin in her hands. 'Then why aren't you? Why follow Taropat's mad dreams? If the queen of Mewt favours you, I'd imagine you could have an extremely comfortable life there. And you were a friend of Darris Maycarpe. It makes no sense to me, the path you've chosen. Surely you've alienated your powerful friends, and for what?'

Shan sighed, his hands dangling between his knees. He contemplated the ground between them, then said, 'It isn't easy to explain. I have seen and experienced things that few people have. When the Crown was revealed to us at Recolletine, it changed my life. I had a vision of all that could be. Taropat is damaged and eccentric, but his drive and determination led us on our quest. I believe there is redemption for all of us in the future. The ideals behind the Crown exist, because we can imagine them. The True King is a symbol of all that is good in humanity. If I found him, I would serve him unquestionably, even if he were your son, a Malagash and a Palindrake.'

'But what if it is my husband?'

'No,' said Shan. 'It is not him.'

'You make inferences with only half the facts,' Varencienne said. 'Valraven was as damaged as Taropat is, but he overcame some of his dilemmas.'

'He still serves the empire.'

'He finds it difficult to believe in magic,' Varencienne said, with a rueful smile. 'If he could only let go of his disbelief and experience the legacy of his blood, he might not serve the empire so willingly. He believes he has no power and that he is doing what is right to keep his family safe.'

Shan hesitated, then said, 'Do you miss him?'

'No,' Varencienne replied at once, 'because I do not believe we are apart. Valraven will not cease looking for us. He will find us.'

'You speak of a great love.'

'If you think that,' said Varencienne, 'you know little of love. Val and I are friends. We are family. I suppose I am like a sister to him.'

'Given what I have heard of him and his sister, it seems his relationships are somewhat mixed up.'

Varencienne laughed. 'I can imagine what people think, and I expect Taropat has told the most grisly version of the tale to you. I think differently. I like to believe that in another life, Val and Pharinet weren't related, but were lovers. They cannot help what their souls feel now or, I should say, used to feel. After what happened to Ellony, Khaster's sister, Val ended the physical relationship with Pharinet. I have always found that very sad, for they shared the great love you spoke of. I wouldn't have minded if Val had wanted to continue his relationship with Pharry, but he doesn't. He feels guilty for it, not because they were related, but because it helped destroy his first wife.'

'You are trying to give me another picture of him, aren't you?' Shan said. 'I am not so easily swayed.'

'You have never met Val,' Varencienne said, 'so your opinion of him derives solely from Taropat's. Surely it is better to form judgements from more than one opinion?'

'Palindrake is a Dragon Lord of the empire. That fact speaks for itself.'

'And you are a kidnapper.' Once again Shan did not respond. Varencienne smiled to herself. He was quite adept at hurt silences. She rolled over onto her back and stared up at the sky. Huge clouds massed against the distant peaks. 'Look at that,' she said, pointing at the horizon. 'It's easy to see why people imagine that gods live in the mountains. They ooze a strange, supernatural energy. And we are going there . . . '

'It is alien territory for both of us,' Shan said. 'You must have faith in the future. Something will happen to us there.'

'We know so little about it, and what we do know does not inspire confidence. We may be killed on sight.'

Shan laughed. 'Do you really believe your magnificent history could

be ended quietly? You are still part of the world, Varencienne Palindrake, even when you are hidden in one of its wildest corners. If
anything, you are our insurance for survival.'

She laughed. 'I feel greatly reassured by your confidence!'

Shan was quiet for a moment, then said, 'There's something I've
wanted to ask you . . . '

'Aha,' she said, 'and you fear my response, clearly. Ask me. Go on.'

'Why did you bow down to Taropat when you first saw him?'

Varencienne had been ready to make a jovial reply to whatever Shan
might say, believing it would involve some shy admission of his
admiration for her. Her laughter died in her throat and she went
momentarily cold. 'Is that what it looked like?'

'Yes. That's what it was.'

'I see.' She stared at him for a while. 'Very well, I will share something
with you, but please respect its confidential nature.'

He coloured. 'Of course!'

'It sounds ridiculous now, but at one time I admired Khaster Leckery
very much. I'd never met him, of course, and I was young and full of
romantic fancies. When I saw his face, which before I'd only ever seen in
paintings, I was taken back for a short while, that's all. As I said, it's
ridiculous.'

'But he's not Khaster.'

'I know that now.'

Shan chewed the inside of his cheek. 'Do you still feel the same about
him?'

'Of course not, the man's a pompous, overbearing and arrogant fool.'

'I wouldn't want to see you hurt,' Shan said. 'You are a . . . unique
person, Ren. I feel privileged to have met you, to be here with you now. I
would defend you with my life.'

Varencienne stared at him and, for a moment, she sensed a connection between them. She felt she could see into the future or the past. 'I
know you,' she said.

Shan returned her stare. 'Do you?'

The air hummed between them, as if the energy of the mountains had
poured down upon them like an avalanche, engulfed them in its flow.
We are not here, we are not now, Varencienne thought. Unconsciously,
she had moved towards Shan, aware of a high-pitched sound reverberat-
ing through her head. She would reach out to him, touch him, unify the
chaotic moments of past and future.

Then Taropat's voice came stridently across the meadow. 'Shan!
Come here!'

Varencienne drew in her breath sharply. The moment was broken,

130

but she could tell that Shan was perplexed by it. 'You'd better go,' she said.

Shan jumped to his feet and ran through the grass towards his mentor. Varencienne rose slowly and ambled along behind. She called to Ellony, who rose, alert, like a startled animal, half hidden by spiky shrubs covered in scarlet flowers.

Taropat had summoned Shan because a pilgrimage of holy men had paused to refresh themselves at the farm. They were on their way to Hanana, the holy city of the Hamagarid peaks, for an annual ceremony, celebrating the marriage of Paraga and the earth goddess Venotishi. By the time Varencienne and Ellony reached the well at the centre of the community, Taropat was already deep in conversation with these men. They were frightening to behold, like mad shamans from some primitive tribe, who would cast evil spells and perhaps sacrifice and eat people. They were led by an ascetic sage called Snopard, who was dressed in filthy brown rags, his bare feet as hard as hooves. And yet, despite this attire, he was adorned with a treasury of jewellery: multiple strands of beads fashioned from semi-precious stones hung from his neck to his knees. His ears were pierced a dozen times by heavy hoops of gold, fashioned into the shape of serpents. Gold bangles inlaid with malachite and jade gloved his arms to the elbow. His eyes were like black opals, nearly hidden by the matted locks of hair that fell over his face and which covered his back like a rough shawl. His three acolytes were similar in appearance, but minus the adornments.

Snopard could speak a pidgin form of Caradorean, which Taropat was able to understand. To Varencienne it sounded like gibberish. Occasionally, while he spoke, his companions would burst into spontaneous song, throwing up their arms and wailing like lamenting women. Ellony laughed in delight at this, but Varencienne saw only madness in their behaviour.

The householders had brought out a meal for their visitors and it was obvious they held the travellers in high esteem because much bowing and gesturing was going on. Snopard, clearly interested more in Taropat, ignored the obeisances and sacred genuflections. Possibly he was so used to this he barely noticed it. To Varencienne, it appeared that Snopard was angry with Taropat, for his speech was harsh and punctuated with emphatic air-punching and facial grimaces. However, once Taropat deigned to approach her and Shan, he was obviously pleased with the interview.

'Snopard is a great holy man,' he said, 'and is happy to allow us to accompany his party to Hanana. This will save us considerable time. I have learned of the boy king that rules there, named Aranepa, who is an incarnation of Paraga. He, surely, must be the one I saw in my vision. We must go to him.'

Varencienne eyed the holy men shrewdly. They were now consuming voraciously the relatively sumptuous repast that had been presented to them. 'They look as if they'd slit our throats in the night,' she said.

Taropat made a dismissive sound. 'I'm not surprised you judge people by appearances,' he said pompously. 'These men are Par Sen adepti, known as Nugrids. It is true that they are warrior shamans, but they will not kill us for gain, only if we cross them, or should someone else pay them for the service.'

'I am much assured,' Varencienne said dryly. She noticed that Ellony had sidled up to the Nugrids and was paying great attention to their guttural exchanges. From what Varencienne could tell, they now conversed in Hamagarid. 'Elly, come here!'

Her daughter looked up slyly from beneath her lashes and then helped herself to a hunk of dark bread which had been laid out on a platter before Snopard.

'For Foy's sake!' Varencienne muttered under her breath and made to go and drag her daughter away.

Taropat grabbed hold of her arm to restrain her. 'No, let the child do as she pleases. She will learn much for us.'

'She is not your servant!' Varencienne snapped.

'Indeed not,' Taropat said reasonably, 'but she has a way with these people. Haven't you noticed? Perhaps it is because she is so young, but the Hamagarids take to Elly easily, more so than they do to the rest of us.'

It was the first time Taropat had referred to the girl by that name, at least in front of her mother. 'Is she like your sister?' Varencienne spat cruelly.

Taropat considered for a moment, then said, 'No, she is a wise little thing, like an elemental or a changeling. My sister was naïve in all respects. I have no doubt that if your daughter had been in her place all those years ago, she would not have perished. Exactly what she might have changed into, however, I dare not conjecture. She has no fear.'

'Not in this place,' Varencienne said, 'but she was a different child in Magrast, believe me. The city intimidated her.'

'Then she rises in my estimation again.'

Varencienne was astounded by Taropat. Khaster was not present today. He was like a ghost within Taropat, haunting him occasionally. At times like this, Taropat barely resembled the old portrait at Norgance. The face was the same, yet not. Varencienne realised that the essence of

Khaster was the feeling that had emanated from his painted eyes, and perhaps that was only the opinion of the artist.

'This country is changing Elly,' Varencienne said. 'It worries me. She *will* return to her proper life one day, and perhaps then she won't be able to readjust.'

'You mean she likes this life,' Taropat said without sarcasm. 'Surely you should let her choose her own path?'

Varencienne visualised an older version of Ellony, dressed as a Hamagarid, refusing to return to her old home. She shuddered, mainly because she recognised that she herself had broken away from her family and its traditions. It wasn't entirely unlikely that Ellony might be the same. 'You want her to deny what she is, don't you?' she said. 'You encourage her. It's all part of avenging yourself on the Palindrakes.'

'I understand why you think that,' Taropat said, and then dismissed her from his attention, turning to Shan. 'We should ready our belongings. The Nugrids won't pause here long and I doubt they will wait for us if we tarry.'

It was Ellony who learned the myths of the mountains. She walked beside Snopard, who talked to her constantly. Later, the girl related what she had learned to her mother and their companions. The peaks were the palace of Venotishi, a mother goddess of ferocious aspect. While she nurtured the land and its creatures, she was particularly harsh upon the human inhabitants. Snopard explained that this was because humanity, in achieving conscious awareness, had removed themselves from the natural order. It was the task of the adept to rediscover this lost heritage and attune himself with the land once more. Venotishi did not seem to appreciate this effort. She beset the Nugrid with obstacles and trials continually, sending demons to lure him from the spiritual path, or else inflicting him with maladies and curses that would render him helpless. Venotishi's embrace was the avalanche and the punishing winter winds that snarled among the crags. Her daughters, all cruel, were the rivers that gushed from the high glaciers. The points where water emerged from the citadels of ice were regarded as the sexual organs of the goddess, of which she had many. Taropat said that Venotishi and her children resembled Foy and the dragon daughters. The latter could not be considered benign in any respects. Venotishi was the consort of Paraga, the dragon of the peaks. Paraga had many aspects. In one, he had the appearance of a beautiful youth with indigo locks who played upon a flute carved from human bone. Then he was known as Hava, and his music encouraged the river goddesses to flow abundantly. He was a trickster, but should he be encountered amongst the lonely passes, he might grant wishes or bestow favours. Paraga's cockatrice aspect was of a serpent covered with feathers, whose wings were of skin and who had the eyes of a cat. His claws were made of ice and he could project them like daggers into the hearts of the unwary. Snopard spoke of many pilgrims who had been found upon the mountain paths, dead, but with no marks upon their bodies. Paraga had taken them, commonly because they were deluded fools who were vessels of human corruption masquerading as adepts. As to what constituted human corruption to a Nugrid, this was rather vague. They called themselves ascetics, yet indulged in drink and narcotics and were far from celibate. They did not appear to hold human life as particularly sacred, although they would kill only to avenge a wrong, or if someone petitioned them to scourge an enemy. The enemy, regardless of guilt or innocence, might convince the Nugrid assassin, if they had a chance, that the original client should be killed instead. The Nugrids were not driven by greed or desire for wealth, but ceremonies and sacrifices to Paraga and Venotishi would sway their favour. Ultimately, the person who could afford the most lavish ritual would be the one to gain, or at least survive. The Nugrids relied on people's fear of and respect for them to acquire food and lodging, clothes and supplies. Hamagarid princes, hidden in their citadel eyries high in the mountains, would sometimes reward Nugrids for services with jewels. Snopard counted seven princes amongst his patrons. The value of the jewels meant nothing to him, but he liked their beauty, which he called the Get of Venotishi, who fashioned all precious metals and stones in her fecund womb, the earth.

To Varencienne, the Nugrids were merely brigands, posturing as priests. When she pointed this out to Taropat one day, he replied, 'Much like the Magravandian fire mages, then. All priests are bandits. They can function no other way. At least Snopard has a certain authentic quality to him. He is not dishonest about what he is.'

From early in the journey, Snopard communicated to Varencienne and the others through Ellony. Once he'd established a rapport with the girl, he no longer bothered with Taropat. Varencienne was concerned about this at first, wondering whether the Nugrid had some evil carnal intention, but as time went on and there was no inappropriate behaviour, she had to revise this view. The holy man, terrifying in aspect, would hold Ellony's hand as they trudged along the ascending paths through forests. He'd bang his carved staff against the earth and smile down upon the child, with a sweet adoration that clearly came from the heart. Wonderful stories would spill from his lips that held the girl entranced. Ellony appeared to have no problem understanding his thick accent.

'She is special, your daughter,' Shan said one day, as they walked along behind.

'I know,' Varencienne replied, 'but I feel she is being taken from me.'

Shan did not respond to that. It must be the truth.

The group paused regularly at the strange cairns that had been built beside the path. Here, the Nugrids would perform short ceremonies, which involved much wailing and shouting. Ellony explained that the rituals were designed to appease the guardians of the path, who were all servants of Venotishi and therefore disposed to waylay and mangle travellers. New stones would be added to the cairns before the party departed. Sometimes Varencienne was sure she could feel the presence of these malevolent spirits. The further they travelled, so the atmosphere of the landscape became more alive. Occasionally, they'd encounter groups of other travellers, Hamagarid traders or bandits, who would offer gifts to the Nugrids. The hospitable farmsteaders of further south were long gone. Everyone they met looked wild and dangerous. Varencienne was glad they were travelling with the holy men, otherwise they would be in constant fear for their lives. Now the legendary Hamagarid temples began to appear, clinging to sheer mountainsides, cupped by crashing waterfalls and soaring forests. They were shambling single-storey buildings of white stone, roofed with gem-inlaid domes or complicated peaks and spires. Flags and banners fluttered from them in profusion, bearing the symbols of demons and demigods. The temples had been constructed by Hamagarid princes on sites that were designated as places of power by the Nugrids. The men and women who lived and worked in these establishments were not Nugrids, who were habitually nomadic, but Vanas, sorcerer priests and priestesses. The temples, or gats, were villages and small towns in their own right. The high priest or priestess of the gat was responsible for the welfare of the lay-people who worked there. Strangely enough, it was not required for the workers to be spiritually inclined, although the priesthood were governed stringently in this respect. Neither did any worship take place within the gats. The priesthood's function was to regulate the excesses of the local demons, to restrain them with spells and force them to grant boons.

At one small gat where the company had paused for the night, Varencienne witnessed a statue of a demon being whipped by two priestesses, who screamed out what sounded like the direst of curses. So hectic was their assault that their robes came adrift, revealing their chests, where the breasts were marked with curling black tattoos. While this was going on, others continued their daily domestic duties with barely a glance towards the demented priestesses. Later those same women sat drinking tea with the Nugrids, as demure as royal virgins, with veils over their faces.

The gats were autonomous, subject to no outside government, not even by the princes whose wealth had built them. They were cut off from the rest of the country for months at a time during the winter, and visitors other than nomadic Nugrids were rare. Occasionally people from the isolated citadels might come seeking priestly aid, or a few travellers from far lands might find their way to the isolated peaks. Each gat had its own laws, customs and beliefs. Par Sen was not a unified religion and did not seek to control the Hamagarid people through fear, guilt or any other psychological means. Varencienne found it bewildering and sometimes frightening, but respected its power, which permeated the walls of the gats and shone from the inscrutable countenances of the priesthood. Few Hamagarids knew anything of the world outside their inhospitable land. The hostile nature of the terrain had ensured it had remained isolated for millennia. Neither were the Hamagarids curious about foreigners. They lived in simple acceptance of everything, whether that was the malevolent actions of a demon or a face very different to those around them. They were dangerous because they were unpredictable, but foreigners were no more at risk than natives. It was a world of harsh survival.

After more than three weeks of travelling, the company arrived at the mountain Venotishi's Eye. Here a magnificent High Gat had been built and the priestesses who lived there were renowned as seers. The gat, Vereya, was the largest Varencienne had seen yet, comprising many storeys hewn from the mountainside. It was a living sculpture, rather than a building. As they climbed to the temple gates, up the thousand steps carved from the bare rock, priests upon the jutting roofs of Vereya blew upon great horns to entertain the spirits of the sunset. The mountains were gilded in mellow light and gigantic eagles wheeled on the warm air that rose from Vereya's stark white stones. Varencienne was struck by a feeling of déjà vu. She had a slight headache, which was unusual, for over the past month she had suffered from no hurts or maladies. She had become inured to hardship, much in the same way as when she'd first arrived in Caradore and her new life there of outdoor activity had made her fit and healthy. Now she felt disorientated, unsure of her place in space and time. Something would happen here.

The High Vana of Vereya was a middle-aged woman named Mother Mavana. Taropat requested an audience with her, to ask her advice about his purpose for being in Hamagara. Observing the size of the temple and the multitude that lived within it, Varencienne doubted whether his request, delivered via Ellony through Snopard, would receive a favourable response. Surely simple travellers would be beneath the notice of the venerable holy mother. But no, Mavana would happily receive guests the following afternoon.

Varencienne and Ellony were given quarters next to a walled garden. Young Vana novices prepared a bath for them, not in the manner of servants, but as hospitable hosts. Ellony acted as interpreter and told her mother that the young women had made suggestions about their pale hair and skin. All Hamagarids were dark-skinned. They believed the Caradoreans to be the victims of a demonic curse and offered to reverse it so that colour could be restored to their bleached bodies. Ellony told them that their appearance was normal where they came from. Again, this did not provoke curiosity. The girls just nodded in acceptance.

Varencienne luxuriated in the warm scented water, wriggling her toes and fingers and sighing deeply in contentment. Never had a bath felt so wonderful. Few Hamagarids were overly concerned with personal cleanliness, but those at Vereya were an exception. They believed that dirt could not adhere to the bodies of gods and demons and that in order for the humble Vana to approach a celestial state they must emulate this trait through bathing. Even the Nugrids would be required to cleanse themselves while within the gat walls, Ellony told Varencienne as the young Vanas massaged soap into her mother's hair. Varencienne had worn it as an oily coil pinned up on her head since the early days of their travels, which meant, mercifully, that it was not too tangled. The Vanas' hair was like black unravelled silk, scented with the essence of mountain herbs. As they combed out the freshly washed locks of their guests, they sang a bittersweet melody that filled Varencienne with a strange, sad joy. She was consumed by a feeling of love and regret for – she knew not what.

After the bath, dressed in embroidered robes, Varencienne and her daughter consumed a meal of nuts, cheese and warm goat's milk out in the garden, which was lit by mellow lamps hanging from the eaves of the colonnade that surrounded it. Fireflies flickered between the lamps and a choral chant drifted from somewhere else in the complex, lulling the senses. This high place was paradise on earth, Varencienne decided, however peculiar the customs of its inhabitants. It seemed to her that the Hamagarids were a species of humanity completely different to any other, because they had evolved in isolation, free of the influence of other cultures.

Lost in these thoughts, lying back upon a cushioned couch and chewing upon a sweet of minced sugared nuts, Varencienne did not notice Shan come into the garden. It was only gradually that she became aware of his scrutiny. Her flesh responded to his presence. She could smell him before she sat up and turned to look at him. He smelled clean and masculine, a scent that was almost astringent.

She smiled at him and he came towards her, his hair as pale as her own. She could imagine now how he might have appeared in the Mewtish court. The Hamagarids had dressed him in a tunic and trousers of dark blue brocade, encrusted with embroidery. His hair lay in a banner over his shoulders. He looked as natural in costly garb as he did in his normal clothes. To the Hamagarids, he and Varencienne must appear brother and sister, because their colouring was so similar. He looked like a Magravandian warrior prince: not a modern Malagash, but a man from ages past, when Magravandias had been more like Hamagara. When they left Vereya, both Varencienne and Shan would have to surrender their borrowed clothes and don once more the simple attire of travellers, for that was the custom. But for a short while at least, they would both be dressed in the finery of princes and could live a dream in this high dreaming land. He was coming to her as her lord, and she was his lady. This moment had been preordained.

As he approached, Varencienne could not speak, for a harsh human voice would ruin the blessing of the evening. Instead, she rose languidly from her couch and climbed the rough wooden steps that led to her chamber, on a gallery above the garden. She knew he would follow. At the threshold, she glanced down and saw Ellony sitting where she'd left her, making a sign upon the air with both hands. The priestesses would come for her soon, put her to bed to the sound of their songs. After Shan had entered the room, Varencienne closed the door.

He came to her and laid his hands upon her arms, looking down into her face. His expression was enigmatic, but she thought he felt he had a right to her and that he was prepared to give himself wholeheartedly to her in return.

As they began their first kiss, Varencienne was assailed by a fleeting image of Valraven, climbing rugged mountain peaks, searching for her, calling her name, while she drew the veil of Venotishi over her, hiding herself in the land. In her mind she whispered, 'Don't find me too soon.'

CHAPTER FOURTEEN

Waking the Dragon Queen

The following afternoon, a priestess came to escort the visitors to the High Vana. Varencienne was sitting with Shan in the garden, watching Ellony play. It was strange how quickly it had become natural to lean against him. It was as if they had been lovers for years. Few words on the subject had passed between them. There was – as yet – no need for them.

Taropat had kept his distance, presumably having spent the previous evening with Snopard, interrogating him about Hanana. Now he turned up with the priestess and gave Varencienne and Shan a sour glance. No doubt he'd have something to say to Shan once he got him on his own again. Varencienne could imagine the kind of words that might emerge, but this did not make her angry. Today she felt like smiling at everything. She had a lover again. Merlan had been the last man she'd slept with – over four years before. Her sensuality, long dormant, had woken up. It seemed inconceivable that she'd lived without physical love for so long and not even missed it.

'Hurry up,' Taropat said. 'We haven't got time to waste.'

Shan pulled a face behind Taropat's back and Varencienne laughed. Taropat stalked from the garden.

Visitors entered the audience chamber of Mother Mavana amidst a cacophony of clanging gongs. The ceiling was low, supported by thick columns, which were carved to resemble trees. Walking amongst them was like negotiating a petrified forest. This was no sanctuary of quiet contemplation. Many Vanas were present, some sitting cross-legged, rocking and chanting, others standing to play the discordant musical instruments of the gats: bellowing horns, cymbals and eerie flutes of plaintive voice.

A row of oracles sat to the left of the main dais at the far end of the room, all gibbering in loud voices and throwing handfuls of coloured sand and dried rice over their heads. Mother Mavana sat on the dais like a serene goddess in the midst of the pandemonium. She was a thin, stick-like creature who looked older than her supposed years. She wore robes and veil of a deep cyclamen fabric and heavy gold jewellery at wrists, ears and throat. Her feet were bare, the soles coloured ochre, while her toenails were decorated with purple sequins. An enormous painted statue of Venotishi coupling with Paraga dominated the wall behind her, surrounded by a flickering sea of candles. Mavana appraised her approaching visitors with black, expressionless eyes.

Snopard had agreed to accompany them, and he now bowed several times to the holy mother, his hands steepled at his brow. After a moment, Mavana lifted a rattle carved into the shape of battling serpents and shook it vigorously. At once, all noise within the chamber ceased. Mavana addressed Snopard in abrupt, almost aggressive tones. She rocked upon her cushions, her head weaving upon her neck like that of a snake.

Snopard indicated Taropat, who stood a few paces behind the Nugrid. Mavana stared at him beadily for some moments, then closed her eyes. Her weaving motions became more agitated. Beside her, the row of seers began to utter high, wailing cries, their hands thrown up over their heads. Mavana, shuddering as if in the throes of a fit, barked out a furious stream of babble. It sounded as if she were damning Taropat with a curse. This continued for several minutes, during which the other Vanas present became increasingly excited and noisy. Then Mavana slumped with a sigh and silence descended.

Varencienne glanced at Taropat. He was smiling slightly, but surely he must be unnerved by what could only be bad news?

Snopard, who had been standing with head bowed, straightened up. He spoke to Taropat in a soft voice.

Varencienne moved closer to them. 'What did she say?' she asked. 'It looked as if she was banishing us from her lands.'

'She says that we will find that which we seek,' Taropat replied. 'Apparently if I only pay the proper reverence to Paraga and his consort, all my hurts will be healed.'

'That is a stock answer,' Varencienne said. 'It could apply to anyone.'

Then the High Vana spoke again, and Varencienne knew instinctively that the words were addressed to her. She heard nothing but a series of syllables that made no sense, but she turned to the woman. The Vana beckoned. 'Come here, my child.' She spoke Caradorean.

Casting quick glances at Shan and Taropat, Varencienne went to kneel before the dais. Mother Mavana stared at her inscrutably for a few moments, then made a jerky movement with her chin. 'People come here in search of answers, of knowledge, of wisdom,' she said. 'You come here for none of those things. Neither were you brought against your will as you wish to believe. Hamagara is not part of the world in which you live, and your world may not touch us. You are an avatar of the greedy Foy, who coveted our lands and sought to subdue Paraga. Foy has learned hard lessons and now lies disempowered. It is the will of They of the Peaks that she should rise from her maundering lair and take her place, as is right, in her quarter. Too long has she lamented over her defeat, which her pride brought upon her. Her self-pity turns bitter the oceans. You are touched by her feelings and do not know it, yet you are strong and can overcome this weakness. You will go to Aranepa and he will give to you something of worth, which you will carry back to Foy. Know now that your son acts in your place and that Paraga is with him. Your son is in danger, for the one who directs the forces is ignorant, a proud and vain woman, who believes she has great knowledge and experience, but who in fact is lacking both. Paraga is his only defence, for Foy is weak. You should make offerings to Paraga before you leave here, for in his wisdom he bears no grudge or malice to the covetous mistress of the waters.'

Mavana dipped her hand into a bowl of dried rice dyed blue and green. She drew out a handful and threw it into Varencienne's face. The grains stung as if they were a host of tiny insects attacking her. Varencienne gasped and put her hands to her eyes.

'Pay attention to your calling,' Mavana said. 'The Dragon Lord turned his back on his queen, in the name of giving her peace, yet he was afraid. He is a man of this world, comfortable only with what his senses can perceive. You too are afraid. This land is full of the memories of Foy, her journey here. Remember her. Come to Paraga and Venotishi as an ally, not a foe. They will help you.'

Varencienne was compelled to press her forehead against the floor. The ancient wooden boards were warm beneath her flesh. She was trembling uncontrollably. 'Thank you, holy mother,' she said.

Mother Mavana now spoke in a thick Hamagarid accent, but Varencienne perceived that she was calling for tea to be brought for her guests. Varencienne felt hands upon her shoulders and glanced round. Shan had come to her. It took all her will not to fall into his arms. She felt as if she'd been beaten, her mind buffeted by invisible blows.

'She knows so much,' she said as she got to her feet.

Shan led her back to Taropat and Snopard, who were seated upon cushions. 'It sounded like the grunts of an animal,' Shan said.

'She speaks Caradorean well,' Varencienne replied. 'I think the earlier part, with Taropat, was a sham.'

Shan frowned. 'I've heard Taropat speak his native tongue. What I just heard didn't sound at all like it.'

'Well, it was,' Varencienne said. She sat down next to Taropat. 'What did you think of the Mother's words? She does not regard you as a kidnapper, clearly.'

Taropat gazed at her, a strange tight smile on his lips, and did not speak for several seconds. Then he said, 'You had better relate what you heard. To us, it sounded as if the High Vana spoke only in the most unintelligible Hamagarid.'

That night Varencienne dreamed of Foy. She woke in the middle of the night, Shan's arms still about her, shuddering at the memory of the dream. Surely the images had been evoked purely by what Mother Mavana had said to her earlier in the day? She dearly wanted to believe so, but the chill in her flesh advised her otherwise.

In the dream she had swum once more in the brooding underwater temples of the Ustredi, dwarfed by the cyclopean stones. She had found the great bulk of Foy sleeping amongst her treasures, at first indistinguishable from the broken spars of ransacked ships. Varencienne, small as a minnow, had swum to one of Foy's spined, equine ears and whispered into it. 'We must both awake,' she had said. 'It is time now to reclaim the seas.'

Foy had exhaled plumes of bubbles from her nostrils and her body had heaved in a gigantic sigh. Slowly one of her enormous eyes opened. 'I am broken,' she said in Varencienne's mind. 'My body ruined. The Dragon Heir forsakes me.'

'There is a smaller, younger voice,' Varencienne said. 'Our son. I know that he is ready and willing for you. Can you hear him, oh queen?'

Foy breathed out bubbles until she and Varencienne were surrounded by them. 'Yes,' she said at last.

'Go to him, oh Foy,' Varencienne said. 'I am apart from him and cannot help him. I have learned he is in danger.'

'I have no power to go to him,' said Foy. 'But I will send my daughters. They will be pleased to do this, for they already know and love him, as they love his father.'

'No!' Varencienne cried. 'You must not do that. They are unpredictable and terrifying. He is only a child. They will swamp him.'

But Foy exhaled furiously and pushed Varencienne away from her. Perhaps, as a mother, even a divine mother, she was blind to the faults of her children. Before Varencienne woke from the maelstrom, she fancied she heard an echo of mordant laughter: the joyless hilarity of Misk, Thrope and Jia, dragon daughters, mistresses of chaos and ruin.

CHAPTER FIFTEEN

Family Business

Pharinet came to meet her brother in the stableyard of Caradore Castle. All he noticed before he concentrated wholly on unstrapping his meagre luggage from his horse was that his twin's countenance was wild, her fists clenched by her sides. Her hair was a riotous black mass around her shoulders and she wore the garb of man, which, if anything, accentuated her femininity. 'Val, thank Foy you are here!' she exclaimed. 'What is going on? Ren and Elly are snatched on the road, with no explanation. What steps have you taken to get them back? Oltefney is virtually mindless with fear and we can get no sense out of her. We've heard nothing since the kidnap, no ransom demand, no threats. Everna and I cannot sleep for worry. Is this connected with Gastern's coronation? Is Bayard's hand behind it?'

'Hush, Pharry!' Valraven said. 'I have much to tell you, but you need have no fear that Bayard is involved in the kidnap.' He hoisted his bags onto his shoulder.

'You know something, though, don't you? I can tell.'

'Yes, I do, but I want to speak to you and Everna together.'

'No, tell me now! I demand it! Who has been here for your wife and children while you spend all your time away? I know them better than you do and I have a right to know what's befallen them. And I can't believe you left Rav in Magrast.'

'If Rav hadn't been in Magrast, he would have been taken along with his mother and sister,' Valraven said. 'I will get them back, Pharry, but none of us can act in haste and panic. Allow me some time to refresh myself and I will tell you and Everna all that I know.'

Pharinet exhaled impatiently through her nose and folded her arms. 'Don't play with me, Val.'

'I'm not playing with you. Grant me some mercy, will you?'

He marched towards a side entrance to the castle, Pharinet following. He was not looking forward to telling his headstrong sister that the husband she had believed to be dead was very much alive. It was inevitable that old hurts would be revived.

Valraven went alone, after much protesting from Pharinet, to Varencienne's chambers in the castle rather than his own. He had visited these rooms too seldom and now might never have cause to again. For some minutes he stood in the window alcove, gazing down upon the beach below the castle. On this side, Caradore almost hung over the sea. Today it was tranquil, as if it couldn't care less whether he'd come home or not. Waves flung themselves lazily into the sea caves and amongst the spires and tunnels of rock. How he'd loved that beach as a child. It had been his make-believe fantasyland. And Pharinet had shared it with him. Sighing, he went back into the room. The sight of his wife's cosmetics and hair brush on the dressing table made his heart clench. What if she never came back to use them again? He must not betray his doubts to his sisters, but part of him was afraid that Khaster would kill Varencienne. It was perhaps a senseless fear, because the last time he'd seen Khaster, he'd been the man he always was, lacking in courage and self-confidence. Apart from what was required of him as an officer in the imperial army, Khaster would never have harmed another living creature. Valraven was unsure why he thought this had changed.

His limbs were heavy as he changed his clothes. Goldvane, the castle steward, brought him a hot drink and a snack to fortify himself for the impending meeting with his sisters. He prudently made little reference to the kidnap, other than to assure his master that he would do anything that was asked of him, if it would be any help.

Mustering his strength for what he knew would be an onslaught, Valraven went down to the sitting room where his sisters awaited him. Everna looked so much older, perhaps dragged down by worry for Varencienne and Ellony. It shocked Valraven to see how emaciated her tall frame was, dwarfed in its chair. Her face was pleated with deep lines. Pharinet too had changed. Although he had sought to avoid her eyes out in the stableyard, now he appraised her directly. There were a few streaks of grey in her abundant black hair and she was carrying slightly more weight about the waist and hips. For a fleeting moment he recalled the girl she had been, how he'd held her in his arms on the eve of her wedding to Khaster. He remembered their forbidden love, even though he had blotted it from his mind for many years. How could he have abandoned her? He'd shut her out of his heart, even his life, when

145

they'd both been victims of Bayard's power plays. Yet, staunchly, she had remained faithful to him. Everyone had believed her to be a widow, so she could have married again easily. Any number of local men would have eagerly taken her for a wife, and he knew she'd had offers over the years, yet she'd refused them all. Now, blindingly, he could see why, as if she was speaking the words aloud to him. Pharinet's love for him endured and she would fight like a dragon to protect all that was his, including his wife. Both she and Everna were growing older, gradually, inexorably, and he was barely here for them. How would he feel if, in the future, one of them should die during one of his long absences? There was so much unsaid between them. Still, now was not the time for such considerations.

Valraven went to Everna's chair and bent to kiss her cheek. 'I'm sorry I couldn't come sooner. It was difficult to get away before.'

Everna's eyes filled with tears and her hands gripped each other in her lap. 'Val, what are we to do? Why has this happened?'

'Yes, spill everything,' Pharinet said.

Valraven went to the dresser and poured himself a glass of wine from the carafe that stood ready. Goldvane had made sure his favourite vintage was on hand. He took a large mouthful before he answered, 'This is no easy way to say this. We all believed that Khaster Leckery was dead. We were wrong. It is he who is behind the kidnap.'

There was a moment's stunned silence, then Pharinet spat, 'Rubbish! What are you talking about? Khaster is dead, Val. If he'd lived, he'd have sent word to his family. Hamsin would have recognised him.'

'Hamsin *did* recognise him. He thought it prudent to keep the information to himself until he had spoken to me. I assure you there is no mistake. Merlan too knows his brother is alive, and in fact spent some time with him last year. He has spoken to me about it.'

Pharinet sat down heavily in a chair. 'This can't be true.'

'It is. I'll tell what I know.'

Both Pharinet and Everna interrupted Valraven's narrative continually, so it took some time. Pharinet, particularly, remained sceptical. She grudgingly accepted her husband was still alive, but would not believe any of the story about Taropat, perhaps because she didn't want to. 'Sad though it is,' she said, 'Khaster is obviously living a fantasy. He must have been extremely damaged by what happened to him, and now believes he is someone else. I imagine any physician would tell you that is the explanation.'

'Merlan is convinced,' Valraven said, 'and as none of us has actually seen Khaster since his disappearance, we're really in no position to judge.'

'But why would he kidnap Ren and Elly?' Everna asked querulously. 'It isn't like him.'

'Not like the person we knew, no,' Valraven agreed, 'but we have to accept he's changed.'

'But there's been no ransom demand,' Everna said. 'What does he want with them?' An obvious thought occurred to her and her hands flew to her mouth. She stared wide-eyed at her sister.

'I know what you're thinking, Evvy,' Pharinet said, 'but I think we can comfort ourselves in one regard. If Ren and Elly had been harmed, I'm sure this new Khaster wouldn't have been able to keep from gloating. He'd have made sure news reached us. Don't you think so, Val?'

'It seems likely,' Valraven agreed.

'What will you do now?' Everna asked.

'I must go to Cos,' he answered. 'Evidence points to the fact that Khaster – or Taropat, as I suppose we must now call him – is in league with Princess Helayna. I have tolerated her presence in Cos, because since her brother's capitulation she has been no threat. Now, it seems, I must root her out.'

'They're not in Cos,' Pharinet announced.

'What makes you say that?' Valraven asked.

Pharinet clawed her fingers through her hair. 'I don't know for sure. Just a feeling. From what you've said, it's obvious Khaster – sorry, I won't call him anything else – was after Rav. He is the heir to Palindrake. Instead, he's ended up with your wife and daughter. Now, why would he want the heir? Think about it. He's now calling himself a great magus, so we must suppose he has mystical ambitions. He hates the Malagashes, who are followers of fire, the people who effectively vanquished Foy. I think he means to create a weapon to attack the Malagashes. He failed to secure the Dragon Heir, but now he has the Sea Wife. How better to attack the realm of fire than through reviving the power of water?'

'He would require Ren's co-operation,' Valraven said. 'He'd never get it.'

'I wouldn't be quite so confident,' Pharinet said, glancing at her sister. 'I have no wish to speak ill of Ren, but I'm afraid she was quite smitten with the *idea* of Khaster for some years. He was a fantasy to her, when she was still hardly more than a young dreaming girl. Ren is strong and capable, and no fool, but what if the reality of Khaster awakens those old feelings?'

Valraven was shocked by the chill that pierced his heart. Pharinet's words were totally unexpected. He felt betrayed. Varencienne had never spoken of Khaster to him, apart from once, years ago. 'I find this difficult to credit,' he said.

'She used to spend hours gazing at his portrait in Norgance,' Pharinet said. 'She once even thought she saw his ghost. Ask any of the Leckerys. They'll tell you.'

'But she is first and foremost my wife and a Palindrake,' Valraven said. 'I will not believe she'd forget that.'

Pharinet shrugged. 'Think what you like. Facts are facts. Let us suppose, however unlikely, Varencienne is sympathetic to Khaster. Where would they go?'

'I will not countenance that possibility,' Valraven said. 'Khaster will have taken Ren and Elly to Cos, to sanctuary with the Cossic resistance.'

'*She* would take *him* to Old Caradore,' Pharinet said. 'Wouldn't she, Evvy?'

Everna's fingers were still pressed firmly against her lips. Now she lowered them slowly, her expression deeply troubled. 'Yes. I would say so. Yes.'

'So forget Cos,' Pharinet said. 'Ren *is* the Sea Wife, Val. You refuse to accept your role, even though the secret heritage of the Palindrake males has been revealed to you. Ren was given her role, and lived it fully, yet once that ritual at Old Caradore was complete, you wouldn't continue the tradition with her. She never spoke of it, but I believe it was always on her mind. Her view of reality was destroyed and a wondrous new world revealed to her, but you would not share it. I think Ren might even welcome the co-operation of a man who is mystically inclined. If she does ally with Khaster, it's your own fault.'

'Pharry, don't!' Everna said. 'This will not help.'

'The Dragon Lord, though magnificent on the battlefield, runs from many other things,' Pharinet said coldly.

'It is easy for you to speak this way,' Valraven said. 'Out here, in the wilderness of Caradore, magic is alive for you. In Magrast, I have to tread daily through a pit of poisonous vipers. There is no magic there. It is all down to human greed and ambition.'

Pharinet uttered a scornful sound. 'Tell that to the empress.'

'Don't bicker!' Everna said. 'All that matters at present is to restore Ren and Elly to their home. Send people to Cos, Val, but bear in mind what Pharry has said. Old Caradore should also be investigated.'

The following day, after what could only be described as a difficult evening with his sisters, Valraven steeled himself for the next unpleasant interview. He must ride over to Norgance and speak to the Leckerys. Pharinet wanted to accompany him, but he could envisage too easily her abrasive interjections while he related his news to Saska and refused firmly to let her ride with him. 'This will be hard enough without your personal opinions colouring the occasion,' he said. 'I must do this alone, Pharry. As you know, Saska considers I owe them a debt.'

'The loss of a son and a daughter,' Pharinet said dryly. 'Yes, that could be considered a debt.'

Valraven ignored the jibe. 'This will have to be handled carefully. We don't know how Saska will react.'

'I do,' Pharinet said. 'There will be a storm of tears, possibly a fainting fit, and a great kerfuffle of Leckery women. On reflection, you are welcome to it, but return tonight. I want to hear what happened.'

All the way there, Valraven composed speeches in his head. Mordantly, he considered how he would find it easier to lead his troops into battle than face the widowed Leckery matriarch with upsetting news. Perhaps he should have ordered Merlan to break it to his family after all.

All around, Caradore was coming to bloom. It reminded Valraven of the time before his and Pharinet's weddings to Ellony and Khaster; the scents and colours aroused poignant memories. In his mind's eye he saw Saska's laughing face, a reflection of her joy at the union of the houses of Palindrake and Norgance. Then he remembered Pharinet's pained scowl and recalled his own frustrated anger. Those marriages had doomed both families to terrible pain.

Predictably, Valraven's arrival at Norgance caused a stir. He had not been a casual guest at the estate since Ellony's funeral. Servants were thrown into a flurry when he presented himself at the main door and left him waiting in the hall for some minutes as they undoubtedly went seeking instructions from their mistress. Eventually Saska received him in her salon, accompanied by her daughter, Niska. Since the death of Saska's elder sister, Dimara Corey, the previous winter, Niska had taken on her aunt's position as Merante, or High Priestess, of the Sisterhood of the Dragon. She was young for the title, but of all the women involved, the most mystical. Valraven knew little of it, as it was women's business, but Pharinet had told him some time ago that no one had contested Niska's appointment. The Sisterhood was dedicated to reinstating the Dragon Heir as the spiritual and temporal leader of Caradore. As such, Niska could be seen as his personal priestess and advisor. Previously, Valraven had avoided any contact with the Sisterhood. It discomforted him, because they wanted something from him he was ill prepared to give. Ligrana, Saska's eldest surviving daughter, was now married to a local landholder. Foylen, her youngest son, was out on the land somewhere. No doubt he would soon be called to Magrast, as his elder brothers had before him. Norgance felt empty and sad, where once it had been a busy household, full of Leckerys.

The habitually fey Niska looked even more like a drowned revenant than usual and Saska's once beautiful face was set into a hard expression. Valraven sighed inwardly. He felt like delivering his news bluntly and then leaving without having to bear their response.

'Valraven,' said Saska crisply, 'this is unexpected. What brings you to us?' She knew there would be a reason for his visit, of course. Socialising was a thing of the past.

Valraven bowed formally. 'I have some news,' he said.

'Merlan?' Saska demanded, her hands flying to her throat. Fear made a distorted mask of her face.

'No, no,' Valraven reassured her hastily, 'this is not bad news. At least, it is not news of a death. Merlan is very well. I have recently left him in Magrast.'

'What is it, then?' Saska said. As soon as she'd uttered this peremptory command, she grimaced and shook her head in self-chastisement. 'Forgive me. Where are my manners?' She flapped a hand at one of the sofas. 'Please, sit down. Refreshments will be here shortly. You must understand that I always fear news, because so often it has brought me grief. First my husband, then my beloved Ellony, then Khaster . . . '

'It is of Khaster I wish to speak,' said Valraven abruptly, wishing to stem the course of Saska's recollections, which he knew from experience could go on for some time. He sat down.

'Khaster?' said Saska in a small voice. 'What is there to tell me of him?'

Valraven shivered instinctively and glanced at Niska, realising the cause of his discomfort was the scrutiny of the young woman. Her sea-coloured eyes were staring at him intently and he knew from her expression that what he was about to reveal was not news to her. Perhaps Merlan had contrived to send word to her, but for whatever reason – and he could think of many – she had decided not to reveal what she knew to her mother.

'You must prepare yourself for a shock,' he said, wishing immediately he'd used one of his gentler scripts. But it was too late to change it. 'Khaster is alive, Saska.'

As in Caradore Castle, there was a short silence after his words, but instead of denying the news, as Pharinet had done, Saska suddenly expelled a great wail and went rigid in her chair. Niska rose fluidly and went to her mother's side.

'Saska,' Valraven began, wanting to finish what he was going to say, but Saska was making too much noise for him to be heard. It was an absurd reaction, more in keeping with the news of the death Saska had feared. Valraven had no idea how to cope with it. The doors to the salon flew open and Saska's personal maids came hurrying in.

Niska took control. 'Terralee, Morla, take my mother to her rooms and give her a posset. I will join you shortly.'

'What has happened, my lady?' asked Terralee, the older of the pair.

'We have just heard that Lord Khaster is alive,' Niska answered. 'The news has been a great shock. Now, I need to know the details. Please see to my mother at once.'

Saska virtually had to be carried from the room. She uttered a continual moan, which gradually trailed away to silence as she was taken further into the house.

'Well,' Valraven said, awkwardly, 'it is clear I should have handled that differently.'

'Console yourself,' Niska said. 'Whatever way you presented it, Mother would have reacted fiercely. The deaths of Ellony and Khaster are still open wounds in her heart.'

'But I'd have thought she'd have been glad to know Khaster was alive.'

'Perhaps she will be, once she has got over the shock. You have to realise how difficult it has been to her. Grief has become her whole being, her religion. Now she has been told that, in part, it was a false belief.'

'I'm sorry . . . '

Niska sat down. 'Now, tell me the rest of it. I said that Mother might be pleased once she'd got used to the facts, but we both know that might not be the case.'

'You know something already, clearly.'

Niska put her head to one side and assumed a dreamy expression. 'Mmm. I would not be worthy of my role as Merante if I did not.'

'Do you know that Khaster has a new identity and that he has recently kidnapped Varencienne and Ellony?'

Niska's eyes widened in surprise. 'He did what?'

'I think you heard me. The reason why has yet to be revealed to us, but we suspect he was really after Rav.'

Niska's brow creased into a deep frown. 'That I did not know. I hope you believe me.'

'Then what do you know?'

'Last year I had a vision while at the Chair. I saw Khaster, alive and well. He did not communicate with me, but I sensed he had received some kind of occult training. I presumed he had staged his own death in Cos, because he was so sick of the life he'd been forced to lead. I also had to presume he had not contacted us because he feared being dragged back into that life. Naturally I could not tell Mother this. You saw how

151

she was just now. It would have been cruel to raise her hopes without physical proof, or any promise that Khaster might return to us.' She folded her hands together on her lap. 'So, tell me all you know.'

Niska listened with few interruptions. Occasionally she asked a question about specific details, but Valraven could not satisfy her in that respect. He admitted that he himself knew only scant facts. Despite his recent dissatisfaction with Merlan, he decided not to mention that Merlan had known that Khaster still lived. Let Leckery deal with that if it ever came out through other means. Valraven concluded his narrative by telling Niska of Pharinet's suspicions that Varencienne might even welcome Khaster's involvement and could have taken him to Old Caradore.

'I'm not sure about that,' Niska said. 'Pharinet does tend to be led by her passions, if you know what I mean.'

Valraven nodded shortly in embarrassment. He knew exactly what Niska meant.

'But, that said, I do think it's essential you go to Old Caradore. I will apply myself to discovering any helpful information on a psychic level, and will accompany you to the old domain.'

Valraven frowned. 'I don't think that will be necessary. Anyway, why do you think I should go there if Ren isn't there?'

'Because it is time for you to stop procrastinating and fulfil your destined role. I have no fear for Ren. What has happened to her is right and preordained. I am more concerned about you.'

Valraven laughed awkwardly. 'Niska, please don't make this a crusade for the Sisterhood.'

'You scorn us,' Niska said. 'I understand why. Four years ago, the Sisterhood was little more than a pantomime, but I have made changes. I have made the sisters work to hone their magical abilities. We are not playing at it any longer, Val. We are worthy of you and your heritage. If I have had a crusade, it has been making sure of that. You must go to Old Caradore to take back what is yours, fully and completely. You must become the Dragon Heir, as you are meant to be. It must be done before anything else.'

Valraven was taken aback by the strength in her voice. Where had the delicate, silent child gone, who'd been more like a mute mermaid stranded on land than a human being? What he saw now was a determined young woman who, despite the passion of her words, spoke clearly and firmly. 'Niska, this is a difficult time,' he said. 'Magrast is unstable. Gastern is emperor, but for how long? I have to act very carefully now. Ren and Elly's rescue consumes my attention. I know you mean well, but . . . '

'Mean well?' Niska rolled her eyes in their sockets. 'Val, how do I convince you? The only way you will understand that what I propose is right is to actually go through with it. Then you will know for certain. But it requires a measure of faith from you, which I see you are unwilling to give.'

'I can't go to the old domain and lark about doing rituals on the beach while my wife and daughter remain captive. And, I have to be seen to be taking action, otherwise my superiors in Magrast will wonder why I haven't returned to my duties.'

'I appreciate your reservations,' Niska said, 'but I'm not asking you to do this because of my personal ambitions for the Sisterhood. I know how unstable everything is, but I also know it is the right time for you to act. You need only send word back to Magrast that you are following a promising lead. Send men to Cos. You might uncover helpful information there. Khaster will have come by sea. If I were you, my first priority would be to seek the vessel he chartered.'

'I had thought of that,' Valraven said stiffly, 'and have already sent men to investigate the matter.'

'You don't have a hope of rescuing Ren and Elly unless you go to Old Caradore and accept your heritage,' Niska said. 'Trust me, it is the only way to restore your family and bring stability to the empire. I have no doubt you will discover Ren's whereabouts at the old domain, and also the true reason for Khaster's behaviour. He is part of your destiny, as you are of his. Every event is part of a grand design. I know that you and my brother are inextricably linked. It is almost mythical, the replaying of an ancient saga. This too, I believe, will be discovered, or remembered, at Old Caradore. You and Khaster are moving towards a certain point, and we must look upon every occurrence as part of a great ritual.'

Valraven was silent for a moment. Conflicting feelings coursed through his body. He remembered the moment when he'd stood over Leonid's corpse and had wondered, for a scant moment, whether he could reclaim his family's power. Niska's eyes were fixed upon him. Her gaze was without heat, but held the power and might of the ocean itself. Valraven swallowed, found his mouth dry. He rubbed a hand over his chin, cleared his throat. 'Then I had better tell you of the Crown of Silence,' he said.

CHAPTER SIXTEEN

Wolves Hunting

Tatrini stood in the shady cool of a small parlour just off her private garden, where she had chosen all the trees and shrubs herself, favouring those that drooped and swung like dryad hair: willows and tender birches. Summer had almost come to Magravandias and Magrast shimmered in an early heatwave. Tatrini watched Tayven and Rav as they sat on the lawn, talking: a picture of contentment and innocence. Her plans appeared to be progressing well. Tayven was co-operating, which she hadn't expected so soon. There was no doubt he had an agenda of his own, but for the time being, he appeared content to go along with her. Now it was time to set other schemes in motion. Before the year was out, she would change the known world, but it would look as if others' hands were responsible.

Already Gastern was initiating changes in Magrast. Madragorean churches that still retained ancient fire-drake altars in underground shrines had been ordered to dismantle the altars. The fire-drakes were a remnant of pagan superstition and therefore did not belong in Gastern's vision of a modern Madragorean world. His decision had alarmed the Order of Splendifers who, despite being Madragorean knights, held dear the ancient beliefs. Their own site of initiation was the fire pit of the drakes just outside Magrast. Tatrini had no doubt that before long Gastern would decree that the Splendifers should discard any pagan leanings. Soon her eldest son would begin to extend his influence into the empire. She could visualise easily what would happen. Local belief systems would be pronounced heretical and be banned. Allegations of blasphemy and stringent punishment for heretics would follow. For centuries, foreign gods had been regarded as Madragore's subjects; in much the same way as conquered countries had been the emperor's subjects. Allowing people to retain their own customs of belief had kept dissension to a minimum. Nothing good could come of Gastern's pious innovations. It was time now for the Grand Queen Mother to make moves of her own.

She heard a movement in the room behind her and turned from the window. Grisette Pimalder stood at the threshold. She curtsied. 'My lady, Prince Almorante is here.'

'Good. Show him in.'

'Shall I order refreshments?'

'That won't be necessary. Thank you.'

Grisette curtsied once more and backed away. Moments later, Almorante came through the door. 'Mother,' he said and executed an abrupt bow.

Tatrini smiled gently at him. 'Mante, thank you for coming. I have delicate business to discuss with you.'

She could almost see the suspicion oozing from every pore of her second-eldest son. Not once, in the thirty-six years of his life, had she summoned him to her private apartments. As a child, he had played there with his brothers and nursemaids, but once the military academy had claimed him at fourteen – as it had claimed nearly all of them – he had gradually become distant. Family closeness was not an attribute that could be applied to the Malagashes. Now she and Almorante met only at functions. Once he had grown as a baby within her body, inconceivable to her now. He was virtually a stranger, a man she barely knew, but whom she had heard much about. Of all her sons, only Bayard and Leo had remained intimate with her. They were her golden boys. Almorante was dark, where the rest of her brood were fair. When he'd been a small child, there had been gossip concerning his parentage, but it was unfounded. Almorante was a true son of Leonid, but perhaps a throwback to an earlier generation. Tatrini gestured for him to sit in an armchair by the unlit hearth.

Almorante perched on the edge of his seat, saying nothing. His long dark brown hair hung unbound about his shoulders and his attenuated hands were clasped loosely in his lap. He did not look much like a Magravandian prince, resembling more a brigand lord. Glittering hoops of gypsy gold glinted in his ears and his clothes were functional rather than decorative: soft deerskin that still smelled of the forest. Almorante had changed over the years. Tatrini could remember the times when he'd dressed more like his brothers. He'd looked older then. Now he gave the impression that he was totally relaxed, but Tatrini was not deceived. He had his camp, she had hers, but she must convince him they could help one another. It would not be easy.

She too sat down and took a few moments to arrange her gown about her feet. Almorante waited patiently, exuding a fog of silence that seemed to condense the air. 'There is a task I would like you to undertake for me,' Tatrini said.

Almorante shifted slightly. 'And what might that be, Mother?'

'I would like you to go to a small province southeast of Cos and recover an artefact for me.'

Almorante stared at her, his hooded eyes inscrutable. 'Why do you want *me* to do this? You have many able men in your employ.'

'It is family business.'

'Then send Bayard.'

Tatrini drew in her breath slowly. 'I would prefer you to do it.'

'I am loath to leave Magrast at your directive,' Almorante said. 'I wonder why you want to send me away and what you will do in my absence.'

Tatrini smiled ruefully. 'You think so badly of me, Mante. I have no wish to get you out of the way. My request is genuine.'

'It is uncommon. You have never asked for my aid before. What is this artefact?'

'I can tell you about it only once I have your oath you are committed to my desire.'

Almorante laughed coldly. 'What do you take me for? I need more coercion than that.'

Tatrini inclined her head. 'Of course. However, you must appreciate why I am wary of taking you into my confidence. What I have to tell you must go no further. The future depends on it.' She had his curiosity now. He would think that she needed him, and that she had asked him here out of desperation.

'Then I will speak frankly,' he said. 'It is no secret you'd prefer Bayard to take Gastern's place on the throne. You must know I oppose that plan . . . '

'You have your own aims, of course,' she interrupted.

He dismissed her words with a curt gesture. 'Whatever my aims, it is doubtful they are in accord with yours. I have to ask myself what you seek to gain by asking this of me. Naturally, my first assumption is that you need to remove me from Magrast to initiate some scheme or another, which I might otherwise obstruct. If this is not the case, then I can think of only three alternatives. One is that you genuinely need my aid, another is that you seek to discredit me in some way, but the third is more sinister. Perhaps you plan for me never to return from wherever you send me.'

Tatrini laughed lightly. 'Oh, what a warren of intrigue and suspicion

156

Magrast has become! I am your mother, Mante. Are we really deadly rivals?'

Almorante's eyes were cold. 'I hope that was an attempt at humour. Now is not the time to act the part of doting mother. You have too many sons and in circumstances such as ours, competition is inevitable, as is favouritism Your own security rests on such matters.'

He had always been the outsider, the dark one, eyed with suspicion. Tatrini did not resent his words. She respected his honesty. Her other sons, including Gastern, would not have spoken so bluntly and would have attempted to pander to her. She drew herself up straight. 'I thank you, Mante, for being yourself. Now, I will speak frankly too. I do not think Gastern is the most suitable inheritor of your father's crown, but you are mistaken if you believe I am motivated solely by a desire to see Bayard take his place. The truth is: I care very greatly about the fate of our empire, which is fragile at present.'

Almorante pulled a sour face. 'I do not totally agree with that statement, but *we* perhaps are in a precarious state. Gastern, once he settles into his role, will seek to root out any potential adversaries. Dare I consider you have decided we should close ranks? If so, what can I gain from the alliance? You don't want me to become emperor.'

'Perhaps it is irrelevant who actually becomes emperor,' Tatrini said. 'We should think more about our dynasty and its continuance. By that, I mean our *true* dynasty and not the ascetic travesty represented by Gastern.'

'Yet you championed Rinata to become empress. Why do that? You have only given both of them more power.'

'I was simply laying the way for the future. Rinata is a cipher, a nothing, and will never be anything else. Her watery blood has created Linnard, who will grow into a mean and spiritless man. He must never take his father's place.'

'He is your grandson.'

'Are you attempting to question my morals?'

'No. You have none and that is that.'

Again Tatrini laughed. 'You have created an image of me, Mante, but it lives solely in your frightened head. And you *are* afraid, my son. You cannot hide it from me.'

'I am cautious, that's all. Again, I have to ask: why should I help you?'

'Perhaps I have something you want.'

'And what is that?'

'Tayven Hirantel,' she answered.

Almorante shrugged. 'If you thought that would come as news to me, you're wrong. It is very difficult to keep secrets here. I've known for some time you had him concealed somewhere. Why do you suppose I want him? We have had no contact for a long time.'

'Some years ago, you attempted a quest with Hirantel. I have no idea what you sought to gain from it, because you certainly were unaware of why you *should* have been undertaking it. But perhaps Hirantel was more astute. Last year, he undertook the same quest with Khaster Leckery.'

'Leckery?'

'Yes.' Tatrini made a languid gesture. 'Two men supposed dead reappear in our lives. They are difficult to kill, it seems.'

Almorante's expression had changed from bland condescension to something far more animated and bare. Tatrini's spies had informed her that after Leckery's supposed death, Almorante had searched Cos thoroughly for traces of both Leckery and Tayven. The latter had eventually surfaced in Mewt, but Leckery had managed to remain hidden. Clearly Almorante had not known he had survived. 'The artefact you want,' he said. 'Tayven found something in Recolletine, didn't he?'

'You are correct,' Tatrini replied. 'It was left in the keeping of a sorceress of Bree. I expect you would like to speak to Tayven about it, wouldn't you? That quest was stolen from you. You were led to Recolletine with a desire to experience the lessons of the lakes. Consciously, you didn't know why, but perhaps you were driven by ancestral memories in your blood. At that time, you lacked the knowledge to complete the quest, and in your disappointment sought never to attempt it again, but Tayven used the experience to his advantage.'

'I admit I knew none of this. All I sought to achieve was to instil Tayven with the properties of the lakes, to make a magus of him.'

'You succeeded in that, my son, and never knew it. Now you must talk to him about it.'

Almorante grimaced. 'He will not speak to me. Since I learned he'd been paying visits to our governmental offices in Akahana, I asked Darris Maycarpe many times to arrange a meeting, but Tayven wouldn't hear of it.'

'Perhaps,' Tatrini said, 'but it may be that Maycarpe himself was opposed to your seeing him. Tayven was both your concubine and your most trusted agent. You gave him everything, yet he repaid you with scorn. He nearly lost his life in your service, but that was his choice. He is not stupid and knew the risks. As far as I can see, there is no debt between you. Tayven is older and wiser now. His bitterness has ebbed and, like the rest of us, he seeks only to secure his own future. I have no doubt he will speak to you. He is, after all, reconciled with Bayard.'

Almorante uttered a surprised grunt. 'Impossible! If it appears that way, he is deluding you.'

'I am not easily deluded, Mante. Go to the window. You will see him in the garden. You and he were on the right track all those years ago, and none of us knew it.'

With a hard glance for his mother, Almorante got up from his seat and went to the window. For some moments, he did not speak. Tatrini attempted to divine his feelings. Did the sight of Tayven rekindle old memories? Perhaps he was sad to see Tayven had grown from a beautiful fey boy into a man. It could remind him of his own mortality. When Tayven had first gone into Almorante's service, the prince had been little more than a boy himself.

When Almorante returned to his seat, he made no comment on what he'd seen other than to say, 'What is the artefact Tayven recovered?'

'A crown,' Tatrini said. 'A symbol of kingship. It was found at Lake Pancanara.'

'Tayven reached Pancanara?' Almorante shook his head in wonderment. 'I trained him well, it seems. Why is this crown important to you? If it is a symbol, then a copy could be made.'

'Mante, you talk of training, but where is the fruit of yours? An artefact which has remained inaccessible for centuries, recovered from the most mystical site in our country at this time of flux, will possess magical properties. Influential people believe in its powers. We must have it.'

'We?'

'Yes, *we*. Together we represent a formidable force. I want you to go to Bree and recover the Crown of Silence for the Malagashes.'

'And you trust me not to crown myself with it?'

'Perhaps you are already crowned with it,' Tatrini said. 'Our family is emperor. Our blood is empire. We who are the vessels of it should not spill it in simple spite. Gastern denies all that we stand for. In him, our blood is turned to milk. We must take action, but not in fragmentation. Together.'

Almorante studied her for a moment. 'If you can countenance the disposal of one son, you can countenance the disposal of any of us,' he said. 'And you still haven't denied you want Bayard on the throne. What exactly *are* you offering me, Mother?'

She held his gaze with her own. 'I have favoured Bayard because, of all my sons, he has been the most dynamic. He has proved himself upon the field of battle. He is strong and would hold the empire together, not just through might and ruthlessness, but also from the fire that shines from his eyes. He is like a glorious barbarian in his self-indulgence. But what is the strategic advantage of placing a barbarian upon the great throne of Magravandias? Qualities other than might are equally desirable. I've tried to instil these qualities into Bayard, and to a degree I have been successful, but I do not believe in focusing upon a single goal – a course that seems doomed to disappointment. Go out into the world, Almorante, and prove to me that you too are dynamic, mighty and strong. Earn the prize you think you deserve.'

Almorante's expression remained hard. 'What has happened recently to make you change your mind? You have betrayed no interest in my affairs or wellbeing before.'

Tatrini gestured languidly with one hand. 'There was much for me to consider. Bayard has an interest in magical matters, but as in all things, he tends to charge at them like a berserker. You, on the other hand, are cautious and careful. I know little of your activities, other than that you are involved in the mystic arts. Also, Bayard has scant regard for Mewt and the power it could offer us. You, on the other hand, are inextricably linked with it. You have made firm contacts there. I think you should know that Darris Maycarpe was involved in the lakes quest. He did not participate directly, but he certainly helped plan it. The other names involved are someone called Shan and Khaster's brother, Merlan.'

'Shan,' Almorante said thoughtfully. 'I recall meeting a youth of that name in Mewt last year. I remember him because he reminded me of Tayven and also because he wore a talisman in which Maycarpe showed great interest. Presumably he recruited the lad because of that.'

'From what I've heard, Shan is Khaster Leckery's apprentice. We can only presume a cabal operates from Mewt, whose workings are as yet unknown to us. It might be prudent for you to include an investigation of Maycarpe's activities in your expedition to locate the Crown.'

'This will take time,' Almorante said. 'Bree is a long journey away, and if I am to go to Mewt afterwards . . . '

'There are matters that need my attention here at home that will also take considerable time. Do what is expedient. There is no rush.' She paused. 'Can I take it you are with me, then?'

Almorante's mouth twitched. 'I am surprised at myself, but yes. You have pricked my curiosity, and I appreciate your frankness. But – and I'm sure I don't need tell you this – if you should betray me . . . '

'Mante, please! Let us not talk of betrayal.'

'How will Bayard feel about my involvement? Or aren't you going to inform him?'

Tatrini leaned back in her chair. 'Bayard does not yet know of the Crown. For the time being, I prefer to keep it that way. Bayard does have a role in the empire's future, but I'm not sure of its nature yet. You must bear in mind that whoever sits upon the Fire Throne will not necessarily be the one to wield true power.'

Almorante stood up and bowed to her. 'I will do as you ask,' he said, 'but know that if you attempt betrayal my retaliation will be swift.'

'You are a true son of my heart,' Tatrini said.

Oblivious to what was taking place so near them, Tayven and Rav sat in the garden waiting for Tatrini to come out to them. Over the past few weeks, Rav had spent a lot of time in Tayven's company. He was like an older brother, who always had an answer to every question and never got tired of his queries. Prince Leo had faded in importance since Rav had met Tayven, a fact of which the young prince was well aware. It had made him spiteful, but had also encouraged him to spend more time with Rav. It was hard to shake Leo off nowadays. He was nearby, tormenting frogs and newts in the ponds at the end of the hedged walk. Rav could hear him laughing cruelly and splashing about with a stick.

From Tayven Rav had learned the true history of the Dragon Heir. Sometimes it scared him, because he realised that even by knowing the story he had broken the oath his ancestors had made to Madragore. But when Tayven was around, nothing bad could touch him. Rav had asked questions about the vision he'd seen of Tayven crowning his father, but sensed that Tayven was being economical with the truth in his responses. 'All you need to know is that your father will do all that he can to keep you and your family safe, no matter what happens here in Magrast.'

'But why does my grandmother want us to work magic together? Are we helping to get rid of Gastern?' Rav had learned some of the political undercurrents that tugged beneath the surface of royal family life.

'We are making contact with the elemental dragons,' Tayven said. 'All you need to think about is Foy. If you are strong in heart, there is nothing to fear. One day you will be lord of Caradore, and think how good it would be to have Foy's power at your command. We do not know the future, but we can work towards the best possible outcome.'

Since this conversation, and many others like it, Rav went to Tatrini's regular rituals in the Fire Chamber with less trepidation, because he knew his friend, whom he trusted instinctively, would be there. Nothing as dramatic as the events of the first ritual had occurred, but now Rav had a sense of Foy and felt connected with her. Tatrini had given the elemental avatars speaking parts in the rites. She was training them, and told them their work was going well. When Rav stood up to invoke the Dragon Queen, he sensed her near him, although she hadn't

161

actually spoken to him in his mind since the first time. Prince Bayard had called upon the fire-drakes and it had been magnificent, like a play. Leo had also invested his part with drama, perhaps to make up for the fact that his invocation produced no strange effects like those of the first ritual. But despite the ringing words and staged gestures, Rav knew that only he and Tayven really felt a connection to the dragons. It was their secret.

Garante clearly suspected nothing, which invested the weekly excursions to the Fire Chamber with greater excitement. Rav enjoyed having a hidden life which others knew nothing about. He looked forward to the meetings in the old dark chamber and the powerful and beautiful words Tatrini was teaching them. He enjoyed the shivery feelings that coursed through his body and made the hairs on his arms stand up. But sometimes, alone in his bed, waking from haunting dreams, he was terrified and wish he'd never gone with Leo to the old Fire Chamber. His life had changed, and he knew that it was irrevocable. Tatrini had said to him that his eyes had been opened for ever, and at night that image scared him. He imagined what it would be like never being able to close your eyes, even when something hideous was in the room with you and you didn't want to look at it.

He had not yet told Tayven about the dragon daughters, because some part of him was ashamed of knowing about them, but the dreams were increasing in regularity and intensity. Sometimes Misk and her sisters never quite went away when he woke up. That morning a spectral face had hung over his own for several minutes after he'd opened his eyes, fading gradually until only a pair of serpentine eyes remained, which had eventually winked out like distant lights. He could no longer keep silent.

'Tayven,' Rav began, 'will I always have horrible dreams now? Is it part of what we do?'

'Dreams?' Tayven said. 'What kind of horrible dreams?'

Rav shrugged awkwardly. He still felt embarrassed to be talking about this. 'Well, after the first ritual we did, I dreamed of Foy . . . ' He paused, unable to mention the daughters.

'That is not a bad thing,' Tayven said in a coaxing voice. 'Has anything else happened?'

Rav rubbed his nose. 'I've had lots of dreams of being in a dark cave, and something is in there with me. I've seen them. Three women with scaly skin. Their hair's made of snakes and their teeth are pointed. They circle round my bed, hissing and laughing. I don't like them. The funny thing is, I always *know* I'm dreaming, but it feels like I'm awake.'

Tayven regarded him with a strange, speculative expression. 'A lot of people can sort of "wake up" in their dreams,' he said, 'especially if they're involved in magic.'

'But I don't want to have dreams like that,' Rav said. 'Even if I know I'm really only asleep, I can't make myself wake up.'

'Then just think of me, I will be there with you,' Tayven said, reaching out to ruffle Rav's hair. 'I'll chase your demon women away. They are only faces of your own fear. They're not real.'

Rav thought Tayven was only saying that to comfort him. He could tell Tayven all of it, reveal the dragon daughters' names, and all that they had said to him. Tayven knew a lot about Foy, but seemed to be ignorant of Misk, Jia and Thrope. Rav didn't like the way they made him feel. They belonged to him, yet he felt that he belonged to them.

He became aware he no longer had his companion's attention and looked up from the heap of plucked grass he'd been building. A tall, dark man had come into the garden.

'Almorante,' Tayven said in a low voice.

'Prince Almorante?' Rav said, but did not need an answer to his question. He had seen the prince at both the funeral and the coronation.

Almorante came across the grass towards them and Rav could sense anxiety pouring from Tayven's body.

'*She* brought him here,' Tayven said.

Rav could ask no further questions because Almorante had reached them. He stared down in enquiry at Rav for a few moments, then said, 'Are you not the son of Valraven Palindrake?'

'Yes, my lord,' Rav answered.

'I had heard you were staying in Magrast, but I'm surprised your father has left you in the care of my mother.'

'There are worse people he could have been left with,' Tayven said. 'Go indoors, Rav. The prince has an uncommon interest in young boys.'

'Hello, Tayven,' Almorante said. 'You have lost your honey tongue, it appears. Have you no greeting for me after so many years? I grieved for you and searched for you, always hoping you still lived. How cruel is fate to give me this reassurance, but to put a wasp of a changeling in your place.'

'Rav,' Tayven said, 'go indoors.'

Rav sidled away a little, but he had no intention of leaving. He was too interested in what was going on.

'There is nothing I wish to say that the boy cannot hear,' Almorante said, 'though I am touched you wish to ensure our privacy. The witch of guile, my mother, has persuaded me to assist her. Does this mean we are on the same side again?'

Tayven squinted up at the prince. 'I am tempted to say we have never been on the same side, but of course that is not the case.'

'An obscure reply,' said Almorante.

'What is it you want?'

'For you to tell me about the artefact you recovered in Recolletine.'

Tayven grimaced. 'It is not *yours*, my lord. Did Tatrini tell you about it?'

'I am tempted to say I divined its existence, but of course that is not the case. My mother told me, yes. She wants me to recover it. I can only presume you will tell me everything, simply from the evidence of finding you here and because you took my mother into your confidence.'

Tayven made a dismissive gesture. 'The information was forced from me. It is too late to take back what I said. The Crown of Silence is in the keeping of Lady Sinaclara. Her house lies in the Forest of Bree and I can give you no clear directions to find it. The forest is quite capable of keeping you travelling in circles. So you must use your art to outwit it. That is all I have to say.'

Almorante was silent for a moment. Rav realised there were things he wanted to say but was unsure how to. Eventually he said, 'I never believed you were dead, and I never stopped looking for you. Not until Maycarpe let it be known he'd found you himself. Then it was up to you, and you made your feelings clear.'

Tayven raised a hand. 'Please say no more. I know you never intended to hurt me, but you are a Malagash. I cannot muster warmth for you exactly.'

'Without me, you would not have found the Crown. Who first took you to Recolletine?'

Tayven looked down at the ground and began to run his fingers through Rav's pile of grass. 'The others already knew of Recolletine. It was a help I'd been there before, but even if I hadn't, we'd still have finished the quest.'

'Tell me of Khaster,' Almorante said. 'I had great hopes for him. What happened to him was tragic.'

Tayven shrugged, still staring at the ground. 'You used him. He lost himself because of it. What lives on now is no longer Khaster as we knew him.' He looked up and fixed Almorante with fierce eyes. 'I will tell you all of it, as much as you want to know. The harm has been done. There is nothing more to spoil.' He paused. 'But not here, not now.'

Almorante spoke quickly. 'I will leave for Bree tomorrow. Will you dine with me tonight?'

Tayven considered, then nodded. 'You must send someone for me, clear it with Tatrini.'

'That's settled, then.'

Almorante gave a salute and left the garden.

Rav stared at Tayven, troubled in his heart. He couldn't express what was wrong with the conversation he'd just heard, but it had made him uncomfortable. Tayven had already told him the story of the Crown, and he was sure Almorante shouldn't be going to fetch it. 'Tayven,' he said haltingly, 'why are you going to see Almorante? You don't want to and yet you do. I don't understand.'

'History,' Tayven said, tearing grass from the lawn. 'Almorante and I were once very close. Bizarrely, I was assailed by the desire to discuss things with him, as I always used to. I realise I must have missed it.'

'What will you discuss?'

'The Lakes Quest.'

'Everything?'

'No, of course not.'

There was a tense silence. 'Will Lady Sinaclara be all right?' Rav asked.

Tayven glanced at him, smiled briefly. 'Don't worry, Rav. She will *know*. I speak to her in dreams, like you speak to your demon women. If Tatrini is meant to keep the Crown, she will. If she isn't, she won't. This goes beyond mere desire and greed.'

'What does that mean?'

'It means,' Tayven said, 'that we must prepare ourselves for what will come. I know you don't understand it yet, but that doesn't matter. I will protect and serve you.'

'Why?' Rav asked.

'For your father's sake,' Tayven replied.

CHAPTER SEVENTEEN

The Warning in Akahana

Sinaclara and Nana had made the same journey that Shan had undertaken the year before. The Lady had sent psychic messages to Darris Maycarpe, but had received nothing from him in return, neither in dream nor trance. She could only hope he would be expecting her and take necessary precautions to safeguard the Crown.

Now the two women stood in the dark reception hall of the governmental offices in Akahana, been told by the official on duty that Lord Maycarpe had recently returned from Magrast and was resting, not to be disturbed. Sinaclara fanned herself with a palm leaf she had purchased on the way from the harbour. She was unused to the stifling heat, which bore down upon her like burning fists, stealing the breath from her throat. She wanted to lean against the wall or sit down on the cool flagstones; it took all of her strength to remain standing. Nana, born in Jessapur, was not discomforted. She berated the official in halting Magravandian, trying to impress upon him that no matter how tired the governor was after his travels, it was essential they saw him immediately.

Eventually the man gave in. Sinaclara had the impression he was less concerned with the urgency of their request than with the need to rid himself of the hectoring woman who was ranting at him in pidgin language and who would clearly not be easily moved.

Within fifteen minutes, Sinaclara and Nana were being shown into Maycarpe's private office.

It was the first time Sinaclara had met Darris Maycarpe in the flesh, although they had communicated by letter many times, as well as by more esoteric means. In the dimness of the room, where the windows were shuttered against the beating heat outside, she saw a gauntly handsome man in early middle age, surrounded by a dark miasma of worry. Clearly his visit to Magrast had brought its own troubles. He had not picked up any of Sinaclara's psychic messages. He was preoccupied with his own concerns.

After the customary offering of seats and an order for refreshments, Sinaclara told him why she had come to Akahana. Maycarpe then explained all that had transpired while he'd been in Magrast. Now the Dragon Lord knew of the existence of the Crown and their ambitions for him. He said that Valraven had not received this news well.

'It is too soon,' Sinaclara said. 'The destiny of the Crown has not yet been revealed to us, never mind to him.'

'I think it has,' Maycarpe said. 'It demands to take its place, and this is why the fox has leapt into the chicken coop in Magrast. If we do not act now, we might miss our chance.'

'But Valraven is our true, spiritual king and he has no empathy with us.'

'Perhaps, but you heard what happened. Taropat has taken the Dragon Lord's wife and daughter. This can be no coincidence and must have bearing on the whole picture. We must investigate this by magical means. Palindrake is being forced into play, whether he likes it or not. If Tatrini is looking for the Crown, it's because she wants to crown someone with it. This will undoubtedly be Prince Bayard. Valraven cannot countenance that. No one can. He won't be able to sit on the fence.'

'But surely, from what you've told me, he'll only back Gastern.'

'Not if Gastern is already dead. Where will Valraven's loyalty fall then, eh?'

Sinaclara pondered this. 'Tayven is in Magrast, as is Valraven's son. We can only assume Tayven is our eyes and ears at court and that we have his loyalty.'

'Tayven will be in a precarious position,' Maycarpe said, 'but he's squirmed his way out of worse. Again, we must attempt communication, although the fire mages keep Magrast cloaked. They are the last people we want to alert to this situation.'

'The Crown must be hidden,' Sinaclara said. 'There's a possibility the mages have already uncovered Tatrini's plans and will come looking for it themselves.'

'The Crown will be safe here,' Maycarpe said. 'Will you show it to me?'

Nana went to fetch the artefact from their baggage. She unwrapped it with reverence and set it on Maycarpe's desk. In the dim light, it seemed to glow: a coronet of delicate tall spines fashioned from coral and bone and bound with white metal wire. Maycarpe drew in his breath through his teeth. 'I will call a meeting of the King's Cabal,' he said.

'And who are they?' Sinaclara enquired.

'The men and women who have been your colleagues for many years, but who you do not yet know.'

Evening brought some respite from the heat. Sinaclara dressed herself in the native costume that Maycarpe's servants had left in her room. She went out onto the balcony that overlooked the governmental square and leaned upon the balustrade. She could hear chanting coming from the many temples, the sundry tunes and voices blending into a strange and eerie song. The air was thick with the pungent incense that burned on every altar. Mewt's gods felt very much alive to her. She hoped that they would give her the protection she needed. As if in response to the unspoken plea, Maycarpe's aide came to her door, to inform her a carriage was waiting for her downstairs.

Maycarpe took them to a small temple concealed in a narrow side street deep in the heart of Akahana. Here, an obscure god named Munt was worshipped, although it quickly became clear that this was just a front for more serious commerce. A priest led them through the shadowed temple, where a few elderly people rocked in their evening devotions and paid no attention to the visitors. The priest took them behind the altar and opened a gate of wrought iron. Beyond it, steps led to an underground shrine.

The small, low-ceilinged chamber was already full of people. It had retained the heat of the day and its incense smell was tainted by a musty odour. Maycarpe said they were close to an underground tributary of the sacred river and that deeper shrines contained holy pools for scrying and healing.

Sinaclara felt as if the weight of history was pressing down upon her head. It was difficult to breathe and a band of pressure over her eyes indicated the presence of unseen entities.

Maycarpe began to introduce all the people present, but to Sinaclara they were only names that she could not take in. Some of the faces were Mewtish, others Magravandian, and she was sure there were a few pale Cossics present too. Under normal circumstances, she would be more interested, but the world of the unseen was moving close to her. Soon it would sweep her up.

'We are only a small proportion of the Cabal,' Maycarpe said. 'We have members in all countries of the world, every one of them waiting for the order to act. Agents in Magrast are already setting certain plans in motion. Whether Valraven Palindrake likes it or not, he is soon to become a rebel against the empire.'

Sinaclara rubbed her brow. She sensed Nana's concerned scrutiny and put out a hand to touch her assistant's arm. Maycarpe's voice boomed on, but she could barely understand his words, even though he spoke Magravandian. Her name was mentioned, but it was like listening to a foreign language. It was only when Maycarpe directed his attention upon her that she could comprehend him.

'I think it would be appropriate if we all joined together in meditation,' Maycarpe said to her. 'Would you like to lead it, my lady?'

Sinaclara shook her head. 'No, I regret I am exhausted after our journey. Please let someone else take the role.'

'Of course,' Maycarpe said, inclining his head. 'I will do so myself.' He turned to the others. 'Perhaps if we concentrate upon it, some indication of future action will be revealed to us.'

There was not enough room for the company to sit down, so everyone present stood shoulder to shoulder in a circle, hands linked. Sinaclara was assailed by a wave of cold and began to shiver, even though the air in the chamber was hot. She had never suffered from claustrophobia in her life, but now the confined space seemed to squeeze the breath from her. It was as if her body had forgotten how to breathe automatically. She had to do it consciously, with effort. The people here were in accord with her. They shared her dreams and ambitions. There was no reason to feel oppressed and apprehensive, yet she could not dispel these negative feelings. She wanted to break free and run from the room.

Maycarpe's voice was a soft drone as he instructed the gathering to visualise themselves on the sacred hill in the centre of Magrast. 'It is as it was at the dawn of the world,' he said. 'Go to this place and ask for guidance.'

Sinaclara had no intention of joining in with the meditation. She was prepared to concentrate fully on breathing deeply to calm herself until she could reasonably escape without attracting unwanted attention. Then a splash of red exploded behind her closed eyes. She gasped and clung onto Nana's hand, instinctively relinquishing the fingers of the person who stood on her other side. She could hear voices in the room, concerned mutterings, Nana's soft murmur. But they were receding. She was being drawn away from them, unable to open her eyes. A pinprick of light was drawing closer in her inner darkness, getting brighter. It seared her eyes, which she knew were closed. She heard the beating of mighty wings, which conjured a burning wind that buffeted her body.

The eternal spirit guardian of the Crown of Silence hung before her: Azcaranoth, the peacock angel, to whom she had devoted herself for life. His face was fierce and implacable, violet light poured from his eyes.

'Are you still prepared to pay the price, Sinaclara?' he asked. 'Is your heart resolute, your step firm?'

'I do your will,' she replied, 'as I have ever done.'

'One must die and one must not,' Azcaranoth said. 'When the first death occurs, you must prevent the second. In so doing, you will break your oath to me. But it will and must proceed as I have spoken.'

A blinding flash erupted across Sinaclara's inner vision. She felt the constriction of chains around her, biting into her flesh. Her body was bruised, beaten, and she could hear the passionless, bestial laughter of enemies. Grief clawed her heart for a great loss. If she could only open her eyes, she would see who lay dead at her feet.

Something smacked her hard across the face and she came to her senses. Her eyes opened and she saw a ring of concerned and puzzled faces around her. Nana's arms encircled her body, holding her close. Maycarpe was standing just in front of her and she realised it had been he who had just struck her. 'Forgive me,' he said, 'but you were screaming. We had to break the trance.'

Sinaclara slumped against Nana. The warmth emanating from the woman's body felt so sweet and pure. Sinaclara never wanted to lose it. In the midst of uncertainty, Nana was always solid and dependable. 'I knew something would occur,' Sinaclara said. 'I had a presentiment of it.'

'What did you see?' Maycarpe said.

Sinaclara shook her head. 'Nothing,' she said. 'It was just a feeling that came to me. Terrible.'

'But what was its flavour?' Maycarpe asked. 'We must know, my lady. You must try to tell us.'

'I can't,' she said. 'It was personal. It was mine.'

Maycarpe drew back, eyeing her shrewdly, as if still full of questions.

'I chose my path,' Sinaclara said. 'And it is hard. I must walk it alone sometimes.'

Maycarpe blinked at her. 'I understand.' Clearly that understanding irked him.

Nana rubbed Sinaclara's arm. 'It's over,' she murmured. 'Be at rest.'

Sinaclara could not speak of what she had seen because she knew without doubt that danger and horror awaited her, but that no one could do anything to avert it. She would have to live through it, or not.

Maycarpe and Nana took her back up into the temple, where the air was a little cooler and the serene countenance of Munt gazed down upon the last of his frail worshippers. Sinaclara could only feel contempt for those who rocked and prayed before the cold stone idol. Gods can't help you, she thought. Gods can't influence the desires and greed of humankind.

Beyond the temple door, Akahana was secretive yet serene in the ruddy gleams of sunset, immortal, inviolate. As they walked to the waiting carriage, the last strains of evening song drifted from the multitude of temples, both near and far. Maycarpe took Sinaclara's free arm and sighed. 'The gods of Mewt must be preserved from the inexorable march of Madragore.'

Sinaclara said nothing. She did not fear for Mewt. Madragore was not a threat to them. The threat, as yet, had not revealed its true face.

CHAPTER EIGHTEEN

The Freedom of Mountains

Spring spilled over Hamagarid mountains, seeping through the deep shadowed canyons, smothering the exposed hillsides. Shaggy sheep and goats cavorted in the high meadows, crushing the starry flowers that released achingly sweet scent that dizzied the mind. The new season in High Hamagara was a trumpet blast of nature, inaudible to the ears, but an assault upon every other sense.

Now, as she walked in line with the others along the narrow tracks, Varencienne could taste the air, able to discern every subtle nuance: the resinous tang of pine, the confection sweetness of mountain violet. She could tell when they passed the haunts of animals, the smell of their dung and musk still hanging heavily amidst the undergrowth. The season pressed against her flesh at night like the breath of a lover. She lay in Shan's arms, delirious as a swooning virgin. He was a shadow against the stars, a god of rock and earth come to possess her. I have no other life, she thought. All of it was a dream. She was passing from the real world into the otherlands, the landscape of myth. Hamagara had allowed them to pass across its threshold and now it claimed them. No wonder there were so few tales of people having travelled here. People did not return because they did not want to, could not. They became part of the land itself.

I have a son and husband, Varencienne told herself, but they did not seem real. Was this what death was like? A drifting away from the mundane, each silver thread of connection breaking one by one, until earthly life no longer meant anything and the cries of grief that tugged at you became as thin and insignificant as the far songs of birds?

Taropat became increasingly quiet as the journey progressed. He took to walking ahead of Shan and Varencienne, as if the sight of them together affronted him. Ellony would chatter and skip beside him, her hand in his, but she desired no response from him. Sometimes Varencienne's heart contracted in her chest at the sight of him: she sensed his loneliness and wished she could reach him. They could be friends, if he'd only let her in. As time progressed, she began to see him as Khaster more and more, the idea of Taropat a needless fabrication. His stiff posture and habitual pinched expression were starting to loosen, revealing a man who looked younger and was more lithe and supple. He was, despite his lingering cantankerous moods, a very handsome creature. Varencienne tried to control these thoughts because she knew they marked the boundary to very dangerous territory. When they assailed her, she would look upon Shan and tell herself she was blessed.

Higher up, towards the sky, where the air became rarer, the constructions of personality began to melt away. Varencienne could only assume the others felt the way she did. Standing on a bare crag at dawn with the wind slicing through her hair and her heart soaring with the breathtaking primal beauty of the landscape, she could scarcely feel her body any more. She was pure essence at these times, strands of uncomplicated emotion. The shapes of the mountains, the patterns of the eagles as they surfed the currents of air, were components of the mandala of creation. Everything had its part, each tiny piece making up the whole. Humans thought they were so important, but they weren't. They lived in delusion, trapped in a petty reality they created for themselves. This was real. This was life.

The company had acquired tents at Vereya, using some of Varencienne's jewellery as currency. Varencienne found it did not hurt her to surrender it, even though one piece had belonged to Valraven's mother. The Hamagarids who accepted this wealth clearly were unaware of its value. Perhaps their children would play with the bright baubles, losing them amongst mountain meadow flowers. It no longer mattered. Varencienne did not want material things any more. A stout stave was worth more than any fancy necklace. A meal of rice, milk and cheese was more satisfying than any royal banquet. She could no longer remember being the person she'd been at the beginning of their journey.

Now every morning she rose before Taropat and Shan, at daybreak, when Snopard and his acolytes had already left to engage in morning devotions away from the camp. Varencienne would climb to the nearest crag to watch the dawn slink over the mountains. At first it would come as a black band on the horizon, obliterating the scintillant starshine. Then a soft glow would bloom in the sky, gilding the highest peaks.

When the mountain tops were ablaze, the valleys were still asleep in darkness. Night departed lazily from the canyons, almost reluctant to go. Sometimes there were nomadic tribes to watch in one of the valleys below, communities of two or more families who would begin their day's work at sunrise: seeing to their animals, preparing the breakfast. Through the clear air Varencienne could hear their voices, their laughter. Other times, when there were no humans visible in the landscape, she watched the wild goats and sheep. Occasionally, she saw wolves and once – a moment to treasure – the rare mountain leopard, a creature of silver and snow. It appeared on an overhang above her, observed her with icy blue eyes for a few moments, then disappeared as if it had never been there. Ellony had told her that the leopards were avatars of mountain spirits. They were magical and could grant boons. Merely sighting one was auspicious. When Varencienne reported her experience to the others, Snopard was delighted. He said that their journey was blessed. He himself was a priest of Kakamani, who was the king of leopards and an aspect of Paraga. The Nugrid did not seem the slightest bit resentful that the leopard had appeared to Varencienne rather than to him or his followers. Varencienne could understand some of his talk now because Ellony had taught her what Hamagaran she knew. It was inconceivable that only a few weeks before, Snopard's words had sounded like nonsense. Now it was the bright babble of a swelling river and occasionally Varencienne could make out shapes beneath the hectic surface.

One morning, snow fell in the predawn, a final flurry perhaps. Today, Snopard had said, they might reach their destination. Varencienne hoped the bout of inclement weather would not delay them. She wanted her first sight of the holy city to be in late afternoon or at sundown, when the land became a treasure-house of gleaming colours. As usual, she clambered at dawn to an isolated ledge near the camp. The snow was a thin crust beneath her feet. She saw tracks in it, wolves or foxes. They had camped on a hillside overlooking a wide valley. On the opposite slope was a ruined gat surrounded by cairns built by superstitious travellers who were afraid of the ghosts that might inhabit the ruins. For the first time in weeks, Varencienne found herself thinking of home. Perhaps it was because their journey would soon be over and then they would have to decide what to do next. Their old lives were destined to intrude. She thought of spring in Caradore, of Pharinet and Everna. They would be worried about her, but there was no need. Perhaps, even now, Valraven was following in her footsteps. Was the land affecting him like it had her? She wanted him to see it, experience it.

She heard the crunch of footsteps behind her and turned, expecting Shan. He knew she liked to watch the dawn. But it was Taropat who had followed her. Her body responded with a flood of pure pleasure. This was dangerous. She should guard against these pointless feelings. Shan was hers and he was all that a woman could desire. Taropat was not. If only he didn't look that way.

Varencienne smiled at him and he inclined his head to her, his mouth managing to grimace a greeting. She realised that she was about to experience something preordained and essential. Time had closed upon her in a circle. She thought of the Chair above Norgance, where, some years ago, she had believed Khaster had appeared to her. For a brief second, she could smell the rain of Caradore once more, and heard the clop of water dripping from the leaves. What had he said? 'It will happen regardless of what you think or do.' Something like that.

'I wanted to see what you get up to every morning,' Taropat said. 'You could be casting fire spells or communing with your mother.'

'Sorry to disappoint you,' she said. 'I like to be part of the sunrise, to feel it. The world is reborn every day, and when I'm part of it, I feel I'm reborn too.'

Taropat sighed through his nose, apparently in impatience, but Varencienne was not deceived. He did not walk away or utter a cutting remark. He wanted something, but was perhaps not even aware of it. 'I saw you once,' she said. 'A long time before we actually met.'

Taropat regarded her sidelong in enquiry. His expression was far from friendly, but she pressed on.

'It was at a crucial time in my life, when I had to make important decisions. I had gone to the Chair to find inspiration. A man came to me. I thought it was Merlan, that he had followed me from Norgance. He said strange things to me, and told me someone was waiting for me at home. I went back to Norgance first and found Merlan there. He hadn't followed me at all. I realised then that it was you whom I'd seen. I went home to Caradore Castle and discovered that my mother had arrived. Soon after, we went to the old domain with Valraven and he communed with Foy there.'

'I wouldn't have told you to do that,' Taropat said in a flat tone.

'No, you didn't. You said, "It will happen regardless of what you think or do." And it has, hasn't it?'

'Those words . . . ' Taropat said, gazing out across the valley. There was wonder in his voice.

'You know them? You've heard them too?'

He nodded. 'Yes. Tayven said them to me once.'

There was a silence, then Varencienne said, 'Who are you now?' He would know what she meant.

'I know what I'm not,' he replied. His expression had changed, become softer, although it was as if he was speaking to himself rather than to her. 'I'm not my pain, nor my bitterness. Nothing seems consequential up here. Even Taropat. I see him as a crusty old man, tramping through the dark valleys down there. I've escaped him, like a spirit.'

'Taropat had no reason to be crusty,' Varencienne said. 'Shan has told me all he knows. If anything, I would say it was a damaged shell you've left down there, part of Khaster.'

'But I may walk back down to it. This escape does not feel permanent or real. It is like respite.'

'Isn't that your choice?' Varencienne asked. 'Isn't it your choice who and what you are, how much of Taropat, how much of Khaster? If I've learned anything here, it's that.' She sat down on the cold rock and gestured for Taropat to join her. 'I have a theory. Will you hear it?'

He shrugged, grimaced again and sat down. 'It might be interesting.'

Varencienne's heartbeat had increased. She could hear it in her ears. He might react badly to what she wanted and needed to say. 'When you became Taropat, you were a mixture of conflicting personalities. I think that when Taropat takes a new avatar, much of the previous one remains, but over time it gradually becomes more dormant. What survives is Taropat's knowledge, like a library of books. The old personality does not at first leave the flesh and become one with the universe, which is an unusual condition in any belief system. But maybe, eventually, it does go. It might have to. What is left is a period of transition, of handing over. I don't think you are Taropat. I think you're Khaster, but that you don't want to be. You've created what you think you should be, but you don't like it. When you met Tayven again, it was a great shock, and the man who Shan first knew went into hiding. I've heard the stories many times over these last few weeks. I could see a pattern in them. You are not mad, nor cantankerous. It is against your nature. You don't even want to feel bitter, but you've created a trap for yourself. If you climb out, what is left? Something raw and new and fragile. But perhaps it is time to do so.'

Taropat laughed, a little nervously. He hadn't interrupted her once, and had appeared to listen attentively. 'You have been thinking deeply about me, princess,' he said.

'I was in love with you for a while,' she answered. 'I used to stand for ages gazing at your portrait in Norgance. You were my tragic hero.'

'Really?'

Varencienne clasped her hands about her knees and found the palms

176

were burning hot. 'Yes. I was a lonely creature, married to a cold stranger, dumped into a country I quickly grew to love but did not know, regarded with suspicion by your family and Val's. I had to prove myself to everyone. I had to make Val *see* me. You, of all them, did not judge me. I could look into your painted eyes and believe you saw my soul, that you understood.' She too laughed, but with more sincerity. 'Valraven stole your wife's body whenever he wanted to, but you stole his wife's heart. I would say that makes you about even.'

'Don't joke about it,' Taropat said. 'Remember Ellony. You cannot laugh about that.'

'No,' Varencienne said, unperturbed. 'I can't, but you should know this. The dragon daughters were responsible for what happened. It was they who took Ellony.'

Taropat shook his head vehemently. 'Don't try to justify what Valraven and Pharinet did. They were responsible. There would be no dragon daughters, but for them.'

'They acted in ignorance, yes,' Varencienne said. 'But do you really think either of them wanted that to happen? They have both tortured themselves about it. We all make mistakes, every one of us. If Pharry or Val still revelled in what they'd done, or didn't care, I'd share your view of them, but they don't. You were all young, and victims of tragic circumstances. Val and Pharry could not help what they felt for one another, but tradition decreed that they must marry other people. They did not mean to hurt anyone.'

'It was perverse,' Taropat said.

Varencienne expelled a snort of derision. 'Listen to yourself. What is perverse? A man loving a man, a woman loving a woman, a sister loving her brother? Love goes beyond mere human constructions. When it happens, it happens. True love, utter giving, is never perverse. Perversity is selfishness, cruelty, coldness. It is humans who are perverse in their fear of what they don't understand. Was your love of Tayven perverse?'

Taropat rubbed his hands over his face, made a sound of discomfort.

'Yes, I know. I'm making you think about things you'd rather ignore or bury,' Varencienne said, 'but will you answer my question?'

Taropat was silent for a few moments, then said, 'I remember Recolletine, the first time. I remember hope and warmth. No, it was not perverse, but we were both far from perfect. That time at the lakes was like this: a respite, a dream. It could not last.'

'Perhaps not, but it was a vision of what could be, a dream to aspire to.'

Taropat stared at her. 'What is this insight you are trying to give me?'

177

'Clarity,' she answered. 'True sight. Freedom . . . Silence.'

'Do you have these things?'

'A little. Let's say I aspire to them, that I'm willing to accept what is.' She reached out and took one of his hands. 'At first I was furious when you took me captive, but now I cannot thank you enough for bringing me here. Things are becoming clear. We will return to the world, but we will go armed with new knowledge and insight. We will do what has to be done.'

His hand lay motionless in hers, but he did not pull away. 'Do you know what that is?'

'I think it's the Crown,' she answered. 'You must reform your brotherhood, bring forth the Dragon Queen.' She paused. 'You must face Valraven.'

Now he did pull away. 'Is this what this conversation has been about?' he demanded bitterly. 'You are a dragon daughter yourself to try and seduce me in this way.'

'You have conquered many fears,' Varencienne said softly, 'but this is the biggest. Think where its root really lies.'

He shook his head, his mouth a grim line.

Varencienne reached for his hand again, held it tightly with both of hers. He pulled against her, but she would not let go. 'You came to me once, whether consciously or not. You helped me. Now I'm trying to help you. Let me be your oracle, Khas. Let's work together to create what we desire. Let's change the prophecy. It must happen *because* of what we think and do! We are not helpless. We have will. Surely Taropat knows that.'

He glanced at her, managed a weak smile. She let go of his hand. 'I'm back at the beginning,' he said. 'It's so strange. The last few years might never have been. Has Hamagara done this?'

'You said we were meant to come, remember? You followed a vision and we followed you. I was wrong ever to doubt you. Shan didn't, despite the way you treat him.'

'You and Shan,' Taropat said, an observation rather than a criticism. 'Is he part of the reality you must return to or simply a figment of your dream of Hamagara?'

'I am married to Valraven and to Caradore,' she replied, 'but I will take lovers. Shan is not the first.'

'I would expect nothing else of a Malagash,' Taropat said, but his voice lacked the usual acidity he reserved for talk of her family.

She shrugged. 'Ours was a marriage of convenience. You know that kind. But Val and I have resolved to be friends. Our relationship is perhaps stronger than romantic love, for it is without jealousy or fear. We trust one another.'

'You want him to be king, and for that you need me.'

'I am not my mother,' she said. 'It is not a case of using and needing people. We should work together. I really don't know if Val should be king. I don't yet have all the information and experience I need to make a judgement. I feel I'm travelling towards it, that's all. But what you achieved last year at Recolletine was phenomenal. That company should not have broken up through fear and paranoia. Get over it. Start again. The Valraven that Sinaclara, Merlan and Tayven see is not the one you see. I'm not saying they are right and you're wrong, or vice versa. I'm just saying there are different views, and that you should appreciate that.'

'Valraven is Sinaclara's tragic hero, as I was yours,' Taropat remarked, and Varencienne perceived a bitchy edge to the comment.

'Then I hope she can be there for him as I am for you,' she said.

'You are quite a paragon,' Taropat said. 'Is it real, or are you simply an accomplished actress?'

'If the effect is positive, does that matter?' she asked, then grinned at him. 'Oh, I'm not a paragon, I assure you. I have strong convictions, that's all, and I've learned a few things. Not everything, by any means. I wouldn't want to know everything, because then I might as well be dead.'

Taropat studied her for a moment. 'I'd never have imagined having this conversation with you. I can appreciate why Shan is so smitten with you now. You are certainly adept with words. Valraven is very lucky. I hope he knows that.'

'The Taropat I met a few weeks ago would never have said that,' Varencienne said, getting to her feet. She felt dizzy, exhilarated, because a thousand words she had kept tightly within her had been given their freedom, because he had spoken kindly to her. 'Shall we go and make breakfast?'

The company set off before morning had taken full claim of the sky. They followed a narrow path along the side of the mountain, high above the valley, which looked endless. It was a path that had been cut by a glacier millennia before, and it extended as far as Hanana. Below, a thick forest hugged cleared areas where a few farmers had sown barley fields. Shaggy sheep with huge curling horns grazed on the opposite hillside, their tiny hooves sure upon the almost vertical meadow. Varencienne saw a brightly coloured blur moving amongst the sheep and at first thought it was a spirit of some kind, but then realised it was a running shepherd child, dressed in a brilliant red cape. She looked down at the path, which was littered with quartz chunks reflecting the early sunlight. It was as if she was walking upon water. There was a strand of red upon the path: a ribbon of blood, or a ribbon of wool? She saw that it was made of silk, something that a girl might wear in her hair. Seeing it there was like an omen. It lay perfect amongst the glittering stones: a lost memory, an accidental still life.

By midmorning, there were increased signs of life in the valley, even though the landscape itself was more wild and desolate. Snopard said this was because they were near to the Holy City and that many people had settled in the lands around it in order to supply produce for the Highest of High, Aranepa, Supreme Vana of Venotishi. A tributary of the sacred river Nankara cascaded over a precipice into the valley, filling the air with noise, colour and light. Just beyond the waterfall, the mountains leaned together so that the river valley became narrower. It was here that Varencienne and her companions had to cross to the other side, via a narrow bridge of hairy rope and wooden slats. Anyone with vertigo would have fainted on the spot, as they were hundreds of feet above the valley floor. Between the splintery slats, Varencienne caught sight of crows wheeling beneath, uttering hoarse cries. The river was a muted roar, foaming white and silver over its rocky bed: Lady Yakse, eldest daughter of Venotishi. Snopard muttered propitiatory prayers all the way, running a string of polished black magic beads through his fingers. Varencienne could almost feel the personality of the river goddess, wild and exuberant in her threshing power, ignorant of the small human specks crossing her roiling body.

In late afternoon, as Varencienne had hoped, the party turned a corner on the narrow path and a panoramic landscape opened up before them. They were so high above sea level that the peaks around them were capped in snow, an icing that would never disappear, not even in high summer. But one mountain alone was black and bare at its summit: the Peak of the Night. This was the holy mountain they had sought, and the citadel gat, Hanana, clung to its lower flanks like a girdle of carved stone. Ellony told her mother that the mountain was Venotishi's heart, which held Paraga in tight embrace. The heat of the life blood of the goddess kept the high peaks free from snow.

'Volcanic,' Taropat announced.

'Is that likely?' Varencienne asked. 'Why would anyone build so extensively on the flanks of a live volcano?'

Taropat gave her a withering glance. 'Very well. It is the goddess's beating heart that keeps the stone warm.'

'The Nugrids believe that the prayers of the High Vanas in Hanana keep the goddess in a good mood,' Ellony said. 'Otherwise she might throw burning rocks down onto the citadel.'

'It sounds perilous,' Varencienne said.

'Yet Hanana is hundreds of years old,' Shan remarked. 'If the mountain is active, it can't have erupted for a considerable time.'

The travellers had emerged onto a track that was on an equal level to the city, but to reach it, they would have to descend into the wide river valley below. At this point, Yakse's mood was somewhat calmer than before, for she ran over a bed of shingles as she passed the citadel. A group of goatherds could be seen guiding their flock through the stream, and there was much activity around the banks, which were wide beaches of glittering black sand.

As they made their descent, Varencienne felt, inexplicably, a depression fall upon her. Ellony said that Snopard had warned her to expect this. There was nothing spiritual or magical about it. It was simply an effect of the loss of altitude. Still, Varencienne hoped it was not an omen.

Halfway down the mountain, they came upon a small gat, half in ruins. Poles reared lopsidedly from its crumbled roof, from which a host of red and white flags fluttered. A man and a boy sat before a fire in front of the gat, drinking from wooden bowls. One of Snopard's acolytes approached the pair and asked humbly if their party might share the fire to warm their own milk. The man looked at the boy, who made a quick gesture of assent. Both had a Nugrid look to them, having long braided hair and simple clothes while being adorned with elaborate golden jewellery. Their faces were virtually covered by dark red scarves, which they lifted aside when they drank. Still, it was easy to see, if only from the luminous eyes, that the boy was well-favoured.

Varencienne sat down with Shan and Ellony and remarked to her daughter what a handsome lad the boy was. He looked a few years older than Rav.

'He is not what he seems,' Ellony whispered to her mother.

'What do you mean?' Varencienne asked.

'He does not live *here*,' Ellony replied, but would say no more.

'Aranepa is a boy,' Shan said. 'It's likely others seek to emulate him. I'm sure that's what we have here. These two will make their living from the boy's prophecies.'

The boy kept glancing at Taropat, in a manner Varencienne could not interpret. Was there hostility, pity or respect in his eyes? If Taropat noticed, he gave no sign. The older Nugrid conversed in a low voice with Snopard. He spoke very slowly, as if under the influence of some kind of drug. Perhaps it was another effect of the loss of altitude, but Varencienne swore that the man moved slowly as well – too slowly. The atmosphere felt altogether surreal to her. These people were like figments of a dream that only a wandering subconscious could conjure up.

Taropat looked impatient, clearly eager to tackle the last stage of their journey, but Snopard was intent on speaking with the Nugrid boy. He gestured towards him, but the older man shook his head, raising his hands in negation.

'What's going on?' Varencienne asked Ellony.

The girl screwed up her nose. 'Snopard wants to ask the boy questions about his spiritual path, but the other one won't let him.'

'Then why doesn't he just ask the boy outright?'

'I don't know. Perhaps he's just being polite.'

'Maybe Snopard should offer something,' Varencienne said. She still wore a thin gold chain around her neck, hung with the Palindrake crest. She removed it and handed it to her daughter. 'Give this to Snopard and tell him to use it as currency.'

'That is generous, Mama,' Ellony said in surprise.

'Should you do that?' Shan asked.

Varencienne gestured at Snopard. 'It's just a trinket. Do it, Elly. I'd like to hear a prophecy.'

Shan smiled. 'You're easily taken in.'

'What do you mean? You know the Hamagarids have something special about them. This moment might be significant.'

'As significant as your conversation with Taropat this morning?'

Varencienne bridled. 'You're not jealous, are you?'

'No. Just be careful. Words are cheap.'

Ellony leaned over to Snopard and touched his arm to attract his attention. She whispered in his ear. The Nugrid regarded her a few moments, then took the crest from her hand. He spoke carefully to the boy's guardian, clearly expecting a negative response. But when the boy saw the necklace, he spoke a few short sentences abruptly to his companion. Varencienne could not understand a word of it. Their dialect was different to any other she'd heard on the journey. With obvious reluctance, the guardian took the necklace from Snopard's out-stretched hand and passed it to the boy. He held it before his face, his eyes narrow. Varencienne thought he would speak, but he secreted the necklace into a fold of his robe and grimaced at Snopard, making a dismissive gesture with one hand. Snopard bowed his head and pressed his steepled hands against his forehead. He then spoke a few quiet words to Ellony.

'I've just given something away for nothing, haven't I?' Varencienne said dryly.

'Snopard says the gift was accepted,' Ellony said. 'He said we should leave now.'

Shan laughed. 'There, you see?'

182

Varencienne grimaced ruefully. 'Ah, well, I hope the lad gets pleasure from it, or at least a good meal.'

The group made the final descent to the shingle banks of the river. The water was not quite as calm as it appeared from higher up the path. It roared over the stones, frothing like beaten milk. Ellony knelt down to take a drink from it. 'Fizzy!' she announced.

Shan and Varencienne knelt down beside the girl. 'We should make a wish,' Varencienne said.

Shan glanced sidelong at her. 'No goddess is so powerful,' he said.

'What do you mean by that?'

He did not reply, but bent low to drink from the rushing flow.

Has he asked for me? Varencienne wondered. Does he want us to continue, beyond this journey? And what do I wish for? She glanced up and it could be no coincidence her gaze fell upon an elderly goatherd couple on the opposite shore. Children, perhaps their grandchildren, ran amongst the goats, and the old people smiled upon them benignly. The man had a gnarled hand upon the shoulder of the woman, yet their connection was clearly so deep they might well have been embracing tightly. They were completely present in the world, without anxiety, without resentment. They were one with creation.

There can be no happy ending for you, Varencienne thought. You are Caradore's mistress, Valraven's wife. There is no summer cottage with a loved one beside you and the sun sinking down the sky, slowly and warmly towards a final contented setting, welcomed after long years of happiness. She sighed deeply and bowed towards the water. Spray moistened her face.

'Great Yakse,' she spoke in her mind, 'let all be well. Let harmony be restored. Give us the wisdom of Hamagara to take back with us to the world beyond. Let us do the will of the gods.' She drank.

CHAPTER NINETEEN

A Sacred Beast

The road to Hanana was wide and partly stepped. Many people and animals were coming and going along it. Buildings had been constructed to either side: flat-roofed dwellings and what looked like storehouses. Varencienne thought the road was like a thoroughfare to Paradise. The white citadel reared above them, its domes and turrets fluttering with a thousand flags. The thunderous music of horns boomed down from the high walls. People climbing towards them were like souls arriving from death, while those descending might be others heading off for rebirth. There was a chaotic aspect to the scene, but also, conversely, a pervading atmosphere of great tranquillity and spirituality. The hairs rose on Varencienne's arms and her eyes filled spontaneously with tears. We are heading towards it now, she thought, so close. Soon I will know.

The gates to the citadel were open wide and looked as if they hadn't been closed for centuries. The Hananites were obviously not worried about security. The gates were of carved bare wood, some thirty feet tall, covered in stylised representations of demons and dragons. This was Paraga's capital and his image appeared on the walls of nearly every building within the citadel. He was a delicate creature with enormous wings like sails. His face was almost feline, with long curling whiskers and enormous round eyes with slit pupils. If anything, he seemed out of character with the typically fearsome Par Sen deities and spirits. His benign gaze fell upon the hectic bustle of the streets, which were surprisingly wide. Varencienne felt as if she'd stepped into another world. Hanana was far more cosmopolitan than she had expected. A lot of the people around her – Hamagarid nobility, from the richness of their clothing – appeared to be nothing more than tourists. They were pointing out sights of interest to one another as hordes of children ran about madly. A festival was due to take place very shortly, but Varencienne wondered where the ambience of stillness and magic so present in the eternal mountains and on the road just beyond the gates had fled. From Caradore to Hanana, she and her companions had travelled an uninhabited wilderness. Where had all these people come from? Few of them looked as if they'd be capable of, or comfortable with, the kind of experience Varencienne's party had been through. These were people sleek with good living, who surely wouldn't trek on foot through the high passes.

In response to her questions, Snopard told her that the Hamagarid princes, of whom there were legion, lived mostly in the north, where the mountains petered out towards the sea. They travelled the Wide Road, known as Venotishi's Gullet, with their caravans and entourages. Varencienne's heart sank a little. Within the enclosure of the citadel, it was as if the mountains did not even exist. She wondered, glumly, whether she had already learned all that she was supposed to learn in Hamagara.

Nobody else was affected in the same way. Ellony was excitedly dragging Shan around by the hand, intent on examining the shops in the street, which were filled with colourful wares. Snopard indicated an inn he knew would accept some of Varencienne's remaining trinkets as payment for board and then bowed formally, apparently about to make a departure. Taropat was far from pleased that the Nugrid believed their alliance to be over.

'I wish to secure an audience with Aranepa,' he said. 'You must help me in this.'

'I cannot,' Snopard replied. 'Go to the temple like everyone else and make your request. There is nothing I can do that will alter the Vanas' decision.'

'Thank you,' Varencienne said hurriedly, 'for all your help.'

The Nugrid smiled and bowed again. He bent to embrace Ellony for a few moments, then summoned his acolytes and marched off quickly into the crowd.

Taropat expelled a grunt of irritation. 'I hope you have some baubles left, princess,' he said, 'for I think we'll need them to bribe our way to Aranepa.'

The inn, called simply 'Wind, Rain, Wind', had few vacancies because of the festival, so the party was forced to share a room. It had only two narrow beds, but the proprietress, a thin young woman, offered to supply a couple of floor mattresses, of which she had a plentiful supply.

185

Varencienne now felt exhausted, and it took all her strength to go down to the dining room with the others for an early evening meal. The room was not large and was filled to capacity with diners. The smell of spiced meat filled the air, a welcome change to Varencienne after a mostly vegetarian diet upon the journey.

While they ate, Taropat discussed with Shan when they should go to the temple and request an audience with Aranepa. To Varencienne, this was an impossible venture. Thousands of people would want to catch a glimpse of the High Vana. At best, they could hope only to join a massive crowd, with no personal interaction.

This is the way of things, she thought. We seek answers and enlightenment, and expect to find it in others, but essentially, it is down to us.

She hoped that what she had learned would be of use back in the world she knew. Anything could have occurred while she'd been absent from it. Caradore was like a distant dream and Valraven a figment from her imagination. She could not believe he had followed her trail into this wild country. Perhaps he was caught up now in other dramas, involving her scheming family in Magrast. He might believe she was lost for good. At that moment, she hadn't the energy to care. The idea of leaving Hanana with Ellony, never to return to Caradore, but to find a home in Hamagara, amongst the natives or in one of the gats, was extremely appealing. Perhaps that was why she'd come here, to become an ascetic and renounce her former life of privilege completely.

Her feelings about Taropat and Shan confused her. She was not in love with Shan, but delighted in his body and his friendship. With Taropat, it was another, darker matter. It would be so easy to give in and let the feelings spill out, in all their awful intensity. No matter how much she tried to reason with herself, every day the feelings deepened. She was sure Taropat was aware of it, that it was a prickle against his skin. What she did not know was how he felt about it. As far as she knew – and she had questioned Shan very carefully in the early stages of their relationship – Taropat had had no proper relationships since Tayven. He was still a man. He must desire it sometimes.

After the meal, Taropat and Shan elected to explore Hanana, and Ellony begged her mother to let her go with them. The idea of regular bedtimes was now a thing of the past, but Ellony had intuited her mother's strange mood and asked for permission simply because Varencienne might need her company. Varencienne tousled Ellony's hair and told her to go.

'Will you be all right here alone?' Shan asked.

Varencienne smiled wearily. 'Quite all right.'

He hesitated. 'You look . . . strained, worried about something.'

'I'm just having a few thoughts,' she said. 'I need to be alone.'

'We won't be long,' Shan said.

Taropat gave her a penetrating glance as they left the room, but he didn't ask her what was wrong.

After her companions had departed, Varencienne sat at the table for a while, finishing a bowl of buttered tea. Depression hung over her like an oily fog, an intensification of the way she'd felt on the descent from the mountains. She thought of Rav and imagined him as a little stranger, a Malagash. She shouldn't have left him in Magrast. In doing so, she had torn the ties that bound him to her. He would not know her now. And what of the vision she'd had of sending the dragon daughters to him? She needed to know whether it had affected him. She rubbed her hands over her face, pressed the heels of her palms against her eyes. In the darkness, she was conscious of the soft hum of foreign voices around her, the few other diners left in the room. She didn't understand their dialects. She belonged nowhere.

She lowered her hands, wiped a finger around the film of grease in her tea bowl, licked it, savouring the strong, almost rancid, buttery flavour. In the midst of despair, small pleasures. She must remember that.

As she left the dining room, dim lamps made mirrors of the windows. She caught a glimpse of her reflection. She did not know the woman she saw, her hair wound up in a makeshift turban of tasselled cloth, her body hidden in a swathe of woollen garments.

Upstairs she discovered a communal female washroom which contained a large shallow bath set into the floor, surrounded by wooden decking. Jugs and towels were strewn haphazardly on benches around the walls and bathrobes of cheap rough fabric hung from hooks next to the door. Two older women were sitting in the bath, chattering together, gesticulating wildly. They looked up, immediately silent, as Varencienne paused at the door. Then one of them spoke peremptorily and Varencienne's exhausted mind slowly translated the words. She was being invited to join them. She nodded her assent and went into the room where she peeled off her clothes and left them in an untidy pile near the threshold. Gratefully she eased herself into the warm water, which smelled deliciously of pine and earth.

The Hamagarid women, who introduced themselves as Lady Patar and Lady Sikim, asked her questions, half of which she could not understand, but she answered, haltingly, as best she could. She told them she was a traveller from the south, and that she might never go home. The women did not find this particularly curious and merely nodded, as if it were the most natural thing in the world. They were the wives of rich merchants and their husbands were presently attending a *honsha* at the temple – a mass audience with Aranepa. It would last for several hours, because the High Vana would allow everyone present to approach him, so that he might bestow his blessing via the touch of his hands on their heads. No one was allowed to speak to him, though, which further confirmed Varencienne's suspicions about Taropat's ambition to question the High Vana.

Lady Patar gestured at Varencienne's hands. 'You are of noble birth,' she said, neither question nor accusatory statement. Hands, of course, always gave such things away. Varencienne examined them and found that, beneath the dirt and despite the ragged nails, they were still the smooth unreddened hands of a princess.

She nodded. 'I am.'

'Not many venerables make the *lahta*,' said Lady Sikim. At Varencienne's bewildered expression, she said this was the term for a holy pilgrimage of deprivation, where one could experience the reality of the goddess in her natural environment.

'At first it was not what I wanted,' Varencienne replied. 'I was brought here by a man who . . . *took* me from my homeland.'

The women regarded her for a moment and Varencienne wondered if, by this frank admission, she had finally intrigued a Hamagarid. Then Lady Sikim said, 'He was sent to you, then. You were lucky.'

Lady Patar nodded in agreement.

'You are right,' Varencienne said in careful Hamagarid, 'Hamagara changes me in many good ways.' She poured water over her breasts and belly with cupped hands. 'But now, here in Hanana, I feel strange. My spirits are low. It is not what I expect.'

'Expectation always brings disappointment,' said Lady Patar. 'Let go of it.'

'I try.'

Both Hamagarids appeared perplexed by this statement. Trying was not really part of their vocabulary. 'Go to Aranepa,' Lady Sikim suggested. 'It is what you have come for.'

Varencienne smiled weakly. 'I will.'

She washed her hair in the fragrant water and rubbed off the grime of her journey. Bathing was like a return to the womb, comforting. When she emerged from the water, she felt less depressed and pleasantly drowsy. She dried herself on one of the voluminous towels on the benches and then lifted an item of her clothing from the heap. Now, thoroughly clean herself, she wanted to wear fresh garments. All she could do was stare at the dirty fabric in her hands, helpless and confused.

Lady Patar got out of the bath with a great deal of splashing. 'The innkeeper will wash them for you,' she said, obviously having divined Varencienne's thoughts, 'but a lady like you needs to wear something better than these travelling clothes to meet the High Vana. I would like to give you some of my own garments, for I have many with me.'

'You are very kind,' Varencienne said.

Lady Patar steepled her hands and bowed, a gesture that was faintly absurd in a naked, wet, middle-aged woman. 'It will give me pleasure,' she said.

After Varencienne and Patar had covered themselves with a couple of the bathrobes provided by the inn, Patar led the way to the room she shared with her husband. It was far bigger than the one Varencienne and her companions had been given and contained a huge bed, covered with an embroidered quilt. Open travelling cases on the floor spilled a variety of exotic fabrics: Lady Patar's robes and coats. She picked a few garments up, apparently at random, and handed them to Varencienne. 'You will look beautiful in these,' she said.

The garments were a long gown of soft green wool, the colour of pine leaves, and an overcoat of dark crimson, which was covered in embroidered serpents and birds. Patar also donated some fine silk undergarments, saying confidentially, 'If a woman knows secret richness touches her flesh, she walks taller.'

Varencienne knew she must not mutter an embarrassed offer to make some kind of payment for these gifts. A Hamagarid would be insulted by it. She bowed and thanked the lady again.

'You are not as lost as you believe,' said Lady Patar, briefly touching her shoulder.

Varencienne wished she had the vocabulary to talk in more depth to the woman, but she was so tired, she could not concentrate enough to try.

She went back to her room and lay down on one of the beds in her robe, her wet hair spread out over the pillow. Ellony and the men had not yet returned. Perhaps they had gone to the *honsha*. Varencienne yawned and turned onto her side, her hands beneath her cheek. She could feel herself drifting off to sleep and thought about getting beneath the covers, because the air was chill, but lacked the energy to move.

She awoke in darkness, absolutely alert, at first unable to recall where she was. Her hair felt stiff about her head, because she hadn't brushed it out before going to sleep. She remembered the bath, the Hamagarid ladies. The city was silent beyond the curtained windows. It must be very late. Varencienne lifted herself from the bed and squinted round the room. She could see, vaguely, the shapes of the mattresses on the floor and the bed next to hers. They were unoccupied. Why hadn't Ellony and the men returned? For a moment, she was frozen by the terror of abandonment. If something had happened to them, she would be truly alone in an unknown land.

A noise in the corner of the room made her jump. She peered into the shadows and made out a faint blue glow, but could not discern where it was coming from. The atmosphere in the room was utterly still, yet charged. Nothing felt real.

I am dreaming, she thought.

Something was moving towards her from the shadows, a slinking pale shape. The blue glow had resolved itself into a pair of burning eyes, low to the ground. Whatever – or whoever – approached her was crawling along the floor. She did not feel afraid, even though she was sure she should be.

But you are dreaming, she reminded herself. Whatever it is, it can't harm you. You can wake up.

She saw now that the pale shape was a large cat, a mountain leopard. It exuded a spectral light, which allowed her to see the faint dark markings on its silvery grey pelt, its huge paws, the pink of its nose leather. Only in a dream could such a creature pass through a closed door, or scale a sheer wall. The most sacred creature of the Hamagarids was visiting her dreams. She must use these moments wisely.

Slowly, afraid the vision might vanish at any moment, she rose from the bed to stand before the leopard. She bowed. 'Revered One, reveal to me the reason for my being here.'

The cat made a strange grunting sound and then, with a switch of its long tail, turned round and headed for the door, which now hung open. Varencienne hurried after the creature, pulling the bathrobe more tightly around her.

The inn slept. Varencienne could hear faint sounds of snoring coming from behind some of the closed doors. She followed the leopard to the stairs, watching the svelte movements of its shoulders as it descended.

The front door to the establishment was also open to the night and beyond it the streets were empty and still. The leopard walked with sure tread out into the city, its ears flat against its head in a feline expression of determination. Cat and woman padded through the winding alleys of Hanana, while the inscrutable cats' eyes of the air dragon, Paraga, gazed down upon them from virtually every wall. Flags hung limp in the motionless night, but a faint echo of devotional horns could be heard coming from the direction of the temple. The only light was that of the stars, and a few dim orange glows from the temple windows.

The leopard led Varencienne up a maze of twisting streets, towards a narrow gate in the citadel walls. By now, they were halfway up the Mountain of the Night. Beyond the gate, a pathway snaked towards the summit, lined by dwarf shrubs with shiny pointed leaves, their boughs laden with heavy pursed flower buds. The path was very steep and treacherous with spiky gravel. Varencienne now wished she'd paused to put on her boots, but why should she need boots in a dream?

She told herself she should stop believing the stones could hurt her, but no matter how she tried to convince herself of the aetheric nature of her reality, she could not dispel the experience of physical discomfort.

The leopard loped ahead of her and eventually she lost sight of it around a corner in the path. Shrines of white stone glowed in the darkness, half-hidden amongst the thick shrubs. Varencienne saw statues within them, garlanded with offerings of spring flowers. At some, incense still smouldered in bowls, lit by the last visitors before sundown. Ahead, the trail branched off in different directions. Varencienne paused, wondering where the leopard had gone. It was her guide. It should have waited for her.

She looked down and there on the bare path, which was warmed by the heart of the mountain, were footprints of snow, the spore of an animal.

The footprints glowed in the starlight: a trail leading upwards. They did not melt. Varencienne followed them. Her feet were now numb with cold, even though the stones beneath them were faintly warm.

After what felt like an hour of climbing, the path emerged at the summit of the mountain. Varencienne had expected to find a smoking crater, perhaps with a perilous track leading down into the earth, but instead she found herself before a huge motionless lake, whose waters looked like a reflection of the sky, filled with stars. There was no sign of the mountain leopard. The white tracks simply ceased at Varencienne's feet. She looked around herself, rubbing her arms against the cold. Vapour plumed from her mouth like the breath of an ice dragon.

I am awake, she thought. This cannot be a dream – yet how can it be real?

She heard a movement behind her and turned quickly, expecting to see an aetheric denizen of some kind, but what she saw was Taropat, just his face peering over the crest of the track. Again she experienced a shock of recognition and pleasure, quickly modified by tension.

191

'What are you doing here?' she demanded, followed by, 'Am I dreaming?'

Taropat finished his ascent and joined her on the gravelly path that led down to the lake. 'How can I answer that?' he said. 'If you are, you can't trust the testament of a dream character.'

Varencienne reached out and touched his arm. He was dressed in the clothes he'd worn last time she'd seen him and felt real enough. 'Then answer my first question. Why are you here?'

'I'm not sure,' Taropat replied. 'I followed something, a strange creature.'

'A leopard?'

'I didn't see. It was just a vague, pale shape.'

'We must be dreaming,' Varencienne said. 'Is it possible to share a dream, or are you just part of mine?'

Taropat shrugged.

'When I awoke in the inn,' Varencienne said, 'you weren't there, neither was Ellony or Shan. That cannot have been real.'

'It could,' Taropat said. 'We didn't return to the inn, but stayed in a free hostel near to the temple. It was a pretty basic experience, but we were told it would give us a better chance of attending the *honsha* tomorrow, as the priests allow guests from the temple hostel in first. We are supposed to rise an hour before dawn and spend the subsequent four hours in prayer and meditation. Then we'll have to give four hours labour to the temple. We weren't told what that would involve.' Taropat grimaced. 'But if that is the price of Aranepa's blessing, we decided we should pay it. We have no other currency now. Shan went back to tell you, but you weren't in our room. He presumed you'd gone out for a walk. He left a message, though.'

'I didn't find it.'

'Obviously.'

Varencienne shook her head vigorously. 'No, it can't be real. A mountain leopard couldn't have got into my room. I followed one here. Now it's gone.'

'Perhaps you are awake,' Taropat said, 'but the leopard was some kind of vision.' He reached out and pinched her arm sharply.

'Hey!' Varencienne cried, slapping his hand away.

'You felt that. I'd say you are awake. I know the ambience of dreams and visions. This doesn't feel like one.'

'Then we have to suppose we've both been led here for a reason.' She contemplated the lake for a moment. 'But there's nothing here.'

'There is a lot here,' Taropat said. 'This place reminds me strongly of

Lake Pancanara, where we found the Crown of Silence. It's humming with energy. Can't you feel it?'

Varencienne hugged herself more tightly. Her teeth were chattering from the cold. 'I'm shaking so much I can't feel anything else.'

Taropat hesitated for a moment, then took off his coat. 'Here,' he said.

Varencienne took it and wrapped it round her shoulders. 'It's my feet,' she said.

Taropat sat down and began to unlace his boots. Varencienne glanced at him, couldn't help noticing the way his hair fell around his face, parting at the back of his neck to reveal the precise knobs of his spine. Familiar feelings welled within her and she had to look away.

'Will these do?' Taropat asked.

She turned back to him and saw he'd pulled off his thick woollen socks, which he now held out to her. He had beautiful feet, pale as snow against the black stones.

'Thanks.' The socks were warm and damp. She resisted an impulse to smell them, but sat down beside him and pulled them on, suddenly conscious of being naked beneath her robe. This was not a time for lustful thoughts, even though, with every moment that passed, she felt increasingly that she was with Khaster Leckery, the man of her imaginings, the man she had created in her mind years ago. Perhaps that, more than anything, indicated she was dreaming after all.

'All the way here, I've fought my own mind, my own instincts,' she said, gazing out over the water. It was a test. She knew it was a test. If she was dreaming, it didn't matter, and if she wasn't, then maybe these things needed to be said.

'In what respect?' Taropat asked.

She glanced at him. 'About you. The moment when I stepped from the coach and saw you before me, all I could do was bow to you. It was absurd, but entirely beyond my will. I bowed to Khaster, a symbol.'

'Of what? Cowardice, decadence, pomposity? I could offer more suggestions.'

'No. Blinded honour. You are like a character from a story, who has strayed from the path, but strives for redemption.'

Taropat grimaced. 'That is about as real as your original fantasies about me, Lady Palindrake. I am not Khaster. How many times do you have to be told?'

'As many times as you have to be told otherwise. I have conspired in your fantasy of identity, tried to see this Taropat you insist on being. But sometimes, the veneer slips away and I see Khaster, the man in the portrait at Norgance, the man described to me by his sisters and mother . . . by his wife.'

Taropat uttered a scornful laugh. 'And what does Pharinet say of me? I'm intrigued. Do tell.'

'Are you still in love with her?'

'I was never in love with her. If I've ever been blind, my marriage to her was the occasion of it. I have never been in love. It's far too much trouble. What does she say about me?'

'Good things,' Varencienne said. 'She feels responsible for what happened.'

'Rightly so.'

'Sometimes feelings flow in directions we'd prefer they didn't. You know of this, don't you?'

Taropat considered for a moment, which surprised Varencienne. She had expected a heated response. 'You refer to my affair with Tayven Hirantel,' he said. 'Yes, I know that feeling, but I have no regrets for it now, and never have I behaved remotely like Pharinet.'

'Yes, you have,' Varencienne snapped. 'You treat Shan abominably. You take him for granted, like he's your slave or something. It makes me wince sometimes. What are you punishing him for? Do you love him, and want him in that way, but can't bear a repeat of what happened with Tayven?'

'Your imagination is fecund,' he said. 'Shan is like a son to me. I do not desire him, and never have. He is not Tayven, and I do not delude myself to think that he is. We bicker, as family do. It's no more than that.'

'Yes, it is. You hurt him. He wants you to acknowledge him, be proud of him, but you just carp and criticise and behave as if you're always looking for someone better, an apprentice to take his place.'

Taropat opened his mouth to speak, but Varencienne interrupted him before he could utter a word. 'I know what it is! Everyone you've loved has let you down in some way. So you've built up this defence and refuse to allow yourself to care about anyone. If you showed your feelings for Shan – it's irrelevant whether they're fatherly or otherwise – you're in danger of being hurt again. That's it, isn't it? I dare you to deny it. Taropat is a great magus, isn't he? Doesn't he "know himself", as a magus should?'

'Thank you for the analysis,' Taropat said coldly. 'Perhaps you are right, perhaps not, but ultimately it is not your concern, and I'd be grateful if you'd keep out of my private affairs. You think you know me, because you fell in love with a picture once. You don't know me at all.'

'I do. I've travelled with you for weeks, and in such circumstances people get to know one another very quickly.'

Taropat slapped a hand against the ground, sending up a spray of black gravel. 'Is this what we've come here for? Do you want to be my conscience? Stop trying to make claims on me.'

'I can't stop,' Varencienne said. 'Remember what I said about fighting my instincts? Well . . . ' She took a deep breath. 'I still love you.'

There was a silence.

'I can't deny it to myself,' Varencienne said, 'and whatever you think of it, at least acknowledge I'm brave enough to admit it.'

'Great Foy,' Taropat said beneath his breath. 'You are insane.'

'No, I'm completely sane. I don't expect a positive response from you. Far from it. You're too damaged.'

'Then why tell me of it? What good can it possibly do you? Where's your Malagash pride?'

'At the bottom of that damn lake!' she cried and got to her feet. 'I have shed my pride, along with many other things during the course of this journey. I'm awake, alive, full of feelings and thoughts. They are mine. I am not ashamed of them. I want to *be*. I want to be part of this world, not a spectator. I want to be real.' Her mind was whirling. What had possessed her to speak this way? She wanted to cry, but fought the tears. This was hideous, the worst of bad ideas.

Taropat did not speak and for some minutes, Varencienne stood rigid beside him, but eventually could not resist looking down at him. He held his head in his hands. Varencienne's first instinct was to apologise, but why should she apologise for honesty? 'Just know,' she said, 'that I love you. I will always love you. It's unconditional. There's no cost attached. I expect nothing from you, but I hope you can glean a small comfort from it, knowing that at least someone in the world really cares.'

Taropat did not move.

'Perhaps we should go now,' Varencienne said.

Taropat lowered his hands. 'The blindness,' he said, gazing at the lake. 'There is a message here, but I can't figure it.'

'What do you mean?'

'At Pancanara, I refused to surrender the Eye of the Dragon to the lake, and for a while I was physically blinded. I'd been an irritant to everybody during the quest and Pancanara was the turning point, but I didn't take the right path. This is a replay of some kind, a second chance, but I don't know what to do.'

'I wish I had the answer,' Varencienne said. 'More than anything, I wish that.' She paused. 'What exactly should you have done at Pancanara?'

'We had to surrender the three dragon artefacts in order to acquire the fourth. I was caught up in a frenzy of disillusion, anger and a lust for revenge, and wanted the Crown for myself. I also wanted to keep the Eye, unaware that once I surrendered the physical artefact, its power would be mine for eternity. Merlan took it from me and cast it into the lake. He took on my responsibility. Shan carried me into the water, to the city of angels. There, Tayven was given the crown. We were deemed worthy of having it, for all that we'd been through together. We took it to Bree, to Sinaclara, and that's where everything fell apart for the last time. I, who'd been the curse of the quest, was then responsible for the final destruction of our company. My rage scattered us. My rage at Valraven for always getting the better of me, for always meaning everything to everyone, for being the light that I could never be. *That* is the dark root of it. The rage fed on my terror of being a shadow to Valraven's sun. In denying this fear, I am still blind.' He looked at her in raw appeal. 'How do I reverse that here and now? It's impossible.'

Varencienne spoke carefully. 'Only you can be your liberator. You have come this far.'

Taropat rubbed a hand over his face, shaking his head. 'I don't know. All I do know is that no one, for millennia, had reached Pancanara, but *we* did it. That meant something. We all had our part, but I wouldn't play mine. I'm not in control, Taropat isn't in control, but I know that I, as Khaster, have to take responsibility for everything, and do it now! The sick energy of fear, of all that's happened to me, has dictated how I behave. It's like an outside force, determined to ruin anything good.'

Varencienne was silent for a moment, then said, 'Are we dreaming, Khas?'

'We've been through this,' he said.

'No. I meant that, in dreams, anything is possible. In a dream, you could have the Eye of the Dragon in your hand.'

He stared at her for a moment, then got to his feet. He held out a hand, and she took it, felt the warmth of him course up her arm. Without speaking, he led her down to the edge of the water. He gripped her fingers tightly and raised his free arm. 'I call upon the spirits of the primal waters!' he cried. 'I call upon all the gods and goddesses of the world. I call upon the power of the Dragon's Eye.'

The high cliffs around them rang with the echo of his words. The hair stood up on Varencienne's neck and arms.

'I surrender my power,' Taropat yelled, 'in the name of Azcaranoth, the Peacock Angel, and in the name of the True King!'

He flung his arm outwards, as if casting something from him, and for a moment, Varencienne swore she could see a spherical object shooting through the air. But there was no splash, no ripple. Only the silence of the peaks around them.

'Now you can truly see,' she said.

CHAPTER TWENTY

The Words of Aranepa

Shan was awoken by the sound of a bell. He opened his eyes to find Ellony curled up against him like a little cat. At the doorway to the dormitory stood a robed Vana, ringing a handbell. Around them, people were beginning to stir. The air in the long wooden dormitory was fusty with the smell of humanity, all of whom were bundled side by side like packed fish. Babies began to whine, men to belch and stretch, while the women uncoiled themselves from their sleep-tangled hair. These were not well-to-do people like those who lodged at inns like 'Wind, Rain, Wind'. These pilgrims had no money or goods to barter with the Vanas and thereby gain a good seat at the afternoon's *honsha*. Shan knew that he and his companions were no better than these people. They had used all but the last of their currency to secure a relatively comfortable room, but it was a waste of funds.

Shan glanced at the pallet beside him and saw that it was empty. Perhaps Taropat had changed his mind about attending the *honsha*, although that was unlikely. Shan sighed. He'd given up trying to predict Taropat's movements.

Shaking Ellony to wake her, Shan sat up on the hard bed.

'Where's Taro?' the girl demanded at once.

'I don't know,' Shan replied. 'I think we should go along with the crowd and find some breakfast.'

The horde of pilgrims descended in a slow, babbling mêlée to a vast dining hall on the next floor down, where the ceiling was low and supported by rough beams. The hubbub of their voices filled the air along with the smell of warm milk and oats. This was Aranepa's gift to the devoted: breakfast, but hardly a sumptuous meal. Novices from the temple, dressed in dark robes, came round the long tables to dispense porridge from vast tureens. Each pilgrim had a wooden bowl and spoon before them on the table. Shan bowed his head to the novice who approached him and held up his bowl. Just as the grey-white stream was being poured into it, he saw Taropat enter the room. Ellony waved and called out and Taropat came over to them.

'I thought you'd changed your mind about the *honsha*,' Shan said. He shuffled up the bench so there was room for Taropat to sit down. The man looked haggard, his clothes and hair unkempt. There was, however, a certain shine to him. 'Where have you been?'

Taropat didn't answer for a moment as he held out his bowl for porridge, but then he placed it carefully before him, staring at the table.

'Taropat, what's the matter?' Shan said.

Taropat looked up and fixed him with a rather fevered gaze. 'Have I ever told you I loved you?' he said.

Drunk or raving? Shan wondered. He shook his head. 'What's wrong?'

'I *do* love you,' Taropat said, 'and I want you to know you are more of a man than I ever could have envisaged when I first found you. I have never had a son of my blood, but you are certainly the son of my heart, even though my vanity urges me to remind you I'm not old enough to be your father. Not physically, in any case.' He began to eat.

Shan stared at him, wondering if, at last, the final seams of sanity had burst and what was left of Taropat was leaking out completely. 'What happened?' he asked dourly. Without question, *something* had happened.

Taropat wiped his mouth fastidiously. 'I met Varencienne last night. We were both lured from our respective beds by a strange creature, which to Ren looked like a leopard. I don't know what I saw. But the creature led us up the holy mountain to the lake at the summit. It was very similar to Pancanara. I replayed my part of the Lakes Quest there, the part I played badly before. Symbolically, I relinquished the Eye of the Dragon of my own free will. It was . . . *cleansing*.'

'Hence the declaration of love?' Shan queried warily.

Taropat shook his head. 'No, that is the fruit of a conversation I had with Ren. She thinks I abuse you.'

'I see.' Shan glanced down at Ellony who was frowning at her food, as if it was the most absorbing and interesting thing in the world. She had uncanny awareness for someone so young. 'Where is Ren?' Shan asked sharply.

'She has returned to the inn to sleep. She feels she has nothing to gain from attending the *honsha*.'

'Are you all right, Taropat?'

He nodded briefly. 'Yes, completely. There is something else I must say. You are not my apprentice any more.'

'What?'

'There is nothing more I can teach you. Know that I am fully satisfied with your progress and hold you in high regard. If I have ever offended you, I am sorry. I trust we can now be friends, as equals.'

Shan felt as if he'd woken up into a strange, alien reality. This was more absurd than a dream. 'Are you sure you're all right?' he said.

'Yes. I know this sounds abrupt and you probably think I've lost my mind, but in fact I feel in full possession of it for the first time in years.'

Shan had become inured to Taropat's strange shifts of mood and eccentric behaviour. Now there was nothing else to say. He would just have to wait and see whether this apparent change of heart was genuine. A needle of jealousy pricked him that Taropat had apparently spent the night with Varencienne. He realised that part of him did not want Taropat to change, to become whole again, because then he might be more like Varencienne's fantasy figure of Khaster. A changed Taropat might not be celibate, and in Shan's eyes, no man alive could resist Varencienne.

After the meal, the pilgrims were herded into a temple courtyard, where a high-ranking Vana in ceremonial robes chanted at them. Most of the crowd knew when to mutter responses to the ancient prayers. Shan sat with bowed head. After the space and solitude of the mountain journey, this procedure felt too regulated and perfunctory to be spiritual.

Four hours of this was torture. After only an hour, Shan was ready to fall back to sleep. Taropat's eyes were closed, as if he travelled some inner continent, while Ellony stared at her fingers, which she moved in curling gestures – obviously absorbed in imaginary play. Whatever mysteries Hanana had to impart, Shan was sure none were to be found here. It was a religious placebo for tourists. Only the fact that he would have to fight his way through a huge seated crowd prevented Shan from getting up and leaving. He also suspected he might be stopped by the Vanas. He had been given a bed for the night and a breakfast meal. Labour was expected from them; he was sure the priests would make sure they got it. Unable to pray or meditate, he spent the remaining time fretting about Varencienne. He was terrified he was about to lose her to his mentor and couldn't stop himself visualising a series of upsetting scenarios. He imagined finding Taropat and Ren together, her telling him she no longer had feelings for him. But she had never told him she cared for him, in any case. Once they left Hamagara, their relationship would undoubtedly end. She was Valraven Palindrake's wife and belonged to a different world. Only the magic of this country had brought them together, like shooting stars colliding briefly in the night sky. Shan had enjoyed dalliances with many women during his travels with Taropat, but he'd never experienced an enduring relationship. It was different, terrifying. He hated the power a beloved could have: the power to wound and destroy.

But you have given her this power, he told himself. You allowed yourself to fall in love.

These nagging thoughts, though depressing, effectively passed the time. Shan only realised the torment of the prayers was over when Ellony nudged him in the ribs and hissed, 'I think we can go.' He smiled down at her, his heart clenching painfully in his chest. Ellony was like a daughter to him now. He stretched his cramped legs and got to his feet. Ellony took his hand.

'I wonder what is planned for us next,' Taropat said with a wry smile.

Shan could not bring himself to return it. Despite Taropat's earlier unexpected words, Shan could only look upon him now as a rival. Four hours of concentrated fear had done nothing to alleviate the condition.

The high temple was surrounded by courtyards of workshops. In some of them, yarn was dyed and woven into fabric which would eventually make up the robes of the Vanas. In others, corn was milled, while yet more were concerned with the creation of devotional cakes. The temple complex was vast, and it was clear other areas must be devoted to different industries. Shan and his companions were herded, along with many others, to the bakery. Here, in stifling conditions, they stood in a line shaping dough into flat circular cakes. In the late afternoon, a whistle was blown and several Vanas clanged gongs at the threshold of the workshop. The labourers shuffled past a series of standpipes, where they were allowed to wash their faces and hands of flour. No one looked smartly dressed and nearly every face registered tiredness. Shan doubted that such a scruffy lacklustre bunch would be given prominent positions in the presence of Aranepa.

Shan's suspicions presently proved correct. The *honsha* took place in a vast hall, where everyone was required to sit upon the floor, which was inlaid with magical symbols. By the time the workers reached it, the hall was already more than half-full of the monied individuals who could afford to buy decent positions for themselves and their families. The Vanas were attempting to create some kind of spiritual atmosphere. Some blew upon sacred horns around the edge of the room, while others played chimes. In a corner, upon a low dais, female Vanas chanted in perfect unison. Shan suspected this was as much of a chore for the priesthood as the earlier tedious labour had been for him. None of the

Vanas looked particularly interested in the proceedings. Despite the efforts of the musicians, the hall was dominated by a muted cacophony: children's babble hushed by parents, low mutterings, coughing and shuffling. The crowd had made the air hot and stuffy; now Vanas lit thick, heavy incense, which did not improve conditions.

Shan and the others sat near the door, where at least a fresh breeze made it easier to breathe. After twenty minutes or so, great gongs were sounded and the crowd more or less fell to silence.

Curtains lifted at the back of the hall to reveal a circular gold dais containing a magnificent carved throne of wood, ivory and precious metals. On this was seated a diminutive veiled figure, presumably the venerable Aranepa. On either side stood tall female Vanas, waving immense fans of peacock feathers over their spiritual leader. A severe-faced older male Vana, dressed in dark purple robes that left one shoulder bare, came forward to stand before the crowd. He bowed to them, his long braids nearly touching the floor, and told them that Aranepa would bestow blessings upon them. First, the Revered One would recite a short prayer, which might or might not be followed by prophecies. After that, every person present might come forward to receive the blessing of his touch.

'That can't be possible,' Shan whispered to Taropat, his deliberate ignoring of the man forgotten in a moment of disbelief. 'It will take for ever.'

Taropat shrugged. 'We have paid for it,' he murmured back, 'as has everyone else present. Let's just wait and see.'

The feet of the boy on the throne did not reach the floor. He was dressed in magnificent tapestried robes of emerald and crimson fabric that engulfed his body. His veil was suspended from an ornate headdress and his golden slippers were covered in pearls. Only his small brown hands could be seen, resting gently upon the arms of the throne. And now he spoke. Though he was small, his high voice carried far. He recited in a dialect unknown to Shan, and even Ellony beside him looked perplexed. 'It is the ancient language,' she said.

The prayer went on for some minutes as the musical voice filled the hall. Shan was no longer aware of the vast crowd around him. All he heard was the song of Aranepa. There was no doubt he had conjured a different atmosphere. What had been tawdry only moments before was now sacrosanct and mysterious. The boy stopped speaking for a moment and raised his arms while the officiating priest dropped to his knees, his arms spread out upon the floor in front of him.

'The age of the dragons approaches,' Aranepa said in a clear common Hamagaran tongue. 'All that was sundered will unite in the cauldron of

202

the heart. The air will come to the water and the fire will make steam within it. Air dries water, but water quenches fire. Earth suffocates air, yet can be burned by the flames. If the elements are not in accord, then the world weeps. But one will come who is the avatar of Venotishi, who controls the elements. Look for his sign, in the skies, in the oceans, in the spoor of the beasts, in the smoke of the hearth fire. For he must come, this man of silence who will govern the elements.'

Shan's flesh went cold. It seemed as if the boy was speaking directly to him and his companions, but surely this could not be so. Perhaps every nation on earth desired a deliverer to rid them of chaos, disharmony and fear. It was not surprising that the Hamagarids desired the same as he did. He glanced at Taropat, who returned his gaze as if to indicate he shared the same uncertainty.

Then Ellony said, 'He knows us. He knows we're here.'

There was silence now, as everyone present absorbed the meaning of Aranepa's words. Perhaps each person perceived a personal message within them. Then Vanas came forward to conduct people to the dais. Shan watched the processions of oldsters, lurching lame, blind people, young children, pregnant mothers, as well as ordinary men and women go one by one to kneel before the High Vana. Aranepa said nothing and his face could not be seen. Only his hands, somehow grave in the precision of their movements, rested briefly upon each bowed head. The devotees were not allowed to speak, even to thank the boy, but ducked their heads in gratitude and went back to their place. But Shan would never forget their faces. As each person turned away from Aranepa, they were radiant with pure joy, compassion and understanding. These qualities shone from them like a magical light. It brought tears to his eyes.

It took over an hour before the devotees at the back of the hall started to make their way to the dais. To Shan, the whole room had become charged with ecstasy. He was no longer cynical. He wanted to feel the touch of those hands himself, discover whether it would affect him in the same way.

When it came to their turn, Taropat indicated that Ellony should go with the priest first. Children were allowed to take an adult with them, so Shan stood up hurriedly before Taropat took the opportunity. The crowds parted as he and the girl followed the Vana to the front of the hall.

Aranepa was a statue robed in veils, motionless, somehow inhuman. They knelt before him and Shan could hear the swish of the fans as the Vanas wafted them through the air. He bowed his head and from the corner of his eye saw the boy reach out to touch Ellony's dark head.

After a moment, the High Vana withdrew his hands quickly and turned in his seat to the officiating priest who stood next to him. This action conjured a ripple of concerned muttering from the crowd. The priest leaned down to the boy, listened to words Shan could not hear. Then he spoke quietly in Shan's ear. 'He asks, where is the other one?'

Shan stared at the priest dumbly for a moment, then pointed back up the hall. 'He will come next,' he said.

'No,' said the Vana, 'not a man, a woman. Aranepa asks where the woman is.'

'Mama,' Ellony breathed.

'Does he means Varencienne?' Shan whispered to the priest. 'Varencienne Palindrake?'

The Vana murmured in the boy's ear, who said something in return.

'The sea dragon woman,' the Vana said to Shan. 'She is the one.'

'She is at an inn,' Shan said, 'nearby. Must I fetch her?'

The Vana looked into his eyes, his expression as inscrutable as the face of the mountains. 'You must come to the Gate of the Sky, to the east of the temple, in two hours' time,' he said. 'Aranepa has blessed you. He would speak with your party in private.'

'All of us?' Shan asked sharply.

'Your party,' said the Vana. 'This is what is asked of you. Depart at once.'

Shan took Ellony's hand, bowed his head in respect, and rose to his feet. Behind him, he found a sea of curious faces, all of whom must be wondering what the whispered conversation had been about. Shan and Ellony were outsiders, foreigners. Why should they be singled out for privilege? A host of eyes watched them as they picked their way back to the door. This was far more than they could have hoped for. It proved to Shan that their journey had not been in vain.

CHAPTER TWENTY-ONE

Hamagarid Magic

Varencienne spent the day investigating the city, her spirits considerably higher than the night before. She replayed constantly in her mind the events at the mountain top, the brief closeness she'd shared with Taropat. In fact, she found it difficult to think of him as Taropat now, convinced that the man who'd shown himself to her the previous evening was really Khaster Leckery, the core of him that remained. Buoyant, she smiled at stall-holders in the market and got into conversation with a family of farmers at an inn where she paused to take lunch. At breakfast, Lady Sikim had told her of a broker where she might exchange her remaining trinkets for coin. The lady accompanied her to the exchange office, saying she was quite happy to do the negotiating for her new friend, and Varencienne believed she'd received a very good rate because of Sikim's involvement. Her purse was comfortingly heavy at her belt. After lunch she visited the city gardens and spent a carefree hour feeding some exotic birds with a group of children she met. The birds were similar to peacocks, with trailing tails of crimson and gold. Tame as dogs, they came to take seed from her hand and eyed her sideways with uncanny wisdom.

She returned to 'Wind, Rain, Wind' in the late afternoon, having been invited to dinner with the ladies Sikim and Patar and their families. Walking through streets that had begun to empty for the night, she took pride in having spent the day alone in a strange city. She had met people, talked to them in their own language, made friends. She had done it by herself. The old Varencienne would never had been able to do that. She'd have been like a fish drowning in air, ignorant of what to do and how to behave. Now she would spend an evening in Hamagarid company and, being more alert and joyful than when she'd met the ladies, derive more pleasure from their company and show them she could be good company too. She could not help feeling slightly disappointed when she went into her room and found Taropat, Shan and Ellony waiting for her. Taropat and Shan were sitting on one of the beds, while Ellony was sprawled on a mattress at their feet.

'Where have you been?' Taropat demanded. There was no hint of Khaster in his voice.

'I thought you were spending the day at the temple,' Varencienne answered, taking off her coat. Shan and Taropat shared a conspiratorial glance. The atmosphere in the room was tense. She guessed they'd been speaking about her just before she entered.

'Something quite amazing happened,' Shan said. 'Aranepa has asked to meet you.'

'Me? Are you sure?'

'It's true,' Ellony said, propping herself up on her elbows. She told the story quickly before the men had the chance. 'We must go back there now, Mama. It's very important.'

'I'm just about to have dinner with friends, though. I met a couple of Hamagarid women here and they've been very kind and helpful to me. I don't want to appear rude by not turning up for the meal.'

'Don't be ridiculous,' Taropat said. 'If you let them know the reason, they'll more than understand.'

'You don't *want* to go, do you?' Shan said, accusingly.

Varencienne shrugged. 'The worship of individuals makes me uneasy,' she said. 'It all seems a bit false.'

'But the boy's asked for you!' Taropat said. 'Doesn't that mean anything to you?'

'We're foreigners, unusual,' Varencienne replied. 'It's not unlikely Aranepa and the Vanas have already heard about us and are curious, that's all.' She smoothed the new clothes Patar had given her; Taropat looked her up and down.

'Where did you get that fancy outfit?' he asked severely. 'I hope you haven't spent the last of our funds.'

'*My* funds, if you don't mind!' Varencienne spat. 'In fact, these clothes were given to me by one of the women I told you about. They looked after me while you were off seeking enlightenment from the master.'

'You should have come with us,' Shan said.

Varencienne laughed coldly. 'After what Ellie just told me about your day? I think not!'

'It was worth it,' Shan said. 'I was just as sceptical as you are. Don't you trust my word?'

206

Varencienne sighed heavily. 'All right, I'll come. Don't look at me like that.'

'Aranepa did appear to speak directly about our situation,' Taropat said. 'We might be reading things into his words that we want to find, but I think we have to go and find out for ourselves.'

'I suppose you're right,' Varencienne said. 'He could have been talking about Val.'

Taropat gave her a hard glance, but said nothing.

'Aranepa touched my head and filled me with light,' Ellony said. 'I didn't imagine it. I think he has a lot of power.'

Varencienne looked into her daughter's eyes and saw the pleading there. Ellony wanted her to soften, to share the adventure. 'I know, sweetness. I do want to meet him. It's just that I've had a good day wandering around by myself, and I was looking forward to this evening. But perhaps we can have dinner tomorrow with the Hamagarid ladies, then you can meet them too.'

'We might not still be here by tomorrow,' Taropat said. 'It depends on what Aranepa says to us.'

'I presume any decisions we make will be by consensus,' Varencienne said.

'You were the one anxious to get home a few weeks ago.'

'And you were the one who forced me to come here. Accept there are unforeseen consequences to your actions. I might choose not to return to Caradore at all.'

'But what about Rav and Papa?' Ellony cried in alarm. 'What about Everna and Pharry? We have to go home, Mama. They'll be worried about us. We can always come back another time.'

'I know,' Varencienne said. 'I'm sorry, Ellie. I didn't mean to scare you. I'm afraid your uncle Taro is getting on my nerves and I over-reacted. I know we have to go back, but in some ways it would be nice to stay, wouldn't it?'

'Hamagara is part of us now,' Ellony said. 'We'll never really leave, and we know the path, so we can find our way back.'

'Wise words,' said Taropat, ruffling Ellony's hair.

She smiled up at him. 'Don't make Mama angry. She won't do what you want otherwise.'

'That is simple feminine behaviour,' said Taropat. He looked up at Varencienne, grinning. 'Are you ready to leave, princess?'

Varencienne went to Lady Patar's room and told her what had happened. The woman hugged Varencienne tightly. 'I knew there was something special about you,' she said. 'I hope you will tell me what occurs at your meeting.'

'I will,' Varencienne said. She hugged the woman in return. 'Thank you, Lady Patar. You and Lady Sikim have done so much for me.'

'A pleasure,' replied the Hamagarid. 'It is Venotishi's will.' She smiled wryly. 'But we didn't do that much!'

'To a stranger, the smallest gesture of friendship means a great deal,' Varencienne said, proud of the fluency of her words. She steepled her hands and bowed, and Patar did likewise.

Varencienne and her companions found their way to the Gate of the Sky on the east side of the temple. It was a magnificent carved arch, covered in representations of boiling clouds, which were painted in bright cerulean shades of blue. The heads of wind dragons could be seen poking whiskery snouts between the folds of the clouds. The Vana who had been officiating at the *honsha* earlier was waiting for them near the gateway, in a room that overlooked a garden of drooping evergreens and ponds. The man bowed to the visitors. 'I am Khanak,' he said, 'servant of Aranepa. He will meet with you in the garden.'

Without further explanation, the man led the way through a red doorway onto the soft turf beyond. In the twilight, white cranes high-stepped through the pools, like girls clad in flouncy ball gowns. Moths fluttered dizzily across the lily pads. A pagoda-like summerhouse nestled amongst trees, its verandah hanging over the water of the largest pool. Here, by the light of lanterns, a small figure could be seen sitting in a high-backed wicker chair.

Khanak crossed an ornamental bridge that led to the verandah and the visitors followed. They found cushions had been set out on the floor at Aranepa's feet for their comfort. Incense that smelled of flowers burned in a bowl beside them. The boy was still veiled, but once his guests were seated, he carefully revealed himself: a delicately handsome creature with serious eyes. He looked directly at Ellony and said, 'Do you know me?'

'Yes,' Ellony replied gravely. 'You are the one we met on the mountain.'

Varencienne recognised him now. The priest was he whom they had taken to be the boy's guardian, divested of the cumbersome garments and the scarves that had all but obscured his face.

'I knew, when I first saw you, that you were entrusted with a great responsibility,' Aranepa said to them. He gazed directly at Varencienne. 'You are she who is the avatar of Foy. You have come to this land, as others came before you, but where they sought to conquer, you seek to understand and to heal.'

'I did not intend to come here,' Varencienne said, feeling she should be honest. 'In fact, I was brought against my will.'

Aranepa closed his eyes briefly, during which Varencienne felt that other, non-physical, eyes gazed upon her. 'You come in rags, all of you,' Aranepa said. 'You come in rags of the soul: a broken company and a disillusioned priestess. Barefoot you came to the mountain and showed your innermost selves to it. Whether you know so or not, you come with good intention.'

'Do you know of the empire beyond your boundaries?' Taropat asked.

Aranepa inclined his head. 'We know of it. We know too that even though it has ignored us for centuries, a new emperor has come to the throne who is in the cacophony of madness. He is driven by a single vision of fear, and will seek to impose his beliefs upon every corner of the world, in order to feel safe. His darkness would have found its way here.'

'Would have?' Taropat said carefully.

Again Aranepa blinked slowly and inclined his head. 'There are darker forces, those that threaten Paraga himself. Long has the Lord of the Sky hidden in the furthest peaks of Hamagara, fleeing the tumultuous desires of the Sea Dragon Queen. But the time has come for him to re-emerge, to clothe himself once more in his full glory. The emperor of fire cannot save himself, no matter how he tries, but what comes after may be worse, unless those with clear sight work in unity to prevent it.'

'You spoke of a man of silence earlier on, one who would come to vanquish chaos,' Taropat said. 'We believe in a True King, a man who embodies all that is divine kingship, the link between the people and the land. Are these two the same?'

'They are. But the True King must first wander the tunnels of the underworld and experience the noise of his own madness. Unless he knows the nature of what he opposes, has smelled its foul breath and clasped it to himself, he cannot overcome it.'

'Do you know who he is, this man of silence?' Shan asked.

'Yes,' Aranepa replied.

For a moment, no one spoke, but Varencienne knew in her heart what Aranepa would say. She was afraid of Taropat's reaction.

'The True King,' said Aranepa, 'is the Lord of Caradore to the south, a son of the sea people. He has men of secret sorcery behind him, whom he cannot see. Their cunning moves the wheels of fate in their favour, for his power over the elements will bring them greater power. This the spirits have revealed to us. The Dragon Heir will hold the banner for the new aeon.' He turned to Varencienne. 'You and your kin, and their empires, are on the path of the Way of Light. It is the great stillness, the great chaos. It is the ultimate harmony born of the terrible conflict of the elements in their eternal becoming. Within this state, the silence can be born, where the cruel line of time which promises only death becomes like Paraga, a form of flux, a circle, wherein all things do not perish, but flow into birth and constant rebirth. All beings borne upon this ocean of silent becoming are on the Way of Light. It is not the long path, it is the short path, and that is the most perilous.'

Varencienne was overcome with emotion. These words, coming from the mouth of a young boy, were more real than any she'd heard before. She put her hands to her face, covered her nose and mouth with her fingers. 'Thank you,' she said.

Aranepa beckoned her closer and she knelt before him. He placed his hands briefly on the crown of her head and a shiver of heat coursed down from his fingers through her spine. 'You have seen it,' Aranepa said. 'Foy has shown you the image of empires rising and falling. The tension that both binds and repels them is the path to the Way of Light. You are here for a reason, for you are one of its most important avatars.'

Varencienne knelt with bowed head, her hands clasped in her lap. Light coursed through her, held her in its radiance. She wondered whether finally Taropat could feel what was right and true. Aranepa had never met the Dragon Lord, and was free of prejudice. If only Valraven could be here to hear these words and feel the truth of them.

In the silence, Taropat cleared his throat and then spoke guardedly. 'There are others who believe Palindrake should be king,' he said, 'but you should know that the lord of Caradore is . . . damaged. Dark influences of the empire corrupted him. I question that he is the right choice.' For Taropat, these were measured words.

Aranepa nodded thoughtfully. 'I am aware of the Dragon Heir's path,' he said, 'but it changes nothing. No man is fit to be the light of the land if he has not looked into the darkness. It has always been this way. The True King is beyond ordinary human considerations, he is beyond good and evil, this is why he can bring the silence, for the conflict of right and wrong is surpassed. In silence, he is both good and evil, and also neither of them. He must be larger in spirit than any other man and know all of creation. Like the gods themselves, he must be capable of the ultimate in cruelty and compassion. He should not seek to rule to gain power but to embody the divine, its tension and its flow. That is a lesson learned by only the hardest trials. The man of silence sacrifices himself to the land. It is his duty and his purpose.'

Taropat sighed, but Varencienne butted in. 'What if the Dragon Heir is afraid?' she asked.

'Only a fool would not be at first,' Aranepa replied, 'a fool or a person seeking vainglory, power over others and riches. The Lord of Caradore does not seek these things, and never has done, not in his darkest moments of isolation and ignorance. That is why he is the one.'

'You do not know him,' Taropat said. 'In visions, you see a possible future, a possible perfection, but that future has been spoiled.'

'Look within,' said Aranepa. 'Once you were driven by your passions and terror. Now they have become ingrained, a habit. In the light of dawn, free of all fear, there is no reason to hate. Hatred fades away like the dew.'

Varencienne glanced at Taropat's frowning face. She could not believe he was ready to relinquish his hatred of Valraven. It would be too easy.

'What must we do, Lord Aranepa?' she asked, breaking the silence. 'Can you tell us how to proceed from here?'

Aranepa turned to her. 'I cannot see the whole design. When you leave this land, you are beyond the influence of its spirits and gods, except for one. All I can tell you is that I have consulted the guardians of Hamagara and that a gift will be imparted to you, a gift that will be a great responsibility.'

'What is it?' she asked.

Aranepa reached into the neck of his robe and removed from his throat a pendant hanging on a golden chain. It was the seal of the Palindrakes that Varencienne had given to him on the mountainside. 'I have worn this since I received it,' Aranepa said. 'I learned much from its memories. Khanak and I will take you to the Mountain of the Night through the underground path. You must take the amulet with you, for at the holy lake the essence of Paraga will return to Foy. He will go with you to the land beyond. This is our gift to you, for the elemental dragons must be reunited by the man of silence.'

'I will do it,' Varencienne said.

Shan reached for her hand, squeezed it. She turned to look into his face, wondering what he thought about Aranepa's words, but all she saw in Shan's expression was devotion. He might well end up loyal to Valraven simply because of her. If so, she could not see that as a bad thing.

'Aranepa,' Taropat said. 'If Valraven Palindrake *must* be king, how can he be healed?'

'In the same way you will be,' Aranepa replied. 'It has already begun.'

Varencienne would carry the image of Taropat as he was then for the rest of her life. He knelt upon one knee, the other raised, upon which he rested an arm. With the other hand, he cupped his chin, shaking his head. He considered, for the first time, whether Tayven and Merlan were right after all. It was a historic moment.

The underground tunnel to the mountain top had at one time been used intensively as a ritual road, but since the days when Foy had brought her influence to Hamagara, some of the old ways had been abandoned and the veneration of Paraga had been superseded by that of Venotishi, who was regarded as equal to Foy in both fierceness and power and therefore able to keep the Dragon Queen under control. The walls of the tunnels had been carved and painted in antiquity and, owing to the subterranean conditions, had been preserved almost in their entirety. Aranepa and Khanak did not appear to be in any hurry. They allowed their guests to stroll slowly through the passages, examining the images of dragons, spirits and deities. The inscrutable mask of the mountain leopard was represented often.

Varencienne told Aranepa what had happened to her and Taropat the previous evening. 'Did you send the leopard to us?' she asked.

'Not consciously,' he replied. 'I have been aware of your presence in Hanana, and knew a certain event had to take place before we could meet.'

'Then it was one of many such events,' Varencienne said. 'Taropat should tell you about his quest for the Crown of Silence.'

'It's a long story,' Taropat said.

'I do not know it,' Aranepa replied. 'Please tell me.'

By the time Taropat had finished his narrative, they had come to the end of the tunnel and emerged into the crater at the summit of the mountain. All was still and the surface of the lake reflected the stars like a gigantic scrying bowl.

Aranepa came to stand beside Varencienne. 'You must not worry about your husband,' he said. 'He will wear this crown.'

'He does not want to,' Varencienne said. 'That is the problem.'

'You cannot convince him. Foy will do that. I can tell you little, but I know that beyond this land, events are in progress. When you return, all will have changed.'

'I hope so,' Varencienne said. She glanced at Taropat. 'There may be other difficulties to face.'

Aranepa made no response to this, but Khanak came forward and placed a hand on Varencienne's shoulder. 'Are you prepared to undertake the responsibility now facing you?' he asked.

Varencienne frowned. 'Mine alone? I thought it belonged to all of us.'

'You, as the passive avatar of Foy, must be the one to channel Paraga,' Aranepa said.

Varencienne studied him for a moment. 'What must I do to achieve that?'

'I will call upon the winds, who are the servants of Paraga,' Aranepa replied. 'Paraga will ride them and enter the talisman at your neck, but he must be conducted in the correct manner, through the *migra*.'

'What's that?' Varencienne asked.

Aranepa gestured to Khanak, who produced a pouch of dark cloth from the belt of his robe. This he unwrapped and held the contents out for display. Varencienne saw a few pale objects in the dim light.

'What are they?'

'Fragments of bone, said to have come from a wind-drake,' Khanak said. 'However, we now regard all spirit beings as aetheric in nature and do not believe they have physical bodies as such. These bones undoubtedly are avian in origin. They are very ancient.'

Varencienne shivered. The bones, though small, were sinister. 'And what must I do with them?'

'To conduct the essence of Paraga, they must be inserted into your skin, at the neck,' Khanak said.

Varencienne laughed nervously. 'I don't like the sound of that.'

Aranepa touched her reassuringly with light fingers. 'There is nothing to fear. The bones are sharp and Khanak is skilled at inserting them. You will feel hardly anything.'

Varencienne rubbed her upper arms. 'Even so . . . '

'The shards are kept scrupulously clean,' Khanak said. 'They are wrapped permanently in antiseptic leaves. There will be no risk of infection.'

Varencienne uttered a sound of discomfort.

'I will do it,' Ellony said suddenly, in a determined voice.

Varencienne glanced down at her daughter. 'No, Elly. If anyone has to do this, it will be me.'

'But you don't want to.'

'I'm just nervous,' Varencienne said. 'I don't want you to be burdened with this heritage until later in life.'

'I already am, and it is not a burden,' Ellony said. 'I'm not afraid of having the shards in me.'

Varencienne detected a slight note of criticism in Ellony's voice. 'I will do it, Elly,' she said, severely. 'Say nothing more.'

Ellony opened her mouth to protest, but Varencienne gave her a stern glance, which was enough to keep her silent.

Khanak said everyone should arrange themselves in a circle, but for Varencienne, whom he placed in the centre, facing Aranepa. Once this was done, the Vana positioned Varencienne's arms away from her body, bent at the elbow, the palms facing upwards.

'Now we must meditate together,' Khanak said, 'and enter the realms of the unseen.'

Softly he began to speak, instructing the company to regulate their breathing and become aware of the life essence coursing through their bodies.

Halfway through, Varencienne opened her eyes and looked around. Everyone else still had their eyes closed. Taropat and Shan stood to either side of Aranepa, Shan with his head bowed. He had been un-characteristically quiet for some time. Varencienne sensed he was unhappy that she had become closer to Taropat. Perhaps she should reassure him later. Would that be dishonest?

She gazed beyond the group to the walls of the crater, where ancient, wind-sculpted temples glowed faintly in the darkness. She imagined silver-pelted leopards prowling amongst the intricate carvings, their hot breath steaming, their eyes shining.

Now Khanak and Aranepa began to chant softly in an ancient tongue, and a gentle breeze lifted Varencienne's hair from her back.

Gradually the chant became louder, more aggressive. Their voices seemed to gust from their bodies like an approaching storm. A wind had started up to stir the still air.

While Aranepa continued to chant, Khanak stepped forward, the shards of bone in his hands. Varencienne, extremely squeamish, instinc-tively closed her eyes again. Khanak touched her shoulders briefly, then pulled the neck of her robe apart. Varencienne swallowed convulsively, wondering whether she would faint. She felt the prick of sharpness against the soft skin of her throat and braced herself for pain, but all she could feel was a slight pressure. This was repeated in three other places. Her flesh tingled, but pain still did not come.

Now Khanak placed his hands gently against her neck, filling her with a burning heat. She felt lightheaded, sure she would lose consciousness.

After a few moments, the Vana stepped away from her. The wind rushed around her in a circle, as if she stood in the eye of a tornado. Its voice was becoming louder and it was now difficult to hear the Hamagarids through it.

Varencienne opened her eyes and thought she could actually see the hurtling element of air. Shapes writhed within the wind, creatures of dust and flying leaves. The Palindrake crest was hot against her skin: a necklace of fire.

Aranepa and Khanak were shouting now, commanding the spirits of the air to manifest. Even though they still chanted in an ancient Hamagaran tongue, Varencienne could understand it. Aranepa and Khanak were ordering Paraga to come to them. It was unlike anything she'd heard before. These were not prayers or gentle entreaties. There was no sense of abasement or respect in the invocations. The

Hamagarids were powerful magicians, to whom the elemental beings were subservient. If Paraga did not come, they would send torments to him. They would bind his creatures to the earth and torture them. If he did not come, they would silence the voice of the wind for eternity.

The maelstrom was so strong now, Varencienne could barely stand within it. Its voice was an angry scream. The chanting whirled in a circle around her, an elemental shout upon the maddened air. Then the Hamagarids screamed out a wordless climax to the chant. The wind dropped abruptly, so completely, it was as if it had never existed.

Varencienne fell back, as if she'd been struck hard by a heavy flying object. The breath was punched from her and she lay on her back, on the lake's gravel shore, gasping and spluttering. Her neck pained her greatly now. She was conscious of the sharp bones stuck into her. She could feel the wet warmth of blood on her skin.

Varencienne drew in a long, racking breath, blinking at the sky. She saw Taropat standing over her, staring down in a kind of morbid curiosity. Shan was there too, gazing in concern and love. Yet it was Taropat's eyes she met. He held out a hand. She took it and he hauled her to her feet.

'What do you feel?' he asked.

'Beaten to within an inch of my life,' she said.

CHAPTER TWENTY-TWO

Return to the Old Domain

Many centuries before, the grandfather of Valraven I, Lord Katerfel Palindrake the Third, had begun work on the great thoroughfare which he named Palindrake Way. Later, Valraven the First had finished the project and renamed it the Lord's Road. The idea behind it was to link the northern parts of Caradore with the south, to encourage trade from Magravandias and also countries across the sea, for ocean passage was far easier further south.

Ironically, it was this road that had facilitated Cassilin Malagash's march to Old Caradore, where he had directed his army to smash through the walls of Caradore Castle, slaughter any opposing male Palindrakes and take the survivors captive. If the Magravandian horde had had to traipse through tangled forest, they would have taken longer to reach the castle, and the Palindrakes might have been more prepared. Local allies could have been summoned, resources gathered. But in trying to make Caradore more accessible, Valraven I had unwittingly created an easy passage for his enemies. Since then, when the surviving Palindrakes had been herded away from their ancestral home to the newer castle further south, the Lord's Road had fallen into disrepair. Over the centuries, locals had heaved up entire sections of flags for personal use, and a stone that bore an imprint of horses' hooves ridden by forgotten warrior heroes might now serve as a lintel over a farmer's cottage door.

This was only the second time Valraven had journeyed to the old domain. Some dark and unspoken superstition had kept both him and Pharinet away from it as children, even though both of them had been inordinately curious about everything and had loved secrets and intrigue. The family curse, though never mentioned, had hung over them; a vaguely threatening ghost.

Valraven the First had once been made to swear that if he, or his line, should ever attempt to rekindle the Palindrakes' relationship with the sea dragons, their entire domain would be consumed by flame. Four years previously, Valraven had dared to challenge that oath, but he had not realigned himself with the dragons. Far from it: he had found the Dragon Queen, Foy, to be a disempowered and withered entity, who craved only release from human concerns. He had given her that peace. But now he must go against his earlier decision and perhaps invoke the curse into the bargain. Niska seemed unconcerned. Valraven could not be so sanguine.

Pharinet had, of course, wanted to join the party to Old Caradore, and a heated argument had ensued between her and her brother. Niska had made it clear to Valraven that the experience that lay ahead for him was far from easy. He must undergo certain spiritual trials. He must venture into the mystical underworld of Caradore, find and reawaken Foy. The curse must be invoked, but also negated. Valraven must purge himself of all past conflicts. These would be perilous tasks. The Dragon Lord would inevitably be changed by them, and the risks involved were great. And he must face the trials alone. Niska could not go into the dark with him. Her only function was to guide him to the portal that led to it and be there for him when he re-emerged. Pharinet questioned why any of what Niska proposed was necessary at all, then completely went against her own arguments and insisted that she, as a Palindrake, should be the one to lead Valraven back to Foy.

'You are risking everything,' she said to him. 'If you make a mistake, then Caradore might be lost. You should not do this alone.'

'Niska feels that I should.'

'Niska?' Pharinet snapped. 'What does she know that I do not? She is not a Palindrake. It is not her place to guide you.'

Privately, Valraven had more faith in Niska as a guide than Pharinet. Niska was cool, centred and had a certain distance from the proceedings. Pharinet, on the other hand, was passionately entwined with them. 'Niska is your Merante,' he said. 'You must trust her.'

Pharinet uttered a snort of sarcastic laughter. 'Trust her? It seems to me she's all too eager to get you alone out in the wilderness.'

Valraven felt his whole body slump in an inward sigh. He lacked both the patience and vocabulary to soothe Pharinet's insecurities. 'I must go alone,' he insisted, and so a second assault from Pharinet began. Valraven went to his bed feeling as if he'd been interrogated by a host of Jessapurian torturers. He'd eventually shouted an order for Pharinet to stay at home in the morning, which was victory of a kind, but he knew he would be made to suffer for it in numerous small ways thereafter.

Now, the further he rode away from Castle Caradore, the fainter the memory of his sister's voice became in his mind. Niska drove a covered wagon, which she had filled with supplies. The journey would take the best part of a day, as the wagon would slow them down, but Valraven would have time to appreciate the landscape: he might never ride through it again. Niska had not actually said what he was about to do would be life-threatening, but Valraven guessed that it would be. He also knew that the Merante of the Sisterhood would not put his life in jeopardy unless it was essential. How different he was now from the man to whom Khaster Leckery had appealed for help on the battlefield in Cos, when Bayard had taken Tayven prisoner. That Valraven was nothing more than the memory of a stranger, who had been possessed by the dragon daughter Misk. Foy's daughters were dangerous, capricious entities, but Valraven was aware that he must eventually tame, master and use them, as they had used him. Only through their co-operation and might could he dare to challenge the ancient oath, reclaim his heritage and negate the curse of the priests of fire.

Valraven and Niska arrived at the old domain late in the afternoon, crossing the ancient bridge that spanned two bastions of rock, between which a canyon road snaked in darkness far below. Mellow sunlight kindled a host of gold and scarlet colours in the lichened castle walls and the crumbled towers reared against a sky that was strangely dark, a peculiar purplish blue. It was as if a storm approached, yet there were no thunderheads massing on the horizon. The sun was a weird fierce disc in the eerie firmament.

Valraven felt as if a host of ghosts were appraising him from the battlements, where crows argued irascibly and lizards crawled amongst the swaying weeds. It was hard to imagine that this had once been a thriving citadel, almost a town in itself. It would be impossible for the horses and wagon to enter the castle yard, as the main entrance had been partially blocked long ago by a cascade of rubble. Niska hobbled the horses on the natural lawn outside, which overlooked the beach below. Sea birds circled and mourned above them while the waves crashed against the massive jagged rocks on the shore, sending up great banners of achingly white foam. A faint mist hung above the tide line.

Valraven helped Niska carry some of their belongings over the rubble and into the yard. The massive walls, even after all this time, still stood intact against the elements. Once inside, the sound of the sea receded. The Magravandians had breached only the main entrance. Valraven had hardly explored the place last time he'd visited; his mind had been preoccupied with thoughts of the task he'd been there to perform. Now there would be time for investigation and acclimatisation. He would be able to meld with the ancient domain, sense it moods, perhaps catch echoes of its memories.

Within the high walls, the air was perfectly still, as if the wind dared not venture there. This was indeed a haunted castle. Even a sceptic could not dispute that.

'We should make camp within the main keep itself,' Niska said. 'The family home.'

Valraven eyed the great building dubiously. Its turrets rose above the wall that surrounded it and its gardens. Varencienne had told him in detail of her visit some years before, and he remembered vividly her tales of ghosts and strange atmospheres. The old Palindrake dwelling had been, in the story, a sentient being, ready to engulf and devour. This might be because of Varencienne's ability to tell a good yarn, but Valraven would still have felt happier sleeping beyond the keep's influence.

'I can tell you are wary,' Niska said, 'but we must open ourselves up, fully and willingly, to whatever walks here.'

Valraven suppressed a shudder. 'It will come at night, won't it?' he said, in a deliberately melodramatic voice. 'I can see it now. I'll wake up and there'll be something there, the ghost of my ancestor, dripping with blood.' He laughed. 'The script for this drama is preordained.'

'We have no way of knowing,' said Niska, somewhat disapprovingly.

'How strange it is,' Valraven said. 'I have led men into battle against impossible odds, with no fear either of losing the fight or for my personal safety. I have faced assassins who were prepared to sacrifice their own lives to end mine. Never have I flinched. But here, I have this unknown feeling stealing through me. There are no assailants, armed with knives or poison darts, to slay me. There is no physical threat. Why should I feel unnerved? It doesn't make sense. What has no corporeal form surely cannot harm me.'

'You have partially opened yourself up to the possibility that another side to life exists,' Niska said. 'You have experienced vivid visualisations of Foy and her underwater realm that have felt to you like physical events. But, in a way, it was safe, because it took place in the realm of the mind, the realm of dreams. Even when Misk took possession of you, it wasn't a physical act of a strange dragon woman marching up to you and forcing herself into your body. It wasn't something you could see with your eyes, or feel with your physical sense of touch. It was subjective. It could just as easily have been delusional madness as reality. If Foy, or any of her daughters, should manifest here and now, in the flesh before you, you would have no choice but to accept that dragons, ghosts and unseen entities – magic, in fact – exist. Your whole concept of reality must change to accommodate the new information. That is what scares you. Our view of what the world is keeps us sane. No one wants that fundamentally challenged. We don't want our image of the world to leak.'

'Your words make sense,' Valraven agreed. 'The experience of Misk was very real, but I suppose that could have been a dark aspect of myself, conjured up by the right stimuli. I have yet to see a ghost or a dragon in reality, and I have yet to receive physical proof a magical spell can work.'

'You use magic all the time!' Niska said, smiling. 'When you stare at a subordinate soldier with those terrible dragon eyes, and he quivers and soils himself in terror, you use magic. Your will has affected his. It's all the same.'

'A picturesque analogy,' Valraven said. 'Well, we shall see.' He looked up at the solid walls around them. 'Do your worst, Old Caradore. Show your ghosts to me. Challenge my sanity!'

Inside the keep, Niska and Valraven made a makeshift camp in the cavernous great hall, round the inglenook of an immense fireplace where the black spectres of old fires had soaked into the cold walls. Valraven and Niska collected wood and kindling from the wild garden around the keep, then built a fire in the hearth. The quick flames were dwarfed by their surroundings that looked as if they had been con-structed to accommodate entire trees, but the fire was efficient enough for cooking. Valraven helped Niska prepare a meal. He was conscious of the shadowy vastness of the room around him, the half-ruined storeys of the building that towered overhead. He wondered whether ghosts were already prowling round the perimeter of their fire, like wild beasts waiting to make a kill.

Before they went to sleep, Niska insisted they conduct a short meditation in order to connect with the spirits of the place and to ask them if they wished to make themselves known. While their fire crackled reassuringly, there were no other sounds from the castle: no groans or strange knockings, not even the creak of ancient timber. Niska opened her eyes and reported she'd picked up nothing on a psychic level.

'This place is crawling with aetheric energy,' she said, frowning. 'I can't understand why it's not drawn to us.'

'Perhaps it is waiting for a more appropriate moment,' Valraven said dryly.

That night his sleep was undisturbed by dreams and he did not wake till dawn.

After breakfast, Niska wanted Valraven to relive the vision he'd experienced four years before, that of the Ustredi sea people and Foy, the Dragon Queen, to help create the portal they needed for the otherworldly to flood through into their reality. Niska discussed such things without qualms, in an almost scientific manner. Valraven, who had experienced the devastating power of the dragon daughters first-hand – whether subjectively or not – could only view the creation of a portal with apprehension. They had no way of knowing what might choose to make use of it.

Despite these misgivings, he lay down on the floor and allowed Niska to put him into a light trance. Her soft voice whispered over him like a spirit of the wind. She conjured in his mind images of the city beneath the sea, Pelagra, where the Ustredi lived, the ancient ancestors of the Palindrakes. He could only visualise Pelagra as empty, an undersea reflection of Old Caradore, ruined and inhabited by fishes. Perhaps the Ustredi did not wish to communicate with him. Was it possible that this was proof he was doing the wrong thing, and that his actions would bring only doom to his home and his family?

If you can tell me anything, he said in his mind, at least let me know the answer to that.

But there were no answers, only vague images of cyclopean ruins and waving weed.

The meditation took only an hour or so. After they had discussed the results, or lack of them, Niska and Valraven set out to explore the keep.

During Varencienne's visit a few years before, she had found Lady Ilcretia's apartments and had seen ghosts there, but Niska was more interested in discovering the entrances to the cellars, which might lead to the legendary underground lagoons where once the Palindrakes had communed with the denizens of the sea. Valraven felt as if they were observed by hostile and affronted presences every inch of the way. They found the remains of the kitchens and the ancient blackened range where once splendid banquets had been prepared. Here, much as could be expected, was a door behind which was a flight of steps leading down to a cellar. Dank foetid air emerged from this lightless pit.

'Foy knows what lives down there,' Valraven said at the top of the stairs, 'but I would imagine it has many tentacles and a general antipathy towards human kind. How many people have died down there? I am far from eager to join them.'

'There are only storage cellars down there,' Niska said. 'The Palin-drakes would have kept wine and meat in them. Things with tentacles undoubtedly live in the dungeons proper, where people were tortured and killed. It's unlikely they'd be found off the kitchens.'

'Do you want to investigate this hole or not?'

'I think we should. It's more likely the passages to the caverns run from the storage cellars, in any case.'

They had brought torches with them, which now they lit. As they descended the steps, the leaping flames looked ghoulish in the darkness rather than cheering. The cellars themselves, a series of linked chambers, were completely empty. Whatever they'd contained had either been ransacked by the Magravandians or else conveyed to New Caradore by the Palindrakes. It was clear it would be easy to become lost in the warren of passages and chambers, so Valraven made marks upon the wall with a sharp stone he found. He was conscious of the great weight of the keep above him, its brooding memories, its twisted bitterness in defeat: Old Caradore was insane, driven mad by all it had witnessed. It was like a mother who'd been forced to watch her children murdered slowly, one by one. Now a wild-haired, rolling-eyed hag, it was dangerous and unpredictable, unable perhaps even to recognise its surviving children.

The floor became wet underfoot, eventually leading to a flooded passage. 'The lagoon lies beyond here,' Niska said. 'We should press on, or at least spend tonight down here.'

'No,' said Valraven emphatically. 'That is beyond folly. This place is a reeking den, and we'd have to swim to reach the lagoon, if it exists at all.'

'You have no sense of adventure,' Niska said.

'And you have rather too much,' Valraven replied. 'I am a strategist, and my instincts tell me this: we shouldn't attempt to bludgeon the spiritual entities of this place into taking notice of us, we should blend into their environment slowly, become part of it.'

'Aha, you are beginning to talk like a true magician,' Niska said.

Valraven glanced at her askance.

That evening they cooked their meal once again in the great hall, crouching in the inglenook, their own small, cosy room within the cavernous ruins.

'I still feel I should be doing something to help Ren and Elly,' Valraven said. He was conscious of feeling guilty. The simple food they had prepared tasted so good. So far, this excursion had been enjoyable. That didn't seem right under the circumstances.

'You *are* helping them,' Niska said. 'Please, trust me when I say you must not fear for them.'

Valraven glanced around the hall. 'Well, the old place hasn't revealed its secrets to us yet. Perhaps we're in the wrong place. The ritual I did with Ren to commune with Foy took place on the beach below.'

'We are not here to re-enact that rite,' Niska said. 'I am convinced we need to be here, in the castle itself. We should perhaps give it more time.'

But time was a precious commodity. While they waited to see whether Old Caradore had anything to show or give to them, Varencienne and Ellony's fate remained unknown. Valraven knew it was pointless to keep mentioning this. Niska was unmoveable in her conviction that Ren and Elly were not in danger. Valraven wanted to share her certainty, but he was a man of action, and to him inactivity was wrong and discomforting.

Presently both Niska and Valraven composed themselves to sleep beside the embers of their fire. Valraven lay on his back, his hands behind his head, gazing up into the darkness of the vault above, which appeared to be haunted only by owls. His mind was curiously empty of thoughts. He listened to the rhythm of Niska's breathing as she descended into slumber and smiled to himself when she began to snore softly. Now he was truly alone. He considered whether he should get up and do some exploring by candlelight – surely the best way to invoke any wandering ghosts. But his blankets were warm around him and he felt comfortable in their swaddling. Also, his eyelids were beginning to droop. Perhaps tomorrow . . .

Valraven was jerked back to full consciousness by the unmistakable sound of footsteps nearby. He opened his eyes, but at first did not move, wanting whoever, or whatever, approached to believe he was asleep. In the shadows he perceived a figure walking towards him from the direction of the main door. It appeared to be a woman, dressed in a dark travelling cape. Something about her suggested she had just finished, or was just about to begin, a great journey.

Valraven sat up and the woman did not falter in her swift approach. Her face, now revealed in the dying firelight, was pale and set into a determined expression. She was a handsome creature in early middle age.

'Madam, are you a ghost?' Valraven said. 'Are you about to walk right through me? If not, I suggest you slow your pace to avoid collision.'

The woman was silent until she stood over him. Then she folded her arms and said, 'I have come some distance to find you.'

'You know me?' Valraven said. 'I regret I cannot return the sentiment.'

'I know you, Valraven Palindrake,' she replied.

'And you are?'

'A relative of yours.'

Valraven frowned. 'I do not think so. The Palindrakes are a notoriously small tribe.'

'I am Ilcretia. You will know me as your great-great-grandmother.'

Her announcement seemed so absurd, Valraven laughed. 'Then you are a ghost, and my perception of the world has just been doomed to change, or I am dreaming, or you are lying.'

The woman smiled. 'Yes, you are in a strange circumstance, but the explanation lies in none of your suggestions. I expect you know that I own the reputation of a sorceress, which I have earned through hard work. I know the real nature of time, and that sometimes you can influence the past by working upon the future.'

'I *am* dreaming,' said Valraven. He lay down again and pressed his hands against his eyes.

Ilcretia leaned down and shook him roughly. There was no doubt she was a creature of flesh and blood. 'Heed me! We have work to do. We don't have much time.'

Valraven lowered his hands. He thought Ilcretia looked nothing like her statue in the castle further south, although she did have an undeniable resemblance to Pharinet. 'If you really can manipulate time,' he said, 'then surely we have as much of it as we need.' He laughed in incredulity and sat up once more. 'I can't believe I'm saying this. You can't possibly be who you claim to be.'

Ilcretia squatted down beside him, her cape a pool of darkness around her. 'You affect levity because you cannot countenance I might speak the truth. Let us make this easier for you. If you want to, then believe that you are dreaming, but that you will remember it and know you learned something important. I have worked long and hard to discover how the curse upon our family might end. I know that one day a boy will be born who will be the one to lift it. You. The fifth Valraven. I also know that events are reaching a climax in your time, which is why both you and I are here.' She looked up briefly and gazed around the ruins of her home. 'It is much as I expected.'

Valraven exhaled slowly through his nose. 'Very well, for now I will accept you exist and that I'm talking to you. So tell me what to do.'

Ilcretia composed herself more comfortably upon the floor. 'Good. This is the problem: the curse still exists, as it was when it was first enforced. I know you have begun the process of reacquainting yourself with Foy, which so far has not attracted any dire consequences, but to go further you risk bringing the full force of the fire mages' curse into effect. There will be no conflagration, no wall of flame, but you will lose yourself. You will die.'

'This is not encouraging news. Why and how will I die?'

'It is in the very bones of your family's being to believe in this curse. To put it simply, you would kill yourself. I do not mean literally, although that is not unlikely, but that a madness would seize you. Your home and your family would be under threat, because in your insanity, you would seek to destroy them.'

Valraven frowned. 'I cannot feel this threat. I am in control of myself, and have worked hard to achieve that.'

'The trigger has not been activated,' Ilcretia said. 'It would be unwise to believe it would have no effect.'

'Then what must be done?'

'The important thing to remember is the exact words of the curse, for then you will know how not to trigger it. I took the precaution of memorising it and writing it down exactly as soon as I could. The fire mages said, "As the heir bears the mark of Madragore, we say unto you, should he not serve God's avatar in life, should he forsake the banner of Magravandias, the fire now within him will consume his body and all in his domain."'

Valraven considered these words for a moment. 'Cassilin was Madragore's avatar, but was that state necessarily passed onto his heirs? Is Gastern the god's avatar?'

'Yes,' said Ilcretia, her face screwed into an expression of irritation.

'I do not seek to forsake the banner of Magravandias. Some say it should become my banner.'

'I have seen this too, but even so, it does not get around the first clause.'

'Then what does?'

'Stoke up the fire,' said Ilcretia grimly, pointing at the embers in the hearth.

Valraven frowned. 'For what purpose?'

'Remember the exact wording, my son. "As the heir bears the mark of Madragore . . ." You, of course, bear this mark upon your neck.'

'I have a birthmark there, yes.' Realisation coursed through him. 'Wait a moment . . .'

'Yes,' Ilcretia interrupted. 'It must be removed. That is the simple and obvious answer to playing the mages at their own game, which is literally playing with words and meaning.'

'You will burn the mark from me? Are you sure such a trick would work?'

Ilcretia gestured expressively with both hands. 'Of course. Nowhere in the curse does it say, "and even if the heir should remove his mark, the curse stays in place". We have to regard these things as literal.'

Without saying more, Valraven got up and put some more faggots on the fire. He did not fear pain and saw the sense in Ilcretia's idea. Niska was still fast asleep. He wondered if Ilcretia would vanish if he tried to wake her. He might even wake up himself.

When the fire was burning high, Valraven removed a smouldering brand from it, which he passed to Ilcretia.

'Now, kneel,' she said. 'Remove your shirt and hold up your hair.'

Valraven complied and braced himself for the shock. Ilcretia thrust the burning wood against him and the pain was so sudden and intense, he cried out and jerked away. The air filled with the stink of burning flesh, but Niska still did not stir.

'There,' said Ilcretia, 'it is done. Hold still. I have salve with me.'

Valraven's head was reeling. His vision was blurred and, for some moments, he was out in the open air, on a rain-drenched shore, with tall, dark people all around him. He could smell his own burned flesh, and also the embers of the fire, which presently the sea would engulf and drag away. He turned and saw his mother standing with her daughters some distance away, her face as hard as the cliffs behind her. Then he blinked and that same face was revealed to him in firelight, indoors, in the old keep. 'I was back there,' he said hoarsely, 'for just a moment. I was your son.'

Ilcretia nodded shortly. 'Good. It proves we made the connection.' She pushed aside his hair and dabbed soothing ointment onto the burn. At once the flesh went cold.

'That salve is uncommonly effective,' Valraven said. 'I thank you.'

'I am a witch,' Ilcretia said. 'You should expect nothing less.'

'So is the curse inactive now?' Valraven asked, gingerly touching the burn, which now was numb.

'We must assume so.'

Valraven stared at her for a moment. 'Why me, my lady? There have been others before me, whom you could have visited and helped.'

Ilcretia smiled. 'Must you ask that question? The Palindrakes were crippled by what happened to them; their heirs were melancholy, bitter men. Remember your father. I have watched them all, in their suffering and isolation. I have watched you too, knowing I must choose the right moment to come to you. That moment is now.'

'I must return to Magrast,' Valraven said. 'I have been absent too long. If the curse no longer exists, then I must see how events have progressed there and plan my next move. I will need allies.'

'You are running ahead,' Ilcretia said. 'There is more to come before you take action.'

'What?'

'You must accompany me on a journey into the soul of your own people,' she said. 'I can guide you to the portal, but once beyond it, you will be alone.'

'For what purpose?'

'Knowledge, experience, wisdom. There are things to learn. The journey is not without danger, but would be worthless otherwise, in any case.' She learned forward and embraced him briefly. 'Ah, Valraven, I would go with you if I could. But I have faith in you, as do many others. Find the answers, my son, and bring them back with you.'

'How will we enter this place? Through meditation?'

'No,' Ilcretia said. 'Simply take my hand and come with me. When we walk from this place, we walk into dreams. Before you take the final steps to power, we must spend time together alone, and this cannot be done here.'

Valraven put on his boots and coat. For a moment he stared down at the sleeping Niska. 'Will she know I've gone, or will we both wake in the morning for me to tell her a fabulous dream?'

'Come,' said Ilcretia, holding out her hand. 'You must not think of her, or anyone else. You must leave your people for a while. I can't tell you how long. Your friend will wake alone. She will search for you in this world and the subtle planes. She is an adept and will understand you were taken for a reason.'

'I don't envy her having to return to my sisters without me,' Valraven said. 'They will blame her.'

'That is not your concern.'

Ilcretia hooked a hand through one of Valraven's elbows and together they walked out of the keep into the grey twilight of the predawn. The smash of waves was a muffled roar beyond the castle walls. Ilcretia led him out to the cliff top and for some moments they stood in silence, gazing down upon the beach.

'I have walked there so many times,' Ilcretia said in a wistful voice. 'The sea has always soothed me. Its voice and its beauty bring solutions to most of life's problems.'

'It must pain you to come here now and see what has happened to your home,' Valraven said.

Ilcretia smiled up at him. 'It endures,' she said. 'Look.'

He turned and saw the walls of the old domain beginning to glow in the first light of dawn. They reared tall, intact against the sky. Flags fluttered from the highest turrets, their cables cracking in the wind. It was a sound that was achingly reminiscent of the newer castle, his home. 'We are back in time,' he said.

'We are in no time,' Ilcretia replied. She squeezed his hand. 'Welcome home, my son.'

CHAPTER TWENTY-THREE

Theft of the Crown

Gastern, emperor of Magravandias, Lord Protector of Magrast and the fifteenth avatar in his line of the great god Madragore, stirred in uneasy sleep. He dreamed of a forest sward, with tall trees all around, whose trunks were hairy with ancient lichen of richest green. There was a castle in this forest, hidden at the edge of the glade by tangled shrubs with knobbly branches and glossy leaves. Here, a drama was taking place. There were three queens, each a different colour. Somewhere outside the glade, a green queen knew that trouble was afoot, but she could not reach the castle, and a weaker red queen trembled upon the velvet grass before the raised portcullis. A black queen lurked in the shadows of the trees, a sharp spiky presence to Gastern, who was an invisible observer of the event. He realised that castle and glade were surrounded on all sides by a moat, also filled with huge and ancient trees. At the bottom of the moat was a depthless ring of water and the slope down to it was treacherous with rock. Now the black queen edged forward, an amorphous shape that vaguely resembled some kind of dragon. The red queen was a mere girl with a swatch of red hair, who knew she was helpless before the might of the other. Gastern knew this because he could see into her mind. He could feel the presence of the green queen nearby, who was unable to breach the natural fortifications of branch and thorn, and who also knew she was not yet powerful enough to defeat the black queen in any case. The black queen advanced, slowly, greedily, and the red queen rose from the grass in a fluid motion of flowing robes and hair. She cried out, 'For queen and country!' and ran to the edge of the glade, where she threw herself down upon the cruel rocks. Gastern heard her body tumble to the bottom, and then a distant splash.

For just a moment before he was yanked sweating and panting from sleep, Gastern's attention was riveted upon the black queen. He felt he was in the presence of ultimate evil, and before then he had never quite believed in such a thing. He believed in ignorance and stupidity and greed, all of which resided in abundance in the human soul, but not in an external, calculating force. Its presence was anathema to him. He forced himself to wake.

At once he sat up in his wide bed, where the damask coverings were barely wrinkled and the vast cumulus of pillows behind him bore only the single imprint of his royal head. A glimmer of light from lamps in the gardens outside offered a meagre illumination to the room. Gastern's breath steamed on the air, for it was chill. He put his hands together in prayer and called upon Madragore to protect him.

Did this dream portend evil within his empire? He knew there was much ignorance to root out, areas of darkness where the clear light of Madragore must be made to shine, and he knew some of his brothers were greedy enough to be a threat to him. But he was well protected by powerful men, who had much to lose if he should fall. The significance of queens could mean only one thing to him: his mother. Also his wife, of course. Was she the trembling red queen? That was hard to imagine, but neither could he see her as the green or the black. He wondered whether Tatrini was capable of murder to get her way, and whether she would countenance the assassination of her own sons. He did not want to think that, but he was aware that he did not have a nurturing, loving relationship with his mother. Royal life had precluded that. As soon as it was possible, Tatrini's sons had been taken from her side. There was no closeness between them. Conditions were changing in Magrast, but there were still many legacies of the past.

Gastern pulled on his robe and then tugged on a tasselled rope by the bed canopy to summon Horgan, his chamber valet, for he felt in need of some warm milk to calm his nerves. Perhaps in the morning he should speak to Grand Mage Alguin about the dream. Alguin supported Gastern's vision of a new Church of Madragore, which would do much to correct mistakes of the past. In Gastern's opinion, Archimage Mordryn, though loyal, was too interested in currying favour with the military, which was riddled with pagan superstitions that needed to be rooted out. Mordryn would not risk upsetting the generals, but Alguin had no such fear. He shared Gastern's dream of a new, enlightened empire, where the tyrannies of war were a thing of the past. In Madragore's cleansing light, all humankind would be united.

Gastern heard light footsteps approaching down the corridor outside his door. Horgan was brisk and efficient; he could wake fully in an instant. Reassured, the emperor lay back on his coverlet. It was then he became aware of scrutiny.

At once his spine coursed with shudders and he sat up straight, peering into the shadowy corners of the room. Was someone there? He could perceive no movement, but thought there was a column of blackness by the wardrobe, darker than the shadows around it. For the briefest instant, Gastern felt once again the presence of evil. He suppressed a cry and at that moment, the door to his chamber opened and mellow light spilled into it, past the familiar figure of his valet. The light dispelled any shadows and there was nothing in the corner to worry about, nothing that could be seen with the naked eye.

Across the world, in the land of Mewt, early evening wafted across the temples and bazaars of the city of Akahana, carrying with it a threnody of music and the breath of a thousand perfumes. As usual, the plaintive voices of priestesses called out from the sanctuaries of a multitude of goddesses. The songs seeped into the governmental building like ghosts. Dining with his guests, Lord Maycarpe identified the devotions to the cat goddess Purryah, who was dear to Merlan Leckery. Merlan was still in Cos, looking for traces of his wayward brother and Varencienne Palindrake. Only that day, Maycarpe had received word from Merlan that King Ashalan's agents had tracked down Princess Helayna, but that the Palindrakes were not being held by her. The princess had admitted that she'd seen Taropat and Shan, but that she'd not had word from them since they'd left for Caradore. Her men had returned to Cos without them, and had revealed that Taropat had taken his captives into High Hamagara. In this action, Maycarpe did not see the workings of a kidnapper or a killer. He was fairly sure Taropat had good reasons for what he was doing, whether he was consciously aware of them or not. From what he knew of Varencienne Palindrake – through stories Merlan had told him – he suspected she would not be a passive captive. She was the Sea-Wife, after all, and would no doubt have some effect over what Taropat did in Hamagara.

Maycarpe and his guests had spent most of the meal discussing the Crown and its possible future. 'Valraven Palindrake is aware of our aspirations for him,' Sinaclara said. 'That must be seen as a step forward.'

'Aware and unimpressed,' said Maycarpe, refilling glasses. 'But that is hardly a surprise.'

'Indeed not,' agreed Sinaclara. 'If he were straining at the leash, eager to become the True King, then, paradoxically, he would not be the right candidate. We must woo him carefully.'

'True,' said Maycarpe, 'but I wonder how much time we have. Gastern has been emperor for several months now. We can only presume Tatrini has set plans of her own in motion.'

'We should guard against rashness,' Sinaclara said. 'That's why I took my time coming here. I'm sure no one could follow our trail. It is far too convoluted.'

Nana smiled. 'And she confounded the ground with potent cantrips at regular intervals.'

Maycarpe pulled a wry face. 'You can be sure Tatrini will have sent no ordinary person to secure the Crown for her. Cantrips, however deviously applied, may not be enough to deter them. Personally, in your place, I would have come to Mewt by a direct route. Here, at least, you are assured some safety.'

'I had to follow my instincts,' Sinaclara said.

Maycarpe nodded. 'I understand.'

In the silence that followed, a commotion could be heard coming from beyond the door. Maycarpe frowned. 'What, by the gods, is that infernal racket?'

Sinaclara turned in her seat to face the door. 'It sounds like some kind of argument.' She exchanged a puzzled glance with Nana.

Maycarpe rose from his seat, but before he could reach the door, it was flung wide and a group of Magravandian soldiers marched into the room.

'What is this?' Maycarpe demanded, involuntarily stepping aside.

The soldiers stood to attention on either side of the door and a tall, dark man dressed in black leather came into the room.

'Prince Almorante,' Maycarpe said. 'This is a . . . surprise.'

Almorante inclined his head. 'Darris, forgive this intrusion. I am here on serious imperial business.'

'So serious that you breach all protocols of etiquette and virtually break down my door? Why not have yourself announced by my chamberlain as usual? This is outrageous!'

Almorante's glance slid past Maycarpe towards the dining table where the two women sat tense in the candlelight. 'I presume one of your guests to be the Lady Sinaclara of Bree?'

Maycarpe had more sense than to deny it. 'You are correct. This is she.' He gestured with a languid hand and Sinaclara inclined her head. 'My Lady, this is Prince Almorante of Magrast.' He turned back to the prince. 'What is it you want here, Mante? Is all well at home?'

'Gastern is still on the throne, if that's what you mean,' Almorante replied laconically. 'I am here, as I said, on imperial business. It has

232

come to our attention that the Lady Sinaclara is in possession of an artefact that was found on Magravandian soil, and is therefore the property of the Crown. I am here to demand that she relinquish it.'

'What property is this?' Sinaclara asked in a sweetly feminine voice. She rose from her chair and came to stand beside Maycarpe. 'I am sure I have nothing that was obtained illegally.'

Almorante regarded her with cold eyes. 'My lady, do not seek to play games. You know very well to what I refer: the artefact in the semblance of a crown that was taken from Recolletine last year by a group of adventurers, who at the very least could be termed looters. I have lately come from your mansion at Bree, which I and my men found locked and abandoned.'

'You followed my trail?' Sinaclara asked sharply.

Almorante smiled, an expression devoid of humour. 'Actually, no. I was on my way here on other business, but the official on duty at the door knows me well and happened to mention Lord Maycarpe had female guests. He was most excited to inform me that they had travelled all the way from Bree. It did not take genius to work out your identity.' He glanced at Maycarpe. 'Why did she come to you, Darris? I feel you should impart this information at once, because her presence here does not cast a good light upon you.'

Maycarpe shrugged insouciantly. 'I can't see why that should be. Sinaclara is an old friend of mine, that's all. I invited her to Akahana for a holiday. Is that so heinous? Has Magrast become so paranoid it sees deceit and conspiracy in every corner?'

'Of course not. However, your official did mention that the ladies had arrived somewhat unexpectedly.'

'I do not inform every lackey of all my plans,' Maycarpe replied stiffly.

'Naturally not,' Almorante said. 'Still, seeing as good fortune has put the lady in my path, I must now interview her on the matter I mentioned earlier. Would you be so kind as to provide me with a private room?' Threats dripped from every word.

Maycarpe felt Sinaclara's body tense beside him. He wanted to say to her, 'Give him the crown now, for he will have it eventually.' In fact, he could go to the safe in his dressing-room himself and retrieve it. He could say, 'A curio, my lord. I was intrigued by it, but of course I happily surrender it to you.' But at that moment, he felt he and Sinaclara shared a single mind, determined that the Crown of Silence should not fall into Malagash hands.

'I did have the Crown,' Sinaclara said, 'but it remains in Bree, locked in a safe in the cellars beneath my house.'

'You are mistaken,' Almorante said. 'We searched the house –

thoroughly. Your strong-room, though stocked with many curious items, lacked a crown. We did find an empty safe, however.'

Sinaclara put a hand against her throat. 'Then I have been robbed!'

Almorante regarded her with a flat serpent gaze. 'You do not deceive me, my lady. For some reason, you want the crown for yourself.' He glanced at Maycarpe. 'Darris, if you are involved in this, I strongly recommend you re-examine your position. Whoever conceals the crown from me commits treason and I'm sure I don't need to remind you of the penalty for that.'

'Do you want this crown for Gastern?' Maycarpe asked. 'Is that why you're here? Or do you come as your mother's creature?'

'Silence. Treason is treason. That's all you need to know.' Almorante turned and grabbed hold of Sinaclara's arm, twisting it severely. She winced and cried out. 'Lady, tell me where the artefact is. Now. I assure you that obstinacy will not reward you. Eventually, you will break. Why not save yourself the torture?'

'Dragons take you!' Sinaclara cried. 'I do not have the crown. I cannot give it to you.'

Almorante twisted her arm a little more. Sinaclara released a sobbing moan. 'You know where it is. Tell me its location.'

'I don't know. That is the truth.'

Almorante flung Sinaclara away from him. She crashed into a tall dresser and then slid to the floor. The prince glared at Maycarpe for a moment, during which time the governor's heart nearly ceased beating. Then Almorante clearly came to a decision. He gestured to one of his men and then to Nana, who had run to administer to Sinaclara. 'Who are you?' he demanded as the man tore the Jessapurian away from Sinaclara's arms.

'I am an employee of the Lady of Bree,' Nana said.

Almorante glanced down at Sinaclara. Blood ran down her face where she'd hit her forehead on the dresser. He looked back to Nana. 'Kill her,' he said.

Sinaclara screamed, 'No!' and leapt wildly to her feet. Soldiers' hands reached to restrain her. Maycarpe could only look in horrified disbelief as two Magravandians took hold of Nana. They forced back her head while one of their comrades, with chilling, wordless precision, drew a blade across the woman's throat. It happened so quickly. There was not a spray of blood, but a gush of it, like a waterfall or a flash flood. The soldiers released her. Uttering a hideous gurgling sound and desperately trying to hold her opened flesh together with blood-slick hands, Nana staggered off furniture and then sank to the floor. She lay on the carpet, moving feebly, in a widening pool of gore.

The sound of Sinaclara's stricken weeping seemed to come from very far away. Maycarpe had seen – and done – terrible things in his time, but he could barely believe what had happened. Only minutes before, he had been dining with this woman, delighting in her vibrant beauty and wondering whether, at some point during the ladies' visit, he might seduce her. Now all that had been Nana, her hopes, her thoughts, her feelings, had vanished. She was a lifeless corpse, empty meat. It was inconceivable.

Almorante stepped up to Maycarpe and looked directly into his eyes. 'If you think anything of the Sorceress of Bree,' he said, 'you will reveal what you know to me. I am quite prepared to kill her. You too, if necessary. I know you value your own life, Darris. You are a survivor. What is this crown to you? Is it worth lives, especially your own?'

Maycarpe swallowed painfully, tasted bile. 'Strangely enough, it is,' he said. 'Do your worst, my lord. Kill me. The knowledge of the crown's whereabouts will go with me to my grave. Sinaclara knows nothing. I deliberately hid it without telling her where it lies. What she does not know cannot harm her.'

'But her pain, perhaps, can harm you.'

Maycarpe shook his head. 'She, like me, is willing to die to protect the crown. You can torture her to death before my eyes. I will not speak. We are both disciplined adepts of the inner arts. Should we wish to, we can vacate our bodies at will. You cannot threaten us with torture, nor death, for we know that life is an illusion, and that we go on to greater things.'

'As you will,' said Almorante. 'It is a great shame, because I admire you greatly, Darris. The world will be impoverished by your loss.' He gestured to one of his men, who took a step towards Maycarpe, unsheathing his dagger.

'No!' Sinaclara cried. 'No more killing. The crown lies in the safe in Lord Maycarpe's dressing room.'

There was a brief silence. Maycarpe was astounded by Sinaclara's outburst, mainly because he had not told her where he'd hidden the crown. He stared at Almorante. He could almost see the workings of the prince's mind. He watched him toy with the decision to kill the governor anyway. He could see, as if those thoughts were his own, how Almorante remembered the past, all the memorable evenings he'd spent in Maycarpe's company. They had acted as if they were great friends. Almorante had not lied when he'd said he admired the governor. Maycarpe knew this fact saved his life.

Eventually, Almorante said, 'The woman has sense. You should value it. Take us to the crown, Darris. Let us end this unpleasantness.'

Almorante took only two of his men with him as they escorted Lord Maycarpe up to his dressing-room. Out in the hallway, there was a reek of blood. Maycarpe glanced up the corridor and saw huddled shapes on the floor. He paused. 'What have you done?' His voice sounded high and plaintive in his own ears.

Almorante shoved him on. 'Do not look, Darris. I regret what has had to be done. I regret your involvement in treasonous schemes. I take no pride in the events of this night.'

'These are your people,' Maycarpe said, stalling and pointing back with a shaking hand at the bodies on the floor. 'They know nothing of treason. This is murder.'

Almorante took his arm firmly. 'The few have to be sacrificed for the good of many. My presence here must remain unknown. Those whose fate led them to duties elsewhere this night may praise their fortune in the morning.'

Later Maycarpe would barely remember the short journey to the dressing-room. The only image that stayed with him was the moment when he handed the Crown of Silence to Almorante. It was still concealed in its wrappings, which the prince peeled away. A weird greenish light emanated from the coral spines, rendering Almorante's face demonic, filling it with hungry longing. Then he sniffed and abruptly flicked the coverings back into place.

'Do you intend to wear this crown?' Maycarpe said.

Almorante gave him a hard glance. 'It belongs to the Malagashes,' he replied. 'That's all you need to know.'

'What do you intend to do with me, Mante?' Maycarpe asked. 'I cannot imagine you will simply leave me here with a fond farewell.'

'You are correct,' Almorante said. 'Both you and your sorceress friend will return with me to Magrast. You know many interesting things, which we are eager to learn. If you behave well and co-operate, your life will be easier and – need I say – longer.'

'There are those in Magrast who will not look kindly upon your actions.'

Almorante smiled in a hard, feral way. 'And they will not learn of your presence there.' He gestured to his men. 'Fetch the woman. We leave for the docks at once.'

Maycarpe and Sinaclara were shackled in a cramped cabin upon a Magravandian galleon bound for Magrast. Sinaclara would accept no physical comfort. She was numb from shock, her hands still covered in Nana's blood. Maycarpe guessed she had tried to help her friend while he'd taken Almorante to the dressing-room. It had been obvious there was nothing that could be done.

'You should not have stopped Almorante killing me,' Maycarpe said to her. 'I was prepared to die for what I believe.'

Sinaclara sighed heavily and made a clear effort to rouse herself from her daze. 'He would have found the crown anyway,' she said in a slurred voice and rubbed her face with her stained fingers. 'The world cannot lose you, not yet. There is work to do and for that you need this incarnation, this mind, this body, as do I. I received an intimation of this in the temple of Munt. But I could not speak of it.'

'You should have done,' Maycarpe said. 'We could have been prepared.'

Sinaclara closed her eyes. 'I know,' she whispered.

'I, at least, should have foreseen this. I thought my plans were so carefully constructed, but there is always a random component. Always.'

Sinaclara pushed the heels of her hands against her eyes. Maycarpe imagined that in her mind she was seeing Nana's death repeated, over and over. 'Azcaranoth told me what would happen, that someone would die. But he also told me I must prevent a second death, which is what I did.' She shook her head, her eyes still tightly shut. 'But I have broken my oath to him, as he said I would.'

'How?' Maycarpe asked gently.

'I vowed to keep the crown from enemy hands, to give my own life to guard it.'

'But Azcaranoth advised you what to do.'

Sinaclara opened her eyes and fixed him with a bloodshot stare. 'I know that, but it doesn't make it any easier. Nana was my rock, my closest friend. I should never have let her travel with me. She could now be in Jessapur with her people, safe and well.'

'My dear,' Maycarpe said in a soft voice, 'if Nana had not been present tonight, it might well be you lying dead in my dining-room now. And however terrible it sounds, I am relieved that is not the case.'

Sinaclara sighed heavily. 'I must accept that what has happened was preordained. I didn't realise how badly the Malagashes wanted the crown.'

'But what will they do with it now?' Maycarpe mused, daring to put an arm around Sinaclara's shoulder. She did not pull away. 'That is the great question. And is there anyone left to stop them?'

It was not unusual for the emperor's chief vizier and the head of the church to be seen together in public. Quite often they shared a box at the theatre or the Terpsichareon, neither being family men, and there-fore free of an entourage of relatives eager to take advantage of complimentary seats. But Senefex and Mordryn were not at the Magrast Hippodrome to spend a leisurely afternoon studying the horses or placing reckless bets. They had come to talk, away from the palace and the governmental offices. Privacy was essential.

'A wave is building up,' murmured Senefex, peering at the course below. 'It is a great black wave.'

'We should guard against overreaction,' said Mordryn. He took a few spiced nuts from the paper cone in his hand and threw them into his mouth.

'We have to face facts nonetheless,' Senefex said. 'The evidence cannot be ignored.'

The evidence derived from Gastern's chamber valet, Horgan. He had approached Senefex the previous week and had, in nervous tones, said all was not well with his master. The emperor had taken to absenting himself from his room at night. Horgan had been woken on a number of occasions to catch glimpses of Gastern leaving his chambers by several of the secret exits which had been built into the palace for security reasons. At first, the valet had believed the emperor to be sleepwalking and had hurried after him, but when he had placed a hand upon Gastern's arm, the man had turned on him with a snarl and ordered him to return to his chambers. Horgan spoke of the bad dreams that had come to plague the emperor and asked Senefex's advice as to how to proceed. Should the royal physicians be called? It might be difficult and invite Gastern's wrath, because physically there seemed nothing wrong with him. Polite enquiries as to the state of his nerves had provoked nothing but an angry response.

Senefex had done what he could to calm Horgan's fears. 'I will speak to his mightiness,' he had said. 'But keep a record of any unusual or eccentric behaviour. Report to me personally on a daily basis. Speak to no one else about this matter, upon pain of death. Especially, do not speak to Grand Mage Alguin. Is that clear?'

Horgan had obeyed the vizier. Meanwhile, Senefex had put plans of his own into operation. He'd had the emperor followed on his nightly jaunts. Gastern, adopting a cursory disguise, wandered the streets of the city. He went from church to church, inspecting the ancient warding hexes that had been carved into the walls and doors, as if to assure himself the city was safe from evil. Sometimes whores and beggars would accost him, unaware of his identity: his best disguise after all was that no one would expect the emperor himself to be abroad in the city, alone. Gastern worked holy symbols on the air before their faces, which adopted expressions of astonishment or scorn, depending on their character. He spoke prayers aloud and called upon the fire of Madragore to purge the city of sin. Hearing of these events, Senefex suspected Alguin's influence at work, but the emperor had spent little time with his priestly mentor recently. Horgan reported that on two occasions Alguin had been turned away from Gastern's chambers.

Senefex listened to his spies' reports with an increasing sense of unease. He did not know whose hand was behind it. Gastern's rapidly deteriorating condition might interfere with his and Mordryn's own plans.

The archimage, apparently unconcerned, munched his spiced snack and watched the horses career around the dusty track, their jockeys reaching out to snatch red marker ribbons dangling from posts stationed at regular intervals. 'Of course, we had anticipated that, in later life, Gastern might become eccentric,' he said, 'but this comes too soon. I believed he would be content with building new cathedrals and spreading the word of Our Lord abroad. What you describe suggests a neurosis, and this could be inconvenient. It will fuel arguments against Gastern's tenure. His eager brothers are waiting in the wings for him to fall. The slightest chink and they'll be in through the defences like famished wolves.'

'It has crossed my mind that one of them may be behind this,' Senefex said. 'Too many of the Malagashes are proficient with toxins.'

Mordryn considered these words. 'The idea is appealing, because it suggests the condition might be reversible, but I do not think poison is responsible. There would be other symptoms, surely? And the staff around Gastern are hand-picked, trustworthy. I hope you don't think one of them might be less loyal than we think.'

'I did consider that,' Senefex replied, 'and made sure the situation was explored, but all seems in order. If there is a spy amongst our people, they are extraordinarily adept at concealing themselves. However, there are many methods of administering poison. I don't think it should be discounted.'

'Perhaps Gastern should take a holiday with his family,' Mordryn said, 'accompanied only by those we know to be trustworthy. Let us see if his condition improves outside Magrast. A trip to the Lakes might be a good idea.'

'It is indeed,' Senefex agreed. 'We should approach the emperor directly and suggest it to him.'

'If his affliction cannot be cured,' said Mordryn, 'then we must consider how to use it to our advantage.'

For some moments, the two men were silent as the race below them came to its climax. The afternoon was dreary so there were few patrons in the circular seats, but those who were present now got to their feet and yelled or else held their heads in their hands in despondency. Only hardened gamblers visited these training races, or men with things to hide.

'Another thing disquiets me,' Senefex said, as the hubbub faded away. People were leaving their seats now, and below, trainers threw blankets over the steaming horses before leading them away. The races were over for the day.

'And what is that?' Mordryn enquired.

'The Dragon Lord has been absent from Magrast for too long. He should return. We need him by us at this time.'

'When we recalled him,' Mordryn said, screwing the paper cone, now empty of nuts, into a tight ball, 'the only response we got was a report from his family that he is engaged upon a search for his missing wife.'

'I sympathise with his dilemma,' Senefex said, 'but he has responsibilities. He should use his own trained men to retrieve his wife and return to us. I feel we must issue a command to this effect. The Fire Chamber will be in accord over it. Many of the councillors are beginning to fret.'

Mordryn threw the ball of paper into a rubbish bin nearby. 'No one knows where Palindrake is exactly, so he can hardly be ordered back to Magrast.'

Senefex frowned deeply. 'People will say that this is not like him. He has never shown himself to be a devoted family man before. If anything, rumour suggests he barely shares the princess's bed. His son and heir is safe in Magrast. The extent of his personal involvement makes no sense. People will begin to wonder whether there is more to this than it appears.'

'Palindrake knows where his grain is safely stored,' Mordryn answered. 'He will not decide independently to change allegiance. We should be more concerned about how Palindrake might easily be kidnapped or disposed of himself out in the wilderness of Cos.'

'That is a perturbing thought,' Senefex said, 'though I have always believed him to be charmed against ordinary danger.'

'Every man's luck runs out on him at some time or another,' Mordryn said. 'Still, we cannot worry about that now. Palindrake is not here, but has left Captain Lorca in command. We must make proper use of him in the Dragon Lord's absence. Palindrake's son is too young to be of use.'

'Lorca must, of course, accompany the emperor on his holiday.'

'Naturally. We must take him into our confidence. Palindrake is no fool. In his absence, we will trust whom he trusts. I am sure he will

240

return to Magrast the moment he has concluded his personal business and that this will be soon.'

'Perhaps,' said Senefex. 'But the wind is blowing hard and who knows how the chaff will fall?'

'I will speak to Gastern this evening,' Mordryn said. 'Perhaps you should join me.'

'I will do that,' Senefex said.

Ponderously, Mordryn rose to his feet and began to leave the Hippodrome. Then he paused and looked back at Senefex, who had remained seated. 'Find out whether the Grand Queen Mother is aware of her eldest son's nocturnal peregrinations,' he said. 'If there is anyone we should keep a close eye on in Magrast, it is her.'

Tatrini was aware of Gastern's new habits, and like the archimage and the vizier, wondered about them. Was Gastern simply manifesting his own madness, or was someone else behind it? She could not imagine who that might be, other than herself, and in this instance, her hands were clean. If Gastern had begun the long dark journey into madness, it could only help her cause, but for the time being she must put it from her mind. She had more important and immediate matters to attend to.

After an absence of six weeks, Almorante had returned to Magrast. He had travelled quickly and had been successful in his quest. Tatrini was very pleased with him. The prince had brought Maycarpe and Sinaclara to the city in utter secrecy, which suited the Grand Queen Mother very well. They were now incarcerated near the old Fire Chamber, where Tayven had begun his residency in the palace. To prolong the time before news of Maycarpe's taking occurred, the prince had taken the precaution of slaughtering any of the governor's staff who had seen him in Akahana. Tatrini knew that it was virtually impossible for someone to cover their tracks completely, and that eventually it would be known that Almorante had brought Maycarpe to Magrast, but she aimed to keep her own involvement out of it.

Now she had the Crown of Silence.

Candles burned in her bedroom, and salt lay in a circle upon the carpet. In the middle of it Tatrini crouched, the crown in her lap. She sought to conjure forth the spirit of the crown. All artefacts of power possessed such guardians. So far, despite her potent conjurations, nothing had manifested. Were any of her sons fit to wear it? For just a moment, Tatrini lifted the crown in her hands. Her fingers tingled as if with currents of subtle energy. She held the artefact out before her, heart beating fast. She raised her hands and the crown hovered over her head. So easy just to lower it now, claim the power for herself. But no. Such action might bring unwelcome consequences. She put down the crown. All around her, in the world of the unseen, events were moving towards a specific point. She wasn't yet sure herself what that would be. The preparatory rituals were almost complete. Tonight she would conjure all four elemental dragons together. Gastern was moving inexorably away from the centre stage. Perhaps it was simply meant to be. But what was Almorante's role? In some respects, he would make a better emperor than Bayard, but if he did take the throne, there was no certainty he would allow his mother to have a prominent role in government.

These boys, Tatrini thought, they are a menace. It should be possible for me, or even Varencienne, to take the throne of the empire. Men, in their fear, have shorn us of temporal power. It must change.

For a moment she reflected on what it must be like to have a conventional mother's role. She had watched other women, the way they doted on their children. Tatrini could not share those feelings. She cared for certain of her offspring, and admired those who deserved it, but she could not experience, nor imagine, the fierce tug of love that other women demonstrated. In her position, it would be a weakness, in any case, because any one of her sons would dispose of her should she stand in their way.

Only that afternoon, she had interviewed Darris Maycarpe, who had said, 'You are the lioness who devours her cubs.'

He was not afraid of her. 'You would kill to see your own dreams realised,' she'd said. 'Climb down from your pious throne, Darris. We are two of a kind.'

He'd affected levity, pretending his interest in the crown was academic, and that he was merely playing with people when he declared he supported Palindrake as king. 'You know me, Tatrini,' he'd said. 'Wherever the cards fall, there I shall be, waiting to collect my winnings.'

'You are in a cell deep beneath the palace,' Tatrini had replied. 'No one but me, Almorante and his trusted men know you are here. You have little to gamble with now.' She smiled. 'Except perhaps for the little sorceress.'

She could only admire Maycarpe's control of himself. He didn't betray anything in his expression. 'Really? What do you mean?'

Tatrini made an airy gesture with one hand. 'Oh, you know. She is the guardian of the crown, and is therefore connected with its spiritual protectors. You will persuade her to work with me.'

Maycarpe laughed. 'You know little of Sinaclara,' he said. 'It is beyond my powers to persuade her to do anything she doesn't want to. We are not allies in the way you think.'

'I could kill her.'

'You could,' Maycarpe said, 'but that doesn't seem to be your style. It would be the petulant and pointless act of someone who is afraid. I don't believe you are.'

'Then tell me what you think I should do with her. You clearly have your own ideas.'

Maycarpe considered. 'You have Tayven Hirantel, don't you? He and Sinaclara are close. Perhaps that relationship could be of benefit to you. Perhaps Tayven has powers of persuasion that I don't.'

Tatrini stared at Maycarpe for some moments, and he did not flinch beneath her gaze. Eventually, she said, 'I am glad I am not a person who believes you to be my loyal friend.'

He inclined his head. 'Likewise, my lady. You flatter me too much.'

Sinaclara had not been as cooperative. She'd had to be physically restrained and gagged and refused to speak when Tatrini visited her. Bayard would probably have advocated torture at that point, but Tatrini could tell that would get her nowhere. She found Sinaclara's hostility tiresome and kept the visit short. There was plenty of time to devise a strategy.

When Almorante returned to Magrast, Tayven knew he had to find out the results of the prince's quest to secure the crown. The work he had put in before Almorante had left now bore fruit. Tayven did not have to do anything to arrange a meeting. A formal invitation to the prince's apartments arrived only hours after Almorante had come home. Tayven did not tarry in responding to it.

At first Almorante was cagey. In response to Tayven's question about whether he'd been successful in Bree, he replied, 'I've had a long journey and am looking forward to my dinner. Let us enjoy this time together. We can talk later.'

This was not quite what Tayven had hoped for, but he could tell Almorante was full of questions about what Tatrini was planning, and hoped that Tayven would be able to enlighten him. Tayven realised a trade was in order. He must offer enough to generate a useful reward, but not too much that might jeopardise his position. He was now allowed a certain amount of freedom within the palace. It was essential Tatrini believed him to be totally compliant.

After a candlelit meal, which suggested what Almorante had in mind for later in the evening, the prince suggested they should take a few snifters of merlac before the fire in his study. Here, he opened up about his recent trip.

'The Forest of Bree is an enchanting place,' he said. 'I would like a retreat there, similar to the one I have in Recolletine. Perhaps I should appropriate the house of Lady Sinaclara.'

'The Lady might disagree with your plans.'

'She is no position to do so.'

Tayven paused, caressing the stem of his glass. Almorante wanted him to ask the right questions. This was nothing more than a game. 'Do I take it the Lady opposed your desire to claim the Crown for Magravandias?'

'When my trackers found her domain, she had fled from it. I found no Crown there.'

'So you returned empty-handed?'

Almorante smiled. 'Far from it. I went on to Mewt, to interview your friend, Lord Maycarpe. As fate would have it, I discovered the Lady Sinaclara there. She had taken the Crown to Akahana.'

'And now you have it?'

'Yes.'

'What of Maycarpe and Sinaclara?'

'At the very least, they were traitors.'

'Were?' said Tayven, a chill filling his breast.

'They are not yet dead,' Almorante replied. 'I have brought them to Magrast.'

'For a public trial? Is that possible? I would have thought your mother wished to keep the Crown a secret.'

'There will be no public trial,' Almorante said. 'You know how the Malagashes operate, don't you? Did you ever get a public trial?'

'What will you do with them?'

'Their fate has yet to be decided. I admire Darris Maycarpe and wish to know his thoughts and desires. I hope there is still an area of accord between us. It would not please me to have him executed.'

'What of the woman?'

'She is a fascinating piece, but I shall leave her future in the hands of my mother. Maycarpe holds more interest for me.'

How blind he is, Tayven thought, nodding as if in agreement.

Almorante sipped his merlac in silence for some moments, then said, 'What are your plans, Tayven? I cannot believe you agree with my mother's. What game are you playing?'

'That of survival,' Tayven said. 'It is the game I have always played.'

'I have heard that Gastern had adopted peculiar behaviour. This is the prelude to his disposal, of course. Do you know how she's doing it?'

'As far as I know, she is not doing anything. Gastern's demons are entirely his own. It hardly comes as a surprise, does it? Who in Magrast ever thought he was the right man to take his father's place? In my opinion, he is not strong enough to withstand the pressure. He is afraid, and his fear will take his mind.'

'How convenient that would be,' Almorante said.

'Indeed,' Tayven said.

'How does she propose to get Bayard on the throne?'

Tayven laughed uneasily. 'You cannot believe she takes me into her confidence over such matters.'

'You are astute. You intuit the truth. I think you know the answers I seek. What does she use you for? What service do you perform for her? Think carefully before you prepare to lie to me. There is no certainty my mother will win this contest. One day, you might need my favour.'

'She wants me to work magic with her, to reinstate the fire-drakes and prevent Gastern from eliminating them. She believes the drakes to be essential to Malagash fortune. That is all I can tell you.'

Almorante stared at him intently. 'You are a snake, Tayven. You have no loyalty to my mother, nor to me. What is the price of your loyalty? Are you prepared to sell it?'

Tayven hesitated before responding, 'I care about survival, my lord. This you know. As such, it does not have a price.'

Almorante reached out to take his hand. 'We have a history, Tayven. Is that worth nothing to you?'

Tayven rose and went to stand beside Almorante's chair. He leaned down, took the prince's face in his hands and kissed him deeply. When he drew away, he said, 'Can't we forget this talk of intrigue, suspicion and betrayal? I'm sick of it to my bones. It tires and bores me. I play your mother's game because it keeps me relatively safe. When I'm away from her, her schemes mean nothing to me. I hunger for simple pleasure.'

Almorante was a difficult man to fool, but his desire clearly overcame his misgivings. 'There is much to catch up with,' he said. 'It's been too long.'

In the morning, Tayven returned to his chamber to find Lady Pimalder waiting for him. 'The Grand Queen Mother is annoyed,' she said. 'She wanted you to take breakfast with her.'

'Tell her I've been working,' Tayven said dryly. He wanted a bath and some hours of sleep. Almorante's demands, though inventive and pleasurable, had exhausted him.

'She will be interested to hear your report,' Grisette said.

Realising he had no choice, Tayven went to Tatrini's apartments and there learned she wished him to persuade Sinaclara to work with them. It was not a request, but an order. 'Did Almorante have anything interesting to say?' she asked.

'No. He's concerned only with discovering your true ambitions for him.'

'I hope you allayed his concerns.'

'I did my best.'

Tatrini laughed. 'Your skills are unparalleled, I'm sure.' Her tone darkened. 'Talk to the sorceress, Tayven. I want her ready by tonight.'

Tayven accompanied Lady Pimalder to a room near the old Fire Chamber. It was clearly not a cell, for there was no bed in it, simply a bare table, around which was placed a set of ill-matched chairs. Tayven sat down with Lady Pimalder while they waited for Master Dark to bring Sinaclara to them. 'You can speak to the sorceress for a few minutes only,' Lady Pimalder said. 'So make your request clear. You must use your arts of persuasion to sway her quickly.'

It was clear that Tayven wouldn't be allowed to speak to Sinaclara in private. This interview would not be easy.

When Sinaclara arrived, she went directly to Tayven and hugged him. 'I am so glad to see you,' she said. 'Darris and I were worried about you.'

'I'm fine,' Tayven said.

She stood back and regarded him, no doubt taking in his fine clothes and groomed appearance. It would be clear he was not a prisoner as she was. 'I can see that! I presume you know what happened?'

'Yes,' he said. 'Clara, we don't have much time, but I need to ask you to do something.'

She sat down wearily on one of the chairs, which rocked dangerously beneath her. 'Of course.' She glanced at Dark and Lady Pimalder then back at Tayven, her expression slightly troubled.

'I am working with the empress,' Tayven said, gazing directly into her eyes and hoping she would understand the truth behind his words.

She stared at him without expression for some moments, then said, 'I am surprised to hear that.'

'It is expedient,' he said. 'I am given freedom within the palace. Also, like Tatrini, I would like to see Gastern removed from office.'

'What do you want me to do?' Sinaclara asked. There was an edge to her voice, indicating she sensed he could not speak openly because of Dark and Pimalder's presence, but that she was still not too happy about his choice of action.

'You must summon the spirit of the Crown for the Grand Queen Mother.'

Sinaclara continued to stare at him. 'You know I cannot do that, Tayven.'

'You must,' he said. 'I want you to trust me now, more than you've ever trusted anyone.'

'When?' she asked.

'Tonight.'

Sinaclara twisted her mouth to the side. 'You must give me good reason why I should comply with your request.'

Tayven scraped a hand through his hair. 'You must do it for the world, for the True King.'

'There are no true kings in Magrast,' she said coldly.

'I am the Bard of the King,' Tayven said. 'I speak only truth. You know that. Trust me, Clara. I can explain no further.'

'I shall see,' she said.

Tayven realised that was the best he could expect from her. 'Thank you,' he said.

She nodded shortly. 'Have you seen Darris?'

'No. I'm unable to, but I'll speak to Almorante about it.'

'Almorante had Nana killed,' Sinaclara said. 'He must die for it.'

Master Dark shifted slyly in the corner of the room.

'I have to go,' Tayven said, standing up. He felt as if Almorante's fingerprints were all over him, clearly visible to Sinaclara's eyes. 'I'll see you later, Clara.'

'I shall look forward to it,' Sinaclara said without warmth.

Back in his own chambers, Tayven lay down on his bed, fully clothed, conscious of a weight of depression. Even if Sinaclara knew the truth, he was sure she'd disapprove of what he was doing. She would loathe him for the fact he had started another affair with Almorante. He couldn't help it, though. Part of him still cared for the prince. They'd grown up together as both brothers and lovers. Whatever Almorante might do to other people, he was loyal to Tayven and always would be. It was not a good situation to be in, because one day there would be a conflict of loyalties. But for now, Tayven was prepared to ignore the possible consequences, even though he knew it was unwise. He realised that part of him had rekindled the relationship with Almorante as a form of vengeance on Taropat, which was absurd. When he lay in Almorante's arms he wanted Taropat to see it. Sometimes he even tried to project the image across space and time. He pressed his hands against his eyes, aware that his circumstances must only get worse, and there was no guarantee they'd ever get better.

He drifted into an uneasy half-sleep, where dream fragments floated across his mind. From a haze of meaningless images, three figures came softfootedly towards him: female, sinuous creatures with waving hair and sly reptilian faces.

'Who are you?' he asked them.

'We are the dragon daughters,' one of them replied. 'You know of us.'

'Yes. What do you want?'

'Your compliance. You are the servant of the Dragon Lord.'

'Compliance in what?'

'You must allow us to direct you in certain matters. Our mother, Great Foy, has sent us to guard and guide the heir to Caradore. Tonight you must allow us to act through you.'

Tayven could tell these creatures were unpredictable and dangerous. He had no desire whatsoever to relinquish control to them. 'You must tell me why,' he said.

'It is not your place to question. You are only a servant of the Light. You must do as we ask. If you refuse, we will act through you in any case, but you may well be lost.'

Tayven became aware of a pounding ache that had started up behind his eyes. He had no choice. The day he had chosen his path and made his covenant with the cosmos had been the day he had made himself a channel for higher powers. The dragon daughters were Valraven's creatures. He had to trust they would act only on his behalf.

'You have my compliance,' he said. 'Do as you will.'

At once he was awake, blinking at the ceiling. Afternoon sunlight carved patterns on the walls. All was peaceful. After tonight, Tayven thought, there would be no peace. The battle would commence.

CHAPTER TWENTY-FOUR

Conjuring Dragons

In the centre of the old Fire Chamber stood a woman whose shoulders drooped despondently. Her red hair hung ragged down her back, dark with grease. Rav could hardly bear to look upon her, for every contour of her body was etched with despair and defeat. She had already been present when he and Tayven had come through the great doors. Tayven had held Rav's hand tightly all the way there, which only contributed towards Rav's uneasiness. Generally, on their way to meetings with Tatrini, Tayven would try to make Rav laugh. Tonight he was tense.

'Who is that lady?' Rav asked.

'Her name is Sinaclara,' Tayven replied in a whisper. 'She is the blue lady who came to us that first time. Do you remember?'

'She looks sick,' Rav said.

'She's tired,' Tayven said.

The woman raised her head and looked at them with reddened eyes. Rav thought she was only half there. Her face looked puffy. It was more than tiredness. He shivered.

Tatrini was arranging some magical paraphernalia upon a newly erected wooden altar next to the fire pit. The altar was rectangular and each of its sides was carved with representations of the elemental dragons. Tonight, the flames in the pit looked purple rather than blue.

Tatrini directed Rav and Tayven to assume their accustomed positions upon the thrones. Bayard and Leo were already seated.

'Now is the time,' said Tatrini, 'for us to witness the culmination of our labour. The dragons are present, to a greater or lesser degree, within each of you. I have secured a powerful artefact to aid us in our cause, and this woman you see before you is its guardian, a sorceress.'

249

'What artefact is this, Mother?' Bayard asked.

Tatrini gestured towards the altar, on which lay an object wrapped in indigo silk. 'It is a crown, my son, an ancient crown, forged at the time when the dragons were present in the land.' Her hands skimmed lightly across the silk. 'This woman, Sinaclara of Bree, is here tonight to act as a channel for the power of the crown and the essence of the dragons.'

'One might say she appears reluctant,' Bayard drawled.

Tatrini glanced at the drooping woman. 'She knows what is best.'

Rav gripped the arms of his throne. He felt slightly nauseous. Often there had been strange energies within the Fire Chamber while he'd been present, but tonight it felt particularly dark and threatening. He realised that the crown hidden in the purple silk was the same one he had seen in his vision during the first ritual. It could be no other. It was the crown he had seen Tayven place upon his father's head.

Tatrini began to utter invocations. She threw incense grains onto a bowl of smouldering charcoal and thick grey smoke billowed into the room. Presently it reached Rav's nostrils and he almost gagged on the acrid perfume. It stole into his body as an invading gaseous serpent. By the fire pit, Lady Sinaclara shuddered and sank to her knees.

Rav looked across at Tayven, seeking reassurance, but Tayven's eyes were closed, his brow furrowed.

In between her invocations, Tatrini continued to feed the fire with grains of incense. The smoke became so thick it filled the centre of the chamber to a level of around six feet. Rav could no longer perceive any of the others as more than vague shapes within it. His eyes were streaming and it was difficult not to cough. Power was building up around him, living, writhing, hissing power. This was more immediate and real than anything he'd experienced before. He felt the dragon daughters very near. They still invaded his dreams and sometimes he felt them during the day, lurking in the corners of his classroom, hiding in the curtains of the dining room, spooking his pony when he was out riding. He talked to Tayven about them often, who had said Rav should not be afraid of them. But Rav had noticed that Tayven never came into his dreams to chase the dragon daughters away. Perhaps he couldn't.

His eyes hurt so much he could hardly keep them open. His vision, what there was of it, had become blurred. The walls of the chamber were glowing through the smoke, dissolving into light, as if the chamber had moved to a place beyond the real world. The radiance increased in brightness until it turned the smoke to brilliant fog. The thrones had become visible within it and also the pit at the centre of the room. Tatrini still stood before her altar, but it looked as if she floated in the air, because the floor could not be seen. She raised her arms and her voice became a wordless shout, full of commanding power. Rav was sure that no entity in creation could resist her charge.

Then, out of the radiance behind Tayven's throne, stepped an immense figure. It was not a cockatrice, but a man who stood at least twelve feet high. He was clothed in a grey shimmering armour that looked as if it had been fashioned from toughened reptile skin. He wore a helmet of black and white feathers which swept down on either side of his face and a cloak that was also made entirely of feathers. This figure stood motionless with folded arms. His eyes were shadowed by his helmet, but Rav could perceive his gaze, which was like that of an eagle.

Behind Leo's throne, another figure had appeared, this a gigantic woman, who was clad in a ragged robe of dark brown and forest green. Leaves and cascades of dark berries were woven into her russet hair. Her eyes were unnaturally large and dark, reminding Rav of a doe. He realised that these visions must be representation of the elements, as the dragons were. The figure in the east, with his feathers and eagle-eyed stare, was an avatar of air, while the woman in the north represented earth.

To the left, another spirit form had emerged to stand behind Bayard, an angel of fire, clad in burning armour and wielding a flaming sword. His hair was a furious red and sparks leapt from it.

Finally, Rav turned and saw behind him a monstrous woman, wearing nothing but a frothing waterfall. Living water cascaded round her towering body, splashing down, but also rising up as fountains of light. Her eyes were dark, liquid pools, reflecting starlight and her hair was green like seaweed. She was so close, Rav could reach out and touch her. He wondered whether he was the only person present who could see these beings; neither Tatrini nor anyone else appeared to be aware of them.

Tatrini was swaying now, her arms held lower, the palms displayed. She was singing in a low voice. Sinaclara knelt near to her, her hair hanging forward to touch the invisible floor. Tayven's eyes were still closed, although his brow was no longer furrowed.

Something touched Rav on the shoulder and he jumped in fright, but when he turned fearfully, expecting to see the huge countenance of the water woman looming at his side, he saw it was a man of normal proportions, dressed in dark clothing. It took some moments for him to realise he was looking at his father.

'Papa!' he whispered, and held out his hands, but Valraven raised a finger to his lips.

'Don't be afraid, Rav,' he said. 'No one can see me but you.'

251

'How did you get here?' Rav said softly. 'Will you take me away with you?'

Valraven touched his son's head. 'You must be brave now. I cannot be with you in the flesh, but know my spirit watches out for you constantly.'

A worm of hideous cold squirmed through Rav's spine. He could barely utter the question, because he was so frightened of the answer. 'Are you dead now, Papa?'

Valraven smiled a little. 'No, I'm not dead. I'm just in another place, Rav, but I will come to you soon. I just want you to know you are not alone. Tayven is with you and you can trust him. You must help him now, as he will help you. Do whatever he advises.'

'Will you be king, Papa?' Rav said. 'I think that's what Tayven wants. There is a crown he wishes you to have. I've seen it.'

'I don't yet know,' Valraven said, 'but we have a great destiny, Rav. It is our fate, but not our curse, for I have broken it.'

Before Rav could respond, the image of Valraven disappeared abruptly and it was as if he'd never been there. Rav's heart was beating fast. He was no longer afraid. All that was strange, unworldly and unknown was familiar to him. He was part of it.

The elemental avatars had started to change form. As if shaped by Tatrini's insistent song, their substance became gaseous. Rav saw dragons coiling on the air, then boiling columns of smoke, then tangled hanks of indescribable monsters. He glanced over his shoulder and saw the snout of Foy poking out through a writhing mass of strange spined fishes. She blinked at him and although she lacked expression, he felt comforted by it.

She is mine, he thought. Great Foy.

Tatrini had ceased her song and had begun to unwrap the artefact lying upon the altar. The smoke had dissipated a little, so Rav could see the crown clearly, emitting its own radiance. Its light pulsed in time to the sinuous movements of the elemental spirits.

The atmosphere had felt dark and threatening before, but now Rav was aware that something of great significance was taking place. It was so powerful, he wanted to weep. Then Tatrini fractured the atmosphere with a loud and forceful voice.

'You!' she cried, pointing at Sinaclara. 'I charge you now to call upon the power of the Crown.'

Sinaclara expressed a sighing moan and raised her head, tendrils of damp hair hanging over her eyes. 'You will achieve nothing by this,' she said.

'It is not your concern,' Tatrini snapped. 'Comply!'

'You know I'd rather die than help you,' Sinaclara said.

Tatrini did not respond to this, but looked towards Tayven, who was watching intently.

'Clara,' Tayven murmured, his low voice carrying far. 'Remember what I said to you. Do as she asks.'

'Listen to him,' Tatrini said. 'He is one of your chosen ones, isn't he? Yet he sits here in the Fire Chamber, an avatar of air in my service.'

Sinaclara did not comment on this. 'I cannot connect with the spirit of the Crown for you,' she said.

Tayven raised himself from the throne a little. 'You should,' he said, and Rav perceived a peculiar constrained urgency in his voice.

Sinaclara turned her head slowly to regard him. An unspoken communication seemed to pass between them. Without taking her eyes from Tayven's steady gaze, Sinaclara began to chant in a low, guttural tone. 'Nee-ee-ess, zohdee-leh-dar, gar, buh-zod-deh, nee-ee-ess, lah-ee-ah-deh. Nee-ee-ess, gar, oh-tzee, moh-mah-oh, ah-leh-meh!'

Her voice became deeper and louder as the chant progressed, repeating the same lines over and over. All the while she kept her eyes fixed on Tayven. Rav saw attenuated eels of vapour slither from between her lips to fly upon the air, twisting up and up. Power flexed within the tattered incense smoke. It poured into the room through the walls of light. The form of the elemental avatars condensed once more into the semblance of humanoid giants. They stood motionless behind the quarter thrones, their arms folded before them.

The light within the Crown of Silence changed from white to indigo and the artefact began to emit a high humming tone. The vaporous serpents of Sinaclara's breath weaved fluidly towards it.

Tatrini threw up her arms and cried out, 'Paraga, Lord of Air; Foy, Queen of the Waters; Hespereth, Lady of Earth; Efrit, King of Flame. I call upon thee! I conjure thee into the avatars that await thy essence. Be present amongst us, oh mighty ones! Bring forth the power of the ancient dragons! Give us command over their being.'

It was then that Rav realised Tatrini was not aware the avatars were already present.

The creature of air behind Tayven raised its arms and its essence began to dissolve. As a curling torrent of vapour it writhed towards the centre of the chamber, where it was joined by the essence of earth, water and fire. As one spiralling column, the elementals rose to the ceiling of the chamber. Tayven stood up. He was cloaked in incense smoke that hugged his body like fabric.

Rav's heart was beating painfully fast. He was sure that at any moment Tayven would take control. All the time he had been lying in wait, pretending to be something he wasn't. It was so clear to Rav now. Tayven directed a piercing glance at Rav and mouthed the words, 'For your father.'

Tayven held out his arms, his head thrown back. At once, the essence of the elements swooped down and crashed into him as a bolt of pure energy. His body jerked backwards, but he did not fall. He absorbed the essence, his mouth wide in a rictus of agony.

'Tayven!' Tatrini cried. The Crown was now surrounded by an expanding bubble of indigo light that spat out sparks of a brighter purple radiance.

It seemed that Tayven had become taller, but physically he appeared no different. Power coursed through him, made lanterns of his eyes. He raised an arm and pointed at Tatrini.

Rav wanted to close his eyes. He couldn't say he was fond of his grandmother, but he did not want to see her hurt. He knew there was nothing he could say or do to influence Tayven. The man before him now was not the gentle friend he knew. Perhaps this had been part of Tayven all along, hidden in secret. Once he had spoken with the voice of Paraga, but now he was a vessel for all the elements. He was no longer human.

A lance of energy exploded from Tayven's outstretched fingers, but it was not directed at Tatrini.

Sinaclara staggered to her feet, cried, 'Tayven, no! No!'

The elemental charge, perhaps invisible to all but Tayven, Sinaclara and Rav, jetted across the room and hit Bayard hard in the centre of his chest, in a more powerful re-enactment of the first ritual they'd performed together. The prince's body flew up into the air and then crashed back down onto the throne, where it jerked around in a hideously mechanical way.

Leo leapt from his throne and ran to Rav's side, climbing onto the seat with him and hugging him fiercely, burying his face in Rav's hair. 'Stop them,' he murmured hoarsely. 'Rav, do something.'

As to why Leo thought Rav should have any power to affect events, Rav was unsure. He put a reassuring hand on Leo's shoulder, trying to interpret what he was seeing. He thought that Sinaclara's cry had been to stop Bayard being hurt, but he could see that was not the case. The searing radiance still poured out of Tayven's hand into Bayard, but it was not killing him. It was being *passed* to him. Rav could see this clearly, totally confused by what Tayven was doing. His father had told him he should trust Tayven, but surely Bayard shouldn't be given the combined power of the dragons?

Tatrini stood rigid, her face bleached of colour, her eyes wide and dark. Sinaclara looked like a demented witch, paralysed by what she was witnessing.

After what felt like hours, the energy dissipated from Tayven's body and he dropped his arm. The walls became solid once more and the radiance within them vanished. All was silent, but for the gasping of Bayard. Tatrini stood motionless, her expression that of stunned shock.

'What have you done?' Sinaclara cried huskily, shaking her head.

Tayven continued to stare at Bayard. 'I have done what must be done.'

Sinaclara staggered forward. 'Bayard must not be emperor. He is not the True King!'

Tayven glanced at her. 'It is what they want,' he said. 'And they must have it. I know this now.'

Sinaclara put her head into her hands, her body slumped into a posture of utter defeat.

Tatrini recovered her composure. She went to Tayven and embraced him, although his body remained stiff and unyielding in her hold. 'You have proved yourself this night,' she said, 'although in what way I am not yet sure. Did you channel the power of all the elements into Bayard?'

Tayven put his hands upon her forearms, gently pushed her away a little. 'Yes. He must be the avatar of the empire, but you must not crown him.'

Tatrini frowned. 'Why not? We have the Crown. It is alive amongst us.'

'Look at him,' Tayven said.

Bayard drooped over his throne, his limbs still shaking. His eyes were unfocused. Tatrini uttered a sound of distress, or perhaps merely annoyance, and hurried to her son's side. She put her hands upon his face and glanced round at Tayven. 'Will he recover? Or have you destroyed him?' She did not sound so grateful now.

'He will recover,' Tayven said. 'But if you believe in him, and your work, you must abide by the rules of the contest. There will be an ultimate choice to be made, an ultimate conflict to endure. If Bayard is victorious, then Sinaclara must crown him, as she vowed to crown the True King last year.'

'I will not!' Sinaclara spat, new strength coming to her voice.

'I have the dragon's breath,' Tayven said calmly. 'I speak only truth.'

'Once you did!' Sinaclara said coldly. 'Now, I am not so sure. You lied to me. You did not tell me the true reason for coming here tonight. I would rather have died than have assisted in this matter. You knew that! You are despicable. I can't believe I trusted you!'

Rav, watching this exchange in shocked exhaustion, noticed three shadowy shapes slinking out of the darkness amongst the columns. Dragon daughters. They were creeping up behind Tayven, as real as Rav had ever seen them. He could tell they were attracted by the energy of conflict in the air, that it was food and drink to them, and that they had been there all along. They seemed drawn particularly towards Tayven, reaching out with their clawed fingers to touch him. Rav tried to utter a warning, but as in a nightmare, he could make no sound.

Tayven glanced at him and blinked slowly, as if to communicate he was aware of what was happening. He did not turn to confront the shadows that clustered behind him, just spoke to them softly. 'Jia, Misk, Thrope. Go now. Do your work, as I have done yours this night.'

'What did you say?' Tatrini snapped.

Tayven shook his head. 'Nothing. Let me take Bayard to his chamber. I will do what I can to restore him.'

'Despicable beast!' Sinaclara snarled. 'You are the lie, Tayven, the only lie in creation.'

Tayven ignored her angry words. Behind him, as wisps of vapour, the dragon daughters spiralled out of chamber, seeping beneath the closed doors.

Gastern had visited the bedchamber of his wife and now lay sleepless in his own room. He had been visited by a powerful urge, which he told himself was sexual, but in reality, it was something entirely different. He had wanted Rinata to give him some kind of assurance and comfort, to tell him he wasn't going mad. But the empress, as she always did, had remained passive beneath his body, her eyes glassy like those of a corpse. For one hideous moment, Gastern imagined she was indeed dead, and had always been so. His lust dissipated. He rose from her bed and rearranged his robe. Rinata said nothing, turned onto her side. So the emperor had returned to his own empty chambers, awaiting shadows.

When the night-time visitations had first occurred, Gastern had imagined that an avatar of Madragore was attempting to communicate with him, to show him the way for the future. He had followed vague longings out into the city streets and sometimes it seemed to him that a network of light connected all the shrines and churches of Magrast, each emanating from a great node of radiance that was the high cathedral. As guardian of this light, Madragore's representative on earth, Gastern checked the lines and where he perceived a dimming of the brightness, he stretched out his hands and sought to increase it, investing it with his own life force. But now there were too many weak areas for him to cover. Each night, the flaws grew more numerous.

Perhaps he needed to confide in Alguin or Mordryn so that the fire mages could help him in his work. But a rational part of him was afraid that the clergy would not be able to see the spirit light and certainly could not heal it.

What had begun as a holy quest had slowly mutated into a torment. There were shadows ahead of him, evil shadows, who sought to undo his work as quickly as he could make repairs. He could see them now, beginning to manifest in the dense black corners of the room. They filled him with a terrible primal fear that reminded him of how he had felt in the dream of the three queens. This was the black queen made manifest.

He'd never been able to see anything with his physical eyes, but tonight the suggestions of shapes were more defined. They were slowly spiralling columns of darkness that in their lithe movements suggested the forms of sinuous women. Gastern wanted to look away, but could not. He swallowed and his throat was dry, the windpipe sticking together painfully. He coughed, swallowed twice more. He could see arms now, lissom limbs waving upon the air, darker than the blackness from which they derived.

'Come now, mighty emperor,' a voice hissed in his mind. 'Come with us. Follow us.'

Gastern made a sacred sign and uttered the first few lines of a prayer. 'Madragore, Lord of Flame, Destroyer of all Darkness, attend thy son and servant.'

The shapes in the shadows uttered tittering sighs, like a windchime of thin dry bones clattering together in the breeze. 'To understand light, you must first understand the absence of light,' they whispered. 'The emperor is lord of all, is he not? He should be afraid of nothing. Come forth, mighty emperor. Follow us.'

He could see them now, the three of them, standing at the foot of his bed. They were black goddesses with blue fire for eyes, necklaced with the bones of serpents.

'You are no creatures of Madragore!' Gastern cried. 'I exorcise you, in the name of the lord of flame.'

'You are wrong,' said one of the creatures. 'We and Madragore are one, as are all beings of subtle essence. Know us, and you know him. But only the bravest may endure the lesson we teach. An emperor must be that brave, must he not?'

One of the creatures extended an arm that was so long, the fingers nearly touched Gastern's cheek. 'Come with us. Take the test of fire.'

'There is only one god,' Gastern said, 'and his name is Madragore.' But still his limbs moved involuntarily. His feet felt around on the floor for his jewelled slippers, his hands moved like spiders on the coverlet seeking his robe.

All the while, his eyes were fixed on the undulating shapes in front of him.

Beyond the imperial bedroom, the palace lay in silence, as if every servant and guard slept in the arms of a magical spell. Gastern followed the floating wisps of darkness along the labyrinthine corridors, down breathless flights of steps, beneath ceremonial arches where banners hung motionless, thick with the dust of ages. He crossed stark parade grounds, where the moonlight fell down like hard rain. Shadows were sharply defined, the world black and white.

Out through the many gatehouses Gastern went. No one saw him pass. Three women walked upon the broad road ahead of him, women who left misty footsteps, whose dark hair swung down their backs like dense incense smoke. He could see their tiny waists, their swaying hips, their little feet. Surely they were beautiful, but they could not be good, nor part of Madragore's design. Gastern was aware of a yearning within him, which was the need for an answer, for union. He could not stop himself following the shadow women, because he dared to hope they could lead him to it.

They passed the slumbering churches and the great hunched bulk of the cathedral that squatted in the heart of the city like an obsidian demon with wings folded over its face. Gastern could see now that the sacred building was composed entirely of petrified gargoyles. Their grimacing faces peered out from every eave and spire. If the right words were spoken, perhaps they would come to life and fly away in all directions. People would wake in the morning and there would only be an immense crater where once the cathedral had stood.

The shadow women did not pause here, but led Gastern onwards, out to the artisan quarter of the city and beyond. He passed through the shantytowns of itinerant workers who laboured at the fisheries around the canal docks, but he did not see his surroundings. His jewelled slippers trod through mud and sewage that lay reeking in the rough streets, but he did not see it. He passed a gallows where an angry mob had lynched a child-killer, but he did not see it.

He went out of the city to where huge black crags reared against the stars, their striated folds glowing in the moonlight. They looked as if they were streaked with white bird dung, but this was in fact a natural formation of the rock. At their feet, yellowish vapour coiled up from the earth and there were pools of milky liquid. This was the holy place of the Splendifers, the pits of the fire-drakes, where initiates were required to spend a night alone.

258

Gastern clambered over the sharp rocks, ripping the fabric of his slippers and the palms of his hands. Pearls rolled from his feet and sank without a ripple into the pools. The shadow women lured him on, into the heart of the pits. They walked backwards, facing him, never once missing a step, but moving surely from rock to rock amongst the deadly pools. He could see them clearly now. Their faces were sharp-featured, the almond eyes slanting like a cat's or a snake's. They had vertical pupils that were windows into oblivion amidst a smoking blue. Their hands were clawed and covered with strange patterns. Their arms moved continually upon the air, so that it looked as if they had multiple limbs.

They were motionless now, standing before him, fixing him with their radiant eyes. Gastern panted and gasped; the acrid smoke rising from the pools seared his lungs. He knew of this place, and considered it damned. He wanted to prohibit anyone coming here, because it was soaked in pagan heresy. Now he must experience it for himself, for only by knowing it could he gain authority over it.

'Who are you?' he wheezed.

One of the women stepped towards him and extended four arms. Four hands gripped his shoulders. 'We are the dragon daughters,' she said, 'I am Jia, daughter of Foy, the Lady of Water. Worship in the spirit the things of the spirit.'

Another of the women came to him and stroked his face with the tips of her claws. 'I am Thrope,' she said 'Worship in the mind the things of the mind.'

And the last came forward, grinning, revealing pointed teeth. 'I am Misk. Worship in the body the things of the body.'

'No,' Gastern said weakly.

'Yes,' hissed the dragon daughters in unison.

Gastern tried to push them from him, crying, 'I exorcise thee in the name of the true god, Madragore, Lord of the Fire of the Sun!'

The dragon daughters released him, but stood in a circle around him. 'You are afraid,' said Jia, 'and an emperor cannot be afraid.'

'You are weak,' said Thrope, 'and an emperor must not be weak.'

'You are blind,' said Misk, 'and an emperor cannot be blind. We come to open your eyes, to give you strength and freedom from fear. You should thank us. The True King welcomes these things, and you believe yourself to be the True King, do you not? Dwell in the darkness of thought and drink of the poison of life.'

'Get thee from me, unwelcome spirits!' Gastern cried. He slipped on the rock and his right leg sank slowly into one of the pools. A puff of evil vapour rose up to fill his eyes and nose, burning down into his chest. He coughed until he thought his lungs would burst and could not open his eyes for the burning pain, but gradually the smoke dissipated and his vision cleared. He drew in a desperate lungful of air and blinked. There were no shadow women before him. He was alone. Awareness came back with speed and he realised the danger of his situation. He must leave here at once. Scrabbling, he sought to retrace his steps, all the while cursing himself for his folly. Demons had led him here, adversaries of his god. They sought to seduce and destroy him.

Clear ground was in sight. He had only a few more feet to go. Tomorrow he must convene a meeting of the fire mages and tell them everything. They would have to believe him, trust his vision. Danger lurked at the heart of the empire, and it must be rooted out and destroyed. The Order of Splendifers must be broken up and reformed in the name of Madragore, with new healing rituals to cleanse them of the taint of evil. Valraven should be here. Perhaps this was happening because of his absence. Lorca was no substitute.

Gastern was just about to step over the last pool to safety when a jet of yellow steam erupted from the rock ahead of him. He dodged to the side, determined to leap the rest of the way and run back to the palace, but the steam did not dissipate. It hung on the air, expanding and changing colour to a deep luminous scarlet as he gazed at it. He saw eyes within it, burning terrible eyes, and a long-snouted head from which a crimson tongue flicked forth.

Gastern cried out in horror and raised his hands before his face. A firedrake, the king of all fire-drakes, hung before him, towering up to the sky, scarlet wings held wide. It exhaled a gout of fiery breath that enveloped Gastern entirely. He experienced its icy burn, which was nothing like the natural heat of flame. It was full of voices, of cries and screams, of prayers and laments. It was full of truth, too much to bear. Gastern saw himself for the small puny creature he was, and realised that all humans were small puny creatures. He became aware of the immensity of existence and the complex web of energy that connected every living thing. He saw all the ignorance, stupidity and cruelty of the world and how it was intricately connected with everything that was enlightened, aware and holy. There was no division. To be Madragore's avatar, he had to be Madragore's bane and that meant bearing every terrible thing in the world with full awareness. *Dwell in the darkness of thought and drink of the poison of life* . . .

Gastern uttered a scream, his mind aching as if it was about to explode. He wanted to tear out his eyes, stop his ears. There was no point to anything. His rule was a sham, his empire a conceit. To believe otherwise was an illusion, the worst of all lies.

Then he was running, running, through the streets of Magrast. He passed the dangling corpse of the child-killer and the terrified screams of the murderer's victim assailed his ears like burning needles. He was swamped by images of poverty, desperation and despair, and over all hung the petrifying stink of human ignorance. Onwards, to the cathedral, which reared as a testament to humanity's blindness against the seeing sky. From every house in the city came the sound of cruel, passionless laughter and the whimper of utter desolation. Ahead, the palace was a rotten honeycomb sprawling over the central hill. Gastern could see now that at one time it had been a sacred place, where the first kings of Magravandias had made their pledges to the land. All that was buried now and forgotten. Forlorn ghosts of noble men and women thronged around it, singing a sad lament for all that was lost. Gastern pushed through them and it was like fighting wet sheets of cobwebs. There was no sanctuary now. Even dawn could not dispel the unseen darkness that shrouded the land. That shrouded life itself.

In the morning, Gastern's valet summoned Lord Senefex and Archimage Mordryn to the imperial chambers. Horgan was in a state of severe distress and showed them directly into Gastern's bedroom the moment they arrived. The sight that greeted them there would never leave them and both men had to pull handkerchiefs from their pockets to cover their noses, for the stink was terrible.

Gastern had torn down all the ornate hangings from his bed and the windows. He had scored the tapestried wallpaper with his own hands. He had broken every ornament and had defecated in each corner of the room. He had smeared himself with is own faeces and now sat naked, rocking, in the centre of this reeking devastation.

'Gastern!' Mordryn shouted, as if loudness could reach a sane part of the emperor's mind. 'What is this?'

Gastern looked up at the archimage with strangely milky eyes. 'We live in the hell we have made,' he said, thick spittle flying from his lips. His rocking motion became more agitated. 'The truth lies in that which is not bestial, for that is our nature, the core of our brains, the only union is with lies, lies are really the truth. We arose from the slime but have never left it. Slime is everywhere. Everything else is illusion. At the end of creation lies destruction and, behold, I know the darkness that lies behind the sun.'

Mordryn turned to Horgan. 'Call the physicians at once,' he said.

'At once, your holiness.' The valet bowed shakily and ran from the room.

'What, in Madragore's name, has happened to him?' Senefex said. 'Is this poison?'

Mordryn flicked a glance towards his colleague. 'If it is, I've seen nothing like it before.' He began to pick his way fastidiously through the mess, holding up his robes of office to avoid soiling their hem. 'Gastern,' he said gently. 'What has happened, my son? You can tell me.'

Gastern began to titter madly and scrabbled backwards, crablike, on the floor. 'Oh, you can't touch me. I know what you are. I've seen you in the smoke. You are the deceiver, who has built an unholy edifice in the name of God. If you touch me, I will burn you.'

'I am your holy father,' Mordryn said. 'Be at peace, my son. Speak to me. I am here to help and comfort you.'

Gastern bared his teeth. 'I know what you are. The dragon daughters showed it all to me. You want me dead. They all want me dead.' He began to laugh hysterically. 'But I am already dead, so what can you do about it now, eh? Nothing! Nothing!'

Mordryn sighed and backed away. 'He has gone,' he said.

Senefex drew in his breath through his nose. 'We need Palindrake here,' he said. 'We need him back in the world.'

'We do indeed,' said Mordryn. 'Our work in this noisome room is done. Let Alguin come here and work his art, though I doubt even he can reach Gastern now.'

'He mentioned dragon daughters,' Senefex said. 'That is interesting. Who is at work here?'

'Perhaps there is a component we don't yet know,' Mordryn said thoughtfully.

'Palindrake?'

'I don't think so. It could be his sisters, perhaps, or even his wife. We should not underestimate the women.'

'A meeting will be convened.'

'Of course. And we must attend to matters of state.'

'I will make the necessary preparations,' Senefex said. 'Would you care to share breakfast at my residence?'

'That would be delightful,' Mordryn said.

Together they left the room, while Gastern sat rocking, muttering at the walls, lost in the terror of reality.

Prince Bayard awoke from unsettling dreams, but he felt clear in mind and healthy in body. Although he'd been virtually unconscious when Tayven had put him to bed, now he was totally invigorated. It was strange the way things turned out. Bayard would never have imagined that Tayven Hirantel would assist him in any way. In Tayven's place he would not have done so. He could not be so forgiving and tolerant. But perhaps Tayven recognised that Bayard should be emperor. Everyone had always said Hirantel had the clear sight. As Bayard truly believed in his right to be king, he did not question why others might disagree. Anyone who did was a traitor and would be dealt with accordingly. He rose from his bed, smug with satisfaction.

The night had been long and Bayard's dreams had been detailed and exhausting. He had travelled the world, aware of every seed of iniquity within it. He had gazed upon brutality and chaos from the highest peaks, but it had not shocked him. Unlike his elder brother, Gastern, Bayard was already aware of what humanity's dark side comprised and accepted it. He worked with it and recognised it within himself without judgement. He also believed he had the capacity to be light as well as darkness. His mother had ingrained into him since birth that he was a potential sun king. Looking at himself naked in the long cheval glass of his bedroom, Bayard saw nothing to contradict that. He was magnificent. He had won everything he had set out to gain. The ritual at Caradore all those years ago, when he, Valraven and Pharinet had attempted to conjure up Foy, had been a pathetic travesty in comparison to what he and Tayven had achieved last night. Foy was in him now, as were the other elemental rulers. He also had Tayven at his side, despite all that Almorante and Khaster Leckery had done to try and prevent that. Almorante, once a bitter rival who had sought to assassinate his brother, had served Bayard by securing the Crown of Silence. Whatever ambitions might remain in Almorante's heart, no one could stand in the way of the True King. The whole world would soon be his.

CHAPTER TWENTY-FIVE

Man from the Sea

Pharinet brushed out her hair before her dressing-table, which stood between two tall windows in her bedroom. She yawned as she yanked the brush through the tangles. Outside the morning was foggy, even though summer graced the land. The fog must have rolled in off the sea in the night. Sound was muted, but Pharinet could still make out the vague outlines of the beach far below the castle, where the great black rocks looked like sleeping dragons. She could see a white wrinkle where low waves broke against the sand. And there was something else: a dark figure walking through the mist, head bent as if in introspection. Was that Everna out there?

Pharinet went to the window, rubbed it and peered more intently out at the beach. No, that could not be Everna. The fog might have skewed perspective, but it looked as if the figure was unnaturally tall. Without pausing for further evaluation, Pharinet pulled on her clothes: trousers, shirt, boots and coat. She ran out of her room and down through the castle, startling servants and guards in her passage. Voices called out to her, but she paid them no heed.

Outside, the air was humid and muggy, difficult to breathe. Hamsin stood talking to a couple of his men near the main gate.

'My lady!' he cried as he caught sight of Pharinet charging towards him. 'Is all well with you? What's happened?'

'Stay here!' Pharinet commanded. 'I will speak to you presently.'

Without pausing, she ran under the arch of the gate and onto the cliff path. Quickly, she went to the place where a narrow staircase cut out of the rock sloped steeply to the shore. The figure was still there, standing motionless. Pharinet could not see whether it was staring out to sea or up at her. The ocean was strangely quiescent, moving sluggishly. Fog rolled off it like young wood smoke, thick and white.

By the time Pharinet reached the sand, she could no longer see the figure, but she was sure it had been female. A female Titan, too tall to be human. It must have been a vision, then, a portent. Pharinet stood upon the beach, gazing up and down it, but could see nothing unusual. What did this mean? Was it to do with Ren and Elly, or Val himself? She had no doubt it meant something.

Disconsolately, she walked up the shore, following the tide-line towards her favourite cave, where as a girl she had spent a lot of time fantasising about the future. It was also the place where she'd first made love with Valraven. Now she craved its memories, caught in the fabric of the rock.

The tide was lapping at the outer stones of the cave, which were covered in bright green weed known as mermaid's hair. Pharinet climbed to one of the larger rocks and sat down upon it, her chin in her hands.

Valraven had been missing for a couple of months now, and there was still no news of Ren and Elly. Niska had assured her she shouldn't worry, and the conviction in the Merante's voice had comforted Pharinet for a while, but now, as time went on, she felt her optimism begin to fray. Everna felt the same, she knew, although her older sister would not speak of it. Pharinet was aware Everna was nervous of inviting bad luck by voicing negative thoughts. Pharinet had come to trust Niska implicitly, but was it possible she might be wrong? The Sisterhood of the Dragon had met twice a week since Niska had returned from Old Caradore alone. They had pooled their strength and projected it to Valraven, wherever he roamed. Niska said that this was all that they could do. She spoke of having seen Varencienne and Ellony in visions and insisted they were not in danger. The rest of them could only take her word for it.

Pharinet picked up a pebble and cast it into the advancing water below. This time of waiting was a torment. What if it never ended? Many years ago she'd learned of the heritage of the Dragon Heir; so many terrible things had happened since then. Mistakes had been made in ignorance. She did not regret what had happened between her and Valraven, because it seemed as right to her now as it had when they'd first become close, but she mourned their estrangement. That should not have happened. They should have handled things differently. She should not have let Bayard seduce and deceive her in his desire to take command of Foy. It was too late, though, for these regrets. Nothing could wipe away the past and she was sure that whatever Valraven and his wife and daughter were going through now was the result of her past actions with Bayard and her brother, the ritual which had resulted in the death of Khaster's sister Ellony. A thought occurred to her. What had happened to Val's first wife had been terrible, but if it had not happened, then Varencienne would never have come to Caradore. The ritual with Ren at the old domain, when Valraven had made the first tentative steps to embrace his heritage, might never have taken place. Pharinet saw Varencienne in her mind's eye. She pictured her sister-in-law's laughing face, the brightness she had brought to Caradore that had healed so much. She was not jealous of Ren, because she was not a rival for Val's affections. No one was. That was the pity of it.

Pharinet picked up another stone to throw into the water, but her hand stilled before she could release it. Something was moving in the fog, just a few yards from where she sat. Something was dragging itself from the water, a dark, hunched form. Holding her breath, Pharinet scrambled to her feet and narrowed her eyes. What was it? Just a bundle of flotsam rags, or something else? 'Foy, preserve me,' she whispered and, dropping the stone, made a sacred sign with three fingers against her brow and lips.

A figure was walking out of the sea, its footsteps slow and heavy. Water weighed down its dark clothes and its pale hands felt the air in front of it, as if it were blind.

'Halt!' she called, attempting to invest her voice with authority. 'This is the land of Palindrake. Who goes there?' Her voice sounded muffled in the fog.

The figure did not pause, but tried to increase its pace. Pharinet felt a *frisson* of fear. It was a man, she could tell that much. He might mean her harm.

'Halt!' she called again. 'I will call the guard!'

'Pharry!' The voice was hardly more than a wheeze, but it carried far. She knew it.

In an instant, Pharinet threw off her coat, leapt into the water and waded out to the man crawling from the sea. The waves, though not as powerful as usual, sucked at her legs, impeding her passage. Eventually she reached him and put her hands upon his arms. She wiped the soaked hair from his face, looked into it. Her brother.

'Val!' She clasped him close and they both sank to their knees in the frothing water. Was this possible? She drew away. 'Are you a dream?'

He blinked at her, his face as pale as bleached bone. He shook his head. 'Help me.'

She hauled him to his feet and, almost carrying him, assisted him to dry land. Here, he sank down on the sand, his body shuddering.

'Get up,' Pharinet said. 'You're freezing. We must get you home.'

'A moment,' Valraven said. 'Give me a moment.'

Pharinet went to fetch her coat, which she put around his shoulders. Then she squatted beside him and stroked his face. 'What happened? How did you get here? Were you shipwrecked?'

He took her hands between his shivering icy fingers. 'Pharry, I have seen such things.' He shook his head. Words were clearly inadequate.

'What things?' Pharinet persisted.

'She is alive, Pharry. She is with us again.'

'Who? Ren? Where is she?'

'No,' Valraven said, 'not Ren. Foy. The curse is broken, Pharry. I have reclaimed my heritage. All that you and the Sisterhood have worked for: it begins from here.'

Valraven's reappearance naturally caused a great furore within the castle. Everna wept to see him, along with Oltefney and most of the female staff. Goldvane, the family steward, began to organise a feast for later in the day. Servants ran along the corridors, and the sound of their laughter made Pharinet realise that few people had been laughing in Caradore since Valraven's disappearance.

All Valraven wanted to do was rest, but before he gave in to sleep, he asked to speak with his sisters in his private rooms. For some moments, he simply sat on the edge of the bed and held onto their hands as they knelt before him, as if he could not believe he was really home. Outside, the mist was slowly clearing. Perhaps it was an occult medium by which he'd returned to Caradore.

He described all that had occurred at Old Caradore, although Niska had already told them most of it. What Niska had not known, of course, was that Ilcretia Palindrake had somehow travelled through time to reach her descendant, and that it had been she who'd taken him away. She walked the way of light, which was not linear.

'Sometimes,' Valraven said, 'it felt completely ordinary. I was taken to a Caradore that was the old domain in its prime, but there were no servants there, no family, only Ilcretia and myself. She explained it was not a "real" place as such, but an etheric representation of the castle. Still, everything felt real enough beneath my hands. I slept in a bed, ate food, walked in the gardens. For what felt like many weeks, Ilcretia imparted some of her knowledge to me. I learned about the life force that animates the entire universe and how an adept can manipulate that force through their own will. I learned to tap into it, to move it with my mind, allow different frequencies of it to be channelled to my body. Ilcretia taught me much about what makes a man a man, and the great

267

fears that lie hidden beneath the surface. I began to see the empire as an expression of these fears, a great conglomeration of them that moves forward in destruction.

'It seemed to me that no sane person would wish to be part of such a thing, and that even Maycarpe was wrong in his desire to find a True King. How could such a man exist? To be a king, he would need the desire to rule others, and that would make him a creature motivated by fear and greed. It was a paradox.'

One day Valraven had asked Ilcretia, 'What are you training me for?'

'To be king,' she answered.

'I have no desire to rule,' he said.

'But you have ruled Caradore for many years,' she said. 'Does the trust and faith of your people offend you so much?'

'That is different,' he replied. 'It is an obligation I have, that I inherited.'

'Just so,' said Ilcretia, and smiled at him. 'Your family live from the land and the produce your tenants grow, make and build. Your obligation is to keep those people safe, to be their link to the land, the spiritual king, who would die for their sakes. The people love you, for you are a fair man. You have earned the right to rule that was passed on in your blood.'

One night, as Valraven was retiring for bed, Ilcretia came to his room, as silent and ghostly as an owl. She beckoned to him without speaking and he followed her down to the cellars of the castle that, in another reality, he had investigated with Niska. Here they were not ruined and dank and empty, but filled with neatly stacked shelves of produce and labelled casks. The floors were swept clean, the walls freshly brushed with distemper. It was as if an army of servants, cooks and cleaners had only recently left – even the air seemed to move faintly with their passing – but of course, other than Ilcretia and himself, the castle was empty, like a painting coming to life.

Holding a lamp aloft, Ilcretia led the way through the confusing warren of passages and chambers, until they came to a wide flight of shallow steps that led downwards into darkness. Here, Ilcretia paused and, without turning to Valraven, said, 'In this place the ancient covenant was observed by our ancestors.'

Valraven peered down into the uninviting gloom and was a small boy beside the towering stillness of Ilcretia, nervous amongst the folds of her skirts. 'Must we go down there, Mama?'

'Yes, my son.' She put a hand against the back of his neck. 'Too long have you been denied. But don't be afraid. The dragons will protect you. It is your right to walk here.'

With a gentle push, she propelled him forward. He could still feel her hands upon him as they began their descent. The lamp cast a dim flickering glow around them, holding them in a fragile bubble of light.

He thought they were on their way to a meeting with the Ustredi, even Foy herself. Years before, he had made a similar journey in his mind with Varencienne. He expected to emerge into a large cave, with a sandy floor and a black lagoon, from where the Ustredi would rise, seeking tribute from their landbound allies. But when they stepped from the final stair and Ilcretia held her lamp higher, he was faced with an unknown place. A spit of flagstones tongued out from the stairs, surrounded by dark water on three sides. The water appeared to be a narrow U-shaped canal surrounded by walls of natural rock. Into the walls, niches had been cut, deep recesses into darkness.

'This is the chamber of dreams,' Ilcretia said. 'Here the Palindrakes communed with their element, the sea.' She gestured at the water. 'Go to one of the niches, Val.'

He looked at her in appeal. 'Must I, Mama? It is dark and cold.'

She nodded, just once. 'You must. You are not a child, Valraven, but a man. Relearn yourself. Face the darkness.'

Reluctantly Valraven went to the edge of the flagstones and gazed down into the oily water. Anything might be lurking there. He shuddered.

'Do it, my son,' Ilcretia said softly.

Without looking back at her, he eased himself down into the water. It came to the middle of his thighs and when he looked up, he saw that the stone spit was about six inches above his head. Ilcretia was standing there, staring down at him. Her face was expressionless, but he got the impression it was taking her a great effort to remain that way. She *was* afraid for him. He had seen that expression before, on the day when the fire mages had marked him, the day his father had died and Caradore had died with him. When had that been? It was all so hazy now. It felt as if it was hundreds of years ago, yet surely it had been only yesterday?

Valraven waded to one of the niches and pressed himself into it. A feathery darkness closed itself all around him. Dimly, he saw his mother moving away from him to the wall near the foot of the stairs. He could no longer see what she was doing, but he heard a strange sound, like metal grating against metal, stone against stone. The earth shuddered beneath him, the walls around him. 'Mama!' he cried, but she was gone.

He was alone in the darkness, and the only sound was the slap of water against rock, and now, another sound, that of heavy stone grinding against the walls. He could no longer see the stone spit clearly, even though the lamp still stood upon it. An eclipse of his sight. It was then he realised he was being walled in. Inexorably a slow-moving slab slid in from the side to entomb him in the water.

Terror engulfed him in a black wave. He beat his fists against the wet rock, cried out, pleaded for help and shrieked with fury. How long this went on he later had no way of knowing, but eventually a thread of light ignited in his mind, telling him Ilcretia did not intent to kill him. He was here to learn to be king.

Shuddering and panting, he leaned back against the far wall of the niche. Ilcretia had called this place the chamber of dreams, so he must dream, then. He closed his eyes, although it made no difference whether they were open or not. A creeping coldness advised him the waters were rising. The tide was coming in. He thought he could hear the far calls of sea birds and the muted crash of collapsing waves. His entire body went slowly numb, until the water reached just below his chin. He felt drowsy now. He would give himself up to sleep and whatever came after.

He could no longer feel the walls around him, but was aware of space and air. Ahead of him, a silvery light appeared, growing brighter and brighter. He saw that it was a silver ship, her tall masts adorned with billowing silken sails. Her figurehead was of a mermaid whose extended arm pointed out the passage ahead. The ship moved towards Valraven swiftly, her unearthly light casting a leprous glow over the sluggish black water. Now she loomed over him so completely he felt he must be drowned beneath her, but then, without warning, a transition occurred and he found himself standing upon the prow, gazing ahead into darkness. He could hear the creak of the ship's timbers and the slow slap of water below, but there were no other sounds. He knew the name of this ship: she was the Dragon Queen. She was an avatar of Foy herself.

His consciousness slipped out of his body and now he hung amongst the rigging, looking down upon a boy with long black hair, clad in dark clothes. Who are you? Valraven wondered. Are you me, or an earlier version of me, or are you all the Valravens who have ever lived since the day Caradore fell to the Magravands?

There is only one, he thought.

With this realisation, his essence was swept with sickening speed out of the vision. He found himself crouching in a corner of Caradore Castle with the sounds of battle all around. He was terrified, his hands over his eyes, his knees up around his ears. He thought he was about to die. Then he heard his mother's voice, scolding him. 'Val, get up! Get up at once!' He lowered his hands and realised another boy was hunched against him, sobbing quietly, a low desperate sound. His mother stood nearby, shrouded in a dark, hooded cloak.

'Come on,' Ilcretia ordered. 'Get up. You must come with me. Now!'

Valraven eased himself away from the other boy, who tugged at his arm. 'Val, don't leave me.'

'I won't, Khas,' he said. 'Come with me. It'll be all right. Mama's here. She'll hide us.'

'No,' Ilcretia said. 'Just you, Val.'

'Mama, I can't.'

'It is what must be. Come now.'

The hideous sounds of fighting were getting closer. Valraven could hear the crash of stone, the hiss of arrows, the screams and moans of dying men, of men fighting for their lives. His mother was holding out her hand to him. She represented an island of safety in a tumultuous sea of terror. The air was filled with black smoke that smelled of burning flesh. Uttering a cry, Valraven pulled himself away from the other boy and ran to his mother's arms. At once she began to drag him away up a passage, towards a door that led to a high tower.

The other boy tried to come with them, but Ilcretia beat him away. 'You cannot come with us, Khaster. Your fate is not the same.'

Valraven had to listen to the cries of his friend as he was hauled away from him. He remembered how Khaster had come to stay with him for a summer holiday, how none of this had been expected, how Khaster's home lay safely to the south, how it might as well have been a thousand miles away. He had not known then that the Magravands had crossed the Leckery land, and that Khaster's father had ultimately surrendered because he feared for the lives of his people. If he had sent a messenger ahead, perhaps Caradore Castle could have been prepared for the attack, but the Leckery patriarch decided his only responsibility was towards his own people. The decision had cost him dear and haunted him for the rest of his days, but it could not be reversed. These actions had been written in stone, and had cast their dark light upon all future generations of both families. Valraven, becoming aware of these facts for the first time, could see that the legacy of Caradore's fall involved more than the loss of his rightful inheritance. It had involved betrayal, abandonment and the death of trust.

Now he stood upon a bare hill that would become the central mound of the city of Magrast. All around him were ranked the kings and queens of history, the sorceresses, wise women, magi, wizards and shamans of all the ages. He saw the company of divine bards, who could speak only virtue, and the champions of kings, both male and female, leaning upon their swords, clad in shining armour. In the centre of this blessed company stood the first king, who had been little more than a barbarian, but who had sought to unite the warring factions of his country. The magus, who was his counsellor, stood before him, holding out a strange crown of spikes and tines that looked as if it had been fashioned from living coral and bone. Flames danced within it and what looked like sparkling diamonds hanging from it were drops of clear water. A woman with red hair, clad in a dark blue gown, stepped forward and took the crown from the magus. She placed it upon the head of the king, saying, 'Thus do I crown you, Casaban, in the name of Paraga, Foy, Efrit and Hespereth, the elemental dragons who represent the powers of the cosmos and the forces of creation. Rule wisely, oh king, for the land is your flesh, its people your blood. Joy to them who wait to hear the word from your lips. Love is the word, the law that commands time to relinquish its promise of death. For through your countenance, we and the land are immortal.'

Now, before Valraven's eyes, time accelerated. The divine company disappeared and buildings began to appear upon the hill. Valraven hung over it, looking down. He saw crude wattle and daub dwellings replaced by those of stone. He saw castles rise and boats sail up the great river from the sea, bearing produce from far lands. He saw armies form and witnessed the births of mighty men and women in high towers. He saw flags billow on the wind and heard the chants of joy issuing from the sacred temples that were nothing grander than stone circles upon bare hills. Had there ever been such a golden age, or was this merely the hope and desire of humanity expressed within his mind? For surely the darkness in men's hearts prevented any such Utopia. He saw it now, creeping out of every dwelling like a vile-smelling smoke. He saw, as pulsing sickly colours, the fear, greed, ignorance and seeping uncertainty that bred either hate or indifference. But there was nobility too, and love and honour. They were mixed together in a chaotic maelstrom of feeling, of force.

How do we overcome this? he thought. How can the light within us take control? For the fear is always stronger.

Then he was standing upon the hill once more, aeons before the first human had ever trodden there. The land was innocent, clean of humanity. A woman stood before him, the same one who had crowned Casaban. 'The answer lies in silence,' she said, 'and in the Way of Light. If you serve the light and hold the silence of awareness within you, you become your own Golden Land.'

'Awareness of what?' he asked.

'All that is. You cannot change the hearts of men and women, but you can live an example of all they aspire to be, a reflection of life and their connection to it.'

Now the dawn broke over the hills in the east. Valraven stood next to the red-haired woman and watched the sunrise. He heard a heavenly chant as of the voices of a thousand angels raised in song. He saw the elemental dragons rise from the land to hang above the hills. The light of the new sun became brighter and brighter and suddenly a bolt of searing radiance shot out of the dawn and struck Valraven on the forehead. He was filled with the light, part of it. He wanted to weep with poignant sadness and sheer bliss. Before him, in the light, hung the Crown of Silence. He saw Khaster, Shan, Tayven and Merlan upon their quest to locate it. He saw all that they had suffered and learned.

'The Crown of Silence is yours,' the woman said to him, 'as is the Way of Light. You are the Sea Dragon Heir. Take this light away from this place and use it to heal through awakening. Before the dawn, there will be darkness. Take your people to the old domain, for that is where the darkness will come for you. This time, the outcome must be different.'

'Who are you?' Valraven asked.

'I am Sinaclara,' she replied. 'And I am with you always. Soon I will come to you in flesh, as will your wife and daughter, and all those who must walk the path with you.'

Valraven had many more questions he wanted to ask, but before he could form any of them, his consciousness was yanked away once more. He found himself flailing in water. For a moment, he thought he was back in the chamber of dreams, but then realised he was out in the ocean surrounded by thick fog. Desperately he paddled water to keep afloat, looking around himself, seeking land. If he was near it, he could not see it through the fog.

Instinctively, he remembered the light within him; thinking of it filled him with warmth. He cried out, 'Foy! Attend me! I am in need!'

For a moment, nothing happened, but even so, Valraven did not fear. He felt as if the divine light burst out of him, from his eyes, his crown, his hands.

And then the water was boiling ahead of him. White foam burst through the surface, along with flotsam from long-sunken ships. In a mighty eruption of weed and spray, the dragon queen rose majestically from the sea. This was no vision, but reality. Valraven could see her wise serpent eyes looking down upon him. He realised he could call upon her now whenever he wished.

'Foy, we are in accord,' he said. 'I once took the decision to lay you to rest, but now I have awakened you, as I will awake the world, and all those within it who are asleep. Your time has come again, and I promise I will not fail you. When you rise, you rise in strength and vitality, for we are one.'

Foy could not speak, but he heard her words in his mind. 'My daughters do your work,' she said. 'We are with you.'

'You must bring Varencienne and Ellony home.'

'There is no need. Paraga guides them. They will come to you with Khaster Leckery, who is to be your Magus, and Shan, who is your Champion.'

'Tell me what has happened in Magrast. You must safeguard my son, or set the fire-drakes to do it.'

'Your son is guarded by Misk, Jia and Thrope and also the man who is your Bard, Tayven Hirantel. The Lady Sinaclara and Darris Maycarpe have been taken captive by the Grand Queen Mother. Gastern rants insane amongst his counsellors. Soon, the wolves will strike.'

'Take me home,' Valraven said.

Everna and Pharinet were speechless with shock. Valraven's throat was dry and sore. He had talked for hours, and yet he no longer felt tired. As if by instinct, Goldvane chose that moment to present himself at the door with a tray of refreshments.

'You know the rest,' Valraven said, gesturing to Goldvane where he should put the tray. 'I found myself at the shore and Pharry was there waiting for me.' He turned to his sister. 'The tall figure you described to me: I'm sure it led you to find me. It must have been an avatar of Foy.'

'I think that too,' Pharinet said. 'I can't believe all this has happened. We have waited so long.' She shook her head. 'Too long.'

'Unfortunately, we cannot sit around congratulating ourselves,' Valraven said. 'I must follow Sinaclara's advice and take our household north at once. I also think we should take the Leckerys with us.'

'My lord?' Goldvane said with frightened surprise, pausing in the act of arranging cutlery.

'You heard correctly,' Valraven said. 'We must leave here. I will explain everything to the staff shortly, but for now I would be grateful if you would meet with Hamsin and begin preparations. Send a messenger to Norgance immediately and tell Saska to do the same. Tell her that the message comes from Khaster.'

'Val!' Pharinet said, a smile hovering uncertainly around her mouth.

He shrugged. 'Well, how else can we get her to move quickly? A little deception is in order, but from what I've learned, it's not too far off the truth.'

'What did Sinaclara mean when she said the darkness would come for you at the old domain?' Everna asked.

'It means that Gastern has fallen,' Valraven replied, 'and that whoever follows him, which I am fairly sure will be Bayard, will realise I am a threat, simply because of the belief certain people have invested in me. I am sure that Gastern's fall will be a trigger for all those who follow

Maycarpe's way. They will begin to put the word about that the heir of Caradore should be the one to take the crown. Bayard will seek to replicate the actions of Cassilin, his ancestor.'

'But Old Caradore is a ruin,' Pharinet said. 'How can we defend ourselves there?'

'We must have faith,' Valraven said, 'and believe that the elements are on our side. We are meant to win this time.'

Pharinet stared at him with a strange expression in her eyes. 'You have decided to be king, haven't you?'

'Yes,' said Valraven.

'How do you know all this for certain, Val?'

'Because I am awake,' he replied.

CHAPTER TWENTY-SIX

Flight of the Dragon Heir

The new Fire Chamber of Magrast was situated in a governmental building annexed to the emperor's apartments in the palace. As Tatrini took
her place, with the morning sunlight falling in benignly through the tall
stained-glass windows, she reflected that few people who would take
their seats here today knew of the original chamber, nor how the
practices and duties of the fire mages had changed over the centuries.

All of the princes were present, every member of the council, as well as
Lord Senefex, who was chairing the meeting, and Archimage Mordryn
with his see of mages. Prince Bayard sat beside his mother and she had
instructed him to maintain a low profile during the meeting. No one
must suspect he had changed in any way. Gastern was notably absent:
the throne used by the emperor looked bleak in its emptiness. And
another seat stood vacant: that belonging to the Dragon Lord. Rufus
Lorca, Palindrake's deputy, had been invited, but for reasons of his own
had elected not to take the seat of his lord. He was positioned between
two veteran generals, who from time to time looked at him askance,
perhaps privately reproaching Palindrake for temporarily appointing
this young, unseasoned man in his place. But the Dragon Lord could
not have foreseen what would happen. Rumours were escalating within
the city concerning Palindrake's continued absence. He might even be
dead. And now there were other rumours to contemplate.

Rinata, as empress, had newly been given a seat in the Chamber. She
sat there now, white of face and troubled, not for her husband, perhaps,
but for herself and her son.

Once everyone had settled to their places and servants had distributed
flagons of water around the table, Senefex got to his feet, placing his
palms upon the polished wood. 'There is no point in temporising. We

are here today to discuss a grave matter that affects the very core of the empire. The royal physicians have confirmed that the emperor is suffering from a malady of the spirit. In short, he has lost his mind.'

A flurry of murmurs swept around the table and people shifted uneasily in their seats. Rinata put her fingers to her mouth, briefly closed her eyes.

Senefex raised a hand. 'This is uncomfortable news, but we must face reality. A number of treatments have been applied during the past week, but the physicians are united in their prognosis. Emperor Gastern's affliction shows no sign of responding to treatment and in fact his condition is rapidly deteriorating. Unfortunately tidings of his illness have spread through the city. It will not be long before it flies to every corner of the world. For the good of the empire, Gastern must renounce his throne. As he is incapable of making such a decision, we must agree unanimously that it is taken for him by the Fire Chamber. Before we proceed, we must vote on this. Is everyone in accord?'

Tatrini presumed everyone present must have already ordered their agents to secure any available information on Gastern's condition. All were aware of the gravity of the situation.

After a short pause, Mordryn said, 'Aye!'

Once the first voice had spoken, everyone else followed suit. Only Rinata remained silent, and no one took any notice of that.

Senefex nodded once. 'That is agreed, then. We meet here today to decide upon a course of action that is best for Magravandias. Unscrupulous individuals could seize this moment to cause disruption, and the losers in that scenario will be the Magravandian people themselves. The empire has been a citadel of reason and peace for many generations. We owe it to the people not to decide upon policies that may be beneficial to ourselves, but what is best for all. The empire stretches to nearly every corner of the earth. Should our government fall, anarchy will take hold. Petty lordlings will rise to take control, unsurping the wise governors, kings and queens who have been part of our empire for years. We cannot let that happen. The emperor is the divine king of the land, a figurehead for the people. He must be replaced with a man who commands the love and trust of the empire. Stability must be shown to have been restored.'

General Leatherer, a heavily bearded man in his late fifties, raised a hand to speak and Senefex inclined his head to indicate permission. 'As far as succession goes, there is only one decision to be made. Prince Linnard is now the rightful heir to the throne, but is too young to assume such a role. Prince Almorante, as next in line, should therefore be made regent until Linnard achieves his majority.'

Again there was a rumble of low voices around the table.

Almorante got to his feet, without asking permission to speak. 'That would seem to be the logical course of action. However, we must first discover whether Gastern's condition is likely to be passed on to his son. If it is my fate to take my father's place, I will do so with full integrity, but I must speak plainly. It is not my desire to succumb to a condition similar to that of my elder brother.'

'What do you mean by this?' Mordryn boomed abruptly.

Almorante's gaze did not falter as he looked upon the archimage. 'In all his years, Gastern has not previously suffered from any mental affliction. We must consider whether an outside agency is responsible, an agency that stands to gain from Gastern's fall.'

Tatrini was aware that more than a few faces turned surreptitiously towards her. Would anyone dare to accuse her outright? She had to suppress a smile. In this instance, she was entirely innocent. But there was nothing to fear. She knew where Almorante was heading with this, having discussed it with him over breakfast.

'These are dire words,' Senefex said. He gestured widely. 'You must voice your suspicions clearly to the Chamber. This is not a time for reticence.'

Almorante nodded. 'I am prepared to take that responsibility. I know that in many hearts lies suspicion that the sons of Leonid are a warring, ambitious rabble, and that any of us here today could be accused of wanting our brother to fall.' He raised a hand to stem the outbreak of denial. 'Gastern is not the most popular of us, and it is no secret – even though few dare to voice it – that his accession was regarded by many as a bad day for the empire. But it is not to me, or any of my brethren, that accusing eyes should turn. I will ask only this. Who is not present here today?'

For a moment, there was silence, which eventually Mordryn broke. 'There are only two absences, my lord. Emperor Gastern himself and Lord Palindrake. Might I enquire where you are leading us?'

'To an inexorable and perhaps unpalatable conclusion,' Almorante replied. 'No doubt everyone in this room will have heard the talk of how Gastern babbled of having been led out of the city by demons. The physicians have personally confirmed to me that his condition resembles that of a person exposed to the miasmas of the fire pits.'

Mordryn sighed, somewhat theatrically. 'They are clutching at straws. It is common knowledge that many Splendifer knights have spent time at the fire pits in meditation. None of them have ever come back raving. These are old wives' tales, the stuff of superstition and ignorance. The worst a man can be affected by the fumes is to be given a sore throat and a pounding headache. If indeed Gastern went to the pits, we can only assume the conditions there exacerbated a pre-existing malady. I am still unsure of what point you are trying to make here.'

'I believe that Gastern was deliberately led to the fire pits by enemies, who exploited his fears and delusions. I believe this was done with the cold understanding that the emperor's mind would be irreversibly affected, that he would have to be dethroned.'

'And who do you believe did such a thing?' Senefex enquired.

'Perhaps you should question Commander Lorca,' Almorante said.

Senefex raised his hands and his eyebrows and grimaced at Rufus Lorca. 'Do you have any idea what he means?'

'None,' Lorca said coldly. 'I too wait to be enlightened.'

'Clearly we are too stupid to follow your thinking,' Senefex said in a measured voice to Almorante. 'Pray stop playing with words and say what's on your mind.'

'It has come to my attention that there exists within the empire a clandestine, treasonous movement that aspires to put its own candidate on the throne of Magravandias. In short, that candidate is Valraven Palindrake.'

At once several people began to laugh, while others glanced at each other in surprise. The generals virtually snarled at the prince, while Lorca shook his head, uttering, 'No!' His face expressed his incredulity and shock.

Senefex rapped the table for order. 'This is an outrageous allegation, my lord,' he said. 'I doubt there is anyone else here who would question the loyalty of the Dragon Lord. The Palindrakes have served the empire for generations. If you are suggesting Valraven is absent today because of guilt, you should consider the tragic circumstances he has recently found himself in. He has good reason to be elsewhere.'

'Yet you have issued orders repeatedly over the past couple of months demanding he return to his post,' Almorante said. 'Were those orders ignored, or did you receive a pleading request he be allowed to continue his search for his family?'

'At this juncture, I shall not question how you assume such orders were sent,' Senefex replied smoothly. 'Valraven Palindrake's character is not being judged today. We are meeting to discuss the future of the emperor.'

Almorante sneered at Senefex. 'Does it pain you so much to consider Palindrake a traitor that you cannot even explore the possibility? How can you deny a conspiracy is afoot? Despite all your best efforts, news of Gastern's decline flies around the city. People are in uproar, vulnerable to any strong voice. My information network is more effective than yours, Lord Senefex. I have recently returned from Mewt, after having been forced to take Lord Maycarpe into custody. He is part of the conspiracy.'

'What?' Mordryn roared. 'By what right . . . '

Almorante cut him off. 'I shall discuss this in due course, but for now it is imperative you realise that the conspiracy permeates the government at very high levels.' He paused for effect. 'A continued resistance to examine the situation suggests you are part of it.'

Lord Senefex got to his feet. 'I will not countenance such outrage! You are not emperor, Prince Almorante, and will show respect to the Fire Chamber! You have no right to accuse Lord Maycarpe in his absence! If you have him in custody, bring him here at once to defend himself. He is one of our most trusted agents.'

All around the table angry mutters supported Senefex's words.

Almorante shrugged expressively. 'I did not mean to give offence. I was merely trying to make you appreciate how serious this situation is. If it takes outrageous words to do that, then I will employ them. Lord Maycarpe is, of course, available for questioning at your convenience, but I feel we should discuss the matter of Palindrake first.'

'You accuse us all,' General Leatherer said, 'for there is not one man in the army who is not loyal to the Dragon Lord. Where did you come by this information? We need all the facts. If there is a conspiracy at work, I'd say it is *against* Lord Palindrake, to discredit him. He is Gastern's champion. Anyone wanting to replace Gastern would do well to besmirch the Dragon Lord. He, too, is not here to defend himself.'

The chamber rumbled with disgruntled murmurs of 'Aye!'

Tatrini got to her feet. Despite her resolve, her heart beat fast. She must remain steady now. The next few moments were crucial. 'The information came from me, my lords,' she said in a clear ringing voice.

'You, my lady?' Senefex said, and there was a taint of disrespect in his tone.

'There is an ancient saying,' she said, smiling wistfully upon the company, 'that a king's troubles will inevitably always lie where he least expects them. With this in mind, I have ever been vigilant for my sons, one and all. Some time ago, I discovered that certain people supposed dead were, in fact, very much alive. One of them was Tayven Hirantel, once an agent of Magravandias, who deserted to the Cossics during the campaigns. I learned that he had recently become employed by Darris Maycarpe in Mewt. I took it upon myself to take Hirantel into custody and it was he who eventually revealed the plan to make Palindrake emperor. The conspirators planned to use the instability of Leonid's death to seize control.'

'There was no uprising,' Leatherer snapped. 'Again, this is paranoid speculation.'

'No, there wasn't,' Tatrini agreed, her voice never slipping beyond the tones of reason. 'That is because Palindrake did not want to be a figurehead for this movement. He was entirely innocent of involvement. But it is now my belief his opinions have been swayed. He saw the way Gastern's innovations were going, and against his better judgement, elected to unite with those who desire radical change. Palindrake would never support Almorante or Bayard, who, as everyone knows, are the only other contenders for the throne.'

'What about Linnard?' Rinata blurted unexpectedly.

Tatrini made sure the repression of her smile was visible to all. 'My dear,' she said kindly, 'any reasonable person can see, even should they be half blind, that Linnard is not made of the stuff of kings.' She knew these words were the private thoughts of everyone present, despite the earlier words of rightful succession. If anything, there was relief in the air that someone had voiced the consensual opinion. She turned her eyes away from the empress and swept her gaze around the chamber. 'Lord Palindrake *has* ignored orders to return, hasn't he?'

Lord Senefex looked slightly troubled now. Tatrini knew her tone of reasonable authority had touched him. 'Lady Pharinet sent a message that her brother had vanished into the wilderness of Caradore,' he said, 'following a lead concerning the whereabouts of his wife and daughter.'

'He knows the empire is threatened by instability,' Tatrini said. 'His first responsibility is to be here in Magrast, and he knows that.' She placed her hands against the table, leaned forward on straight arms. 'Come, my lords, see what lies before your eyes. How many of you here believe his marriage to be one of close affection? He cares only for his son, who is safe in the palace. He has already sent Merlan Leckery – who, incidentally, is part of the conspiracy – out to search for Varencienne. Palindrake has many trusted and able men capable of finding his wife and daughter. I do not personally believe he is emotionally involved enough to warrant this long absence of search and worry. It is not in him, and I believe, in your hearts, you think that too.'

'Bring Lord Maycarpe and Hirantel to this chamber!' General Leatherer cried. 'I want to question these men myself!'

'The general is right,' Senefex said, in a milder tone. 'We cannot go upon hearsay. We need hard evidence and facts.'

Tatrini inclined her head. Much as she felt uncomfortable about it, she could not refuse permission. 'Might I suggest that Lord Senefex, Archimage Mordryn and General Leatherer interview the prisoners and report back to the Fire Chamber?'

'You must hand over these prisoners,' Senefex said. 'We will decide who interviews them and where.'

She paused a moment, as if to consider, then spoke with calm confidence. 'Tayven Hirantel is no longer a prisoner, but is now in my employ, as one of my agents. I have assured him of safety in return for his co-operation. I feel this should be respected, for he has many uses. You may interview him in my chambers. As for Maycarpe, Almorante delivered him into my custody to ensure the news of his capture remained private. I will bow to the circumstances and surrender him, on the understanding you will allow me to be present at all interrogations.' She knew she was taking a risk here. She had no real authority over the Fire Chamber. Senefex could rightly send a deputation of men to her quarters to apprehend Tayven and could also prevent her from being involved in any subsequent discussion with the prisoners.

'We must take a vote on this,' Senefex said. 'Does anyone here object to the Grand Queen Mother's requests?'

The generals and Rufus Lorca registered their objection, as did a few minor councillors, but the majority gave their consent.

'Perhaps we should now return to the matter at hand,' Senefex said dryly.

Tatrini noticed the slight tremor to his voice now. He was shaken utterly. Mordryn looked little better, like a choleric toad spread out in his seat. They would be confused by the apparent alliance of Almorante and his mother. They would be wondering where Bayard, who had kept uncharacteristically quiet throughout the meeting, fitted into this picture. They would be worried that Valraven Palindrake, upon whom so many relied, might have withdrawn his loyalty from them.

'Are all agreed,' Senefex said, 'that Prince Almorante should stand in as regent until further decisions can be made? The people need to be assured the situation is under control. A statement must be issued as to Gastern's abdication.'

Everyone gave their assent, although a few, notably the representatives from the military, clearly did so with reluctance.

'Gastern should be moved to one of the family estates in the country,' Tatrini said. 'We must do what we can for him out of the public eye.'

Mordryn shook his head gravely. 'Nothing like this has happened in the history of the Malagashes,' he said. 'Today is a sad day for all.'

'The only thing certain in life is uncertainty,' Tatrini said.

After the meeting had broken up, Tatrini went to her garden. No doubt Leatherer and Lorca would send panicked messages to Caradore at once, begging their Dragon Lord to return and proclaim his innocence. No chance of that. Tatrini knew, because of what Lady Pimalder had told her, that Palindrake would not return. In some ways, this suited her purposes admirably. Palindrake would be the sacrificial goat. Eventually the Magravandian army would sally north to Caradore to subdue him. She would make sure, by whatever means, that both Almorante and Bayard would be included in that venture. As to what outcome would proceed from it, Tatrini had yet to make up her mind.

Almorante would, in many ways, make a better emperor than Bayard, but he was far less compliant, and although not lacking in charisma, too much of a dark lord to represent the light of Madragore on earth. Yet there was something about him that Tatrini admired; it encompassed the noble will, which Bayard also had, but it was more than that. Tayven had channelled the elemental powers into Bayard, but had indicated that they would be worthless unless Bayard was destined to be the True King. Even now, Tatrini doubted such a man existed. Humans had to make do with what they could. Pure, sacred kings, if they existed at all, were a thing of the past, of innocent times. Now, they had to be tough and dispassionate. They would not rule for long otherwise.

It had almost been too easy to cast doubt upon Linnard as a future emperor, but his blood could not be denied. Mordryn and Senefex, if they secretly agreed that the boy should never assume his father's position, would have some plotting to do. An old decree would have to be unearthed in the archives to uphold their view. The libraries were bulging with impenetrable texts that could be interpreted in any manner desired, but the common people might be uncomfortable with a departure from dynastic tradition. In contrast with whatever Palindrake might have to offer, the Malagashes had to continue standing for continuity and permanence. Still, Linnard was a sickly boy. Anything could happen in the intervening years.

Tatrini leaned back in her chair, her hands folded comfortably on her belly. She had imagined the Fire Chamber and the Church would be an impediment to her plans, but the truth was they were as anxious to secure their positions as she was. Ultimately, all talk of what the people desired was a sham, at best lip service to a potentially ungovernable threat. She imagined that already the worm of paranoia was munching its way into the heart of everyone who'd been at the meeting. While she and Bayard might once have been regarded as a menace, now all that fear would be transferred to Valraven Palindrake. He was adored throughout the empire, regarded almost as a supernatural creature. How many hero-worshipping boys would rise to his banner should he choose to wave it in their direction? Leonid had kept the Palindrakes close to his hearth, but with his death a link had been severed.

Something important had died with her husband, but Tatrini did not regard this as regrettable. They were all facing perilous times, but if handled calmly and with care, a new order could be established to everyone's liking. Well, nearly everyone.

It was possible that Darris Maycarpe would try to incriminate her and Almorante when the Fire Chamber interviewed him. This was why she needed to be present. Would he reveal the Crown's existence to Mordryn and the others? What about Sinaclara? It was possible Maycarpe might start revealing all manner of things in order to win sympathy. Tatrini considered for a moment whether Sinaclara and Maycarpe were rather too much of a nuisance to live. Unfortunately, their demise at this point would cast unwelcome suspicions upon her. No, Maycarpe had to be allowed his say. Tatrini planned to reveal the Crown of Silence just before the next emperor was to be inaugurated. Two men desired to wear it, but which one? Which one?

The same afternoon, Almorante summoned Tayven to his chambers. 'Events are in motion,' he said. 'Give me your insights.'

Tayven had realised something was afoot that morning, but Tatrini has not revealed what it was. 'Be like your father,' he said.

Almorante narrowed his eyes. 'Meaning?'

'It is something you should think about. It came into my head, that's all.'

'I have a feeling you already know the outcome of everything,' Almorante said. 'But I think I have news that you may not have anticipated. You are to be called before the Fire Chamber to give account of what you know about the Palindrake conspiracy. My mother revealed you as her informant at a state meeting this morning.'

Tayven sat down heavily in a chair near to the hearth. 'This is not good news.'

'Not for you it isn't, no,' Almorante agreed. 'I'll tell you everything that transpired.'

Tayven sat in silence as Almorante gave his account. With each word, his heart became heavier. His tenuous security had vanished.

When he'd finished the report, Almorante said, 'So, what will you say to them when they summon you?'

'I do not have a ready answer,' Tayven replied carefully.

'You must contrive one,' Almorante said, 'because you can be sure they'll question you remorselessly. If you fail to satisfy, they will throw you into a pit from which you'll never emerge, and neither my mother nor I will be able to save you.'

'How reassuring,' Tayven said.

'They will question Maycarpe too, and if he chooses to reveal the existence of Sinaclara – which I hope *you* will not – they will interview her as well. They want evidence of the conspiracy to put Palindrake on the throne. If you are wise, you will give it to them in abundance, so that their questioning of Maycarpe will not be as crucial as it could be.'

'That is sensible advice,' Tayven said. 'I'll think about it.'

'On a more cheerful note, the Fire Chamber has appointed me as acting emperor.'

'You must be pleased,' Tayven said.

Almorante grimaced. 'The battle is not won yet,' he said. His gaze, perhaps unconsciously, flicked to every corner of the room.

Tayven rubbed his hands over his face. He would have to take action now, and quickly. He should get out of Magrast. But how could he do that when Maycarpe and Sinaclara were still held captive? It was his fault they were imprisoned. He couldn't abandon them.

Almorante came to his side and put a hand on the back of his neck. 'I wish I could help you,' he said in a gentle voice, 'send you to Recolletine, perhaps. But I have to act carefully. You do understand that, don't you?'

Tayven nodded. 'It is not your responsibility, Mante.'

'Tayven . . . '

There was a silence. 'What?'

Almorante withdrew his hand. 'There is something I wish to say to you.' He walked across the room to the window, gazed down towards the plaza below where palace staff went about their business, ignorant of the storm building up within. 'Since I have found you again, I have thought much of the past, the things we did together. I remember you as you were, and how I believed you to be the embodiment of the magic of the land.' He turned. 'You may have changed, but some things remain the same. You are a creature of destiny, Tayven, and even though as your emperor I should stand by what has been decided for you, I believe strongly that you must not be constrained by those who do not understand your light.'

'What are you saying?' Tayven said cautiously.

'I have given you advice concerning your interrogation. I have told you I cannot help you. There is another course, though it pains me to consider it.'

'Mante . . . '

Almorante held out a hand. 'Come to me, Tayven. Come one last time to my arms.'

Tayven stood up. 'As my emperor, you should advise me to speak honestly to the Fire Chamber, to co-operate.'

'I should, yes, and I have.'

Tayven stared at him for a moment, then said carefully, 'It is not as easy for me as you think. What of Maycarpe and Sinaclara?'

Almorante gestured with both hands. 'Come one last time . . . '

Tayven knew Almorante would say no more. He crossed the room and allowed himself to be enfolded by the prince's embrace. He heard Almorante sigh, heard the great sadness in it. 'I want you to know that I love you,' Almorante said. 'It is a great love, and princes are often denied such a thing. My path is lonely and made all the more so by all that I feel for you and have felt since the time I first saw you. I abused you in so many ways. If I had had any sense, you would not be in this position now.'

'You never abused me,' Tayven said. 'All that was good in you allowed me to make my own choices. I do not regret them.'

Almorante took Tayven's face in his hands. 'I had hoped that, as men, we could learn to love one another, but circumstances have taken that possibility from me. You must go, Tayven. Very soon. I don't know whether fate will allow us to meet again, but I will dream of it.' He pressed his forehead against Tayven's own, his skin burning hot. Then he kissed Tayven's brow and released him. 'I do not feel optimistic about the future. We will ride to Caradore, Bayard and I, to confront Valraven. I do not know when this will happen, but do not think of going to him, Tayven. Do not sacrifice your life. Find another way.'

'You are emperor now,' Tayven said hurriedly. 'You could be the king that everyone desires. There is another way for you too. You could end it, all of it. Do not listen to your mother. *Please*. If you will take on the heritage of the True King, I will remain here, stand beside you as your Bard. There is no one person fit to be king; the potential exists within all of us. It is a choice. This is destiny. This moment. Now. Can't you feel it? Even Palindrake will stand beside you if you make the right decisions.'

Almorante smiled sadly and pushed Tayven from him gently. 'Fly,' he said. 'Use those wings I know you have.'

Tayven walked slowly back to his own apartments through the twisting corridors that linked Almorante's with the main palace. At first his mind was strangely blank of current concerns. He thought about his previous life in the palace and how he had changed. The younger Tayven had been such an idealist, but he'd taken pleasure in the way Almorante praised him to everyone, making out he was so special and different. Perhaps the fact that Khaster Leckery had been such a challenge had been the main attraction to the man. In those days, Tayven could have had just about anyone he wanted. He wondered how events would have proceeded if he'd never met Khaster. It was unlikely Almorante would have sent him on the fateful expedition to Cos. Tayven's role now would be very different. He would be embroiled in some magical plot to put Almorante on the throne, ignorant of everyone else's plans. He would have gone through with it too, in ignorance. He'd thought he'd known everything there was to know about the world of the unseen, but in reality he'd known so little. He was no longer so naïve, but the knowledge he possessed had come at a high price.

Tayven had told Rav the dragon daughters had made contact with him, which had cheered the boy, although Tayven had not revealed the full extent of his dealings with them. The daughters had urged him to pass the elemental powers to Prince Bayard and he had done so without question. He could see the sense of it, even though its logic was somewhat bizarre. The daughters had shaped an opponent worthy of Valraven. It was to be his final test. And in some ways, Foy's daughters were impartial. Should Bayard be victorious, they would be his. The battle was all that mattered, and it was not so much a physical fight as a conflict of souls. The future of the world would be decided by its outcome. The dragon daughters and the other elemental beings did not share humanity's morals. They were not loyal to Valraven because they saw him as a 'better' man than Bayard or Almorante. Ultimately they would work for the one who had the power and will to control them.

Bayard had lain low since the night of the ritual. It could be that the elemental force coursing through his body was changing him, but Tayven could not guess in what way the prince would be affected. Perhaps Bayard was destined to become emperor after all. The future seemed like a chaotic blur to Tayven. All he could think of was that he had to leave the city and before he could do that, there were others to consider. Sinaclara and Maycarpe deserved his best efforts to free them. He knew Tatrini had secreted Sinaclara away in the palace underworld, but Maycarpe would now be out of her control and therefore too closely guarded for Tayven to free him easily. Maycarpe would just have to fend for himself. Tayven had no doubt the man was quite capable of it. There was one other, however, who could be helped at once, and whose flight from the city was more important than anyone else's.

Rav took his daily lessons in a study attached to his father's apartments. In the afternoon, it filled with sunlight and overlooked a pleasant garden where a fountain played. When Tayven presented himself at the open door, he was unnoticed for a moment and observed with a pang of sorrow Rav's young head bent over his notebook, scribbling down what his tutor read to him. It was quite possible that the boy's world was about to fall apart. Garante, the tutor, was a strange sort, being part ascetic, part warrior: a blend that could sometimes generate lunatics. He was cadaverously thin, yet muscular. His dark eyes were deeply set beneath prominent brows and his tawny hair was almost unnaturally thick. It sprang from his scalp as if in surprise, and always looked somewhat dusty. Tayven was not sure whether the man was attractive or repellent; it was a strange combination of both. He did not know Garante personally, and knew he was taking a risk coming here. Nevertheless, he drew in his breath and knocked on the door frame.

Garante glanced up in irritation. He had perhaps expected to see a servant standing there. He would know Tayven's reputation, and also his face, for at one time, Tayven had been a celebrity at court. He often wished he could shed that reputation like a dried-out skin. Few people had known of his less frivolous activities in Almorante's service, and his common designation as whore did nothing to encourage people to take him seriously, which had been a deliberate ploy at the time.

Garante frowned and said, 'What do *you* want?' He clearly disapproved of Rav spending time in Tayven's company, but could do nothing about it, since Tayven was favoured by the Queen Mother.

'Excuse me,' Tayven said, executing a polite bow. 'It is vital I speak to Master Palindrake – to both of you, in fact.'

'It can wait,' Garante said briskly. 'As you can see, we are in the middle of a lesson.'

Rav had turned in his seat and it was clear from his expression that he sensed something was wrong.

'It can't wait,' Tayven said, coming into the room. 'You might as well know this, for soon it will be common news around the palace. Valraven Palindrake has been accused of treason. This will obviously affect his son.'

'No!' Rav cried. 'What's happened, Tay?'

Garante closed the book that had lain open in his palms. Slowly he put it down onto a desk. 'Rav,' he said. 'Please go to the garden for a few minutes. I must speak with Master Hirantel alone.'

'No!' Rav cried again.

Tayven went to the boy's side and placed a reassuring hand on his shoulder. 'He should hear,' Tayven said. 'This concerns him most of all.'

'He's just a child!'

'People in his position are rarely accorded the luxury of true childhood,' Tayven said. 'I think you know this.'

Garante sighed deeply. 'Very well. You must be quiet, Rav. Don't interrupt.'

Tayven did not remove his hand from Rav's shoulder, hoping to extend calmness through the contact. Succinctly, he related all that Almorante had told him.

When the story was out, Garante pressed the fingers of one hand against his eyes for a moment. 'Believe me, I have heard the rumours about Lord Palindrake already. I have not credited them before, and I cannot do so now.'

'It is not for us to decide the Dragon Lord's innocence or otherwise,' Tayven said, 'but he did place the care of his son in your hands. I hope you continue to stand by that responsibility. I too am committed to Rav's welfare. In my opinion, he should return to Caradore at once.'

'They would never allow it,' Garante said. 'I'm not convinced it is the right thing to do, in any case. It might be taken as evidence of Lord Palindrake's supposed guilt. Those who believe in his innocence should surely continue as normal.'

'There is merit in your words,' Tayven said, 'but they will be of little comfort to Rav should someone in authority deem it necessary to place him under more stringent supervision. Then he will no longer have the option to leave, or at least it will be a lot more difficult.'

'Someone will already have thought of this,' Garante said. 'They will be watching.'

'I know. We must act immediately.'

Garante stared at Tayven for a few moments while Rav squirmed beneath Tayven's hand. Tayven could feel the suppressed words that longed to burst out of him.

'Your training in the Cathedral Guard will be of great help in this situation,' Tayven said carefully.

Garante turned away. 'This is sudden. I need to consider.'

'There is no time. What plans do you have for the day? Is it conceivable you could take Rav on an outside excursion?'

Garante nodded. 'It is common for us to ride in the afternoon. We could do so, but in view of what you've just told me, it's likely we'd be stopped now.'

'You have to try.' Tayven looked down at Rav. 'Do you understand what must happen?'

Rav nodded, his eyes wide, face pale. 'But Leo usually comes riding with us,' he said in a shaky voice.

'Not today,' Tayven said.

'He might be waiting for us, or watching somewhere,' Rav said.

'I know,' Tayven said. 'You must talk to Jia and her sisters. They will help you.'

'Who, by Madragore, are they?' Garante demanded.

Tayven had no desire to enlighten him. 'Children often have invisible friends,' he said. 'They are expressions of inner traits. Rav can draw strength from them.'

'I don't want to talk to them,' Rav said. 'You do it, Tay.'

Tayven shook his head. 'I can't, because I have things to do.'

'What things?' Rav demanded. 'You are coming with us, aren't you?'

It tore at Tayven's heart to see the confused blend of trust and fear in Rav's eyes. 'Master Garante will take you out of Magrast. I'll meet you later. Don't be afraid. Be sure your father chose the best man possible to look after you.'

Garante uttered a cynical snort of laughter at these words, possibly amused by the flattery of someone he considered far beneath him. 'It may be no easy task,' he said. 'I'll be surprised if we can just saunter out of here.'

'That is why you must talk to the sisters,' Tayven said to Rav. 'You must ask them to guard you.'

Rav pulled a face of profound discomfort.

'The sisters are your friends.' Tayven knew Rav found that difficult to believe. 'You must be strong,' he said, 'like your father is. You'll be doing it for him.'

'You are obviously speaking of rather more than invisible friends,' Garante said. 'What occult nonsense have you filled his mind with?'

'It's no more nonsense than your daily prayers to Madragore,' Tayven said. 'Rav and his father have beliefs of their own, native to their homeland. You should respect them. I know it is something Lord Palindrake would want.'

'As far as I understand, the Palindrakes renounced their native beliefs a long time ago,' Garante said dryly. 'Still, this is not the time for a theological debate. We must get moving. Rav, put away your things. You'll have to leave with only the belongings you have with you now. It would look suspicious if you carried more.'

Rav opened his desk and put his notebook and pen inside. 'Why can't you come with us, Tay?' he asked.

Tayven flicked a glance at Master Garante before speaking. 'There is someone else who needs my help,' he said. 'I can't abandon her.'

'Sinaclara?' Rav said.

Tayven nodded.

'Is this another invisible friend?' Garante asked coolly.

'Not at all,' Tayven replied. 'If I succeed, you will see her for yourself.'

After Tayven had left, Rav put on his coat, which was hanging on the study door. It was really too hot in the city to wear a coat, but he couldn't travel all the way to Caradore with only a thin jacket for warmth and protection from bad weather. Part of him looked forward to an adventure, while another part grieved to leave Magrast. Why did things have to go wrong? Everyone loved his father. It made no sense to have to leave. Tayven's story of the Fire Chamber meeting had sounded unreal.

'Hurry up,' Garante said.

Rav was unnerved by the tension in his tutor's voice. 'What has my father really done?' he asked.

'Probably nothing,' Garante replied. 'In my view, his sin is simply that he is not here. By that I mean he has laid himself open to become a scapegoat.'

'What's that?'

Garante placed a hand on Rav's back and pushed him gently towards the door. 'The emperor is ill and people are frightened because of it. They think enemies surround them and they need to know who they are. As your father is not here, and has been absent for a long time, someone has decided he's got something to hide. Come along now.'

'I like it here,' Rav said. 'I don't want to go back to Caradore.'

'I'm sure everything will be sorted out,' Garante said. 'Then you can come back here.'

Rav could tell the man was lying.

They went to the kitchen where the cook was sleeping by the stove. Fortunately, no other servants were around, as this was a quiet time of day for them, when they were usually able to enjoy leisure time. The cook did not wake as Rav and Garante stole past her, but as they began to descend the narrow stair that led down to the yard below, Rav heard the sound of people coming into the apartment. A stern male voice called out, 'Master Garante, present yourself to the emperor's guard!'

If they'd lingered a moment longer, it would have been too late. The thought made Rav's throat go dry. He felt slightly dizzy. Garante hissed an order for him to hurry. They ran across the walled yard and passed through a door into a busy service area beyond. Here the servants of the nobles and courtiers who lived in apartments nearby did their laundry and repaired garments. Garante told Rav to slow down. They mustn't look as if they were in a hurry. They often used this quick route to the stables where the Dragon Lord kept his horses, so their presence in the area would not arouse that much interest. 'The fewer people who notice us, the better,' Garante said, smiling at Rav as if they were just having a friendly chat. Steam from the laundry rooms billowed around them and they were soon hidden amongst the sails of wet sheets that hung from a maze of clothes lines around the yard. Rav inhaled the strong aroma of perfumed detergent. Would he ever smell this again? It was the most exquisite scent to him. Tears came to his eyes, but he forced them away, remembering Tayven's words. He must be strong. As he thought this, an image of the dragon daughters flashed across his mind. 'Jia, Misk, Thrope,' he said in his head. 'Help me.'

A shiver coursed up his spine. It would be so easy to imagine shapes in the flapping sheets, the clouds of steam. But now they had reached the other side of the yard. Garante took Rav's hand. It was only a short way to the stables, between high narrow buildings where diamond-paned windows, far overhead, stood open. Rav looked up and saw how the sun came over the complicated roofs of the palace and fell on one of the windows. He saw a vase of flowers, slightly drooping on the sill, and a tabby cat sitting with folded paws, looking down upon him with half-closed eyes full of inscrutable wisdom. Already the warm scent of dung, straw and horse sweat filled the air. Rav could hear the clop of hooves on stone, an occasional whinny, the slam of a stable door. These memories would stay with him always. It was a map of his flight, but also a keepsake. He couldn't imagine returning, for a sense of finality and ending enclosed him, like a farewell murmured in a soft, sad voice.

Garante led Rav across the stable yard to where Valraven's horses were kept. Most were out in the fenced pasture nearby, where the grass had been trodden to dust in the summer heat. A stable girl was cleaning out one of the stalls, but put aside her broom when she caught sight of Garante and Rav coming towards her.

'Prepare our usual mounts,' Garante said to her in a casual manner.

'At once, sir.' She winked at Rav as she went into the tack-room. Sometimes, when they came back from a ride, she would give Rav a toffee wrapped in waxy paper. He didn't even know her name.

After five minutes, Garante uttered a sound of irritation and muttered, 'What's taking her so long?'

Rav shrugged, but Garante wasn't even looking down at him. Then the girl came out of the stable, leading Rav's grey pony and the bay gelding Garante usually rode.

'Help the boy,' Garante said, swinging into the saddle.

Rav's heart had begun to beat fast. The smells in the yard had become stronger, so much so he felt intoxicated by them. He could smell the girl's hair as she helped him onto the pony, the scent of horse that clung to her clothes. Then the afternoon shattered and he could smell nothing at all.

A group of soldiers came into the yard and their captain called out, 'Halt!' It was common knowledge that Rav went riding most afternoons with his tutor. The soldiers must have come here directly from the Dragon Lord's apartments.

Rav barely glanced at them, but put his feet in the stirrups.

'What is it?' Garante called back in a cheerful voice.

'Master Palindrake must return to the palace,' the captain said.

'Why?' Garante enquired. 'What has happened?'

'I am ordered to escort him to the Grand Queen Mother's chambers.'

'Now might be a good time for invisible friends,' Garante said in a lower voice to Rav, then spoke more loudly to the approaching captain. 'What is the reason for this? We are just about to take our daily ride.'

'We have our orders. You must obey.'

Garante had a weapon – his sword – and for all Rav knew might well be capable of fighting off a dozen armed soldiers, but at that moment, as the shivery sound of steel blades being unsheathed hissed around the stable yard, Rav knew true fear. A parade of faces flashed before his inner eye: his mother's, his father's, his aunts', Tayven's and Sinaclara's. None of them were with him. Before him he saw men intent on his capture, whose eyes were cold. He could imagine Garante's death as if it were already happening: a rearing horse, a flash of metal, a falling body. He could smell smoke and the salt of the ocean. In a moment of pure clarity, he stood upright in the stirrups and raised his arms. The afternoon sun was warm on his face, and time was so slow, yet a thousand moments passed in an instant. He cried out, 'Jia, Misk, Thrope, come rise, come unto me! I am your flesh, your voice!'

The captain of the guard yelled, 'Seize the boy!'

'Dragon Daughters, rise!' Rav cried and it felt as if someone else's voice boomed from his body, the voice of a man.

Soldiers ran forward and Garante urged his horse to meet them, drawing his sword. He shouted, 'Ride, boy! Ride!'

The soldiers were almost upon them, some reaching out to take hold of the horses' reins. Then thunder crashed through the summer afternoon.

Beneath clear skies, a storm billowed out from the direction of the service yard: sound and smoke and power. Horses screamed and reared and men fell to their knees on the shaking ground. Steam came in a swelling cloud and filled the yard in seconds. It stank of burning meat and soap.

Garante reached out and grabbed hold of Rav's pony's bridle. Rav kicked the animal furiously and, with its ears laid flat against its head, the pony leapt forward. Both animals clattered out of the yard, heading towards the palace gates. Rav was terrified, sure they would never make their escape. There would be more guards on the gates. But the damp cloud that had erupted from the laundry still seethed around them in a concealing fog. It was as if it were following them. Rav could see shapes within it: people running around shouting, and other, more sinuous, slowly moving forms that made no sound at all. Another explosion shook the palace and nearby some windows shattered. Rav cried out in alarm. He could see the dragon daughters running along beside his pony, laughing madly. This was their doing.

Then the looming arch of the main gates appeared out of the fog and the horses galloped beneath it. Below, the city baked in clear daylight. The horses galloped so fast it was as if their hooves were winged, as if the dragon daughters had taken possession of their pumping muscles. The sound of shouting and the soft thumps of minor explosions died away as Rav and Garante were swallowed up by the labyrinthine streets of the city. There was still some way to go before the walls were reached, but Rav knew that no one would stop them now. The dragon daughters would not allow it. They would guide him home.

CHAPTER TWENTY-SEVEN

Escape of the Sorceress

Tayven forced all thoughts of Rav from his mind as he headed back towards the heart of the palace. He must remain focused now. He walked along the endless corridors, where banners hung motionless in the still air, listening to his inner voice, hoping to divine exactly where Sinaclara was confined. He could not waste time on a search of the underworld. It could be that he was too late, and Sinaclara had already been moved to a more conventional prison, depending on whether Maycarpe had revealed her existence or not. Also, the Fire Chamber had undoubtedly already summoned Tayven to appear before it, which meant that guards would be searching for him.

With this thought in mind, Tayven hurried to the nearest doorway to the underworld. Over the weeks, Tatrini had revealed a few of them to him. She had come to trust him. Tayven did not underestimate her. She might already have guessed what he would do. The door he was accustomed to using lay close to his own rooms. As so many of them were, it was hidden behind a tapestry and required the turning of a carved vine in the wooden panelling to open it. Once the door was closed behind, Tayven leaned on it for a moment. The air in the cramped corridor beyond was musty and hot, heavy with the secret intentions of generations of Malagashes. Tayven felt that if he opened himself up to psychic impressions now, he would be buffeted by a hurricane of whispers, both malevolent and desperate. Dismissing this uncomfortable thought, he lit one of the torches provided and made his way to the lower areas. The palace was like a honeycomb, hollowed out with secret thoroughfares. It was as if two buildings occupied the same time and space.

Tayven tried many doors. Some were locked, but clearly hadn't been opened for years as their locks had rusted into a shapeless mass. Others were open, but empty of anything except for dank atmosphere. He returned to the chamber he had occupied in one of the better-kept areas, and had to suppress a shudder at the threshold. The light of his torch threw grotesque shadows over the meagre furniture of table, chair and bed. There appeared to be dark shapes writhing on the musty coverlet. Quickly he withdrew and closed the door. As he did so, he heard a sigh, as if it had been uttered just behind him. He turned, saw nothing but the wide, swept passageway, the shadowed vaults of its low ceiling, the heavy door opposite. Then he heard another sound, a voice speaking quickly, urgently. He stared at the door across the way for a moment, then went to open it.

Inside, it was very much like his own erstwhile quarters, with bare plastered walls and scant, rough furniture. A tall candelabrum stood on the table and the light of five candles filled the room, which smelled of mice and damp. The Grand Queen Mother sat at the small square table, while Sinaclara was slumped on the edge of the bed, her head hanging low, her hands between her knees. Tayven had the impression that she'd been arguing for hours and weariness had overtaken her. This environment would be like poison to the soul of a woman who was accustomed to living in the Forest of Bree.

Tatrini looked up. 'Tayven! What are you doing here?'

Sinaclara also raised her head. Her eyes looked glazed, and there was no sign of recognition within their gaze. Tatrini had no doubt been administering her potions again.

Tayven regarded the Queen Mother for a moment. Despite their differences, he had respect for Tatrini. She was not just a survivor, but also a warrior, fighting a way for herself in a very difficult world. She had been honest with him, taken him to a small degree into her confidence. Tatrini was no fool, but she had come to trust him. Perhaps he should not be surprised. From a young age, it had been his task to win the confidence of the great and powerful – usually for the benefit of other great and powerful people. Now he was acting for himself. He placed his torch into a sconce just outside the door and stepped over the threshold. 'I have spoken with Almorante,' he said.

'Ah,' said Tatrini. 'In that case, you must know what transpired this morning.'

'Yes. News of these events changes everything.'

'Naturally. We must seize the moment in whatever way we can.'

'Indeed,' said Tayven. 'It is why I am here for Lady Sinaclara.'

Tatrini frowned. 'Does this mean the Fire Chamber know of her existence already? I had hoped we'd be able to keep it quiet, move her to Cawmonel. Have you been interviewed, Tayven?'

'No,' Tayven said. 'This has nothing to do with anyone else. I mean to take Sinaclara away from Magrast.'

Tatrini uttered a small laugh. 'Excuse me? What are you talking about? Who sent you? Almorante?'

'Nobody sent me,' Tayven said. 'It is too dangerous for Sinaclara to remain here. She shouldn't be here in the first place.'

Tatrini straightened her spine and carefully rested one elbow on the table. 'And what is this to do with you? You haven't shown much interest in the lady's welfare up to now.'

'She has been dragged into this. It was my fault, because of what I revealed to you. Now I must repair the damage.'

Tatrini smiled wryly. 'Tayven, must I remind you that you are in my employ? I do not wish Sinaclara to leave, for there are many things she has yet to tell me. It may well be your responsibility she is here, but you should not feel guilty about it. I suggest you and I now sit down somewhere together to discuss how you should respond to the Fire Chamber's questions. Remember, there is still an allegation hanging over you concerning your activities in Cos. It would be most inconvenient should the Fire Chamber panic and decide you should be incarcerated – or worse.'

'I don't intend to endure any interviews,' Tayven said. 'I am leaving.'

Tatrini stared at him. 'You can't. Don't be a fool. My protection is worth more to you than anything else. If you flee now, people will draw their own conclusions and I'll be unable to change them.'

'I've played my part here,' Tayven said. 'I've given you many things you wanted. Let me go without conflict or trying to restrain me. In any event, the outcome will be the same.'

Sinaclara appeared to have come to her senses a little. 'Tayven?' she murmured.

Tayven closed the door behind him and went to the bed, where he helped Sinaclara to stand. She leaned against him, feeling slight and weightless in his arms.

'You can't do this,' Tatrini said. 'How far do you honestly think you'll get? Or do you propose to inflict harm upon me?' The idea clearly amused her.

Tayven did not answer her questions. In an instant, Tatrini was on her feet and hurrying for the door. Tayven was forced to drop Sinaclara on the bed and hurl himself on the fleeing woman. They both fell heavily against the door. Tatrini snarled in Tayven's face, her arms pinned to her side, 'How dare you lay hands upon me! You will die for it!'

'You leave me no choice!' Tayven said, hauling Tatrini upright, while still restraining her arms.

Tatrini shook her head, as if in disbelief. 'You are ungrateful, Tayven, and duplicitous. Tell me now and I will never mention what just happened again: has Almorante sent you here? You mustn't listen to him. Didn't obeying his orders in the past lead you only to pain and ruin? I need to know what he's planning. You must tell me!'

'Almorante has nothing to do with this,' Tayven said. He released Tatrini's arms and without pause she threw a punch into his face that conjured stars. He caught hold of her again before she could open the door, shook his head to clear it and drops of blood flew from his nose onto Tatrini's bodice. 'You have what you want,' he said, blinking away hectic spots of light. 'It may even be what is meant to be. I don't know. I only know I have to get Sinaclara away from here. I can do nothing more for you.'

'Where do you intend to go?' Tatrini asked. 'Whose side are you on?'

'The right side!' Sinaclara cried. Before Tayven realised what was happening, she lunged across the room and hit Tatrini over the head with the candelabrum. Candles rolled across the floor and the chamber was plunged into darkness. Tatrini slumped heavily against Tayven's body, so that he fell back against the door.

'By Madragore!' he cried.

In the darkness, Sinaclara managed to claw and shove Tayven and Tatrini away from the door and wrenched it open. She stood at the threshold, hunched and shuddering in the light of the torch outside, her eyes wild and unfocused. How she'd found the strength to attack the Grand Queen Mother, Tayven could not guess.

'Come on,' she said, swaying and gripping the door frame for support. 'We must go.'

Tayven carried Tatrini to the bed, where he laid her down and felt for her pulse. 'I hope to all the gods you have not killed her,' he said.

'Why do you care about her?' Sinaclara snapped. 'You know what she is.'

'I do,' Tayven said. He was reassured to discover Tatrini was breathing. He covered her with a blanket and then went to pick up the candelabrum and candles.

'What are you doing?' Sinaclara asked. 'We must leave. Her cronies are always hanging around this place.'

'If she wakes in darkness, she might be afraid,' Tayven said.

Sinaclara expressed a snort.

'You seem far from the gentle lady of magic I met in Bree,' Tayven said. 'Is this common behaviour for you?'

'I do what is necessary in every situation,' Sinaclara answered. 'You are mistaken if you believe me to be only a philosophising ascetic.

Neither did Tatrini's potions influence me as much as she thought. I was able to keep a part of my conscious mind in total clarity. I was biding my time, and it was clear to me I needed to take action.'

'The situation was under control. We could have got away without harming her.'

'Now you seem far from the conniving assassin of your reputation,' Sinaclara said. 'Just what are you, Tayven? I'd come to believe you were firmly in the Malagash camp.'

'I will explain my actions in due course,' Tayven said. 'All you need to know is that I want to get to Valraven Palindrake, as do you. We are on the same side, despite appearances or assumptions you have made. We have both learned something about each other, but there is no time for thoughtful reflection.' He put the candelabrum back on the table and arranged the candles within it.

'Let's go, then,' Sinaclara said.

Tayven brushed past her to fetch the torch.

'You are an enigma,' she said, folding her arms. 'Is this the man who professed to detest all Malagashes? You have blood all over your face. She might have broken your beautiful nose. Leave her be, Tayven. I am quite sure that woman is never afraid of the dark.'

Tayven lit the candles. Tatrini looked so vulnerable on the bed. It seemed somehow obscene that such a vibrant force could be knocked out so easily. Still, Sinaclara was right. There was nothing to be gained from lingering here except discovery.

He went to the door and took Sinaclara's arm, for she appeared to be in severe need of physical support. 'We must get the Crown,' she said. 'Do you know where it is?'

'There's no time,' Tayven said, glancing up and down the corridor. 'I need to think of the safest escape route. It would help if it was dark outside, but the sun's not due to set for some hours. We can't wait that long.'

Sinaclara pulled against his arm, refusing to move. 'I'm not leaving without the Crown. We have to have it.'

'No,' Tayven said. 'We can't. Madness is about to break loose here. I'm sure of it. Our only hope now is to go to Palindrake and trust he's prepared to take up the sword for his followers. I've already managed to get the Dragon Lord's son out of Magrast, or at least I hope I have. Our first priority is to leave the city and follow Rav to Caradore. Isn't that what you want – to go to Palindrake and swear allegiance to him?'

Sinaclara ignored the slightly sarcastic tone of his remark. 'Tayven, you know what the Crown represents. I am its guardian. I can't leave it in enemy hands. If the situation is about to explode, we need the Crown. Valraven Palindrake needs it.'

'And if he's meant to have it, fate will take care of it,' Tayven said. 'I don't know where it is, but you can be sure Tatrini will have hidden it well. Neither you nor I can go poking about the palace at will. The Fire Chamber has no doubt already issued orders to apprehend me. We'll be no use to anyone incarcerated in a dungeon here – or dead.'

'Then where will we go?'

Tayven paused, trying to clear his head to listen to his instincts. His nose had begun to throb now and the pain was distracting. 'Down,' he said after a few moments. 'The Malagashes must have had secret exits from the palace incorporated into this underworld. We must use our inner sight to find one of them.'

'Despite what you just saw me do, my inner sight is a fog,' Sinaclara said bitterly. 'Your lady friend made sure of that.'

'Then I will do it,' Tayven said. He pointed to the left. 'This way.'

As they set off, the earth suddenly shook beneath them and the sound of an explosion echoed overhead. 'What in Foy's name was that?' Sinaclara said, steadying herself against the wall. 'Is the palace under attack?'

'I doubt it,' Tayven replied. 'But whatever it was, I don't want to linger here and discover the cause. We must hurry.'

Tatrini opened her eyes to see the concerned face of Lady Pimalder hanging over her. Just behind she caught sight of the more sinister countenance of Master Dark. She uttered a cry and tried to rise, but was thrown back to the bed by a thump of pain in her head.

'Lie still,' Lady Pimalder said. 'Your physician is on his way. Once he's examined you, we'll take you back to your apartments, away from this dank place.'

Tatrini dragged her hands over her face, expelled a moan.

'Who did this?' Lady Pimalder asked.

'The woman, Sinaclara,' Tatrini answered.

'How? How did she overpower you? I gave her the strongest philtre.'

'She is no ordinary female,' Tatrini said. 'We underestimated her. She has a powerful will and is stronger than we thought.'

Lady Pimalder turned to Master Dark. 'The guards must be ordered to search for the prisoner at once.'

'I have already seen to it,' Dark said, 'before I came for you.'

'She will be found,' Lady Pimalder said, taking Tatrini's hands in her own. 'You can be sure of it, my lady. She'll hang on the walls for this.' She placed a soothing hand on Tatrini's brow. 'Rest now. All will be well.'

Tatrini swallowed with difficulty and closed her eyes. She should tell them about Tayven's involvement, his betrayal, but something held her tongue. She felt like weeping.

The physician, Doctor Bugleharp, arrived some minutes later. He diagnosed a mild concussion. 'You were lucky,' he said to Tatrini, 'and, if you will forgive my importunity, should think twice about interviewing prisoners alone again.' He turned to Lady Pimalder. 'Who was the person who did this, anyway?'

'A sorceress,' Lady Pimalder said. 'She was working against certain people at court. It is not a state matter.'

'You must speak of this to no one,' Tatrini said. 'Give me your solemn oath.'

The physician smiled. 'Have I ever abused your trust, great lady? Fear not. I have a very short memory.'

In the early evening, Prince Bayard came to his mother's bedchamber, where Tatrini was propped up on her pillows, being read to by Lady Pimalder. Doctor Bugleharp's effective analgesics had calmed her headache and left her in a serene, dreamy state of mind. Bayard was like an angry buzzing presence in the room, and he had yet to speak.

Tatrini waited until Lady Pimalder had left the room before speaking herself. 'What is it, my son? You look distressed.'

Bayard stood over the bed, his body taut and tense. 'Mother, what has happened today? Dark intimated to me that you'd been attacked.'

'That is true. I was careless. Lady Sinaclara took it upon herself to assault me with a candelabrum and then escaped. She will be hiding beneath the palace and will soon be found. It is of no great consequence.'

Bayard sat on the bed. 'It is of very great consequence. I can't believe that you – the empress – can be so sanguine about it.'

'I am no longer empress,' Tatrini said mildly. 'Anyway, it was my own fault. I underestimated her.'

'This is not like you!' Bayard insisted. 'You should be furious. What's Bugleharp given to you?'

'Bayard, be calm. I am all right. It was wrong of me to assume I was invulnerable. A hard lesson, but perhaps necessary.'

'It comes late in life,' Bayard said in a cold voice.

'It might sound trite, but better late than never. Lady Sinaclara will be found and punished. There is nothing more to say.'

'Actually, there is,' Bayard said. 'There are a few things you should know, which I suspect have bearing on the situation. First, Tayven Hirantel has disappeared.'

'What do you mean?'

'The palace guard have been looking for him all day. The last person to see him was Almorante, around noon. That fact alone is suspicious. Then Master Garante was found trying to smuggle Palindrake's son out of Magrast. A timely explosion in the boiler rooms enabled them to flee. It was no coincidence and has Hirantel's spoor all over it. This is the beginning of it, of course. Somehow Palindrake's supporters got wind of what happened at the meeting this morning. They mobilised, and now four key players have vanished. It's clear to me that Almorante is to blame.'

'He no doubt apprised Tayven of the facts,' Tatrini said, 'but I'm quite sure that was in ignorance.'

'I agree. He is a fool, blinded by lust. Hirantel could always wind Almorante round his finger.' He cupped his chin with one hand. 'Strange, I thought Hirantel was ours. He's a good actor. Not much gets by me. He should be on our side, because his skills and cunning would be extremely useful, but now he must die with the rest of them. A pity.'

Tatrini said nothing.

'You don't seem concerned about what's happened,' Bayard said.

She gestured languidly. 'I always knew that when matters came to a head, something like this would occur.'

Bayard expelled a choked laugh of disbelief. 'Mother! What is wrong with you? Hirantel was supposedly your creature, yet you don't seem at all surprised he's gone. He was our creature of air, and young Palindrake was water. We've lost half our cabal, and you're not at all distressed.' He paused. 'You know something. Tell me. What's the secret you're holding to yourself?'

'First, remember that Tayven channelled the powers of all the elements into yourself. We need no others now, my son. Second, Tayven effectively gave us the Crown. His position is now precarious. It's understandable he'd want to melt away.'

Bayard stared at his mother for a few moments. 'He's spoken to you, hasn't he? You *knew* he was going. Is this your design?' He thumped the bed with a closed fist. 'Tell me! Why is he so precious to you?'

'He has helped you, Bayard,' Tatrini answered and now a dangerous barb came back into her voice. 'Don't forget that. He walks in many worlds.'

'Admit you knew he was leaving.'

'I admit it, yes. I tried to reason with him, but . . . ' She raised expressive hands.

Bayard put one hand against his mouth for a moment, and then spoke softly. 'By the flame, it wasn't *him* who attacked you, was it?'

'No, of course not.'

'You don't *reason* with anyone. You give orders. Something's changed. For Madragore's sake, let me in. I don't like seeing you like this. I'm concerned for you.'

Tatrini smiled without warmth. 'Are you, my son? I think that you are only concerned for yourself. What you really believe is that Tayven and I have a secret agenda. It is not the case. I still have the Crown, even if its guardian has fled. This should be regarded as a beneficial event. In effect, she has abandoned it.'

Bayard stood up. 'I spoke with Senefex before I came here. Already there is talk of sending troops to Caradore. I hope this is not a smoke screen for something else.'

'Speak your mind.'

'I know Valraven, and despite the estrangement between us, I cannot see him as a traitor.'

'Love sees what it wants to see.'

'Don't insult me,' Bayard said. 'I do not look through the eyes of love, and you wouldn't respect me if I did. You suggested we ally with Almorante and soon he will be emperor. This was not what we planned.' He looked down at her. 'You want me to go to Caradore, of course.'

'You should. The past must be re-enacted, for therein lies the magic.'

Bayard regarded her with a cool gaze. 'And there Valraven and I will have our last confrontation. Who can predict the outcome? Some might think we are both being used. Almorante schemed to have me murdered on the battlefield before, remember. And now Tayven, my proposed assassin, who glamorised you enough to win your favour, has fled the city. I cannot help feeling these facts are connected.'

Tatrini put her head to the side. 'Many frightened ideas are roiling in your head, Bay.'

'I am not afraid,' Bayard said. 'Look into my eyes and search for fear. You will not find it. I'll do what has to be done. I simply question your motives.'

'Do you no longer trust me?'

'I think you are floundering,' Bayard said. 'You have lost control and will do whatever you can to salvage your position. This is why you are so calm in the face of all that's happened today. Behind that serene exterior, you are thinking madly, desperately.'

Tatrini lay back against the pillows. 'You're wrong. I believe in us, Bayard. I believe in the Malagashes. We are an ancient line and we are not doomed to disappear from history. I trust in the future, and so must you. Almorante will make a competent emperor, but he is not the beautiful sun king. That role is yours. When you defeat the dark lord, Valraven Palindrake, your name and your reputation will shine. Retake

Caradore for the empire and you will be Cassilin Malagash, the warrior king who first subjugated that realm. You must kill the Dragon Lord and make his son swear the allegiance as his ancestors did. History will begin anew. The empire will be reborn and so will you. I guarantee there will be no obstruction to our designs then. Senefex, Mordryn, the military: they will all see the sense of giving you the crown, and then the true Crown will be revealed.'

Tatrini could see that Bayard was inspired by her words, but she had not allayed his suspicions entirely. 'I hope all you say will come true,' he said. 'But it all depends on a single truth, and that is whether Valraven is a traitor or not. I could go to Caradore and find only a household of lamenting women. He could be dead, Mother.'

'He is not,' Tatrini said. 'Of this I am sure.' She held out a hand which, after some moments, Bayard took hold of. 'The elemental power is within you,' she said. 'Experiment with it, feel it coursing through your blood. That is all you should concern yourself with for the moment. Leave the rest to others.'

Bayard stared at her, his expression hard, but Tatrini felt a pulse of energy pass from his hand to hers. It was the start of it.

Tayven led Sinaclara deep into the labyrinth of passages, until they found themselves clambering through areas that had clearly not been frequented for centuries. Sometimes the passages were blocked or flooded, but Tayven insisted they must keep moving. They hauled rubble from their path with bleeding hands and replaced it as best they could in their wake. They waded through stagnant stinking water that exhaled a miasma of disease. Sinaclara clearly had little reserves of strength, yet she did not complain. Sometimes, far overhead, they'd hear the thunder of running feet. 'They are looking for us,' Sinaclara said.

'They will not find us,' Tayven snapped. He felt fully focused now, and kept his eyes closed for most of the journey, feeling the way ahead with his senses. He was fired by a fierce, white-hot hope that he would succeed in finding a way out. He had to believe this completely: to doubt for one instant might mean they'd be lost, unable to find their way forward or back. Tayven had to trust that there wouldn't be soldiers waiting for them should they find an exit. He must believe they were meant to escape, that they were still part of the unfolding story.

Sinaclara wanted to know everything that had happened to Tayven since Tatrini had taken him captive, and he obliged her with the full details.

'I can see why Bayard must have the elemental power now,' she said when he'd finished speaking. 'It will be Valraven's final trial.'

'Let's hope he's up to it,' Tayven said. 'Whatever you think of Bayard, he has great reserves of strength and confidence. He will believe utterly that he can vanquish all enemies, and that might be his most potent weapon. The Dragon Lord must have no doubts.'

'Then we must get to him soon,' Sinaclara said. 'If anyone can help him find his own strength and confidence, it's us.'

Coming to a low chamber where the mould-encrusted walls ran with glutinous moisture, Tayven agreed they could pause for some minutes while Sinaclara caught her breath.

'This place has existed for millennia,' Sinaclara said in a hushed voice. 'The palace has grown upwards from it.' She uttered a soft laugh. 'We might be standing upon the original sacred hill, Tayven, though there is not much sense of it.'

'I think this illustrates succinctly what the Magravandian kings have become,' Tayven said. 'Mouldy, stagnant, rotten and dank.'

There was a silence, then Sinaclara said, 'Where do we go from here, supposing we find a way out? We have no money, no transport, not even any travelling clothes. How can we get to Caradore?'

'I've been thinking about that,' Tayven replied, 'and have come up with a risky plan.'

'Risky? In what way? Any plan at all is to be applauded!'

'Well, we could appeal to my family for help.'

'That doesn't sound risky, but very sensible.'

'I haven't seen them for years,' Tayven said. 'They believed me dead, and even though news must have filtered through to them I'm back in Magrast, they've made no attempt to contact me. This speaks eloquently of their feelings.'

'You haven't attempted to contact them, either,' Sinaclara said. 'And you don't know for definite that they're aware you're alive.'

'My parents have friends at court,' Tayven said gloomily. 'I've hardly been invisible recently. Most courtiers regard me as the worst kind of scoundrel, little more than a criminal. No doubt my family have heard all kinds of rumours about me. They have a great regard for propriety and etiquette. I imagine I've been a great embarrassment to them all round.'

'You still share their blood, Tayven,' Sinaclara said. 'That will count for something.'

'We'll have to see. Are you ready to get moving again?'

'In a moment,' Sinaclara said. 'Tayven, we've got to think about Darris Maycarpe. He's in great danger now, isn't he?'

'I'd rather not think about it,' Tayven said, 'because there's nothing we can do to free him. He's more closely guarded than you were. I should have had more time, or realised sooner that we'd have to leave Magrast. I was stupid.'

'We'd all do things differently if we could foretell every event,' Sinaclara said with a wry smile. 'Even those of us who are psychic! There's no point punishing yourself for it.'

'Isn't there? It's my fault you and Maycarpe were taken captive in the first place. I told Tatrini Darris was a conspirator to get Palindrake on the throne. That, of course, is an executable offence. I only hope he can wriggle his way out of it.'

'He could tell them he was working undercover with the rebels,' Sinaclara said, 'for the benefit of the empire, that is.'

Tayven sighed deeply. 'I hope he thinks of something. I don't want his blood on my hands.'

'It wasn't your fault,' Sinaclara said. 'Tatrini drugged you as she drugged me.'

'I doubt you revealed as much.'

'I'm lucky. I live in the middle of nowhere with only my dreams.'

'Did you tell her you supported Palindrake?'

Sinaclara nodded silently, her expression thoughtful. 'I tried not to implicate anyone else. I admitted I knew the Malagashes would come looking for the Crown and that I went to Maycarpe because he was an old friend who, being Magravandian, might give me some protection. I told her that Maycarpe's interest in the Crown was mostly academic, and that it was I who suggested Palindrake might be the True King to wear it.'

'Then you fought well. I just spilled everything.'

'What does that matter? I took my best friend with me to Mewt and now she's dead. If I hadn't gone to Maycarpe when Almorante was looking for me, maybe he wouldn't have been arrested. Things just happen, Tayven, and sometimes we have no control over them.'

'That doesn't make it any easier to live with.'

'It's past now,' Sinaclara said briskly, 'and we cannot dwell on things that cannot be changed. Come on, let's go. The sooner we leave this disenchanted place the better.'

They set off down a passageway that was an inch deep in water. By this time, their torch was nearly spent and Tayven did not relish the prospective loss of light. He might close his eyes to navigate, but it was a comfort to open them and see Sinaclara beside him.

'There's a glow up ahead,' Sinaclara said.

Tayven held the torch behind him a little so he could see. 'Looks phosphorescent,' he said. 'Could be some kind of lichen.' Even so, they increased their pace.

Within minutes they came to a circular grille that was nearly covered with ferns and moss.

'You've done it!' Sinaclara said and jumped on Tayven's back to hug him. 'I will never doubt you again.'

Tayven laughed in relief and turned to return her embrace. 'First, we have to see where we are.'

Together, they began to tear the plant life from the grille. The bars were extremely rusted and would present no problem to break through. Outside, the sun was sinking through the early evening and a panorama of rust-tinted buildings sprawled out far below them. The grille was positioned about thirty feet above a slow-moving, wide body of water, and there was what looked like a row of abandoned or rundown warehouses on the opposite bank.

'Where are we?' Sinaclara asked. 'Do you recognise it?'

'Miles from the palace,' Tayven replied. 'This looks like Fifer's Scarp, which is a spine of rock near to the Soak, the old docks. It's almost a sheer drop. We'll have to jump down into the water.'

'I don't care,' Sinaclara said. 'Nothing can be worse than this place.'

Tayven wrenched three of the bars aside and they were able to squeeze through them onto a narrow, crumbling ledge. 'Now I feel sick,' Sinaclara said nervously, hanging onto Tayven's arm. 'I've just remembered I dislike heights.'

Tayven took her hand. 'Don't think about it. Jump!'

He leapt into the air, dragging Sinaclara with him, who uttered an involuntary shriek. Then they splashed down into the murky waters, which closed over their heads. Tayven was reminded poignantly of an incident in Recolletine the previous year when the Crown questers had leapt into a dangerous weir. For just a moment he could sense Khaster beside him, then his head broke the surface. Sinaclara came up at his side, still holding grimly onto his hand. He was sure her nails had drawn blood. 'Are you all right?' he asked her.

Sinaclara nodded, her face sickly-pale. 'I think so. I thought we'd hit the bottom.'

'This is a tributary of the Leonid Canal,' Tayven said. 'The tributaries were constructed deep enough to take ocean-going ships – mercifully.'

They swam to the opposite bank and hauled themselves from the water. Sinaclara's gown hung soddenly around her body. One arm of her dress had nearly ripped away, while the hem was a lace of rents. 'You look drowned,' Tayven said. 'Still, in the Soak that will not be an unusual sight. Its natives are forever staggering drunk into the waters.'

Sinaclara gave him a bleak glance. 'This is where you met Khaster Leckery, isn't it?'

'How do you know about that?'

She shrugged. 'Shan's friend, Nip, spent many happy evenings with me supplying me with gossip. Shan had given her a detailed account of all Taropat told him.'

Tayven grimaced. 'I see. Well, yes, this is the place. What you've just experienced gulping in the polluted waters of the canal has given you a taste of those happy memories.'

Sinaclara sat on the bank and began to wring out her skirts. 'It's not an irretrievable circumstance, you know.'

Tayven hunkered down beside her and was silent for a moment. Then he said, 'There isn't one day that passes I don't think of him, but what's the point? I have to accept the man I loved is dead – at least to me. I think the phrase is: "I will carry him to my grave". Sometimes the burden of it isn't that heavy.'

'I'm sure he thinks of you too,' Sinaclara said.

'There are more immediate concerns,' Tayven said. He stood up and bowed. 'Madam, now it is my pleasure to escort you to the domain of my family.'

Sinaclara scrambled to her feet and took his arm. 'Charmed, sir.'

The Hirantel manse stood on a wide avenue called The Cloudcaps, which was situated on one of the high hills of the affluent residential district. By the time Tayven and Sinaclara reached this area, the sun had nearly sunk. Tayven suggested they make use of the service alleys that ran behind the estates out of sight, because the vision of soaked, ragged individuals in this place was not a common one. Tantalising cooking smells made both their stomachs roar with hunger. The servants of the houses were preparing their employers' evening meals. Because it was summertime, many families were eating outdoors. Between the high railings and hedges, these genteel gatherings could be glimpsed. Girls in white dresses sat demure with their smart brothers and elegant parents. Lanterns hung in the trees attracted moths and rare birds dragged extravagant tails along the dew-kissed lawns.

'It is a true enchanted place,' Sinaclara said. 'I lived in a big house, but it was a proper home, not like this. These people look like actors and their domains are stage sets.'

'Here we are,' Tayven said laconically. They had reached a tall wrought-iron gate, beyond which lay an ornate landscaped garden. Tayven gave the gate a push. 'Luckily it's not locked yet.'

They walked up a gravel path surrounded by sculpted hedges. 'You grew up here,' Sinaclara said. 'It's hard to believe.' She chuckled. 'I can just see you as a pretty little blue-eyed boy, scampering away from your nurses. You would have been given every luxury, you spoiled creature: a blessed childhood.'

'My eyes are grey,' Tayven said. 'Here I was reared and trained to be the boy who would go to Almorante's bed. My parents considered it a great privilege to give me away.'

'How did it happen?' Sinaclara asked. 'Why you?'

'A friend of my father's needed to curry favour with the prince over a business deal concerning land the emperor had bestowed upon his son. Almorante was very young then himself, but already embroiled in court intrigues and schemes. My father's friend brought a member of Almorante's staff here and showed me to him. The rest of it is irrelevant.'

'I thought you said your parents were sticklers for propriety and etiquette.'

Tayven gave her a pointed glance.

'Ah, I see. That *was* etiquette.'

'Precisely. My mother was overjoyed for me. She thought it would be my making. And it has, though not in a way she would have desired.'

Sinaclara was silent for a moment, then said, 'I think we should take your delightful family for every coin we can. And good horses. And clothes.'

'We could steal the silver too.' Tayven smiled. 'Don't think too badly of them. What happened to me is not uncommon here. Almorante was only in his mid-teens when I went to him. He could have been vile, but he never was. Despite the obvious things to the contrary, we were mostly like brothers. He treated me with respect and was never cruel to me.'

'Until he decided to turn you into a spy, perhaps.'

'I wanted to be that,' Tayven said. 'I didn't want to be a pretty bauble. I craved to be far more dangerous.'

'There are few things more dangerous than a pretty bauble, as Almorante well knew. By now, I expect Tatrini does as well.'

'I have fulfilled my vocation then.'

They followed the path until they reached a door in a wall that led to the kitchen garden. Beyond lay the servant quarters. The kitchen was a blaze of light and through the windows, a scene of intense activity could be seen. Tayven drew in his breath. 'Here goes,' he said.

Sinaclara squeezed his arm. 'Trust yourself,' she said. 'You have already proved what that's worth today.'

Tayven went to the back door and looked into the kitchen. It was like

309

going back in time because so little had changed. The cook, Merry Attercorn, looked older, but was still intensely industrious as she'd always been, barking orders at the staff, moving like a blur amongst the cauldrons. The steward, Barlock, had lost much of his hair and had gained a paunch, but his expression of resigned distaste was the same as Tayven remembered. He sat with his feet up on the great table, which was laden with vegetables in various states of preparation. While Merry shrieked and spun, he smoked reflectively on a pipe, ignoring her imprecations.

'Mister Barlock,' Tayven said, in a voice just loud enough to reach him.

The steward looked up, took the pipe from his mouth, stared.

'Can I speak to you?' Tayven asked.

With a brief glance at the cook, Barlock unfolded himself from his chair and loped to the door. 'Be off with you,' he hissed. 'If the termagant catches sight of you, she'll whip you with a pan. There are no scraps to be had here for vagrants, whether you mend shoes or tell fortunes.'

'Barlock, it's me,' Tayven said urgently. 'Master Tay.'

Barlock peered at him for some seconds, then his face broke into a series of expressions, encompassing most human emotions. 'What are you doing here, lad? They said you were dead, then you weren't. Your portrait was taken down, then up, then down again.'

'It's a story,' Tayven said, 'but I've no time to tell it. Who's at home?'

'Everyone,' Barlock said. 'It's your sister Armancia's birthday.'

'This is a surprise present she can't possibly have anticipated,' Tayven said dryly. 'Will you fetch my brother Jadawyn? I have a friend here too. We're desperately in need of help.'

'I'll do what I can, discreetly,' Barlock said. He paused. 'It is a joy to see you, lad.'

'I hope my brother feels the same,' Tayven said. 'I'll wait out here. Tell no one but Jadawyn I'm here.'

He went back to Sinaclara and they sat in the yard, on a bench, mostly hidden by an exuberant spray of honeysuckle that released its scent subtly into the night. Tayven was too tense to speak. Sinaclara held his hand, occasionally squeezing it. Tayven could barely breathe.

The silhouette he saw in the doorway to the kitchen was not one he remembered. Then he realised that Jadawyn had aged, like he had. He was a man now, not the puppy-like thirteen-year-old he'd been when Tayven had left Magrast before. There was four years between them, but they looked similar enough to be twins. Now this mirror image approached him cautiously. He halted some feet away from the bench and murmured, 'Tay?' as if invoking a ghost.

310

'Yes, it's me,' Tayven said. 'The prodigal.' He stood up.

Jadawyn uttered a strange laugh that was almost a lament, then ran forward to embrace his brother. 'Not dead!' he said fiercely. 'I never believed it. Mother thought it was a fetch in your place at the palace, or an impostor seeking royal favour. She couldn't credit you'd stay away all this time and not contact us. When you were killed – when you disappeared – Almorante assured us he would find out what had happened. He visited us personally and gave us many gifts. He gave mother a necklace of black Mewtish opals for her grief, but it never went away.'

Tayven interrupted this babble of words. 'Father knew I was back, didn't he? He knew it was no fetch or impostor.'

Jadawyn drew away. 'Yes, with an attempted assassination charge around your neck. They said Tatrini had hired you as a cut-throat, that her patronage protected you from the law. They said you'd defected to become a terrorist in Cos, a traitor to the empire. Is any of it true?'

'Against my intentions, yes,' Tayven said. 'But there is more to it than that. I need help now, Jad. I need to get out of Magrast. The Grand Queen Mother's patronage has suddenly been withdrawn.'

'Why didn't you come or contact me? I thought that, if you lived, you'd gone mad. The fact you never came here suggested the worst.'

'Let's just say that being in Almorante's service had unexpected consequences.' Tayven gestured towards Sinaclara. 'This is my friend, a lady of Bree. We've recently had to escape the palace, virtually through the sewers, which is the reason for our dishevelled state. We need money, clothes, horses.' He paused. 'Has anyone from the palace come looking for me here?'

'Not yet,' Jadawyn said. 'I can't tell Father about this. You can't see any of the others. I'm sorry. You do understand why, don't you?'

'If you can help us, that's enough,' Tayven said shortly.

Jadawyn went back into the house, telling his brother to wait with Sinaclara further away from the kitchen. By this time, some of the staff had worked out something was going on, and inquisitive faces peered occasionally from the wide window, hastened away only by Merry Attercorn's sharp bark.

Tayven led Sinaclara to the bottom of the garden, to a line of potting sheds that smelled strongly of soil and wood in the warm evening. The roofs of the sheds were covered with a blanket of the climber known as night-blooming bane rose, a vine whose trumpet flowers were of startling white and whose winding cable stems had no thorns at all. Tayven plucked one of the blooms that hung down the wall. 'Ancient shamans would eat this stuff to see the gods,' he said.

311

'You and I can do so without it,' Sinaclara said lightly.

'I saw your peacock angel with my own eyes at Lake Pancanara,' Tayven said. 'But I feel the privilege has a high cost. We were all cursed as much as blessed by the Lakes Quest.'

'Our paths were never destined to be easy,' Sinaclara said. 'It is our choice. Remember it was you who wanted a dangerous life.'

Tayven laughed softly, bleakly. 'My family will never know the least portion of it. If they did, they'd only think I'd been stuffing myself with bane rose.' He crushed the petals in his hand. 'It could never be real for them.'

'The path I chose cost me my family and the life I knew,' Sinaclara said. 'But I would change none of it.'

'The compensation is that we are drawn to others like us,' Tayven said. 'At this moment, I am grateful for your company.'

It took half an hour or so for Jadawyn to return, accompanied by Barlock. They had brought food and a selection of garments, the latter of which derived from Jadawyn's own wardrobe. For the journey north, Sinaclara must dress as a man. While they ate, Tayven told as much of his story to Jadawyn as he could. Being unsure of where his brother's political loyalties lay nowadays, he edited the tale severely and omitted any reference to occult practices or his association with Palindrake. He emphasised the fact that Almorante had told him to leave.

'You may take two of my horses,' Jadawyn said, then sighed heavily. 'In the morning, I will have to tell the family what has happened. Most of them will punish me for not telling them sooner. They would want to see you, Tay. It's just that Father . . . '

'I know,' Tayven said. 'I hope that one day I can come home through the front door.' He reached out and squeezed his brother's shoulder. 'Don't worry, Jad. As soon as this is over, I will get word to you.'

Jadawyn shook his head, smiling wryly. 'You haven't changed much,' he said. 'Still the figure of mystery.'

'It is an image I've spent a long time cultivating,' Tayven said.

When Sinaclara had finished eating, she went into the shed to change, while Barlock went to prepare the horses.

'I wish you could stay overnight,' Jadawyn said. 'I want to hear the rest of your history – the bits you've left out, which I'm sure are the most interesting.'

Tayven laughed. 'Another time, Jad.' He paused, then said, 'If you are able, send word privately to Almorante that you've seen me and that we got away. But perhaps you should tell no one else of his involvement in my disappearance.'

'Where are you going?'

'North,' Tayven answered.

Jadawyn stared at him for a few moments. 'How far north?'

'It's best you don't know.'

Jadawyn hesitated before speaking. 'You're going to Caradore, aren't you? You're going to look for Khaster.'

'Perhaps.'

'But the Dragon Lord is there, and Khaster will probably be with him.' Jadawyn sounded bewildered. 'Or is that part of the plan?'

Tayven stood up. 'There's nothing for you to worry about. One day, if I can, I'll tell you everything. Trust me.'

'Perhaps you are what everyone says you are,' Jadawyn said, then grinned. 'But I wouldn't want you to be any other way.'

CHAPTER TWENTY-EIGHT

The Empty Castle

From a distance, the pale towers of Caradore looked unfamiliar. Rav felt he'd never seen them before. Everything about the flight from Magrast felt unreal. First it had been coloured by the terror of being followed by a horde of soldiers, who would fall upon them with merciless retribution. Then he had to suffer the exhausting journey, which was hard because Garante pushed the horses to their limit. Sleeplessness and the rigours of long-distance riding dragged Rav's mind into a kind of surreal limbo. The dragon daughters were around him constantly. Sometimes he could see them clearly, then would jerk wide awake with a start only to realise he'd been half asleep in the saddle, assailed by dream images. He could not speak of these things to Garante; he wished that Tayven were there.

Fortunately, Garante had funds with him, which meant they could stay at inns along the road rather than sleep rough. Garante made sure Rav ate good meals to keep his strength up. He was concerned that the size of Rav's pony meant they couldn't travel as fast as they should, and debated with himself aloud about whether he should spend a large amount of money on buying a larger, faster mount. Ultimately, he decided against it.

Rav felt safe with Garante, but lonely. He looked forward to seeing his aunts again. At night, he found himself crying softly for his mother.

Now home was in sight. The days in Magrast might never have happened, but nothing in life was comforting and familiar any more. The towers ahead, poking above the trees on the road, looked stark and unwelcoming. No flags fluttered from the turrets.

Garante realised something was amiss before Rav did. They

approached the cluster of dwellings and workshops that surrounded Caradore Castle and Garante said, 'There is no smoke.'

All was quiet. The village around the castle was as devoid of life as if a plague had seized every man, woman and child. Garante urged his horse to a canter and, with Rav's mount following, clattered up the sloping road to the castle itself. Rav saw something he'd never seen in his life before. The great portcullis was down across the archway that led to the main courtyard.

Garante pulled his horse to a halt before the gate and called out, 'Hoy! Valraven Palindrake, heir to Caradore, demands entrance!'

There was silence.

Rav pulled his pony up beside Garante's snorting horse. 'The portcullis is never down,' he said.

'They're expecting trouble,' Garante said shortly. 'No doubt the villagers are all within the castle walls.' He stood in the stirrups and yelled again, 'Hoy!' The only sound was the lament of the wind and the crash of waves from the shore below.

For a while, nothing happened and Rav was privately beginning to fear that something terrible had happened, which had killed his aunts and all their household, but then a face appeared over the battlements and a voice cried, 'Who goes there?'

'I am Garante, employed by the Dragon Lord as guardian to his son. I have brought the heir home. There is trouble in Magrast. Give us entrance!'

Without further words, the face disappeared and after some minutes an elderly soldier appeared in the yard beyond the thick iron grille. He bobbed arthritically towards them.

'Jomas!' Rav called. 'It's me. Let us in.'

Jomas was a guard who had been with the family for many years. He was more or less retired, and used to spend most of his time before the fire in the barracks mess room, regaling anyone who would listen with the exploits of his youth.

Slowly, with knobbly hands, Jomas operated the mechanisms that lifted the portcullis. When it was just above the horses' heads, Garante urged his mount through, ducking low to miss the steel points of the gate. 'Close it again,' he said to Jomas, dismounting from his horse. 'It's likely we will have been followed.'

Rav looked around the yard. Normally it was filled with servants and guards going about their business, but today all was still and silent. 'Where is everyone?' he asked, a note of fear in his voice.

'Gone,' said Jomas.

'What's happened?' Garante demanded.

315

'Lord Palindrake has taken the household north, to the old domain,' Jomas said. 'I'm here to keep watch and send messengers when the Magravands come.'

'Then it is true,' Garante said softly. For a moment, even in the midst of this strange situation, he became lost in his thoughts.

'Why have they gone?' Rav asked.

'It's what must be, or so the master told us,' Jomas said. 'Lady Pharinet said the time had come for Caradore to take back what is hers. Someone had to stay behind and watch. Someone did. I'm too stiff for travel.'

Rav realised the possible consequences of Jomas' decision. He could not imagine Magravandian soldiers arriving here and regarding the household's departure without fury. They would vent their wrath on whoever they found. 'Will you hide?' he asked.

Jomas grinned. 'Aye, lad. They'll not take me!'

'We must follow Lord Palindrake,' Garante announced, coming out of his reverie. 'Are fresh horses available, or have they all been taken?'

'I can get you horses,' Jomas said. 'But you'll need a guide. It's a straight road to Old Caradore, but you have to know the land. Inns are few and far between there.'

'Then see to it, man. We can't lose any time.'

Jomas unlocked the main door to the family living quarters so that Rav and Garante could find something to eat. Most of the food supplies had been taken north, but a modest amount had been left for his use. Inside, the castle was a haunted place. It felt damp and forbidding, even though it was summertime. The heart of the place was gone, or at least in hiding.

'Go to your old rooms,' Garante said to Rav. 'You might find your clothes have been left behind.'

Rav was almost afraid to do so. He could sense the dragon daughters slinking through the draughty passageways, conjuring ghosts of the past. Every time he turned a corner, he half expected to run into a phantom of a family member.

As Garante had predicted, Rav's possessions had been left in his room. He found this upsetting, as if his father hadn't expected him to need them again. Mournfully, he changed his clothes for attire more suitable to travel. He imagined that the old domain was very far away in a cold country, where it was never summertime.

By the time he went back downstairs, Garante had prepared a cold meal in the kitchen. Rav had never seen the old range black and chill, nor the great table in the centre of the room empty of pans and produce. Most of the cooking equipment had been taken.

'Come along, eat,' Garante said briskly.

Rav sidled up to a chair and sat down, regarding the meal before him with a dry mouth. He wanted to cry, but felt he shouldn't in front of his guardian. He could tell that Garante was perplexed and upset by finding Caradore empty. He hadn't believed what Tayven had said about Rav's father. He'd thought there would be an explanation awaiting him here. Rav knew little of the complexity of loyalties, but recognised that Garante was torn. He was a Magravandian, a devotee of Madragore, and now the man he served had been proved to be a traitor. Perhaps he would consider it his duty to take Rav back to Magrast now, or even kill him. Rav couldn't eat. He stared at his plate in misery, fighting tears.

'Rav,' Garante began sternly, then paused. 'I know you're worried,' he said in a softer tone, 'but you've got to be strong now. We must eat and then leave. It's dangerous to linger.'

'You're angry,' Rav said.

Garante did not answer at once. 'I have a responsibility to you,' he said eventually. 'I swore to keep you safe and I will do as I promised. I can't pretend I'm happy to discover the allegations against your father are true, but neither can I go back on my word. I will deliver you to him and then consider my future actions. You must not be afraid of *me*, Rav. There are too many other things for you to fear.' He managed a smile. 'Come on, now. Eat. We have a long ride ahead of us.'

They were not able to leave as quickly as Garante hoped. Jomas reported that a local farmer would be happy for one of his sons to take them north, but that they'd have to wait until the late afternoon for the youth to return from the hills, where he and his brothers were rounding up sheep. Garante was not pleased by this news. 'The Fire Chamber are bound to guess I'd bring you here,' he said, thinking aloud. 'We'd only have had a few hours' lead on them, if that, and their horses will be faster. If anything, they should have overtaken us by now.'

'Then perhaps they're not coming,' Rav said.

'If they're not,' Garante said, 'then it means they're planning something worse. The full might of the army could soon be marching on Old Caradore, then Madragore help your father.' He stared at Rav and shook his head. 'If I were a true guardian, I'd take you far from here, to somewhere where you'll never be found.'

'I want to go to my father,' Rav said.

Garante sighed deeply. 'But what am I sending you to, eh? That's the question.'

'They'll not kill *me*,' Rav said, and he wasn't sure where the words came from. He simply knew them to be true.

Before the farmer's son arrived, the sound of clattering hooves rang out upon the road approaching the castle. Garante and Rav were standing on the battlements above the gates, Garante scanning the road to the south nervously. Jomas had joined them and was relating tales of his youthful exploits. Rav found the familiar stories comforting, but it was clear Garante hadn't heard a word. Now, at the sound of horses, he hissed the old man into silence. 'Not many,' Garante said, his voice tense. 'If this is trouble, then you and I should be able to take them, with the help of these walls.' He thumped the thick stone as if to test their mettle. 'Bring longbows. It's our only chance.'

Without a word, Jomas hobbled off to search for weapons.

The thick trees hid the approaching riders until they reached the village at the castle walls. There were only two and Rav quickly recognised them. 'It's Tayven and Sinaclara!' he cried, virtually jumping on the spot. 'Let them in, Garante. Let them in!'

Garante leapt down the steps that led to the yard and raised the portcullis. Tayven and Sinaclara rode into the courtyard on sleek thoroughbred horses, which perhaps explained why they'd caught up so quickly. Rav threw himself at Tayven as soon as he dismounted, filled with a relief so profound it was beyond words or feeling. After the greetings were over, Tayven spoke to the stern-faced Garante. 'What happened here?'

'Palindrake has fled,' Garante said. 'We intend to follow him.'

'He has gone to Old Caradore,' Sinaclara said. 'I knew he would.'

'Yes,' Garante confirmed. He glanced severely at Tayven. 'The Fire Chamber are correct in their assumptions, it seems. Palindrake intends to make a stand at his family's old domain.'

'Thank you for bringing Rav here,' Tayven said. 'If you wish, you can return to Magrast now. There is no point in compromising your position further, if it isn't necessary.'

'It is neither your place to thank me for my actions nor to discharge me of my duties,' Garante snapped. 'We will travel together. Rav is my responsibility, not yours.'

CHAPTER TWENTY-NINE

Stolen Time

Coming down out of the mountains of High Hamagara was like waking from a narcotic dream. As the road descended, so the land became more populated: first villages, then towns, and traffic upon the great road that led to the northern sea.

Varencienne savoured these last stages of her travels. Not only was she going home to Caradore, but Khaster was escorting her there. She had stopped referring to him as Taropat, and he had voiced no objection. Ellony and Shan had not changed the way they addressed him, however. Varencienne could not imagine what would transpire when he returned home. He had a wife there, a grieving family, another life. These would be the last quiet weeks for a long time, Varencienne thought. There were emotional battles to face, as well as physical combat.

The Hamagarid ladies and their families did everything possible to make the journey comfortable for their unexpected companions. Ellony and Varencienne travelled in one of the carriages with the other women, while Shan and Khaster rode with the men, on horses decked out in tasselled livery.

For the first few days after leaving Hanana, the group camped out, now in much more luxurious accommodation than Varencienne and the others had endured upon the way. The merchants' servants would erect a small village of spacious peaked tents and then build a fire, where the evening meal would be cooked. After eating, everyone would sit around the fire and talk. At these times, the Hamagarids showed interest in the affairs of the outside world, and asked questions about them. For the first time, Varencienne encountered what appeared to be curiosity in a Hamagarid. There was something in their manner that suggested

319

they were more concerned about the manoeuvres of the empire than she'd first thought. But these people were traders, not holy ascetics. Civil war, either in the eastern continent of Cos and beyond, or south in Caradore and Magravandias, would affect their livelihoods.

Lady Patar's eldest son, Purna, showed great interest in befriending Khaster and Shan. Amused by it, Varencienne thought the youth saw the fair-skinned foreigners as exotic and strange. They had visited many far lands and, after consuming vast quantities of the walnut liquor the rich Hamagarids favoured, were disposed to talk about their adventures. To Varencienne, Purna was one of the most exotic people she'd ever met. He was around eighteen years old, with black hair plaited to his waist and a sculpted face with high cheekbones and the large dark eyes of a stag. His proud bearing and inscrutable expressions were those of a noble warrior shaman, yet in the men's company he became more amiable.

One evening, as they waited for the servants to erect the pavilions in a fragrant grove, Lady Sikim told Varencienne, with obvious relief, that this would be the last night they'd have to sleep outdoors. Now that summer had truly come to Hamagara, Varencienne enjoyed camping out. She felt close to the land, sensitive to its moods. The idea of comfortable inns and carefully prepared meals no longer held the appeal they once had. She also felt that out in the wilderness she was becoming closer to Khaster. In the evenings he would catch her eye across the fire and smile. It was as if they shared a secret, and perhaps they did. She felt he saw her properly as a woman now and so many times wanted to speak bluntly to him about it, but was afraid of being too forward, which might scare him off. She must nurture their relationship slowly, be patient with him. But the end of their journey was so close and Valraven waited there for them. She knew Khaster would not touch her then. It would take all of their strength for him to steel himself for the inevitable meeting. Then there was Shan, her staunch ally, a true friend who wanted only to be her lover. Why is it, Varencienne thought, that the people who are best for us are rarely the ones to capture our hearts?

That last night, while the murmuring forest exuded its panoply of fragrances into the warm night and fireflies were brief stars amongst the swaying branches, Varencienne watched Khaster carefully. A nexus point was approaching. His face was thoughtful in the orange light and his arms were wrapped around his raised knees. He looked young and innocent and seemed to be conducting a great debate within himself. A pang of pure nameless emotion pulsed through Varencienne's heart. This was one of the timeless moments that are never forgotten. Perhaps

Khaster was conscious of her scrutiny, because he rose to his feet and went into the shadow of the trees. Once, he glanced back.

Varencienne held her breath. She could go after him. He might want her to do so. Or he might only be leaving the fire to obey a call of nature. She hesitated, argued with herself, a dozen unlikely scenarios flashing through her mind. Then she caught Shan's eye across the fire. He was watching her as closely as she had observed Khaster. She smiled at him weakly, but he did not smile back.

Lady Sikim tapped Varencienne's shoulder, then launched into a description of the inn they would stay at the following evening. Varencienne could barely concentrate on the woman's words. She was thinking of Khaster walking soft-footed through the forest. If he was waiting for her and she did not follow, she might never get the chance again. Impatience and anxiety built up within her. Eventually Varencienne got to her feet, avoiding Shan's gaze. Pleading she needed to excuse herself for a moment, Varencienne hurried into the trees. Don't you dare follow me, she thought angrily.

It would soon become clear she had not left the fire simply to relieve herself.

For some minutes she followed a path near to where she had seen Khaster disappear. He had to have come this way. She was so tense, she could barely draw breath. How should she approach him? With laughter or with silence? What would he desire most? All she wanted to do was to offer herself to him, to give him love and physical comfort and pleasure. He had been alone for too long.

Moonlight came down through the trees, lighting her path before her. She thought she heard the murmur of a human voice and paused. Silence. Perhaps he was praying aloud. Carefully she crept forward. The path had narrowed and thick-trunked trees huddled close together, their roots reaching out to one another through the earth. Varencienne had to tread carefully. It would be easy to trip in the spectral light. Now she could hear the sound of running water. As she proceeded, the sound became louder and she could see that ahead the trees opened out into a natural glade, where a narrow waterfall fell over a low, fern-covered cliff into a pool. She caught a glimpse of something pale, his shirt perhaps. He must have come here to think clearly, comforted by the beauty of the forest. She could not bear to contemplate his loneliness, but would indulge herself and watch him for a while from the shadow of the trees.

Slowly she stole forward, her heart beating almost painfully in her breast. The night was not chill, but her hot breath steamed upon the air.

Then she heard laughter. He was not alone.

Varencienne's pounding heart seemed to still within her and heat fled her body. She felt physically sick, but had to see. There could be any explanation. She crouched down in the dusty branches of a rhododendron and peered into the glade.

Khaster sat with Purna beside the pool, talking animatedly in a low voice. Varencienne slumped in relief, but was unsure whether she should show herself or not. Clearly, with someone else present, she could not voice her desires. The boy really was an annoyance. He should have kept away. Perhaps Khaster would get rid of him soon.

The conversation in the glade had fallen silent. Khaster might be formulating a way to send Purna away. But Purna did not appear to be discouraged. He lifted his long plait of hair and began to unravel it. Khaster just watched him. Varencienne experienced a chill of dread.

Purna shook his head and his entire upper body was enveloped in a shawl of shining hair. Khaster reached out to touch it, ran it through his fingers. Then he leaned forward, put his hand behind Purna's head and pulled it towards him. They kissed.

Half blind with frustration and regret, Varencienne scrambled backwards through the foliage, uncaring of whether she made any noise or not. She ran back onto the path and did not stop running until she reached the edge of the trees where she could see the glow of the fire. Here, she paused and pressed her hands against her face. 'Stupid, stupid, stupid,' she murmured aloud. Her flesh felt hot again now, but with embarrassment. Thank Foy she hadn't reached Khaster before Purna did. A number of excruciating consequences flashed across her mind. She couldn't bear it. But then she realised they must have planned it all earlier and that Purna had been there waiting for Khaster. That was what he'd been thinking about by the fire. She must not let this affect her. Khaster was healing himself. She should be happy for him. Hadn't she told him her love was unconditional?

She smoothed her hair and walked back towards the fire. Shan turned to look at her and she managed to smile. She went to sit beside him. 'I thought you'd got lost,' he said.

She shook her head. 'No. I was just walking around. It's beautiful here.'

'Yes, it is,' he said. 'Very romantic.'

Varencienne saw again the scene beside the pool: two beautiful creatures about to make love in the most glorious landscape imaginable. But it should have been her. Why hadn't she spoken to Khaster before? They had been close. She had felt a mutual attraction between them, but caution and reticence had caused her to miss the tide. Someone else, who was clearly more forward, had sailed upon it. Despite her concentrated effort to be cheerful, sorrow welled up in her heart and overwhelmed her. She felt tears come to her eyes and was unable to suppress them.

Shan peered at her. 'Are you all right? What's the matter?'

Again Varencienne shook her head. She could not speak.

Shan put his arm around her and pulled her close. Her emotions took control. She wept against him, as silently as she could. Shan made a wordless sound of concern, kissed the top of her head. 'Are you worried about the future, Ren?'

She nodded against him.

'You're so strong. You'll be fine. This land, and all that happened here, was just a dream. We always knew it was. We should simply be grateful for the experience.'

Varencienne couldn't help laughing weakly. That was exactly the sort of thing she'd say.

'You have never wept once before,' Shan said wistfully. Then his arm became stiff against her and his voice was hard. 'Ren, why are you crying?'

She pulled away from him, scrubbed at her face. 'I don't know really,' she said shakily. 'I was just overcome.'

'Where's Taropat?'

'How should I know?'

Shan drew in his breath through his nose and Varencienne realised a hurt silence was presaged. 'He's with Purna,' she said irritably. 'I saw them, and yes, that's why I'm crying.'

Shan stared at her fiercely.

'I woke him up, Shan. Don't you realise that? Khaster has come back, but he doesn't see me.'

'Don't ask me to comfort you about this,' Shan said. 'Just don't.'

'I wouldn't,' she said, 'but I respect you enough to tell you the truth. I care for you, Shan. You're my rock.'

'I thought I was your lover,' he said. 'I thought I'd have to deliver you back to your husband, who it seems I must serve, not watch you make a fool of yourself with my mentor.' He smiled coldly. 'Taropat – Khaster – doesn't want you, Ren. That's what hurts, isn't it? You brought him back to life as he really is – the man who fell in love with Tayven Hirantel. How ironic.'

'He's never loved anybody. He told me so.'

'That's right,' Shan said sarcastically.

'And I have not made a fool of myself.' She sneered at him. 'I thought you were my friend. I thought you understood. But it's all about male jealousy, isn't it?' She realised they had attracted the attention of some of the Hamagarids by the fire. This was not desirable. 'I'm going to sleep,' she said and stood up.

'Sweet dreams, princess,' Shan said.

Varencienne went to the tent she shared with the others. Ellony wasn't in bed yet, and would no doubt be out chattering with her new Hamagarid friends for hours. Varencienne indulged herself in the act of crying herself to sleep, wrapped in a warm if prickly cocoon of self-pity. When someone shook her roughly awake, it took some time for sleep to fall from her body.

'What . . . ?' She pushed the hair from her eyes, expecting to see Shan. She didn't want a fight. But it was not Shan.

'Val?'

Her husband stood over her, his dark hair hanging down. He looked at her with affection. 'Ren, it's me, yes. We have to speak.'

She sat up. 'How did you find me? What's happened?'

He squatted down beside her. 'I'm not really here, Ren. I've just come to give you a message.'

She reached out and touched him. 'You *are* really here, Val!'

He shook his head. 'You're dreaming and I've invaded your dream, taken control of it.' He laughed. 'You won't believe how much I've learned since we last saw each other.'

'You seem very different.' She had never heard him laugh so freely before. His face appeared less severe.

'I am. I've taken the family and the Leckerys to Old Caradore. You must come to me. Bring Khaster and Shan with you. As soon as you can. Bayard will come there with the Magravandian army. We all need to be together, for only in unified strength can we win this battle. I need the Brotherhood of the True King around me.'

She opened her mouth to speak, but he had vanished. 'I'm awake,' she said aloud. 'What in Foy's name was he talking about? I'm awake!' She threw back her blanket and leapt up. Grabbing a shawl, which she cast around her shoulders over her clothes, she ran barefoot out of the tent. There were still quite a few people sitting around the fire, but Varencienne did not pause to look at them. She ran straight into the forest down the winding narrow path to the waterfall glade. She knew it could wait until morning, but the urge to tell Khaster that Valraven had appeared to her was too great to ignore.

Before she entered the glade, she called his name, to give him a few moments to compose himself. Half of her expected to see the pair of them still sitting by the pool as she had left them. But they were lying naked together, both faces turned towards her in surprise.

'Khas, I'm sorry,' she said, 'but I have to speak to you.'

'What?'

'Val just came to me.' She gestured emphatically with both hands.

'He's told us – all of us – to go to Old Caradore. He *appeared* to me. It was so strange. He's changed, Khas. He's who he should be. He asked for you by name.' She had begun to shake and realised she was on the verge of tears again. She stood there at the edge of the glade, her face in her hands.

After some moments, during which he must have put on his trousers, Khaster came to her. 'Ren, it's all right,' he said gently.

She lowered her hands. *No it isn't.* 'It was a shock. So real. I shouldn't have come here, I know. I just had to talk to you.'

He lifted her chin with one hand, looked into her eyes. She pulled herself away, sure he could see everything that was in her heart. 'We'll go to Old Caradore,' he said. 'Usually it's me who has the informative dreams.'

'You're distracted,' she answered sharply, then more softly, 'It wasn't a dream, anyway. He said it was, but it wasn't. It was both dreaming and being awake.'

Purna sat observing their conversation, probably understanding none of it because it was in Magravandian. He looked curious rather than displeased.

'I'll go now,' Varencienne said. 'I'm sorry I interrupted.'

'You didn't,' Khaster said. 'We were just about to return to the camp, in any case.'

Varencienne smiled shakily. 'Welcome back, Khaster,' she said. 'Thank you for stepping down out of the painting.'

He put his head to one side. 'Oh, your painted dream man hasn't come back, Ren. He never existed, but thanks for believing in him anyway.'

Varencienne leaned over and kissed his cheek briefly. 'Let's go home.'

Shan was no longer by the fire when Varencienne returned from the forest with Khaster and Purna. It was strange the way feelings could change. Varencienne couldn't bear to lay her eyes on him at present. She realised he had become an ex-lover, without her even thinking about it consciously.

Khaster sat down and told the Hamagarids their new plans. Nobody questioned the fact, or even considered it unusual that Varencienne's husband could appear to her like a ghost.

'At least we know now where we have to go,' Khaster said, 'but our lack of funds will pose a problem. It would help us if we could secure a loan to buy passage south.'

Lord Alak, the husband of Lady Sikim, raised his hands. 'You may travel on one of my ships. I will supply a crew. What about men? I have a trained personal guard who, at my command, will fight for you as if you were their master.'

'I won't refuse your generous offer,' Khaster said. 'If the Dragon Lord is attacked by the Magravandian army, he'll need all the support he can get.'

Lord Turkat, husband of Lady Patar, gestured widely. 'We will go to Prince Kutaka on our return to Nimet. He is lord of our city and will listen to the words of Aranepa. He will give you men.'

Khaster grinned fiercely at Varencienne. 'I'll feel better going to meet Val if I can take him an army.'

'This battle will affect us all,' said Lady Sikim. 'Hamagara stands back from the world, but sometimes it is our place to take a stand with those who fight for what is good.'

Especially when it might affect your income, Varencienne thought. 'This is more than we could have hoped for,' she said. 'We will never forget your kindness and generosity.'

'You have Paraga with you,' said Lady Sikim, to whom Varencienne had told the whole story. 'Never fear the outcome.'

I do not feel him though, Varencienne thought. I'm still too human for my liking.

Purna, who was sitting beside Khaster, took his hand. 'I will be greatly honoured to fight at your side.'

Khaster glanced at Varencienne with a startled expression. She knew what he was thinking.

Later, she was able to talk privately to him about it. The Hamagarids had opened several more flagons of walnut liquor to toast the new alliance and, despite the late hour, no one seemed inclined to go to bed. Purna left the fire for a while and Varencienne made use of the opportunity. She went to sit beside Khaster. 'Purna shouldn't come with us, unless you want to have an added complication. His feelings are obvious.'

Khaster raised an eyebrow. 'You can read my mind.'

'Tayven will be at Old Caradore. I just know it. He is part of your Brotherhood. If you want to mend that situation, you don't need an appendage like Purna.'

Khaster rubbed his face. 'I'm not sure the situation is mendable, Ren, but at the very least I want accord between us.' He sighed. 'Tonight, I felt I was doing the right thing. It was like coming alive again, free of old guilt, pain and shame. It was good.'

Varencienne winced inwardly. She was glad to be his confidante, but this wasn't without pain for her.

Khaster rubbed her arm. 'I'm sorry. You probably don't want to hear this. I can't thank you enough for what you've done for me, but . . . We can't be together, Ren. You do know that, don't you?'

She forced a smile. 'I've awoken the man who fell in love with Tayven. I know.'

'It's not just that,' he said. 'You are beautiful and I find you very attractive. I certainly love you as a sister, and in another world the rest might follow. It's mainly because of Val. It's too complicated.'

'Story of my life,' Varencienne said bitterly. 'Merlan said that too.'

Khaster's eyes widened. 'You and Merlan?'

'Yes. Shocked?'

He laughed uncertainly. 'No, no. It's just that I still think of him as a child, I suppose.'

'Oh, he's very much a man, Khas. The next best thing to you.' She clasped her knees. 'The saddest thing is that Val and I will never share the kind of love I want. He is my husband, and no other man can love me openly, because of my position. I'm doomed to a life of furtive affairs.'

'We have to hope we'll all still have lives to live in the future,' Khaster said, 'whether doomed or otherwise.'

'I know. We could all die very soon.'

For some moments, there was silence between them. Varencienne looked up at Khaster slyly and found him gazing at her. 'Just once,' she said softly. 'That's all. Give us that.'

He continued to stare at her. 'Sometimes the Malagash comes out in you, doesn't it?' he said quietly. 'Bayard's sister.'

She didn't answer.

Khaster ran his hands through his hair and exhaled with a soft groan. 'It would feel as if I were taking advantage of you.'

Varencienne snorted. 'Khaster, really. I'm a grown woman, with my own mind. It's what I want.'

'I've experienced life again tonight,' he said. 'I want more of it. It seems selfish.'

'It isn't.'

'I don't want any regrets.'

'You won't get any. I promise.' She reached out and ran her hand down his face. 'There are many paths in the forest.'

'Shan?'

'Forget him. I have.'

'Malagash!'

'Yes,' she said. 'I am.' She got to her feet. 'Come with me now. I'm not going off alone and waiting for a man who might not join me.'

Without words, he stood up. 'Lead me then, Lady Darkness.'

As they left the fire, Purna approached them. Varencienne's heart sank, but the youth only grinned at them cheerfully and gave them a somewhat salacious salute. Clearly, jealousy was not a part of the Hamagarid character. Unfortunately, it could be a great part of most other people's. Of Shan, there was no sign.

CHAPTER THIRTY

Night of Fire

Although thunderheads had massed on the horizon of the Magravan-dian mountains every evening for over a week, rain had not broken through and the air was sultry, almost unbreathable, conjuring every foul stink from the lowliest quarters of the city. People can be driven to strange actions under the influence of heat. Men and women who'd remained in the shadows came forth, bringing their maledictions with them.

Tatrini was taking a late supper, beneath the quickly waving fan of a page. It was almost too much effort to eat, even though her favourite morsels had been prepared for her. Earlier she'd thought she'd heard thunder, but on going to examine the sky from her parlour window, she had seen only a bloody sunset which turned her garden red. The sun looked as if it was dying as it fell into the arms of the cathedral spires that, even from the high vantage of the palace, could be seen above the walls.

As she slowly ate her dessert – rather flabby strawberries and cream on the turn to rancid – she'd heard distant shouts. She'd not paid this much attention, as there had been a lot of shouting since the incident at the boiler rooms. People were unnerved by the disappearance of Rav Palindrake, and truth had swiftly been distorted into fiction by hysterical rumours. Not least amongst these was the idea that the curse of the Palindrakes had been broken and that the Dragon Lord had secretly been amassing allies within the empire and that soon this horde would march upon Magrast, intent on slaughtering every man, woman and child in the city.

Tatrini had made sure her agents had gathered every rumour and wondered privately whether the Fire Chamber had anything to do with them. It was surely in their interest for public opinion to be against Valraven, and what better way to do it than through the threat of extinction? Valraven had been turned into a dark and vengeful god, but as in the case of every religion, rabid fanatical factions had arisen. All gods have their Chosen Ones who, through devotion and piety, believe themselves impervious to divine plague or curse. Valraven's followers were reputed to call themselves the Dragonards. Whether they actually existed, or whether the slogans that had appeared on walls in the market areas had been written only by troublemakers and youngsters for a lark, Tatrini was unsure. She steeled herself to weather the storm, for every day its potential built in strength and emotion. Gastern had been squirreled away in the country, along with his drooping empress and listless son, and now Almorante was acting emperor. People felt uncomfortable with this. It was a departure from tradition and showed only that the Malagashes were not invulnerable. People became conscious, in dreams or waking reality, of the empire spreading out to every quarter of the world, and the most aware realised that for every subjugated realm there was a potential rebellion and the conquering wave that had surged outward might very well reverse direction.

Tatrini pushed away her half-finished dessert and lay back exhausted in the cushions of her chair. Soon the Fire Chamber would make public that the military was to march on Caradore. Preparations for a campaign were already underway. It was expedient, if only to quash the rumours about Valraven. Without taking any action himself, he had become more than a legend. Tatrini still wondered whether he was lost in the wilderness somewhere, searching for his wife and daughter, completely oblivious to what was taking place at home. That was the true stuff of legend, like an archetypal myth or a moral fable concerned with the evils of gossip.

Tatrini, half dozing, heard the sound of booted feet marching nearby. She heard isolated calls, strange barked orders. Then the crash of doors opening. She sat upright. Within moments, Grisette Pimalder ran into the room, without pausing to knock or request entrance.

'Who?' Tatrini snapped.

Before Grisette could answer, Rufus Lorca strode across the threshold, accompanied by six Splendifers.

'What is the meaning of this?' Tatrini demanded perfunctorily, even as she spoke, wearily aware of the hackneyed aspect of the question. She had to say it: it was her line. Tonight, she felt, there would be many standard lines uttered.

Lorca bowed stiffly. 'My lady, the Fire Chamber has ordered you be taken to a place of safety.'

'I am quite safe here. What has happened? Don't try to fool me, boy. Speak the truth.'

'An attempt has been made on the life of the emperor.'

Tatrini rose from her chair. 'Almorante? Was he harmed? Give me a full report at once.'

Lorca's face was expressionless, but sickly-white. 'The emperor escaped unscathed. He was dining with his brothers, Prince Roarke and Prince Celetian, as well as several of their friends. A group of masked individuals broke into the room. In the scuffle, the emperor's brothers were injured . . . '

'Wait!' Tatrini interrupted. 'How did people get into the palace? Were the guards asleep?'

'My lady, it is being investigated.'

'What of my sons?'

Lorca hesitated. 'The physicians are with them. One of the other men was pronounced dead on the scene.'

'What of my sons, boy?' Tatrini asked in a darker tone.

'The prognosis is not good,' Lorca replied. 'That is all I know.'

Tatrini took a deep breath. Part of her was unsurprised by this news, part was perturbed. Celetian and Roarke were injured badly. They were her sons, but in many ways little more than names to her. What did she feel? Tatrini was aware this was unnatural and was surprised to find herself unnerved by it. Despite this, she spoke with a calm voice. 'I trust Prince Bayard and Prince Leo have been given adequate protection?'

Lorca eyed her speculatively. 'All the princes and their families are now under close supervision.'

There was a tone to his voice that Tatrini interpreted as suspicious accusation. Lorca was wondering whether Bayard was, in fact, behind the attack. He was certainly capable of it, and he'd voiced his displeasure to his mother vociferously over Almorante being given the crown, albeit temporarily. Now it was in place, Bayard could not imagine it ever passing to anyone else – namely himself. Perhaps the heat and fever of the city had driven him to desperate measures.

'Were the men caught who attacked my sons?'

'Most of them, my lady. They claim to be Dragonards.'

Tatrini raised her eyebrows. 'Indeed? Then they do exist.'

'It is what they claim to be.'

Tatrini smiled gently. 'You don't want them to exist, do you? You don't want to believe ill of your Dragon Lord.'

Lorca bowed. 'I must leave now, my lady, but will station two men at your door. Prepare yourself to leave the city. It has been decided your household should be taken to Recolletine, where it is safe.'

Tatrini stood up. 'Soon the order will come to march on Caradore. How do you feel about that, Captain Lorca? How do your men feel?'

'We do our duty,' Lorca replied and the look in his eye informed Tatrini he had her measure. 'You need not fear for your security.' He stalked out of the room, followed by his men.

Tatrini had no intention of being tucked away in Recolletine. She clapped her hands at Lady Pimalder, who was still drooping on the floor in a puddle of skirts, not having risen from her initial skidding curtsey. 'Come, Grisette, see to my face and hair. I must make a social call.'

If the Splendifers were aware of the warren of passageways that burrowed through the walls of the palace, they knew only a few of them. The men on duty at Tatrini's door had no inkling that the Grand Queen Mother had slipped away virtually from beneath their noses. Taking Grisette Pimalder with her, Tatrini hurried along the cramped, creaking corridors where needles of light came through cracks in the walls.

They emerged in a high gallery, a short distance from Lord Senefex's chambers. Long unused, its walls were bare of the portraits that had once hung there and the windows overlooking the city far below were almost opaque with grime. Tatrini glanced out of them and saw that the sunset still raged on the horizon. Then she paused and rubbed the glass.

'What is it, my lady?' Grisette asked.

'Look,' Tatrini said in a flat tone. 'The city burns.'

The cathedral was limned in flame, apparently impervious to Madragore's chosen element. It presided over a realm of fire. Gouts of oily smoke hung like fog above the rooftops of the merchant quarter and occasionally a spurt of sparks would shoot up as explosions some miles away shook the palace walls.

'It was not thunder we heard earlier,' Tatrini said.

Lady Pimalder pressed one hand briefly to her mouth, then said, 'I did not see this.'

'We cannot foretell everything,' Tatrini said. 'Come, we must hurry.'

Tatrini had to shove the guards aside at Senefex's door. Within, she could hear the low hubbub of male voices. It appeared that the Fire Chamber was in unofficial session.

Frightening with a snarl any servants who might have barred her entrance, Tatrini swept into Senefex's office. As she'd suspected most of the Chamber were present, including a clutch of generals and Mordryn.

'Good evening, gentlemen,' Tatrini drawled. 'You have not invited me to the meeting. It is most remiss of you, but I will forgive you, on this occasion. It seems we have trouble at hand.'

'My lady,' Senefex said, hurrying towards her. 'I sent Captain Lorca to explain the situation to you. It is dangerous for you to be here. I've arranged for you to be sent to safety.'

'I know all about your *arrangements*,' Tatrini said. 'It was thoughtful of you, Senefex, but not needed. You act from reflex – what you suppose is best for a woman. I don't need to remind you conditions have changed.' She marched towards his desk where a map was laid out. 'Apprise me of the situation in the city at once.'

She could tell that a large percentage of the men present were unhappy with her arrival but, as she was now an elected member of the Chamber, they could not voice their complaints. Tatrini also took note of the fact that none of the princes were present, nor the emperor himself. What had she interrupted here?

'Frenzy has broken out,' Mordryn said, the first to respond to Tatrini's request. 'The people who call themselves Dragonards, who are acting under Palindrake's name, though most of us believe without his blessing, have chosen to rise up and make a noise.'

'They must have some organisation behind them, then, to reach this far into our sanctuary,' Tatrini said. 'Also, from what I observed on the way here, they are making rather more than just a noise.'

Senefex made a dismissive gesture. 'They have agitated the citizens in certain areas and have set fires. It looks worse than it is. The militia is currently dealing with the crisis.'

Tatrini was not deceived by his apparently unconcerned attitude. 'How have they managed to become this prepared without the Fire Chamber being aware of it? I presumed we had an effective network of agents to sniff out such circumstances.'

There was a rumble of murmurs, but Mordryn stemmed them with his loud voice. 'Your criticisms are justified, my lady. We have been taken unawares, but the situation is now in hand.'

'How exactly?'

'Grand Mage Alguin has deployed the Cathedral Guard.'

Tatrini choked off a laugh. 'Alguin? Are you mad? How can you let him loose on the city? He will make it a religious crusade and no doubt add to the chaos.'

'We have no alternative. Rebellious factions must be contained and eliminated.'

Tatrini experienced a moment of pure psychic intuition. She realised that the fires had not been started by the rebels. She would discover the truth of events for herself in time, but now considered that perhaps Alguin's 'containment' methods involved the suppression of individuals who might not be guilty. Alguin was a man who would make examples. Mordryn and the others must feel extremely threatened to let him have full rein. But perhaps this was part of their plan, a secret plan, known only to the inner cabal of the Chamber. It was extreme if it was just to discredit Valraven further.

'You are right, we must take action,' she said, 'but I can perceive beneficial results from tonight's events. The old order is being shaken up. The Malagashes must now show the people of what we are made. Stagnation must be burned away by fire. I take it plans to march on Caradore are in hand?'

Mordryn regarded Tatrini with a severe gaze. 'That is the gist of our strategy,' he said carefully, for him.

Tatrini was aware she would be saying things that undoubtedly these men had muttered to one another many times, but she wanted them to know how their efforts to exclude her had been pointless. 'Palindrake must be brought back to Magrast in the hands of the Malagashes. If he is dead, his body should be displayed on the city walls. If alive, he must be punished publicly for treason. We can only suppose the Dragon Lord's son has been taken to Caradore. He too must be reclaimed.'

'Figureheads are a difficulty,' Senefex said.

'I perceive implications in your words,' Tatrini said. 'Young Rav is not a difficulty. He is my grandson and Malagash blood runs in his veins. Having foresight, I have trained him myself while he's been in Magrast. We must look upon his disappearance as abduction. Once he's returned to me, you will have your tame Dragon Heir once more.'

The men were regarding her with a certain amount of suspicion. They did not like to hear she'd been 'training' Rav. She was pleased to note they were wary of her power, but in some eyes she saw a grudging respect. They wanted her strengths. They wanted Leonid back, someone who would be decisive and optimistic, who was confident in their own right to rule. This night, some of them, for the first time, would behold a woman with clear sight.

'The army will be deployed to Caradore within the week,' Senefex said.

'Will Rufus Lorca and the Splendifers be part of it?' Tatrini enquired.

'Under the circumstances, no.'

'Prince Bayard should lead the army,' Tatrini said. 'He knows Palindrake well and has fought beside him. He knows the Dragon Lord's strategies and, it must be said, will not be affected by torn loyalties.'

'Are you suggesting any of our officers might turn traitor?' one of the generals asked coldly.

'Not at all,' Tatrini said, 'but I doubt there are many amongst them who would *relish* leading an assault on Caradore.'

'And Prince Bayard would relish it?' Mordryn asked.

'He would do his duty and succeed,' Tatrini replied. 'You need a strong figurehead, because the men will not be comfortable with the Splendifers' exclusion. That simple decision says so much. Soldiers are trained to obey, but they are also men of instinct, otherwise they would not survive. They should have their emperor amongst them. Almorante should not skulk here in Magrast while Caradore is vanquished. Leonid spent far too much time doing that at the end of his life.'

'Some would question the wisdom of sending both Almorante and Bayard into battle at this juncture,' Senefex said. 'We do not yet know what the army will find in Caradore.'

'You should not fear defeat,' Tatrini said.

Before she could offer more persuasive arguments, Mordryn interrupted her. 'We do not disagree with your suggestion and neither do we fear defeat. Senefex means we have to do what the people see is right. Sending Malagashes en masse might be interpreted as panic. Also, Almorante himself might be against it. He is not a man of battle, my lady. His wars have always taken place behind closed doors.'

Tatrini uttered a scornful laugh. 'Since when has the emperor's own desires impeded yours? I am sure you can persuade him. I will help you do so, for I also intend to go to Caradore. And before you bluster your objections, allow me to decide what is right in this matter. It is time you accepted how seriously I take my role within the empire and how dearly I uphold it.'

'No one has ever doubted that, my lady,' Mordryn said, somewhat dryly. 'If you wish to ride with the army, we will not prevent it. However, I hope you are fully aware of the strictures of military travel. It will be no easy journey.'

'I am aware,' Tatrini said. 'You look upon me still as a mere woman, but my presence in Caradore will ensure you get what you desire.'

CHAPTER THIRTY-ONE

Ships from the North

Valraven surveyed the progress his artisans were making with the main entrance to the old domain. Much of the rubble had now been cleared and dozens of builders were already intent on rebuilding the sagging walls. Within them, a shanty village had formed in the main courtyard, while the servants and working folk of Caradore cleaned out and repaired the buildings around it. Only the ground floor of the keep was fit to live in, as the upper storeys were unsafe, and here Everna and Pharinet had set up their household, along with the Leckery women.

A week after their arrival, Rav had come back to them, along with his company of guardians. While the women wept and laughed over the boy, Garante and Tayven told Valraven all that had happened in Magrast. He remembered what Foy had said as he'd floundered in the ocean. He had acted upon her words, but perhaps part of him had never fully believed them. Now it was incontrovertible. A dark cloud, shot with bloody flames, was massing on the far horizon, and soon it would surge north. He thought of Varencienne, how he had failed her, how he might die and be unable to prevent the deaths of all those they loved, without her ever knowing that he'd searched for her.

When he met Sinaclara in the flesh, he felt he knew her already, though she had no recollection of meeting him in visions. Still, it was strange to feel familiarity with a stranger. Pharinet and Niska were not greatly enchanted by Sinaclara. They did not like the way the red-haired sorceress was so proprietorial with him. Pharinet said she thought Sinaclara looked down on them, and who did she think she was? Sinaclara appeared oblivious to this hostility, but Valraven noticed she spent little time with the women. Tayven was her closest friend.

Valraven observed the dynamics of his people with bewildered perplexity. Saska had been told that Tayven was a friend of Khaster's, and naturally wanted to question him extensively. Valraven had told Tayven to be careful with the Leckery matriarch and not to say anything upsetting to her. Tayven commented dryly that Khaster's mother's attitude had no doubt greatly contributed to his fear of love between men, which Valraven could not dispute. Pharinet regarded Tayven with a kind of morbid curiosity and clearly found it difficult to equate the man she had married with the stories she heard about Taropat. She would have liked to get to know Tayven better, but it was difficult for her, because Tayven was rarely without Sinaclara by his side.

Valraven liked Tayven and made sure he sometimes had the man's company alone. But it was clear to him, from various comments Tayven had made, that he was becoming increasingly tense. When Valraven asked him why, he said that he felt sure Khaster would come to them. Valraven had gone over the story of the Crown Quest several times with Tayven, who insisted that the Brotherhood of the True King should be reformed. But Tayven was afraid of it too.

One night Valraven dreamed of finding Varencienne and telling her to come home. In the dream, he had asked her to bring Khaster and Shan with her, as if she was the one who had kidnapped them, rather than vice versa. The dream had been so vivid, Valraven went to tell Tayven about it as soon as he awoke. Once he'd heard it, Tayven become even more restless. 'They are already on their way,' he said. 'The dream is a sign.'

Valraven had more than family problems to deal with. His employee, Garante, was a tormented soul, who felt he was forsaking his god and his country, but who recognised an instinctive loyalty to the Dragon Lord. He wanted to discuss the matter in great depth, with which Valraven had little patience. The man was either with him or not and that was the end of it.

The whole situation frustrated Valraven. Everyone around him was wrestling with personal dilemmas, when they should be focused upon what was about to happen. They would need all their strength for it. Only Sinaclara seemed unaffected and confident. She looked upon him with a fierce and determined gaze and told him that all was as it was meant to be. He should not worry. He was the True King, the Man of Silence. The Crown was his by right and he was destined to crush the Malagashes. Occasionally a spark of hope would ignite within Valraven as he listened to Sinaclara's impassioned words, but he was concerned that everyone was so unprepared. Ironically, he only possessed power over his dreams because he was no longer asleep. His eyes were wide open. It was as if his life before had been the dream, where he'd floated like a ghost with no true will of his own. He'd had no awareness of the dilemmas and feelings of anyone around him. It was hard now to endure the cacophony of so many voices crying out for silence. Sinaclara told him in a portentous tone that silence derived only from the soul light of an heir to the absolute. He did not consider this to be helpful information.

In the cold twilight before dawn, when the ocean held the fragile land in its relentless fingers, Valraven walked the battlements, thrashed by wind. He could hear only inevitability in the crash of the waves below. Nothing endured for ever. In the end, everything would be washed away by time. Time devoured mercilessly, just as the ocean tides could extinguish the most ardent flames. Despite these melancholy thoughts, an instinct whispered that victory was possible, but something was missing. Something. He could not believe it was simply the Brotherhood.

The old castle felt startled to Valraven, as if it had been woken abruptly from a deep slumber: awoken or resurrected. He yearned to sense Ilcretia's presence near, as a spiritual guide to encourage and direct him, but even her ghost was absent. Mother. Where are you?

Every day, while Everna, Oltefney and Saska drank tea in the main hall, as if trying to cling to their lives as they had known them, Valraven and Pharinet explored the ancient passageways beneath the castle. During these dank excursions, a sense of intimacy revived between them. It felt different now, cleansed by tears. They could hold each other's hand without guilt. At the end of time, there is no room for shame, but they resolved they would not touch each other in love until the future of Caradore was secure. Perhaps they were gambling with fate. Valraven thought that, like he did, Pharinet secretly hoped to find in the Caradorean underworld miraculous aid for their situation: a magical artefact, an informative vision, supernatural allies, some undreamed-of truth. They found nothing but damp and cobwebs and the marks Niska and Valraven had made upon the walls last time they'd been there. What they could not speak of was the fact that the combined might of the Caradorean families who supported them might not be enough to hold off the army of the empire.

On the way north, Valraven and his twin had visited together every noble house along the route. Most were willing to send men to the old domain, even though they must have suspected in their hearts they might be sending their relatives and faithful servants to certain extinction. Valraven was not sure how many of these potential soldiers would arrive. It would have been better to take them along from the start, but first he wanted to put the old castle in order and organise supplies. There was no point in taking a huge company if there was no way to feed them. It would take Magrast some time to mobilise its troops, but they would come eventually.

After nearly a month, the first recruits began to trickle in. Representatives from the House of Doomes and Darthenate arrived, galloping over the causeway amidst a forest of banners. Then Galingale, Ignitante and Rook. They brought supplies, men and weapons with them, along with a strange dreamlike enthusiasm, as if they could not believe what they were doing and that flags could not possibly be flying from the craggy towers of Old Caradore once more. These were not young men, though. They weren't the flower of Caradorean youth. Men who were not infirm, mad or retired were in active service for the imperial army, and no doubt most of them had recently been posted far overseas as a precaution. Valraven surveyed the ranks of staunch, elderly men and their life-long servants. He saw younger men who were veterans of battle, some with missing limbs and ravaged faces. It was like a company of the dead, revenants hauled from the grave to re-enact an ancient war. Part of him felt like a deceiver as he walked amongst them, his mouth speaking words intended to inspire and inflame. What could he offer them, really? Would Foy arise from the deeps to breathe icy breath over the enemy?

Communal evening meals were taken in the great hall. They were like a memory of a far earlier time, men ripping meat like barbarians, with their teeth and daggers. After the meal, some of them, who had once been in Magrast and who had long memories, would ask Tayven to sing for them. This, to Valraven, was slightly indelicate, as he was sure Tayven had no desire to be reminded of certain aspects of his past, but he complied without complaint. His was no silvery boy's voice now, but in many ways more poignant. It was often difficult to tell what he sang about, for the words made no sense. The feelings conjured by the songs, however, could make the hairs rise on a man's neck. Sometimes Valraven would stare at Tayven in the firelight and think, 'Are you to blame, fundamentally, for Khaster's madness, for Varencienne's disappearance? If you had never existed, how would it all have been?'

And sometimes Tayven would catch Valraven's eye in return and there was no smile between them, just a bitter knowledge. Once Tayven said to him aloud, across the heads of dozing men, 'I am your Bard.'

And Valraven knew that no one heard those words but him. He said, 'I know.'

At night, Valraven prayed in a small chapel to the Dragon Queen, which he and Pharinet had found at the end of a corridor filled with rubble and desiccated vines. He knelt before the cracked altar, his sword held before him, point against the gritty flagstones. Sometimes he was touched by moonbeams and his ears roared with the song of the ocean, but there were no messages for him, no sense of presence. At these times, he felt utterly alone.

One night, as he prayed, he leaned his forehead against the pommel of his sword. 'Great Foy,' he whispered, 'I once believed I saw you with my living eyes, that you bore me from the sea. The mark of fire has been scourged from me. Speak to me now. What must I do? Have I been brought to this place for a purpose? Is it right? How can I inspire the hearts of men if my own is fearful?'

There was, as he'd expected, no response. The tide was low and the sound of the sea was distant, a mere murmur. Valraven closed his eyes, tried to calm the chaotic tide of thoughts in his own mind. He was angry with Foy, thinking she'd abandoned him. This was the way it must be: he would be king alone. Perhaps he should be thinking about building boats and taking his supporters east to Cos. At least, then, his family might be safe. He wondered about Merlan for the first time in weeks. Had he discovered the whereabouts of his wayward brother and Varencienne? Perhaps Merlan was dead, taken by an assassin's knife. As for Darris Maycarpe, it was unlikely he would survive the disorder, if he wasn't already dead.

For a moment, Valraven remembered a winter festival at Caradore Castle. He could smell the pine logs burning in the great hearth, mingled with the aroma of spiced wine and roast beef. He heard the laughter of women, the chink of glass and then saw his sister's face, full of mischief. How long ago had that happened? Were Khaster and Ellony in this picture?

Then the sound of the door scraping open behind him jolted him from his memories. He turned and saw Tayven standing at the threshold.

'What is it?' Valraven snapped.

'Did you not hear the cry?' Tayven asked.

'No. What cry?'

'You must come,' Tayven said, and turned away.

For some moments, Valraven stared at the empty doorway, wondering whether anyone had actually stood there or whether it had been a vision. Then, a voice came from the corridor outside. 'Hurry. The sentries have seen something.'

Valraven ran across the courtyard and leapt up the steps to the northern battlements. A cluster of men, dark shadows in flapping coats, was clustered at one spot. Wind howled furiously amongst the ancient stones. As Valraven approached, a man turned to him. Hamsin. 'My lord, they come from the north.'

Valraven pushed through the knot of bodies, snatched a telescope from a sentry's hand. The moon was full, so it was possible to make out the ghostly shapes of ships on the horizon. Dozens of them, sailing down a river of moonlight. Valraven strained to make out details, to see a flag or some other identification, but the design of the boats was unknown to him. When he lowered the telescope, Tayven was standing beside him. 'Well, Bard, what do you make of this?'

Tayven shook his head slowly. 'I'm unsure. I feel anxious, but that could mean anything.' His expression was troubled, bewildered even. It was unusual, because he rarely let his mask slip in front of others.

'Does anyone recognise these ships?' Valraven demanded. 'They hail from no province of the empire from what I can see.'

'They could be Cossic,' someone said.

'Merlan?' Valraven said to Tayven. 'Is it possible?'

'I don't think so,' Tayven said.

'Round up the sorceresses, then!' Valraven said, unnerved by Tayven's uncertainty. 'We have need of their sight.'

Valraven's command conjured a ripple of laughter from the men and Hamsin ordered a couple of them to seek out Sinaclara and Niska. Valraven put the telescope to his right eye once more. 'They are coming straight for us. Too much of a coincidence. It's someone who knows we are here.'

'The tide is low,' Hamsin said. 'They'll not get that close. We should have a good look at them walking up the beach.'

'They are not enemies,' Tayven said. 'Their approach is too bold. These battlements could be bristling with cannon.'

'But they are not,' Valraven said. 'Hamsin, I want twenty men and horses made ready. We will go to greet our visitors.'

By the time the men had come down from the battlements, Pharinet, Niska and Sinaclara were hurrying into the yard. 'What has happened?' Pharinet demanded.

'Ships,' Valraven answered. He addressed the other women. 'Can either of you tell me anything about them?'

There was a moment's hesitation, then Sinaclara said, 'I have not picked up anything of importance this evening . . . '

'I must consult with Foy,' Niska said. 'Come with me to the chapel, Val, and we can meditate together.'

'There's no time for that,' Valraven said. 'Pharry, ride with me to the shore.'

*

The way to the beach involved negotiating steep, treacherous paths down which the horses had to be led. In the moonlight, miles of white sand stretched out towards the distant surf. 'The tide is unusually low tonight,' Pharinet said. She looked up at the sky. 'And the stars are so *stark*.' For a moment she was silent, but Valraven was compelled to pause in the act of swinging into the saddle. She was about to say something more, something important.

Pharinet drew in her breath sharply and glanced down at her brother. An expression of surprised realisation formed on her face. She seemed to shine. 'Ride!' she cried.

Before Valraven could mount his horse, Pharinet kicked her mare into a gallop across the sand.

A rowing boat cleaved down the river of silver light to the shore. Valraven could see it clearly, even though Pharinet's horse threw up a spray of wet sand in front of him. He could see the precise black lines of the oars as they dipped and lifted from the water. The boat reached the shallows and men jumped overboard to haul it the final few yards. They wore strange, multi-layered clothing, adorned with tassels and metal ornaments reflecting the light of the moon. A woman stood erect in the boat, holding onto the hand of a child. Valraven's heart nearly stopped. He drove his horse into the water, through the foam. Voices babbled around him in a tongue he could not understand. All he could see was the woman. She wore heavily embroidered clothes, her hair wrapped up in a turban scarf. Valraven jumped down from the horse and waded the last few feet to the boat. The woman did not move, but she was smiling.

'Val, I got tired of waiting for you,' she said lightly. 'I had to rescue myself.'

He climbed into the boat, took her in his arms. 'Ren,' he said. 'By Foy, it is good to see you.' He released his wife and bent to pick up his daughter, held her close to his body. She was heavier than he remembered, and taller. She smelled of the earth and the sea.

Pharinet had also climbed aboard and hugged Varencienne fiercely for a few moments. Her face was wet with tears of joy. 'How did you know to come here?' she asked. 'How did you get away from Khaster? What happened?'

'Oh, it's a long tale,' Varencienne replied, catching Valraven's eye. 'You'll hear it soon enough. These people are Hamagarid. Prince Kutaka of Nimet has sent men to aid our cause. It is a sizeable company, as you can see. Any use to you, Val?'

Pharinet hugged Varencienne again. 'You are a wonder!' she cried and kissed her sister-in-law's face a dozen times. Varencienne laughed and the two women danced in a tight circle in the rocking boat.

Valraven broke into their merriment with a sharp question. 'Where is he, Ren?'

Varencienne sobered and pulled away from her sister-in-law. 'On one of the ships,' she answered. 'I wanted to see you first.'

Valraven put Ellony down, but she remained close to him, leaning against his legs. 'Is there anything I need to know?'

'Val!' Pharinet snapped. 'Let's get Ren and Ellie back to the castle before you start interrogating.'

'It's all right,' Varencienne said smoothly, briefly touching Pharinet's arm. 'What you fear, Val, is not real.'

'And how do you know what I fear?' he asked.

'It's in your eyes,' she said, 'and in some ways I'm gratified it's one of the first things you asked me.'

Everyone in the castle had gathered on the cliff-top to see what was happening. When Varencienne and Ellony emerged from the path, the Leckerys and Everna surged forward to embrace them. Rav ran to his mother, shrieking madly with elation. Tears and laughter transformed every face. Men cheered and whistled, stamping fiercely against the ground and punching the air with closed fists. Their Sea Wife had returned to them, the priestess of Foy. Hope had come to them with a flaming torch.

Varencienne and Ellony were carried high on shoulders into the castle, as were the Hamagarid sailors, who although willing to share in the hysterical delight of the moment, were rather bewildered by it.

Valraven allowed the people their celebration for a while, but then summoned Varencienne to his side. Her turban had come off and now her hair was a mass of tangles round her face and shoulders. She didn't stop grinning.

'Ren,' Valraven said. 'There is something that cannot wait. Speak to the Hamagarids and send for Khaster. At once.'

Varencienne's expression became more serious. 'Of course, if that is what you want. However, I would have thought we should have had a little time together, all of us, before the fateful meeting.' She glanced at Saska who had Ellony in her arms. 'There might be difficulties.'

'I'm aware of that,' Valraven said, 'but we are at war. People can celebrate once certain issues have been resolved. I am not looking forward to this interview. I want to get it over with as soon as possible. Also, convey a message that I will meet with the Hamagarid commanders first thing in the morning. Let them know we have family business to conduct tonight. We will, of course, send anything to the fleet that they require in the way of supplies.'

Varencienne brushed back her hair, sighed and then called for one of the Hamagarids in his own tongue. Valraven listened as she uttered instructions to him, impressed at how proficient she was in their language.

After this was done, she said, 'And now, because you have hastened events, I must speak to our families in private. There are things that must be said.'

'Naturally,' Valraven said. 'I will ask Goldvane to prepare a room for us.'

The makeshift army set about organising a feast in the great yard of the castle, while those amongst them who were musicians started tuning up their instruments. Clearly a night of great festivity would ensue, which Valraven knew would be good for morale. Leaving the celebration for a while, the Leckerys and the Palindrakes retired to a private room in the main keep. Once the festive mood of the yard was left behind, Valraven was acutely aware of the tension. He noticed that Sinaclara had followed him, accompanied by a subdued Tayven. The sorceress came to his side and insisted in a firm voice that she and Tayven should be present at the meeting.

Varencienne took in the sorceress with one sweeping glance. 'And you are?'

'Sinaclara of Bree, guardian of the Crown of Silence,' Valraven said. 'It is right that she hears what you have to say. She is an intrinsic part of our company.'

'She is not family,' Varencienne said. 'What I have to say is personal and sensitive.' For the first time, she directed her gaze at Tayven, who was hanging back at the threshold of the room. 'Perhaps *you* should hear it, though.' Her voice was not exactly warm.

'If Tayven stays, then so do I,' said Sinaclara.

Varencienne raised her eyebrows. 'Excuse me?'

Sinaclara closed her eyes briefly and grimaced in self-deprecation. 'I apologise. I didn't mean to sound so rude. Please allow me to stay, my lady. It is very important to me.'

Varencienne eyed her for a few moments, then shrugged. 'Very well. I would be grateful if you were a silent observer, however.'

Valraven noticed Pharinet smirking. No doubt his sister was relieved someone had come who might put Sinaclara in her place.

'I will tell you my story,' Varencienne said, 'but please, no matter how what I say affects you, do not interrupt me. Time is short and you can ask questions later.'

Listening to his wife, Valraven was torn between outrage at Khaster's behaviour and wonder at how Varencienne had changed him. He

344

remembered uncomfortably what Pharinet had told him of Varencienne's feelings for Khaster. She had made a quest of bringing him back to the fold, a lost lamb bleating on the hillsides of High Hamagara. It was clear that they were now close, for she spoke of him defensively, as if for her husband's ears alone.

At the end of her story, Varencienne said, 'So here I am, bringing Paraga to our company, blessed by Aranepa. Soon Khaster will be here as well.'

Saska uttered a sound and Varencienne turned to her.

'I will be blunt. None of you present, not even you, Saska, must make this more difficult for him than it already is. There must be no recriminations – Pharinet! – nor hysterical displays of emotion. I ask you all simply to welcome him back to your hearts, for he has suffered and made mistakes, but is now redeemed.'

'Val?' Pharinet said in a tight voice.

He shrugged and displayed his palms. 'I am the Man of Silence, remember. Varencienne is obviously the one for words in this situation.'

'Are you going to welcome him back to your heart?' Pharinet said.

'Yes,' Valraven replied, knowing he sounded excruciatingly insincere. 'I will speak to him, Pharry.'

'I am still his wife,' she said.

'Yes, you are!' Saska exclaimed angrily.

Pharinet ignored her. 'What does this mean for me, Val?'

'That is something you will have to discuss with him,' Valraven said.

'There is no time for any of you to lick your wounds and complain,' Varencienne said. 'We have to concentrate on what is important now, namely our victory. Put your feelings aside and know only that Khaster has come to you to fulfil his ordained role. That should be enough. Once Valraven is king, you can worry about petty details.'

'Ren,' Pharinet said, shaking her head slowly, 'don't speak to me like that.'

'I have to,' Varencienne said. 'Khaster is the least of your worries, Pharry, as you are the least of his.' She glanced coldly at Tayven, who was standing with folded arms, leaning against the door with an inscrutable expression on his face.

'Lady Palindrake is right,' Sinaclara said in a ringing voice. 'She is the Sea Wife. Listen to her.'

Varencienne gave her a sharp glance, clearly surprised by the unexpected support. 'Thank you, Lady of Bree. I am glad that someone here has some sense.'

'I also have sense,' said Niska. 'I will behave in whatever way you see fit, say what you tell me to.'

'And I,' said Saska with dignity. 'He is my son, whom I love greatly, whatever he's done. I would be happy to have him home, even if I had to remain silent for eternity.'

The idea of this unlikely possibility conjured a ripple of laughter in the room.

'You win,' Pharinet said. 'I'll pretend nothing ever happened between us. That should be the easiest way.'

'Good,' said Varencienne. She clasped her hands together, stretched the fingers. 'Now, let us go back to our people and join in their celebrations. If Val and Khas survive their reunion, we'll see them later!'

CHAPTER THIRTY-TWO

Opened Wounds

Sitting in the stuffy cabin, Shan felt as if he was the sole companion of a condemned man who was waiting for the summons to the scaffold. Khaster sat at a table staring at his hands, which were clasped before him. Shan had said everything he could think of that might be of comfort, but all of it was trite. The only sounds were the creak of timber and the muffled babble of Hamagarid voices outside.

Khaster heaved a sigh. 'Magic and talk of destiny amounts to nothing in the face of raw human relationships,' he said.

'Ren will smooth the way,' Shan said. 'Don't worry. She's good at influencing people. We both know that.'

Khaster smiled weakly. 'There is so much history, Shan. You have no idea of it.'

'I do. You told me about it, remember?'

Khaster shrugged. 'They were just words. Valraven was my dearest friend, a brother to me, yet we turned upon each other like rival wolves. We could blame Bayard, or the empire itself, but essentially it was down to us. We both gave up on one another, when we should have remained staunch. It will not be easy simply to erase this history.' He looked Shan directly in the eye. 'I appreciate your support. This must be hard for you too.'

Shan looked away. He knew immediately to what Khaster referred. 'It is not your fault what Varencienne feels. I know you did not encourage it.'

'Still, many men could not be so tolerant.'

Shan ducked his head. 'We must forget it. Varencienne was never destined to be mine. She is Valraven's. In Hamagara, we all lived a fantasy – she dreaming of you, while dallying with me. It all came to nothing, and now we must go back to reality.'

347

'That last night in the forest . . . '

'There is no need for explanations. Ren told me nothing happened between you and I believe her.'

Khaster frowned a little, but then the fateful knock came upon the door and the captain was there, telling them the order had come to go ashore.

The Hamagarid company was met at the cliff-top by a group of Valraven's personal guards, who escorted them to a large empty chamber in the main keep. On the way across the castle yard, Shan was conscious of the way voices fell silent and musicians lowered their instruments. People gawped at Khaster, while a few made covert sacred signs as if to ward off evil. No one stepped forward in greeting.

Khaster stared straight ahead, his expression stony.

Then the doors were before them, ancient, iron-studded, bearing the scars of old conflicts. For a moment, Shan was acutely aware of the castle's tragic past. This had once been a place of slaughter, and might become so again.

A man Shan recognised as the old soldier Khaster had spared during the kidnap stood with folded arms at the threshold. He did not look at all welcoming, as if he wanted to prevent this meeting, but was frustrated by his inability to do so. Even if Valraven was prepared to forgive the past, this man must have felt personally responsible for losing the lady of his household to brigands. He would have felt shame for it, even though he had fought well.

Khaster wisely said nothing and endured the hard stare as the man opened the door.

Valraven Palindrake was alone.

Shan found it difficult to believe he was facing the man he'd heard so much about. The Dragon Lord didn't look at all like he'd expected, lacking the imagined hatchet face and demonic expression. He was slimmer than Shan's image of him and perhaps not as tall. His abundant black hair was loose around his shoulders, giving him a more effeminate air than Shan had anticipated. Was this the man who had killed thousands and given the orders to kill thousands more? Shan remembered his old friend Nip's words about how the emperor Leonid probably had no idea what atrocities his armies had committed far afield in his name. Was Valraven Palindrake therefore equally as likely to be ignorant of many things? It was possible, but seemed too convenient an excuse.

Palindrake inclined his head and beckoned. Shan came forward to stand beside Khaster, for no reason other than he wanted to see Khaster's face, his reaction. At the moment, there was none.

'You must be Shan,' Valraven said. 'Is that just "Shan", or are you known by any other title?'

'Just Shan. In my own village I would have been known as Son of Hod.'

Valraven nodded thoughtfully.

Shan realised he must feel as awkward about this meeting as Khaster did.

'I have heard good things of you, Shan,' Valraven said. He would not even look at Khaster.

Shan bowed. 'Thank you, my lord.'

Now he did turn to Khaster, with an attempt at inner steel, which was physically visible in his posture.

Before he could say anything, Khaster spoke first. 'There is almost too much to say between us, Val. A thousand apologies will not change the past on either side.'

Those words appeared to give the Dragon Lord some relief. Perhaps he had dreaded being the one to break the long silence between them. 'Khas, there is only one thing of importance to say. We must live in the moment, because the lives of our families and the people of Caradore depend upon us. We must put aside the demons of the past.' He smiled. 'I am glad you came. We will have our noble company of men, and the women of strength to sustain and support us. There is no other issue. Not at this time.' He stepped forward with open arms. 'Welcome home, my brother.'

Khaster returned the embrace and for some moments they both stood silent and still.

They released each other at exactly the same moment. Khaster rubbed his hands over his face. 'You have made this too easy for me.'

'What did you expect? Having to offer a string of justifications? My black condemnation of both you and myself?' Valraven grimaced. 'No. We have both changed too much, Khas. I trust that we are free of our respective dark legacies. I have learned that some solutions are remarkably simple and require only a choice to be made – the choice between life and death, freedom and fear.'

'And light and darkness?' Shan couldn't help saying.

Valraven considered him for a moment. 'They are the same thing,' he said. 'I think you already know that.'

Shan felt himself redden, as if he were a young boy again.

'Shan knows as much as you or I,' Khaster said. 'He has gone into the darkness and beyond. He is my son.'

'Then he should take your name,' Valraven said, 'and be knighted as a lord of Norgance.'

Khaster bowed his head slightly. 'It would give me great pleasure to do that. Would you accept it, Shan?'

Shan bowed in return. 'With unreserved pleasure.'

Valraven clapped a hand against Shan's shoulders. 'Come, we have much to discuss, but there is one matter I'm sure Khaster wants to get out of the way before anything else. The womenfolk.'

Khaster expressed a groan. 'My mother . . . '

'Varencienne has lectured them all to behave. I'm sure they fear her wrath enough to comply.'

At the threshold, before the door was opened, Khaster hesitated. 'Val, you spoke of a noble company. Who else is here to be part of it?'

Valraven drew in his breath, nodding slowly. 'Tayven is here,' he said. Khaster closed his eyes briefly. 'There is a wound to be healed.'

'Then see to it. Tayven arrived here with Sinaclara of Bree.'

Khaster's shoulders slumped a little. 'That woman . . . ' he said darkly.

Valraven grinned. 'She is a handful, I admit, but important to our cause, nonetheless. Varencienne is in control and will curb any tendency of the Lady of Bree to berate you. You should trust Ren, but I gather you already do so.'

Khaster glanced at Valraven sharply. 'I look upon her as my sister.'

'Just so,' Valraven said.

The women were waiting in a tense silent group in another room. To Shan, they looked like ghosts, because their fine clothes and shining hair seemed out of place against the bare, soot-stained walls. Phantoms from an earlier age. Varencienne was standing with a woman who could only be Valraven's twin, the lady Pharinet, Khaster's wife. Pharinet was dressed in man's hunting garb, without doubt a dashing and bewitching creature. The three tawny-haired ladies who sat together – two younger round an older woman – would be Khaster's sisters and mother. Shan recognised Varencienne's lady-in-waiting from the scene of the kidnap, sitting next to a severe-faced mature woman, no doubt Valraven's older sister. Sinaclara stood slightly apart from the group, with Tayven beside her. She was holding onto his arm as if to prevent him bolting from the room.

Valraven introduced Shan formally to the group and the women bowed their heads stiffly to him. They were like a wall of stone, absorbing everything, yet at the same time impenetrable.

Varencienne stepped away from Pharinet and went to Khaster's side. 'Will you not greet the prodigal?' she said in a light voice, beneath which was a tone of command.

For a moment, no one moved, then the Leckery matriarch rose majestically to her feet. 'Come here,' she said.

Khaster went willingly to her embrace. 'I ask for your forgiveness,' he said.

Saska's face was already wet with tears which rolled uncontrollably down her cheeks, but her voice was firm. 'We want none of that,' she said. 'The past is gone. We must look to the future.' She glanced at her daughters. 'We have been told, in no uncertain terms, that this is what we must do.'

Khaster's sisters rose to their feet and silently joined their mother and brother in a tight embrace. Pharinet leaned against the blackened mantelpiece, her foot kicking at dead leaves in the hearth.

Khaster broke away from his relatives and turned to face her. 'Pharinet, you have nothing to fear. I have not returned to place a claim upon you.'

Pharinet stared at him. Shan could see her thoughts in her eyes, how she was considering that Varencienne stood by Valraven as his wife, even though there was no romantic love between them. She was trying to make herself do the same with Khaster, but pride was strong in her. It wasn't easy for her to speak consoling words. Eventually she walked across the room and slapped Khaster's arm, as a man might in greeting. 'No one has any claims on me,' she said lightly. 'Therefore I do not fear it. I'm glad you're here, Khas. We all need to be together at this time, for Val and for ourselves.' It was, Shan thought, the best Khaster would get from her.

Khaster then went to the Lady Everna and took her hands. Shan could not hear what he said to her because everyone in the room had begun to speak at once. He turned to find Sinaclara at his side, who squeezed his arm. 'How are you, Shan?'

'Fine.' He bent to kiss her cheek. 'I am grateful not to be in Khaster's place.'

Sinaclara smiled. 'It will be difficult to get used to that name. To me he is Taropat.'

'Where is the Crown, Clara?' Shan asked.

Sinaclara grimaced. 'Tay and I were forced to leave it in Magrast.'

'In the hands of the Malagashes?' Shan could not keep the censure from his voice.

'Yes. It's a long story, which I can tell you later. Still, I'm content that all progresses as it should.' She glanced back at Tayven, who still lurked in the shadows. 'There are just a few wrinkles to iron out.'

To Tayven, the whole experience was excruciating. He felt embarrassed to be there, torn between the desire to see Khaster and the urge to flee. Khaster had not looked at him once. It was all very well to put bindings over deep old wounds and pretend that all was healed, but Tayven knew better. He could not bear the mealy-mouthed pronouncements that the future was the only thing of importance. Emotions seethed beneath the surface like pus. The insincerity made Tayven nauseous. He knew why Varencienne Palindrake had told them to behave in this way. It was the only manner in which this injured company could function, and for victory it needed to function well. He did not envy her her role.

It became clear to Tayven that Khaster was not going to approach him and to remain in that room seemed pointless. When Sinaclara went to talk to Shan, Tayven slipped away, out into the dark corridors of the castle, where faint echoing sounds of merriment could be heard from the main yard. Tayven shuddered. What if the Magravandian army fell upon them now? They were so vulnerable. But Valraven had stationed a string of sentries on beacon hills from here to New Caradore. When Jomas caught sight of the imperial army, he'd light the first fire and the message would spread north quickly, literally like wild-fire. Still Tayven felt unsafe. He knew the family tensions had to be addressed before anyone could really focus upon the important business, but there was so much to organise, not least how they would combat magically the elemental avatar that Bayard had become. The dragon daughters had been strangely absent since Tayven and Rav had come to the old domain. He could not summon them for information.

Tayven wandered deep into the old keep. Gaping windows and holes in the ceilings created channels for moonlight to flood the desolate rooms with a spectral glow. Occasionally bats surprised by his entrance would fly up in a squeaking leathery mass or pale owls would hiss at him from high rafters. He was sure he could feel the thunder of the sea beneath his feet, pounding into sunken caves far below. 'Foy, you had better be with us,' Tayven muttered beneath his breath.

He climbed out of a crumbling window casement and then followed a flight of steps up to the battlements. Here wind gusted between the sentries, who called out greetings to Tayven as he passed amongst them. Braziers were lit at regular intervals where the men warmed their hands. Tayven did not want company. He climbed to the highest tower and gazed out to sea where the Hamagarid fleet floated at anchor. His body filled with a sense of imminence. He wondered whether life had come into such sharp focus within him because it would soon be ended.

His spine prickled. Someone was coming, though he could hear no footsteps. His hands gripped the stone battlements. 'Foy, give me strength for this. Give me dignity,' he murmured.

Khaster came silently, like an assassin. Tayven's skin was aware of his presence. He could hear breathing, for the climb to the tower was long.

'Where are you, Tayven?' Khaster said. 'Recolletine, Magrast or Cos?'

Tayven picked lichen from the wall. 'I am in the Forest of Bree,' he said. 'I have come to meet a man I once knew.' He turned. 'Where are you?'

'Standing at the edge of the forest looking at a ghost.'

'If there was a ghost, it was you,' Tayven said. 'I came to you in flesh and blood, only you weren't in your body. Someone else was.'

Khaster sighed. 'Words, words. There are too many of them. They have cloyed in my mouth.'

'I don't want it to be like that with us,' Tayven said. 'That's why I left the room down there.'

'You did that before, remember? When Almorante made you sing for me? You fled.'

'And you came after me, as you have again.'

'Then you took me to your sanctuary, showed me the city from the roof of the palace.'

'This is a high place too, but it's not mine.'

'Perhaps the best you could find under the circumstances.'

'I'm not that boy,' Tayven said bitterly.

'I know,' Khaster said, 'and I'm not that ridiculous youth.'

'Then why are we here together at all?'

Khaster scratched at his hair, inhaled deeply through his nose. 'We're still playing, Tayven. Stop it. Are you with me or not?'

Tayven stared at him for a moment. 'With,' he said at last.

'Good,' Khaster said. 'Shall we return to the festivities?'

'If you like.' Tayven crossed the small space between them. 'After this.'

The kiss was a test. He expected Khaster to pull away from him, utter some feeble excuse. Despite Khaster's blunt words, Tayven expected to play a long, careful game back into this man's heart. Therefore Khaster's enthusiastic response surprised him. It had never been a part of him before.

Tayven broke away first and spoke hurriedly, pressing his hands into Khaster's shoulders. 'Of all of them, we must be the least confused,' he said. 'We and Shan. Valraven needs us. This army he has is a shambles. We do not even know how best to use the elemental powers we have on our side. We are still blind from Pancanara.'

Khaster put his hands on Tayven's face. 'Hush,' he said, 'tomorrow, we begin our work. We will do whatever must be done. For this one night, however, no problems or conflicts exist. We can allow ourselves that.'

'Will we succeed, Khas?' Tayven asked in a hard voice. 'Give me the truth. What are our chances?'

Khaster leaned his forehead against Tayven's own. 'I don't know,' he replied. 'If we follow our will, we will be victorious, but there is a worm in the heart that tells us our will is weak and its desires an illusion. That is our true battle – against ourselves.'

CHAPTER THIRTY-THREE

Hunting the Dragon

Tatrini drew her horse to a halt in the yard of Caradore Castle. Men had swarmed over the walls and lifted the portcullis; there'd been no one to stop them. The Queen Mother had not found the journey north that hard. She had brought her carriage with her, but rode a horse alongside her sons as often as she felt able. She wore half armour, dark skirts and knee-length black boots. Her cloak covered the rump of her mount, which she rode astride like a man.

In her carriage, wrapped in its indigo silk and hidden within a locked wooden box bound with iron, the Crown of Silence lay waiting for what would come. Tatrini had not told Bayard or Almorante she'd brought it with her, and was unsure herself why she had felt it necessary. But the thought of leaving the Crown in Magrast had irked her. She needed it near to her. At night it appeared in her dreams, on the head of an angel or hanging in the sky like a star. It spoke to her, but she could not understand the words. Yet.

Now they had reached Caradore Castle and its emptiness had been apparent from the moment Tatrini first caught sight of its turrets. Almorante strode across the courtyard towards her, his face strained.

Tatrini dismounted. 'They have already gone,' she said, 'and we can guess where. North, to Old Caradore.'

Almorante nodded grimly and looked around himself, hands on hips. 'Someone lit a beacon on the high tower. There's another fire on a hill some miles to the north.' He had gone directly to the tower as soon as he'd seen the smoke, but it was too late.

Bayard had gone into the main keep with his personal guard, but Tatrini knew he wouldn't find anything. Valraven was too clever for that. 'The old domain is a ruin. We can only presume he's whipped up the Caradorean gentry into a patriotic frenzy.'

'There can't be that many of them,' Almorante said. 'The best of their men are on duty with our army.'

'By that, you mean incarcerated in Cawmonel or the Skiterings,' Tatrini said dryly.

Almorante gave her a hard glance. 'I would think less of them if they didn't want to fly home to defend their families. It is best to be prepared.'

'As Valraven no doubt is,' Tatrini said. 'Still, I don't think he'll be able to stand up to us. We have Bayard.'

Almorante smiled cynically. 'Our best asset, of course.'

'You know so little,' Tatrini said. 'Bayard will surprise you.'

'I can't imagine that,' Almorante said. He turned away from her. 'We should rest here for the night and head north in the morning. There may be ambushes ahead. I will address the men.'

Left alone, Tatrini went into the Palindrake house. The draughty entrance hall felt as if it hadn't been moved by human warmth for centuries. She remembered the last time she had come here. If it wasn't for her, Valraven wouldn't be trying to win back his country now. He would still be asleep.

Tatrini sniffed with contempt and peeled off her riding gloves. She still didn't know how this would end, or who would sit upon the throne of Magravandias. All she did know was that she must emerge with the spoils.

Bayard appeared from a corridor and started slightly when he saw his mother standing motionless in the centre of the hall. 'By Madragore, you look like a ghost!' he snapped. 'This place is haunted.'

'For you, no doubt,' Tatrini said. 'We have both experienced life-defining events here.'

Bayard came closer. 'I can feel it moving within me, Mother.'

'The past?'

He laughed coldly. 'Oh no. The future. The power of the elements. On the ride here it has become increasingly stronger.' He held out his right hand before him and flexed the fingers. 'I have experimented as you suggested. If I wanted to I could thrust my hand into solid rock, hold my head under water without drowning and bathe my skin in flame without burning.'

'You have done well, my son,' Tatrini said.

Bayard regarded her coldly. 'I am not just your son any more, but a living God. Isn't that what you wanted?' He folded his hand into a fist before her face. 'I will crush the soul from Valraven Palindrake.'

Tatrini smirked, and did not flinch away from Bayard's aggressive gesture. 'I have complete confidence in your zeal,' she said amiably, 'but gods need belief to exist. That is what you must inspire in every Magravandian heart.'

'The sword will inspire belief in me,' Bayard said. 'I have always been a warrior, but now I am more than that. Fear conceals itself inside belief, and that's all the magic a blade needs.'

The next morning, the army rode north. The mood of the men was difficult to interpret. Tatrini knew there was a danger they'd find it hard to raise arms against the man they admired so greatly, but both Almorante and Bayard had given inspiring speeches the night before about how they had been betrayed and that Valraven cared nothing for them. Even to Tatrini, this sounded unconvincing. The men would think Palindrake was being forced into a corner and could take no other action. It was the truth, of course. Bayard must destroy Valraven quickly. Such an act would sway the loyalties of the superstitious soldiers. These were men whose training had included the magic of the fire-drakes. It was Efrit they invoked before battle, not Madragore. If Bayard could only show them how Efrit was now within him, the men would turn to him. It was a pity he'd spent so little time earning their respect and devotion. Still, that was too late to change now. He'd simply have to make up for lost time.

And what of the new emperor Almorante who, at the very least, was a dark and reluctant general? Tatrini could tell that his mind was turning with a thousand strategies. He did not want to be here and although he had said little, she guessed he disagreed with the campaign. Something had changed him, but she didn't know what. He rode in silence amongst his personal guard at the head of the army, his hair dark down his back, his tall black horse slicing through the morning mist. He was a beautiful man, Tatrini thought, an enigmatic stranger. For a brief moment, she imagined how it might be if Almorante was allowed to be emperor. It was as if the future breathed on her neck. In another world, they would not be marching on Old Caradore now. In that world, Palindrake would be at Almorante's side.

But we are not in that world, Tatrini told herself. We are in this one and I have made it to my liking.

General Leatherer rode just behind the emperor. Tatrini knew he did not relish the task ahead either, but Leatherer was a career military man who had been close to Leonid. It was in his nature to follow orders, however much his heart might flex in discomfort within him.

Caradore drenched them all in a scent of pine. Crows circled round them, calling hoarsely for meat. Anyone watching from shuttered windows or forest hides would see the tall tasselled banners of Madragore heading north, the horses of Magrast claiming the old Lord's Road for its emperor.

As they rode, they saw the smoking remains of fires on every hill. The country had mobilised to alert Valraven of the encroaching threat. That was something his ancestor, Valraven the First, had lacked. That was the difference this time.

In the old domain, the walls had been repaired as well as possible, given the lack of time and resources available. The only real problem had been the shattered main entrance, where the walls had originally been breached. A large section had been destroyed along with the gate and its arch. The Hamagarids showed the Caradoreans how to construct barriers quickly from carefully woven withies. The walls looked flimsy, but they were very strong. They bristled with hidden spikes that any pressure would coax forth at speed. While this was in hand, the Caradoreans dug out the old moat and filled it with more spike traps.

The main entrance was to the north, on the opposite side to the approachway. The narrow causeway that led across the gorge would expose any attacking army, but the Magravandians would no doubt erect their siege engines on the forest side, beyond the range of the Caradorean archers on the battlements, and try to starve their enemy out while simultaneously pounding the walls. Valraven knew that no military commander worth his wage would try to assault Old Caradore without first trying a political solution to the situation. The Dragon Lord would be asked to surrender. When he refused, the Magravandians might well decide just to sit it out. Valraven knew that was what he would do in this situation. A well-constructed fortress could enable a small handful of men to hold off a horde in combat.

Valraven now had a large company to think about. They'd stockpiled supplies and had wells of fresh water within the castle, but food would not last indefinitely, and neither would the walls against Magravandian cannon, should they elect to employ them. The Hamagarids had brought similar weapons with them, but they were not as powerful as those forged in Magrast. As a possible last resort, Valraven had the causeway bridge booby-trapped so that it could be destroyed from the castle. This, however, while keeping the enemy on their side of the gorge, would cut off the Caradoreans as well. Also, to the west, men could climb slowly through the crags to reach the castle. Valraven knew how big and powerful the Magravandian army was. The best he could hope for was that whoever was in charge would believe Old Caradore would be easy to take and therefore wouldn't bring a vast number of troops along. If Bayard led the army, they'd be in for a tough fight. Valraven had fought beside the prince on numerous campaigns and couldn't fault his strategy, his courage or his skill as a warrior. Bayard was not the kind of general who skulked behind his men. He liked to get blood on his hands. If he had been fired up by all the rituals his mother had been performing, he'd be almost reckless in his attack. But within recklessness would lie that cold steel mind and the old issues it sought to avenge.

Within days of the Hamagarids' arrival, the castle had come to resemble a functional fortress once more. Valraven was pleased these practical, cheerful men had come to join him. Without them, he and his supporters would have had very little chance of victory. Once the army had disembarked, the Hamagarid fleet had sailed round the coast to conceal the boats in the honeycomb of coves along the shore. It would be best to obscure their presence from the Magravandians.

Niska and Sinaclara tried to speak to Valraven constantly about magical plans for the forthcoming conflict, but he was too preoccupied with earthly preparations and didn't want to hear it. 'You plan it. Get Tayven and Khaster to help you,' he'd say.

Sinaclara was the most offended by his attitude. 'Don't you know what you are, great lord? Will you not take on your ordained role?'

'I'm doing it,' he said. 'All the rituals in the world won't help if Magravands are pouring in through the walls or watching us starve.'

'And while they are, who do you think will be working in the background, investing all of their life-energy into raising true power?'

In the end, Valraven agreed that as soon as the beacon fires were lit, he would go with his Brotherhood and the Sisterhood of the Dragon to the Chapel of Foy, where Sinaclara would conduct a rite. Until then, they weren't to bother him about it.

Tayven had explained that they had the power of Foy and Paraga with them, exemplified not just by Rav and Tayven, but Varencienne, Valraven himself, and the Caradorean and Hamagarid peoples. With obvious difficulty, Tayven had related how the dragon daughters had inspired him to pass the power of the elements to Bayard. Valraven, who despite everything still had more trust in a sword than a nebulous entity, was not as angry about this as Tayven clearly expected.

'I am loath to trust anything that Misk, Jia and Thrope do or recommend,' Valraven said. 'They are minor spirits, mischievous. I cannot imagine Bayard being a magical threat. Remember, I've seen him in action with the dragon daughters before. He lacks the discipline for true concentration of the will. There is plenty more to fear about him than that, believe me!'

Tayven said nothing, but his expression informed Valraven he thought he was wrong.

Valraven had not been pleased to learn that his son had been given magical training by Tatrini. He considered Rav too young for such things. Varencienne was equally annoyed by it. Still, Ellie had picked up quite a few strange ways herself in Hamagara. It was odd to watch the twins together now. They were clearly confused about the changes in each other and were trying to rebuild their relationship as siblings. But old behaviours had gone and this sometimes led to arguments.

One evening, as Valraven talked with the Hamagarid generals and his own, including Shan, a frantic call came from the yard. Valraven went out at once and climbed to the southern battlements, followed by his closest aides. Just to the west, where stark primordial mountains were black against the setting sun, the sparks of a dozen fires could be seen on the rocky slopes. Beacon fires.

'They come,' said Shan, his voice tight.

'They have reached New Caradore,' Valraven replied. 'I doubt they will travel north tonight. Our men must rest now. No alcohol. See to it. And double the sentry watch as a precaution.'

Shan bowed his head, muttering, 'There will be a few who'll sleep this night.'

Valraven headed back to the yard where the army had gathered, anxiously awaiting his word. Standing on the steps, he raised his arms. 'Hear me, people of Caradore and Hamagara. The beacon fires are lit and soon our enemy will be upon us. Prepare yourselves and pray to your gods. I shall go now with the priestesses and invoke the power of Foy and Paraga, who will stand beside us in the coming conflict. We must be staunch, my people, and know that we are reliving an ancient time. We are about to change history. We have the power! We have the wisdom of silence, but also the thrashing power of the storm and the inexorable might of the waves! We are the ones who will quench the fire of Madragore!' At once, the entire army began to cheer and stamp.

Valraven turned to Shan, who was just behind him. 'Come with me. You must be part of this.'

As Valraven passed amongst the men, many reached out to touch him. He clasped many rough hands, faces a blur before him. Now that the hour was nearly upon him, he had gone automatically into combat disposition; the time for doubts was past. He had become a focused beam of intent, thinking neither of victory nor defeat, only the conflict. His words of inspiration had not come from beliefs of his own, but had been designed simply to uplift and encourage his troops. The original battle of Old Caradore had been fought with the hands of men. This would be no different. He was sure even Ilcretia had known that. The training she had imparted had given him self-control. He could rely upon himself and it was folly to hope that some great magical force would intervene to save them. Still, the ritual had its place if it gave his people courage. He could see the importance of showing them he was a part of it.

Sinaclara and the Sisterhood were waiting for him in the main hall of the keep, along with Khaster and Tayven.

'It is time for you to do your part,' Valraven said to them. 'Lead on.'

Ellony and Rav began to follow the adults, which prompted Valraven to pause. 'No,' he said to them. 'You must remain here.'

Ellony stepped up to her father. 'It is our birthright to be present.'

Valraven stared down into her determined face. Rav came to stand beside her, his expression equally fierce. 'We are coming too, Papa. Isn't it what I've been trained for?' For the moment, the twins had closed ranks.

Valraven glanced at Varencienne, who gestured to indicate the choice was his. She was smiling,

Valraven regarded his children sternly. 'Very well, you may come with us. But play your parts well. No childish larks or questions. Understand?'

Ellony narrowed her eyes at him and took her brother's hand. 'I am your priestess too, Father,' she said.

The company went to the Chapel of Foy, which the women had restored. The floor had been swept and scrubbed clean and all the shattered seats had been removed and burned. What was left of an old stained-glass window representing Foy had been washed, and candles flickered on the polished marble altar, where shells, coral and stones from the beach had been placed in a spiral pattern and partly concealed the cracks in the stone.

Standing amongst the women, Valraven felt as if he were surrounded by strangers. He did not know them like this, so stern and purposeful. Even Saska was different.

Niska began the ceremony by arranging everyone in a circle. Valraven stood opposite the altar with Tayven and Khaster on his left side, Shan on his right.

Once they were composed, Niska uttered some opening invocations and prayers to Foy and Paraga. Then Sinaclara walked to the centre of their circle.

'I call upon great Foy, the Queen of the Deep, to come unto the Dragon Heir, Valraven Palindrake,' she cried in a ringing voice. 'I call upon mighty Paraga, King of the Mountains, to be present at this rite. Bring forth your sister, Hespereth, and your brother, Efrit.'

Valraven's mind wandered as Sinaclara attempted to persuade the dragons to make their presence felt. He did not doubt the power of command in her voice, but couldn't help thinking that somewhere Tatrini might very well be performing a similar ritual. He had no doubt that Paraga and Foy, if they chose to take part at all, would be firmly in the Caradorean camp, but he did not think the same of the fire and earth dragons. Through men, a conflict of the elements would take place.

In his mind, he heard the distant sound of laughter. 'You think yourself greater than I?' a female voice murmured next to his ear. Valraven glanced to the side, but much as he expected, there was no one there. Had Tatrini reached him somehow, seeking to claw at his confidence?

'No, it is I, Foy,' murmured the voice. It came over a vast distance, muted by the muffled roar of waves.

I do not believe myself greater than you, Valraven responded silently, but where are you now? Will you manifest with your daughters before the Magravandians and smite them with pounding waves? Will you turn my small army into a horde of thousands?

No, Foy replied. It will not be necessary.

Why not? Valraven demanded. If you are near, great Foy, speak to me. Give me the advantage through knowledge.

In the end, Dragon Heir, it will be between you and the man of fire. In your heart you know this . . .

'Valraven?'

He realised Sinaclara had addressed him. 'My lady?'

'Where were you, Lord Palindrake?' Sinaclara asked. There was a faint smile on her face. 'Not with us, that is sure.'

'Foy spoke to me,' Valraven said.

'What did she say?' Varencienne demanded.

'Little of help,' Valraven said, 'but at least she is near.'

'After all you've been through,' said Sinaclara, 'you should have more faith.'

'I have been shown that there is more to life than this world,' Valraven said, 'but I eat, sleep and fight in this one. We are men and women, Clara, not spirits or gods. If we were meant to be otherwise, we'd not have flesh and blood. The otherworld might guard our dreams, but it is up to our hands and hearts to realise them.'

Varencienne went to him and took his hand. 'He is right,' she said. 'If I feel Paraga within me, it is as hope and courage. I can't conjure winds to blow the enemy away.'

'What do you think, Khaster?' Sinaclara asked.

'I think Valraven is honest,' he replied. 'We might need more resources to achieve victory than we have at our disposal, but it would be folly to rely upon supernatural aid alone. We should trust in our magic, but act with our minds, hearts and bodies. My recommendation is that we place our faith in the skill and abilities of the empire's most respected battle commander.'

Valraven was grateful for the down-to-earth support. He could tell that the company was swayed by their words; there was little point in remaining in the chapel. Sinaclara was not wholly pleased, but was resigned to the fact that there would be no more rituals that evening.

Varencienne indicated that Valraven should linger behind as the group began to disperse into the keep.

'You are my strength,' he said to her. 'There isn't one moment I don't give thanks for your return.'

Varencienne smiled a little tightly.

'What is it?' Valraven asked, reaching out to touch her face.

'We are rarely together as man and wife,' Varencienne replied, 'but tonight I wish it to be so. I would like us to find a private room.'

Valraven studied her for a moment. He had become used to looking upon Varencienne as a sister and her words surprised him. They had come to an understanding long ago, and he'd believed she had no desire for him. Perhaps this meant she feared death was imminent and wanted to experience the love of a man one last time.

'Is it so difficult for you?' Varencienne asked sharply when he did not answer.

'No,' he said. 'I was considering your reasons.'

She paused, then said, 'If we survive this conflict, there must be another child of Caradore. I feel this strongly.'

Valraven could not suppress a laugh. 'The last time you demanded my services was to create Rav and Elly. You make me feel like a prize stallion.'

'You are that,' Varencienne said. 'And I am a mare. Will you do it?'

'It is a somewhat arid romance, but if you so wish.'

She hugged him briefly. 'I do.'

CHAPTER THIRTY-FOUR

The Heir and the Dragon Daughters

In the morning, a stiff breeze blew in off the sea towards the south. As the morning lengthened, so the wind increased in strength. It would lend wings to the bolts of the Hamagarid crossbows and the arrows of the Caradorean archers. Valraven stalked the battlements, too restless to stand still.

By noon, scouts had returned to the castle, reporting on the advance of the Magravandian army. It was bigger than Valraven had hoped for, but not as big as it could have been. The royal standards of both Almorante and Bayard had been identified. It appeared the brothers had set aside their differences to unite against their common enemy.

By mid-afternoon, activity could be seen in forest on the other side of the causeway. Clouds had massed in the sky making visibility difficult, but it was clear the Magravandians weren't going to risk coming within range of any missiles from the castle.

Tatrini's personal guard had erected a spacious tent for her some yards behind the quarters of the army. Almorante had made sure that twelve of his best men were constantly vigilant. Echoes of the past resonated within Tatrini's heart. She remembered coming to this wild place with Valraven and Varencienne, and how they had conjured Foy upon the shore, far below the castle. In those days, anything had been possible. It was as if they'd stood upon the brink of a vast and devastating change, but it had taken years to manifest. All of them had returned to their habitual lives, even if the events of that time had transformed them inside. It was a shame that the Dragon Lord would have to be sacrificed. In the past, Tatrini had always envisaged the noble house of Palindrake

364

would be her ally. Still, she would have to make do with what she had and trust that Rav could be saved.

For a moment she thought of Varencienne and an unfamiliar pang clenched her heart. My daughter, she thought. Where is she? Will she ever forgive me for this?

Almorante and Bayard convened with General Leatherer and his immediate staff in the grand pavilion that had been erected for their use. Tatrini joined them, but kept a low profile, more interested in hearing the thoughts behind men's words than joining the discussion of siege strategy and assault.

There was a strange, stilted undercurrent to the meeting, which Tatrini found difficult to interpret. She suspected it generated from Almorante. General Leatherer had already made it clear Valraven Palindrake should be given the opportunity to surrender.

'He won't,' Almorante said. 'He knows what would happen to him.'

'Then perhaps the deal should be made more attractive,' Leatherer said carefully.

'The only deal will incorporate Palindrake dead or in chains,' Almorante said. 'Preferably the former. He will always have secret supporters.'

'We can wait,' Bayard said. 'Eventually, once Palindrake's men have been demoralised by the sight of our army beyond their walls and their supplies begin to dwindle, we can smoke them out. Fight with our chosen element: fire!'

Tatrini knew that the only possible end to this conflict must be a confrontation between Bayard and Palindrake. She did not relish the thought of months of inactivity, waiting for the Caradoreans to crumble. In her opinion, the army should start bombarding the walls at once, but she knew that good generals only resorted to combat when all other means of conquest had been explored and exhausted. They took few risks with their men. Someone like Leatherer would have little sympathy with the idea that Bayard was a magical weapon in himself and that the power of the fire-drakes could be thrown against Caradore through his will.

General Leatherer stroked his beard, staring at the table before him where an ancient plan of Caradore Castle was laid out. Tatrini sensed a great tension within him. She supposed he longed to say that, even now, he did not feel Palindrake was a traitor and that some kind of discussion should take place. He was probably right, but that circumstance would not expedite Tatrini's plans. She longed to say certain things herself, but realised this wouldn't help her cause either. The air fairly simmered with repressed words in the confined space of the pavilion.

Almorante obviously felt the undercurrents as well. 'You have something to say, Leatherer,' he said. 'What is it?'

Leatherer shook his head slowly. 'You have heard what I wish to say.'

Next to the pavilion wall, one of his aides shifted restlessly. Leatherer glanced up and caught the man's eye. Tatrini witnessed an almost imperceptible nod of the general's head.

Neither Almorante nor Bayard appeared to notice. 'We should begin bombardment,' Bayard said. 'Old Caradore is a husk. She can withstand little punishment.'

The atmosphere went utterly still. Tatrini could sense tension pouring from Leatherer's body. His fists were flexing by his sides. He was fighting himself. Tatrini became uncomfortably aware of the ring of men around them. She and her sons were not amongst friends. Resentment and fear turned the air sour. Her body went cold, as if she'd been drenched in icy water. Instinctively, she moved very slowly nearer to the entrance.

Almorante looked straight at her, his eyes wide. It was as if the sight of her clandestine retreat gave him a presentiment. Her hand was upon the drapes that hid them from the world outside. She could hear men's voices out there, the sound of heavy items being moved, the steady tock of a hammer against wood as more tents were erected. A different world existed within the pavilion. She had to get out.

The silvery grate of steel blades being withdrawn from scabbards sliced the air behind her. She heard Bayard's shocked exclamation and glanced back just once.

Almorante jerked upright from where he'd been examining the plan of the castle, while Bayard leapt round with a snarl. Tatrini saw a circle of men close in upon her sons, swords drawn, faces intent.

'Almorante Malagash,' said General Leatherer, 'Bayard Malagash, we arrest you in the name of the True King.'

'What?' Bayard roared. 'By what right . . . ?'

Acting purely on instinct with no time for conscious thought, Tatrini slipped like oil through the pavilion entrance. Her heart was pounding. Outside the day was misty, full of the scent of pine. Men and horses moved about the camp slowly, like ghosts. The world inside the pavilion was cut off from her now. She could hear nothing from within.

Tatrini walked very calmly a short distance into the trees behind the camp, aware of the curious eyes upon her. No one tried to stop her. She was only a woman, after all. How many of those who watched her leave the camp were part of what was happening in the pavilion now? She did not know whether Leatherer would kill Almorante and Bayard or not, but doubted whether the old general's morals would allow him to commit cold-blooded murder. She had to rely on that hope and she had to get away. She could not help her sons if she was a captive.

Amongst the trees, Tatrini became acutely aware that this was Ilcretia Palindrake's territory: even though the woman had been dead for centuries, it would never be anything but hers. The land still rang with her outrage and her grief. She had shouted it to the elements. And every blade of grass, every tree trunk, every stone, had absorbed her feelings, making them part of the energy matrix of the land.

Tatrini paused, resting her head against a tree. There was a stitch in her side. Ladies of Magrast did not regularly take exercise. She had come to a circular grove of oaks and could no longer hear the muffled sounds from the camp. The air was very still. It was a woman's place, in which Tatrini knew instinctively no man would find her. Tall ferns grew around the outside of the grove, enclosing it completely. On the opposite side, she caught a glimpse of rock and was drawn towards it. Pushing aside rustling fronds of fern, she discovered a low cave and stooped down to enter it. Beyond a short cramped tunnel, the cave opened out and Tatrini was able to stand. Light came in from holes in the rock overhead, perhaps crafted by human hands. The walls of the cave were carved with patterns: spirals and stylised dragons. Tatrini touched them, ran her fingers through the ancient grooves. She had no doubt that this had once been Ilcretia's haunt.

And now it will be mine, she thought.

She wore neither coat nor cloak and lacked the means to build a fire. She had no provisions, but perhaps this was how it was meant to be. It was time for her to test her powers.

Valraven had not taken his eyes off the Magravandian camp. He had watched men erect siege engines across the gorge, beyond the range of his bowmen. For a while, all had gone strangely quiet, then a lone horseman had ridden from the camp, bearing a standard emblazoned with the image of a white hind: the emblem of negotiation.

Hamsin, standing beside his lord, muttered grimly, 'Now they will ask you to surrender. Their messenger should be shot. Let's show them our opinion of their clemency.'

Valraven, who knew he had probably fought alongside most of the men in the Magravandian camp, had no intention of doing that.

The messenger halted on the causeway and waved the standard.

'Shall we signal?' Hamsin said. 'Or will you take other action?'

Valraven made an abrupt gesture. 'We will at least hear what they have to say. Show the flag.'

Then, without warning, an arrow zinged out and caught the

messenger's horse on the rump. Someone in the Magravandian camp had fired upon their own man. They had not been aiming for the castle. The horse reared with a grating cry and its rider struggled to stay on its back. The standard he held fell to the ground.

'What, by Foy . . . ?' Hamsin muttered.

Valraven became intensely still.

A roar erupted from the enemy camp and even through the veil of trees, it was possible to see some kind of conflict had flared up. 'Open the gate!' Valraven ordered. 'Get that messenger within the walls! Now!'

Without question, Hamsin left the battlements swiftly. It was clear that some Magravandian faction was attempting to prevent the messenger delivering his message. But what was that message?

More arrows flew from the trees and two found their mark. The messenger was staggering towards Old Caradore's walls, shafts protruding from his shoulder and leg.

A Caradorean on horseback galloped out from the castle and, with great haste, amidst a deadly rain of arrows, managed to manhandle the wounded messenger across his mount's withers. Within minutes he was back within the walls and the gates had been barred once more.

'Now we shall see,' Valraven said softly.

Rav and Ellony had found their own private vantage point, on a high tower of the keep, from where they had planned to observe the Magravandian army. They had had to claw away rubble to reach it, and the steps had been perilous, half broken away, but they knew no one would think of looking for them there. The previous night, after the ritual, Ellony had drawn her brother aside. 'They look on us as children,' she'd said fiercely, 'but I know we are as important to this conflict as any man or woman.'

Rav had been awed and surprised by the fire in his sister's eyes. She looked far older than her years – very much like his aunt Pharinet, in fact. Rav had already told her everything that had happened to him in Magrast, but thought she had been jealous, because she hadn't responded with the interest and curiosity he would have expected from her. When he'd heard her story of Hamagara, he guessed she was annoyed their mother had not allowed her to have more of a role in all that had occurred.

'Khaster knows what I am,' she had hissed, thumping her narrow chest with a closed fist, 'but Mama is always scared for me.'

A fleeting recollection came into Rav's mind of certain things Prince Leo had said to him when he'd first gone to Magrast, about how protective mothers could be with their sons. It appeared they could be the same with their daughters too.

'We are the male and female aspects of Foy, as our parents are,' Ellony had said. 'There will be a time for us, when we are needed. We must be awake to it, ready for it.'

Rav had agreed fervently.

That morning, once all the adults who usually supervised them were intent upon their own tasks for the day, Rav and Ellony had slipped away to their eyrie. Ellony had stolen a spyglass from one of the Hamagarids and Rav had had to pull her hair several times before she'd allow him to look through it. Reluctantly, she'd handed it over.

Rav scanned the forest opposite. Through the glass he could see the men clearly and thought he even recognised a few of them from the palace. When the messenger rode out from the camp, he had to shove Ellony away with an elbow as she tried to grab the glass.

'Let me see!' she demanded.

In the event, they did not really need the spyglass. The moment that the first arrow hissed out from the camp, Ellony was on her feet. Rav told her to crouch down again, afraid that some long-distance projectile from the Magravands might find its mark in his sister's body.

Ellony ignored his frantic order. 'Something's happening. Give me the glass.'

'Only if you get down here!'

Ellony pulled a sour face at him and snatched the spyglass from his hands. 'There's fighting in the camp. It's difficult to see because of the trees.' She paused. 'Strange . . . What *is* that? There are smoky things flying around.' Then she drew in her breath sharply. 'The messenger's down!'

Rav's curiosity overcame his fears about missiles and he stood up beside his sister at the crumbling battlement. He saw the messenger struggling to reach the castle, and then heard the groan of the portcullis on the ocean side. Presently a Caradorean rider careered into view around the side of the castle and dragged the injured messenger up across the front of his saddle.

'Let's go,' Ellony said in a determined, adult voice. 'I want to find out what's going on.' She had already run to the steps that led down to the yard.

Despite their excitement, Rav and Ellony knew they'd have to remain alert for adults who would want to restrain their movements and shut them away for their own safety. They had quickly learned to become adept at mingling invisibly within a crowd.

A large group of people had already gathered in the yard and the gallant Caradorean rescuer stood proudly by his stamping horse. The messenger lay on the ground, hidden by others. Rav recognised their father before anyone else, because he always stood out in any gathering. Then, through the shifting bodies, Rav saw that a group of women, amongst them Niska, were administering to the wounds of the fallen messenger. Hamsin, Khaster, Shan and Tayven stood close by. At any moment, Varencienne and other women of the family would emerge from the keep, attracted by the commotion, and neither twin wanted to risk being snared by their mother's hawk-eyed attention. They crept up behind their father, wriggling through the curious mass of soldiers, who barely noticed the children slinking between their legs.

There was not as much blood as Rav had expected, but perhaps that was because no one had yet pulled the arrows out. Niska supported the messenger's head to offer him water, while Valraven asked firm but softly-spoken questions.

'My lord,' the messenger gasped, reaching up to grab Valraven's jacket with a trembling hand, 'General Leatherer made sure that many who were faithful to you came upon this mission. It was our intention to take the princes captive and then pledge ourselves to you. As I left the camp, all had proceeded as we had planned, but then the arrows took me . . . '

'As you left, so the princes' allies staged a counter-attack, that much is obvious,' Valraven said.

The messenger tried to struggle from the women's hold. 'My lord, send out your armies. Aid your allies!'

Valraven drew back a little. 'No,' he said quietly.

The messenger uttered a groan and fell back. 'We are loyal to you. We came to give you aid, to ride back with you to Magravandias with the royal dogs in chains . . . '

'I have no doubt of your loyalty, nor of Leatherer's,' Valraven said, 'but I will wait to see the outcome of this conflict. If we need to fight, then let it be against a fragmented army. I will not act rashly.'

Rav was desperate to hear more of this exchange, but Ellony pulled on his arm, forcing him to stumble back through the tangled scrum of legs and feet. 'What are you doing?' he hissed. 'Let me go.'

'No!' Ellony's eyes were like black flames. 'Rav, now! Come with me! I know what we have to do. Our allies can't win without it.'

She did not wait to hear his protests or questions, but dragged him out of the crowd. They ran back across the yard towards the keep, passing their mother and Pharinet on the way, who appeared not to notice them. Rav felt that a magical light hid them from adult eyes. Energy thrummed from his sister's fingers into his own. Their feet seemed barely to touch the ground.

In the main keep, sound echoed weirdly. Rav felt disorientated and slightly dizzy. He heard the slow call of voices and the clang of iron. Invisible missiles streaked past his head. Horses were screaming in fear, and women were lamenting. The stench of smoke and blood was everywhere. But then reality shifted, and he and his twin were racing through a silent, empty building, where the banners of the Caradorean noble houses and the Prince Kutaka of Nimet shifted restlessly upon the blackened walls and the only sounds came from outside.

Rav did not question where Ellony was taking him. Her body was full of purpose and certainty. There was a certain comfort in being able to rely on her. He could not doubt her instincts. As they ran, he sensed the dragon daughters drawing near, riding a current of time as if it were a wave on the ocean. He could hear their faint siren calls.

Unable to remember how they got there, Rav realised they had entered the cellars of the castle. Here Ellony paused to draw breath. She braced her hands upon her knees, gazing up at him through rags of black hair, her chest heaving. Just beyond her, Rav saw shadowy shapes in the gloom that wove like smoke.

'What is it?' Ellony asked sharply.

'The dragon daughters,' Rav replied, pointing into the dark.

Ellony glanced round. 'I can't see them. Call to them, Rav. They have to lead us.'

'Lead us where?'

'To the place where our ancestors met the Ustredi, the sea people.'

'Why?' Rav said. He wanted to know, as his twin did, what they had to do. He was angry with himself because he had to ask her, yet even in his pride, he recognised that she knew answers he did not.

Ellony straightened up and pushed back her hair. Her skin glowed like phosphorus. Perhaps it would be the only light they had to guide them down there. 'I saw something from the tower,' she said. 'I saw *things* in the Magravandian camp, flying through the trees. Things of smoke and sparks. They were fire creatures. I know now that they are fighting against the men loyal to our father. Someone has called them. Bayard or Tatrini. We have to stop them. This is our task, the one we've been waiting for.'

Rav frowned. 'But how do we stop them?'

'We call upon the Ustredi, Foy's people. We have our elemental creatures as the Magravands have theirs.'

'But how do you know they're real?'

'How do you know the dragon daughters are real?' she snapped scornfully. 'There is a place, deep below this castle, where the Palindrakes used to meet with the sea people. We have to find it, and I'm sure Jia, Misk and Thrope will know the way.'

Rav glanced around the dank chamber. The air resonated with a strange high-pitched hum. 'We have no light,' he said. 'We must find light.'

'Call them,' Ellony said, and now her voice was a low grating rasp.

'Jia, Misk, Thrope . . . ' Rav paused and listened to the eerie, almost subliminal scream of the atmosphere. Spots of colour bloomed before his eyes like spreading ink stains. He could hear the dragon daughters breathing, and could feel the spidery touch of their thoughts. 'Daughters of Foy, take us to the meeting place,' he said, 'the heart of the old domain, where sea and land meet. Call forth the denizens of the deep oceans. Come rise, come unto me, guide me with the light of your beating hearts.'

'That's it,' Ellony murmured. 'Speak to them, Rav.'

Rav could see them clearly now, as if they were real women of flesh and blood. He had never before heard the words he had spoken, yet in some way he was remembering them. His invocation gave the dragon daughters substance. He saw the greed in their glinting eyes, their flexing fingers. He remembered them too, as if they were women he had known in a previous life. Thrope was recognisable by her silvery shimmer. Her hair and body glowed with it and she wore a close-fitting garment of gleaming grey like sharkskin. Behind her stood Misk, who had once been the bane of his father's life. Her hair and skin were dark iridescent green and her garment was a trailing mesh of weed and shells.

'Let us *in*,' said Misk, 'then we will take you.'

'We will walk with your limbs,' said Thrope. 'See with your eyes.'

Jia was close to him, plucking at her skin with long indigo claws. She had dark blue skin as if it was dyed by the ink of an octopus, and her hair was a similar colour braided with turquoise pearls. Her body was swathed in a sheath of fishskin that gleamed wetly in the dim light. 'How empty you are, little man. Let us inside. We will fill you with unimagined strengths.'

'No,' Rav said. 'Lead us.'

The daughters pressed close to him and he knew that if he weakened only slightly, they would seize his body and never give it back. 'I command you!' Rav cried. 'In the name of your mother, Great Foy. Lead the Dragon Heir to the sea!'

The dragon daughters hissed together and drew back. 'You are cruel and selfish!' said Thrope. 'Still, that is the way of men. Take my hand. I am she who is closest to you. I am your guide.' She moved her long fingers in a slow undulating gesture. 'Come . . . '

'No,' Rav said. 'I won't touch you. Just lead us.'

Thrope folded her arms and in the dim light, it looked as if she had more than the human complement. 'If you will not take my hand, how can I lead you? Stupid child!'

Rav hesitated and looked to his sister. 'They want to touch me. They want to lead me by the hand.'

'Do it!' Ellony said.

Rav was sure Ellony didn't know enough about the dragon daughters to give such advice.

'You ask us to help you, yet you hold us in contempt,' said Jia, her grin revealing rows of hooked teeth. 'Such arrogance!'

Tentatively, Rav extended one hand. He could see it was shaking. He could still whip it back.

But Thrope leapt forward and grabbed hold of him. He uttered a shrill cry and Ellony threw herself against him, wrapping her arms around his neck. The whole world spun around them, bolts of bright colour shooting past. Then they were flying into darkness.

There was no ground beneath their feet, no walls around them, just a swirling void, filled with hectic blots of light and the laughter of the dragon daughters. Rav was aware of Ellony's arms around him and even though he could not feel his own limbs, tried to imagine he was holding her just as tightly.

A mighty flash of brilliant green radiance broke over them like a wave. Rav felt pressure against his skin; they were swimming through water that glowed with shooting motes of bright green radiance. He had the body of a fish, and could feel the unfamiliar way its muscles worked. A beautiful creature of long waving fins and shimmering scales swam beside him, and he knew it was his sister. The dragon daughters were undulating shapes to either side, swimming like dolphins, their arms pressed against their sides, their long hair and gowns waving like weed. Exhilaration spumed through Rav's body. He had never experienced such a sense of liberation. It was like flying.

They swam into a forest of vast undersea growths, which might have been plants or creatures. Long stems were rooted to the cyclopean rocks, while immense umbrella-like hydra heads swayed far above. Rav felt other creatures swimming around them, invisible but curious. The dark ocean rang with their resonating calls.

The forest ended at the lip of a precipice. Below, Rav saw a mighty triangular edifice that was unlike any building he had ever seen before. It looked alien, as if it had never really been part of this world.

'The Temple of Foy,' Ellony said, her voice entering his mind.

The walls of the temple were covered with bizarre creatures that clung to it like molluscs, possessing elements of crustacean, fish and human forms. Some adhered to the weed-curtained stone with crablike claws, their bodies emerging from gigantic coiled shells. Others were like little children with perfect human bodies. But their heads were like octopi, adorned with long tentacles that vibrated in the ocean currents. Yet more were like merfolk from fairytales, with fish tails and waving hair, but their faces were terrifying.

'Look who we have brought to you!' crooned the dragon daughters. 'The Dragon Heir and his priestess. It is as it always was.'

At once the Ustredi began to disengage themselves from the temple and pulse towards their visitors. They surrounded a fish-maiden, whose dark green hair was woven with a treasury of jewels. Her face was not ugly, but not beautiful either. It had rudimentary fishlike features, with wide eyes and slits for a nose, which pulsed like gills. Her mouth was wide and thick-lipped adorned with feline whiskers at each corner. A set of lovely fin-like veils, similar to the tails of the stately fish that swam in the pools of Tatrini's garden, hung from her cheeks and chin. Her eyes glittered gold and green like mysterious opals from another world.

'I am Hargat,' she said, 'you may know me as queen of this realm.' Her voice was nothing more than a guttural gobbling sound, but Rav could understand her language. It was clear that Ellony did too, because she was brave enough to answer in the same peculiar tongue.

'Greetings, Queen Hargat,' she said. 'Thank you for this audience.'

'Have you brought gifts, humans?' Hargat asked. 'Where are our gifts?'

'We have no gifts,' Ellony replied, 'for the old domain is under attack once more. We need your help.'

'You are Palindrakes?'

'Yes, we are. Help us fight the creatures of fire and the old contract shall be restored.'

'The Palindrakes closed their hearts and minds in fear,' Hargat snapped, exhaling a plume of angry bubbles from her nose. 'I do not know what I smell in your blood. What happened between your people and mine was before my time.'

'My brother here is the Dragon Heir to Caradore,' Ellony said. 'I am a priestess of Foy. Valraven has returned to you in spirit, to undo the wrongs of the past. Please help us, for we alone cannot combat our enemies.'

'It is in our history that you used to bring gifts,' Hargat said. 'That was the way.'

'We *will* give you gifts,' Ellony said patiently, 'but at this time we come to you in need. Our ancestors came from this realm. We are kin. Do not close your senses to us.'

Rav felt incapable of communicating with the Ustredi queen. She was both enchanting and hideous, and he sensed that she did not understand human morals, as he could not understand hers. She might order her people to devour them.

The Ustredi swam around Rav and Ellony, peering into their faces with wide lidless eyes. 'We want no commerce with fire, great queen,' one of them said, a creature that looked like an ancient merman, encrusted with barnacles. 'We have been estranged from the Palindrakes for centuries. What have we to gain from re-establishing this contact? Think what have we to lose by fighting for the dry-skins.'

'But now is the time to put things right, make them as they are meant to be,' Ellony insisted. 'We are kin.'

Hargat hung in the water before them, her face without expression, as if she lacked the physical ability to show any. 'Fire invaded our realm,' she said, as if thinking aloud. 'The djinn were importunate and never paid for their effrontery.'

'And now they walk upon the soil of Caradore,' Ellony said, 'attacking those who would be my father's allies. If you rise to aid us now, the djinn will not expect you.' She paused. 'You *can* come onto land, can't you?'

'We can come as the mist and the rain,' said Hargat. 'There is no place in the elemental realms where we cannot go.' She threshed her mighty tail, tossing lesser Ustredi aside in the current it conjured. 'We will do this thing, my people. We will quench the arrogance of fire. Although the empty air and the hard rock are not our natural realms, the land of Caradore was once our ally. If the revered kings and queens of ages past still lived this day, they would rise and conquer, avenge the hurts inflicted upon them. Rise, my people, rise!'

As one, the Ustredi surged past the twins, creating a maelstrom of frothing bubbles. Rav was tossed up in the current, no longer able to guide his movements. He felt as if his form was changing back into human. He was gulping water, drowning. Blindly, he groped for his sister's hand, found her fingers firm and sure reaching out for him.

A sharp impact jarred Rav's body and he rolled onto his side, gasping. He found he had fallen to the floor in the old cellars of Caradore. What they had experienced must have been a vision, yet his clothes were wet through, his hair lank and dripping around his shoulders. Nearby, Ellony was dragging herself to her feet, weighed down by sodden skirts.

'I think they will do as we asked,' Rav said.

Ellony wiped her hair from her face. 'They will,' she said.

A voice hissed close to Rav's ear. 'Do you want to see, Dragon Heir?'

Rav jumped in alarm and turned to see the inhuman face of Thrope just behind him. Her sisters stood nearby, watching him with a hungry intent.

These were no spectral creatures of vision or dream. They were real, standing on two feet. He could smell the briny perfume of their skin. Perhaps they would never vanish again. It was clear that Ellony too could now see the daughters. Her eyes were wide, but she was not afraid. Rav saw excitement and awe on her face. 'Do you know me?' she demanded.

Jia stepped towards her. 'You are the future Sea Wife,' she said. 'Yes, I know you. I came to your Aunt Pharinet once. She knows me too.'

'You will not do to me what you did to her!' Ellony said.

Rav was astounded by his sister's courage. He would never dare to speak to a dragon daughter in that way.

Jia merely smiled. 'How wide your eyes are, sea child. They observe so much. Too much. Fear is like wine to us, but the finest liquor is, of course, a free spirit. Share your light with me and I will speak with you. There is much I can teach you.'

'I won't let you hurt me,' Ellony said.

'You have more than enough light for your needs,' Jia said. 'It is the warm human breath that mists from your breast. It is the spark that keeps you alive, the engine within you that creates more and more of it. Can you feel it?'

'Yes,' Ellony replied. 'I have done so for a long time.'

'Come,' Thrope said. 'There will be time in the future for this discussion. You summoned the Ustredi, now observe the results.'

The dragon daughters formed a circle and held out their hands. Tentatively, Rav placed his fingers into the icy damp grip of Thrope on his left and Jia on his right. Thrope took Ellony's right hand, while Misk took her left. Then Misk and Jia completed the circle.

Rav closed his eyes and for a moment felt completely at one with Foy's daughters. They belonged to him and to Ellony, to his father and mother, his aunts, Niska, everyone of Caradore. Whatever had happened in the past had been wrong, but perhaps the dragon daughters themselves had not been at fault. They manifested in the form in which they were summoned. Bayard had called them up full of greed and pride and they had become a reflection of that. Perhaps it was Rav's task now, and Ellony's too, to reinvent the spiritual guardians of their family. As if Thrope could read his thoughts, he felt the gentle pressure of her fingers against his own.

I love you, Rav thought clearly, and he meant it.

At once his essence surged out of his body through the crown of his head. He perceived his sister and the dragon daughters as four balls of spinning multi-coloured radiance around him. Below, he could see their bodies standing upon the cold wet floor of the cellar, hands joined, eyes closed.

As one, the company sizzled up out of the cellars, through the castle, across the yard, unseen by anyone. They fizzed high into the air and for some moments, gambolled around each other, revelling in the freedom and exhilaration of their flight. Conflict and battles were forgotten. This was the heritage of the Palindrakes, this liberty, this joy. Thrope whizzed right through Rav's essence, mingling herself with him, conjuring strange ecstatic sensations. He was caught in the web of her aura and she dragged him behind her, out towards the forest. Men were fighting there, but they appeared insubstantial. More real were the creatures that fought amongst them.

Rav saw the Ustredi attacking the creatures of fire that Ellony had described. Some of the sea people were monstrous crustaceans that could crush and rend with their enormous claws. Others were many-tentacled, and when they grabbed the fire elementals, so they hissed and shrivelled, quenched by the power of water. A soldier, who appeared as no more than a ghostly shadow, flailed his arms wildly against an elemental attacker. Rav saw an Ustredi scuttle towards the conflict and nip off the fire creature's head with its pincers. The soldier continued to wave his arms, yelling, as yet unaware he was no longer under attack. He could see nothing.

At the entrance to the royal pavilion, a group of men were holding off attackers of both human and elemental nature. Something within the pavilion glowed a bright crimson and Rav knew that this was Bayard. The light increased in brilliance as he observed it. He was sure that someone, or something, was feeding him strength. If Bayard got any stronger, he'd burst out of the tent like a fireball. Rav called to Thrope with a loud thought and she was there beside him in an instant.

'I know what you behold and you are right,' she said. 'Your grandmother lies in a cave close by, spawning spirits of fire: the djinn.'

'We must stop her,' Rav said.

Without further communication, Thrope led him out over the trees and then down into the darkness of the forest. She was a spiralling sphere of light ahead of him, leaving a trail of sparkling vapour.

They came to a glade where gouts of fiery light burst like belching magma out of a narrow cave entrance. Thrope and Rav shot into the cave, but the flames tried to repel them. Rav felt their hissing anger as they beat against him. He could feel his essence burning up in their searing heat. Desperately, he called out to Thrope with his soul. At once, her essence expanded around him and enfolded him in cool, comforting light. The flames could no longer touch him.

'This is our land,' said Thrope, a soft whisper in his soul, 'this is our site. What we have here are interlopers, who do not know they lack the power to harm us. It seems we must teach them.'

In the inner chamber of the cave, they found Tatrini lying on her back on the cold stone floor, her body writhing as if in pain. Her hands were hooked above her breast, clawing the air. Thousands of little flames burst out of her skin and danced from her open lips. They flew up into the air and mingled, drawing strength from one another. This was the elemental lava that was erupting from the cave, fuelled by Tatrini's intention.

Thrope released Rav from her essence and manifested as a tall woman of water, who stood over Tatrini's prone form. 'Oh, how you suffer, queen of fire,' Thrope murmured. 'See how your body twists and shudders. This is costing you dear and the full price has yet to be paid.' She extended her hands and a shimmering fluid rained down from her long fingers. When it hit Tatrini, it hissed and turned to mist. Tatrini uttered a hoarse cry, her face contorted into an ugly expression of pain, as if the cold liquid burned her. Her body was becoming drenched, so that she could no longer generate the children of fire. Those that still remained within the cave exploded in sparks, with audible pops and whistles like festive fireworks.

Tatrini opened her eyes. She looked old and tired, as if an inner light had been extinguished. Her hair hung dripping over her face and her hands shook as she pushed it from her eyes. Rav watched his grandmother blinking and gasping in the gloom. Thrope's silvery gleam was the only source of light.

'Tatrini Malagash, you have violated our sacred place,' said Thrope. 'You have no business here in the domain of the women of Caradore with your alien magicks.'

Tatrini sat up abruptly and looked around herself. Rav knew she could not see the dragon daughter, but when she looked in his direction, she murmured his name. He was clearly visible to her.

'We had to stop you,' he said. 'What you were doing was wrong.'

'Rav,' Tatrini said, reaching towards him with a trembling hand, 'my little warrior. Remember your training. This is part of all we have worked for. You mustn't interrupt me.' Her eyes were glazed. Clearly she did not think it strange that Rav should suddenly appear there. In a way, she was dreaming.

'I am not your creature,' Rav said. 'I command the dragon daughters now. This is my father's realm.'

'Rav . . . '

He raised one arm and pointed at her. 'Your fire is quenched, in the name of Foy and all the denizens of Pelagra. There will be no more fire in this place.'

The rock around them began to shake and crack. Tiny fissures appeared within it and then water began to drip down from the roof in a hundred narrow waterfalls. It pushed through the stone, crumbling it, creating wider channels for itself. Chunks of rock fell to the floor and shattered, throwing up muddy spray. The cave was rapidly filling with water, a deluge.

Tatrini looked weak and dazed, sitting in a widening puddle while stone crashed down around her. Rav was suffused with pity for her. 'Get out of here or you'll die!' he cried. 'Get up, Grandmama. Get up!'

At that moment, Thrope seized hold of him. Instantaneously they were transformed once more into spheres of light and together they shot out of the cave.

Rav did not know whether his grandmother followed them or not, but heard a muffled explosion as the rock collapsed behind them. His whole essence shook with it.

'She will survive,' Thrope said grimly. 'She will survive with awareness, and there is no greater penance.'

When they returned to the Magravandian camp, the conflict had ceased. Men sat dazed upon the ground, their weapons hanging limp from their hands, while others lay groaning, bleeding from terrible wounds. Still more did not move, nor make any sound. They were dark husks, empty of the light of life. No elemental creatures remained.

Ellony, Jia and Misk still hovered above the scene, but came spiralling towards Rav and Thrope when they became aware of them.

'It is over,' said Ellony. 'The Ustredi just kept coming and coming. They were so angry. We did this, Rav. Us! Now let our father dare to question our worth.'

Rav could not respond to this, but directed his attention towards the royal pavilion. He could see that Bayard's essence was now a dull crimson glow. It pulsed with fury, but its power had been diminished. 'We must return to our bodies,' he said. 'We must send people to find our grandmother. She's out in the forest alone.'

CHAPTER THIRTY-FIVE

The Death of Kings

In the dark, sagging keep of Old Caradore, the Palindrakes and the Leckerys, along with Sinaclara and Tayven, had gathered around their lord, to listen to what his children had to say. Valraven had observed what he could of the Magravandian conflict from the battlements, and just when it seemed some kind of conclusion had been reached, because everything had gone ominously quiet, Sinaclara had come yelling from the keep, demanding he go inside at once.

When he laid eyes upon the twins, he couldn't help but smile. They both looked guilty, worried whether they were about to be reprimanded in some way. But there was no denying the excitement in their eyes, the frantic desire to reveal a wonderful secret.

'We've met the dragon daughters,' Ellony said, running up to him, her expression showing how much she hoped for approval. 'They took us to the Ustredi. We helped vanquish the Magravandian fire creatures!'

'Hush, slow down,' Valraven said. 'What is this?'

Between them, Rav and Ellony related their experience, although Ellony had to be silenced by her father on several occasions, so that Rav could have his say. The story took some time, because of the many questions that people wanted to ask. The account was rather muddled.

Valraven's first response, once the twins' breathless narrative was finished, was to issue a quiet order for some of his men to search for Tatrini.

Niska interrupted him, saying that only women should venture into Ilcretia's sacred place. Some of her priestesses, who had come north with the Palindrakes, would search there and bring Tatrini to the castle.

Pharinet was perhaps the most surprised by Rav and Ellony's story.

380

'I find it difficult to imagine the dragon daughters as anything but malevolent,' she said. 'It makes me wince to think how you two opened yourselves up to them.'

'They are not evil,' Ellony said bluntly.

'They're impartial,' Varencienne said. 'It makes sense. They manifest as they are imagined by the one who invokes them.' She pantomimed a shudder. 'For years, they have been the image of Bayard's warped imagination. Poor things!'

'This is an immense step forward,' Sinaclara said. 'The dragon daughters should be able to help us regain the Crown of Silence, wherever that Magravandian witch has hidden it!'

'Can you bring them here now, Elly?' Khaster asked. 'How solidly are they able to manifest?'

'They are already here,' Tayven said. 'Not everyone will be able to see them with their physical eyes.'

'Rav sees them the easiest,' Ellony said, 'but Jia has told me she'll teach me.'

Pharinet grimaced. 'I don't like the sound of that! From what I remember of the divine Jia, she is a minx, to say the least.'

'It's all right,' Ellony said. 'It really is, Aunt Pharry.'

Valraven drew in his breath and then spoke in a ringing voice. 'Well, lovely dragon daughters, minxes or not, it seems we are to be reconciled. Despite the sorry history between us, you have my thanks for your part in what has taken place this day.'

Everyone was silent for a moment, perhaps hoping for a tangible response, but there was none.

Varencienne broke the hush by saying, 'Will you open the gates now, Val?'

He nodded thoughtfully. 'I don't see any reason why not. What I've heard from the twins explains some rather peculiar things I observed over the last couple of hours.'

'Are you sure this isn't some complicated, tricky Magravandian plot?' Saska asked in a worried tone.

'It isn't!' Ellony said. 'What we said was true.'

Varencienne put a hand on the back of her daughter's neck. 'I know it is, sweetness. I don't doubt you.'

Valraven smiled down at Ellony. 'I think I should go out to meet our allies, don't you?'

She nodded enthusiastically. 'Yes! Can I come?'

'No,' Valraven said. 'A battlefield offers no pleasant sights for a young lady. And before you argue with me, indulge me. If you remain here, it is perhaps for my sake, rather than yours!'

Ellony smiled and hugged her father's legs. 'I'll stay,' she said. 'This time.'

Valraven went to his son and placed a hand upon one of his shoulders. 'I am proud of you,' he said. 'You have accomplished things that I could not.'

Rav's face flushed. 'I was afraid,' he said, as if in apology.

'Nevertheless, well done, my son. You are an asset to the House of Palindrake.'

Valraven signalled for Shan, Khaster and Tayven to accompany him and began to leave the hall, but Varencienne came after him. 'I'm coming too,' she said. 'Say nothing to contradict me. I won't listen.'

'I wouldn't dream of it,' Valraven said.

Beyond the castle walls, fresh wind blew huge clouds across the sky and cleansed the air of the stink of blood. When the Caradoreans had ridden halfway over the causeway, men came to meet them from the Magravandian camp, led by General Leatherer. Many bore wounds, wrapped with hasty, makeshift bandages.

When Leatherer saw Valraven, he sank to his knees and placed his right fist against his breast. 'All hail, Great King!'

Those who had come with him did likewise.

Valraven dismounted from his horse and went to pull the general to his feet. 'Get up, get up. All of you. Do not bow to me. My hands are clean. This is a battle I have won without a fight because of you.'

'It is my pleasure to deliver the Malagashes to you in chains,' said Leatherer. 'You are the only king, Valraven. Many of us have thought so for a long time. I would gladly have given my life to ensure your victory.'

'Thankfully, that was not necessary,' Valraven said. 'Who else in Magrast was aware of your plans?'

'The most influential members of the Fire Chamber, my lord.'

Valraven laughed aloud. 'Senefex and Mordryn? You jest, surely!'

'No. Once Gastern went into decline, some of us spoke together and decided what needed to be done. We had to act carefully.'

'Senefex and Mordryn always tend to back the winning horse,' Valraven said. 'They change allegiances to save their own skins.'

Leatherer did not comment on this, but his eyes showed that he agreed with Valraven's words.

'Well, there will be time for discussion later,' Valraven said. 'Now you must take me to Bayard and Almorante.'

'The men wanted to string them up,' Leatherer said, 'but I told them to wait. I knew you should witness it.'

Valraven said nothing.

Tayven observed a calm concentrated purpose on Valraven's face. He had a secret.

The Malagashes had been brought out of the pavilion and had been made to kneel amongst their dead, their hands tied behind them. Bayard snarled out imprecations, his face twisted into a bestial snarl. He was like a maddened beast, unchastened, fighting against his bonds.

Almorante was a different matter. He knelt erect, but his eyes were closed. It was as if he was waiting for the executioner's sword and wanted it all to be over. Tayven's heart flexed in his chest. He would ask Valraven to show mercy, even though he knew Almorante might not want it.

Valraven went to stand before them, staring with a calm expression at Bayard, who spat at his feet. 'Untie them,' he said to Leatherer.

The general gestured to a group of his men. 'Keep the fire dog in a firm grip,' he said. 'He has the madness upon him.'

Bayard bared his teeth at them in response. When Leatherer's men tried to lay hands on him, he attempted to fight and had to be knocked almost senseless before he calmed down.

In contrast, Almorante got listlessly to his feet and did not look into anyone's eyes as the men untied him. Tayven knew the prince was aware of his presence, even though he betrayed nothing of his feelings.

'Look at you!' Bayard sneered, shaking blood from his face. 'What a noble company: whores, cowards and traitors!'

Varencienne, who had hung back, now approached her brother. 'And what are you, Bay? Will you tell me that? I see no nobility within you. I see a thuggish brute who thinks with his balls.'

'Such gentle words, dear sister,' Bayard said. 'Are you here to watch me die? Are you here to watch the world die with me?'

'You will not be executed,' Valraven said.

Everyone turned to him in astonishment. 'My lord,' Leatherer began, but Valraven raised a hand to silence him.

'If I am to be your king, then I must prove my worth. If Caradore is to break free of Magravandias, she must vanquish its king. It is a symbolic act.' He glanced at Leatherer. 'Bring him a sword.'

Leatherer frowned, looking very much like he wanted to say, 'Are you mad?'

Varencienne said, 'Val . . . what is this?'

Tayven knew what Valraven wanted to do and why. It was not in the Dragon Lord's nature to accept so bloodless a victory. He wanted to feel that he was part of it, that he deserved it. He wanted to face Bayard, his archetypal opponent, in hand-to-hand combat. Fire and water.

'Bayard is not their king,' Varencienne said, 'Almorante is. Fight him.'

'But Almorante will not fight me,' Valraven said, 'will you, my lord?'

Almorante looked at him for the first time. 'There is no point. If I should kill you, these people would kill me. I am emperor in name only. It is clear to me that since my father died, there has only been one king in the people's hearts and that is you. We did not realise how wide-spread this desire was, and now we have paid for our carelessness. Men who were close to us have betrayed us. The Malagash dynasty died with our father.'

'Of all of your brothers, you are the only true Malagash,' Tayven said, 'a man who shares the spirit of Cassilin and his forefathers.'

Almorante would not look at him or even acknowledge he'd heard the words, but his eyes moved briefly to Khaster, expressionless and dull.

'Listen to your whore,' Bayard drawled. 'Even as he comes to gloat over your defeat at your enemy's side, he has silver words for you.'

'Bayard is the symbol of the Malagash desire and will,' Valraven said. 'Tayven was not wrong in what he said to you, Almorante. I have no desire to fight you either.' He turned to Shan. 'Clear an area for me.'

'If I am to die, I swear by Madragore that I'll take you with me, Palindrake!' Bayard said. 'In your arrogance you have just created your own death.'

Tayven knew that Bayard would fight like a maniac. He had nothing to lose. Valraven was a skilled fighter, but the prince's desperation and fury might give him the edge. There was no way to predict the outcome of such a conflict.

'Val, you can't do this!' Varencienne said. 'It's senseless! Are you still a boy that you have to prove yourself like this?'

'My lord, let me fight for you!' Shan said. 'I am your champion.'

Valraven ignored them both and drew his sword.

It was clear that Leatherer felt extremely uneasy putting a weapon into Bayard's hand. The moment his guards released him, Bayard uttered a roar and charged madly towards Valraven. He did not care about having a prepared field of battle. He just wanted Palindrake blood.

Tayven witnessed the whole event in slow motion. Time seemed to stop. He saw the horror on Varencienne's face, frozen. He saw the men fixed in positions like people in a painting. He saw Valraven turn, enquiry upon his face. He saw Bayard's weapon raised high, shining in the sunlight. Then, before that sword could fall, a dark blur intervened. Almorante threw himself forward, pushed Valraven aside and took the full force of the sword thrust in his chest.

Time swung back to normal speed. Shan and Leatherer ran to grab hold of Bayard, who was roaring incoherently, apparently unaware he had just wounded his own brother and not the Dragon Lord. Almorante slumped at Valraven's feet and Varencienne and Khaster hurried over to him. Valraven appeared stunned, but only for a moment.

'Silence!' he roared and everyone fell silent. 'Shan, take Prince Almorante at once into the castle and tend to his injuries.' He looked at Bayard, his expression serene. 'I have business to finish.'

He indicated that soldiers should manhandle Bayard to a distance around twenty feet away from him.

'Release him,' he said.

As before, Bayard hurtled forward, more animal than man. Valraven did not assume a stance of defence or attack. He stood perfectly still while this raging madman came towards him. At the very last moment, as Bayard made to attack with his bloody blade, Valraven stepped deftly to the side. Bayard lunged past the Dragon Lord, who, with one precise full-bodied swing of his sword took the prince in the back of the neck, partly severing his head from his body. Bayard fell face forward to the ground and lay there with arms and legs outflung, his head twisted grotesquely to the side, his dead eyes frozen in an expression of surprise.

The onlookers were too astounded to react. It was almost comical.

Valraven handed his sword to Khaster, who looked at the weapon as if he didn't know what it was.

'Gentlemen, I invite you into my domain,' Valraven said, addressing the entire company. 'I have concluded my business out here.' With complete sang-froid, he went back to his horse.

Tayven caught Varencienne's eye and saw her total perplexity. She put a hand to her mouth to cover a smile, but Tayven could tell she didn't know whether to laugh or weep.

Almorante was taken to the family living quarters, where the women of both families had gathered.

Tayven sat on the bed and held Almorante's hand. His wound was too deep. It could not be healed. How the prince had survived even this long was a miracle.

'Look at me, Mante,' Tayven said, but still the prince would not acknowledge his presence. Tayven was unsure why. There could be many reasons, all of them complex.

'Is there anything we can do for you?' Valraven said. 'People you'd like us to protect and care for in Magrast?'

Almorante sighed slowly, his breath rattling in his chest. 'There is no one,' he said, 'no one worth the trouble.'

'Is there anything you'd like to say?' Valraven persisted.

Tayven could tell the Dragon Lord felt anguish at Almorante's fate. He was confused by the sacrificial act.

'She brought the Crown with her,' Almorante said. 'She thought I didn't know, but I did. It will be concealed amongst her possessions in the camp.'

'I will go at once and look for the crown myself,' Sinaclara said.

Valraven nodded to her. 'It must not be lost or stolen.'

Almorante's fingers moved feebly in Tayven's hold. 'I could feel its presence, but it did not speak to me. That was when I knew.'

'Knew what?' Tayven asked softly.

Almorante looked at him then. 'You are still so beautiful. You always will be, even when you're old and dying.' His fingers were trembling. 'It is all fading now. My father is here.'

For some moments he was silent, and Tayven wondered if those would be his last words, but then Almorante summoned the last of his strength and his voice was clear. 'I knew that Valraven Palindrake would be king and that he would wear the Crown of Silence. Paradoxically, when I realised this thing I also knew it was the moment when I was most worthy of being emperor myself.'

'Mante, I told you in Magrast,' Tayven said. 'I told you how you could be king.'

Almorante's head moved slowly on the pillow. 'No, it was never for me. A beautiful dream.' He closed his eyes. 'I was never king.'

'You were,' Tayven said. 'The moment you took the sword in your body, you were the only true great king. You gave that title to Valraven. You passed it to him.'

Almorante smiled a little and murmured, 'Kiss me, Tayven. Come one last time to my arms.'

But when Tayven bent down to kiss the prince's lips, he was already dead.

He was an enemy, a scheming Malagash, who had done and ordered terrible things in his life, but everyone in that room gave in to tears of grief. Even Valraven pressed the fingers of one hand against his eyes. Now the Malagash dynasty had truly died, even though the killing was not yet over.

In the Magravandian camp, soldiers attempted to make sense out of all they had witnessed that day. When Sinaclara walked amongst them, they stared at her as if she was a vision. She asked them, 'Where is the Queen Mother's pavilion?', but some of them didn't even answer. Eventually, after piecing together morsels of rather garbled directions, she found her way to a secluded peaked tent of dark blue canvas, its entrance hung with golden tassels. There was something forlorn about the way it was isolated from the main camp. From within, Sinaclara heard the song of the Crown. Her whole body reverberated with it and her mouth was dry as she pushed aside the entrance drapes and entered the dark space within.

With her psychic sight, Sinaclara perceived a silvery violet glow emanating from beneath a pile of folded clothes and blankets. She felt the power of the Crown, which had grown in intensity since last she had beheld it. Perhaps Tatrini's ritual had greatly affected it. She pulled aside the coverings and discovered a wooden box bound with iron, which was locked. The locks would not succumb to her physical assaults or to any tricks of the mind she attempted to throw at them.

Eventually she went back to the main camp and managed to persuade two Magravands, a little less dazed than their fellows, to come and break open the box for her.

'What's in it?' one of them asked.

'A Palindrake heirloom,' she replied. 'A curio.'

The Crown shrieked as the men beat at the locks that protected it. When the lid finally gave way, splashes of fierce spirit light burst out, which made Sinaclara gasp and back away. The men looked at her in curiosity. They saw nothing.

'Go now,' she told them, adding a little more gently, 'Thank you for your help.'

The men suspected that what lay within the box was rather more than a curio, but they obeyed the imperative in Sinaclara's voice. When she was alone, she knelt before the box for nearly half an hour, her hands plunged between her thighs. She listened to the song of the Crown, her body swaying slightly. There was no message for her, but the Crown seemed to understand that something important had occurred and that soon it would fulfil its purpose.

Sinaclara dared to lift it from its nest. She unwrapped the silk from the coralline tines and held the artefact before her. Some impulse made her turn it over and she realised, for the first time, that the frame upon which all the tines and adornments were arranged was the top section of a human skull. She had kept this artefact in her house for months, but had never noticed that before. The most sacred relic she had ever encountered concealed a grisly foundation. It made sense, she supposed.

Sinaclara wrapped the Crown once more in its coverings and went out into the open air. As she left the pavilion, a subtle tension left her body. The two men who had helped her earlier were sitting nearby and regarded her dubiously as she passed them. Sinaclara inclined her head to them. In due course they would see the artefact for themselves, when she placed it upon the head of Valraven Palindrake.

Just as she reached the causeway, Sinaclara saw a group of women emerging from the forest. Between them, they supported a staggering figure. It took Sinaclara a few moments to realise that it was Tatrini. She looked aged and fragile, her hair hanging lank around her shoulders, tangled with twigs and leaves. Her face was sunken and grey, her mouth a withered line. Thrope had savaged her thoroughly. Sinaclara wondered how much the erstwhile empress would be able to recover from the assault.

A compassionate twinge in her breast urged Sinaclara to go to Tatrini and place a hand upon her face. 'Do you remember me?' she asked.

Tatrini nodded slowly. 'Yes. I still bear the scars.'

Sinaclara smiled. 'I never drew blood, my lady!'

'Oh, you did,' Tatrini said. 'More than you ever knew.'

'Come to the castle,' Sinaclara said. 'Varencienne is there, and the children.'

Tatrini closed her eyes for a moment. 'My family is dead,' she said.

Sinaclara swallowed with difficulty. She was not given to feeling sympathy for those she thought didn't deserve it, but earlier she had felt sorry for Almorante; now a similar feeling welled within her for Tatrini. It was difficult to hold onto anger when a person was brought so low, no matter what terrible things they might have done. 'Almorante died well,' she said softly. 'He died as king. Bayard died as he lived, with ferocity and passion. But Ren is alive and well, and so are Rav and Elly. You are not alone.'

'You don't understand,' Tatrini said in a small, cracked voice. 'The blood of my sons fills the rivers of the land. They are murdered, all of them.'

'I'm sure that's not so,' Sinaclara said. 'The conflict is over, my lady. There will be clemency now. Only Bayard was a true threat to the new king.'

'It will happen,' Tatrini said. 'I saw it. My vision was a wash of blood as I fought through the forest. These women found me. Without them, I would have left this world. I was seeking a portal to what lies beyond.'

'Life is not over,' Sinaclara said. 'I believe you can make what you like from what remains. It is up to you. Be thankful that Valraven sent these women to find you. He bears no grudge. Through him, your dynasty will live for ever.'

For a moment, Tatrini became alert and her body straightened up. She became a faint reflection of what she used to be. 'Then stop him sending the bird of death,' she said hurriedly. 'Run, sorceress! Tell him not to send word to Magrast. Let him ride south and tell them all with his own mouth. For when the bird flies, it will be too late.'

Sinaclara regarded Tatrini, and an intense moment of understanding passed between them. She thrust the wrapped Crown into the Queen Mother's hands. 'Give this to Valraven,' she said. 'It will be a symbol of all that must be. In return, I will do as you ask.'

With these words, she picked up her skirts and ran frantically back to the castle. The air was full of screaming gulls. A bird. The bird of death. Not a raven or an eagle, or any other bird of prey or carrion, but a dove. A messenger. The carrier of good news.

Sinaclara hurtled across the castle yard, pushing jubilant men from her path who sought to grab hold of her for a victory dance. Her eyes were upon the sky. Before she entered the keep, she saw it, winging out from a high tower of the Palindrake house. She came to a standstill and directed her will forcefully towards it. Fall! Return! But it was too late.

The dove flew from Old Caradore, south over the mountains, and so into Magravandias. Within a few days, hastened by fair winds, it alighted at its destination on the window-sill of Lord Senefex's office in Magrast.

Senefex saw the shadow of a bird fall over his desk and rose at once to open the window. He lifted the delicate creature in his hands and took the message from its leg. He read it. While the dove strutted over the papers on the desk, purring softly, as if congratulating itself on a job well done, Senefex stood motionless, staring at the wall.

After a few minutes, he came out of his trance and went to pull the cord of a bell that would summon his personal assistant. The man presented himself at the door almost immediately.

'Summon Archimage Mordryn,' Senefex said. 'And tell him to bring Lord Maycarpe with him.'

The assistant bowed. 'At once, my lord.' He hesitated briefly, then said, 'May I ask if you have received news from the north?'

'I have,' Senefex said. 'We have simply to complete the operation here.'

'I understand.'

Senefex sighed deeply. 'This is the lightest and darkest of days.'

The process began at the hour of dinner. Master Dark walked like a ghost through the corridors of the palace, a long black cloak swirling around him. He was accompanied by six men: Splendifers – amongst them Rufus Lorca.

They visited first the apartment of Prince Celetian, who was still recovering from his injuries received at the hands of the Dragonards. Dark and his men forced their way past astonished servants and pushed aside the prince's screaming wife, who instinctively knew why they were there. They went into the prince's bedroom, where he sat propped up by pillows in his bed, eating his evening meal. Celetian uttered a frightened shocked question, but Dark answered it only with a blade. He said, 'In the name of the True King!'

The assassins left the apartment before the first drop of blood hit the floor.

Next, Dark went to the rooms of Prince Roarke, who conveniently was dining with two of his brothers, Pormitre and Wymer. Dark left corpses sitting at the table and another widow to grieve when she heard the news.

Prince Eremore was found tied up in his bedroom, being beaten by a female concubine. His taste for danger and pain was indulged in abundance before he died.

Perhaps then, the assassins' steps became less sure as they made their way to their final destination in Magrast, the college refectory where the younger princes, Leo, Osmar and Parrish, sat taking their dinner with fellow students and masters.

'In the name of the True King,' said Dark. His knife and his right hand were painted red with Malagash blood. He bore down upon the princes with unswervable purpose.

The boys were more difficult than their elder brothers. They neither swore nor attempted to fight back. They pleaded and screamed. Masters tried to intervene, but ultimately it did no good. Later, witnesses would report that the Splendifers accompanying the killer did not turn their eyes once towards what Master Dark did.

'What kind of True King orders this?' the headmaster demanded, his face spotted with young blood, his body shaking as if in the throes of a palsy.

'The orders come from the cathedral,' Dark answered. 'The Malagashes are traitors to the people.'

With these words, he left the building, to the accompaniment of children's sobbing and cries.

The company went at once to the stableyard and mounted fast horses, which would bear them quickly north to Recolletine. Before the dawn, they reached the royal retreat by Lake Anterity, where Khaster Leckery had first made love to Tayven Hirantel. Gastern was still in bed, and no doubt spent most of his time there, but Rinata was taking breakfast with her son.

When Dark came through the door, she knew at once what would happen. Her mind went calm. She said, 'Spare the boy. No one will know. We'll disappear. No one will ever know.'

'In the name of the True King,' said Dark and cut her throat.

Linnard stared up at him from his seat, his expression curiously blank. 'Will you kill me too now, Master Dark?'

'In the name of the True King,' said the assassin, but his face was bleak.

Linnard tried to run from the room, but Dark intercepted him and opened the boy's throat with his knife.

Rufus Lorca backed against the table and said, 'By Madragore, this is . . . By Madragore.' He shook his head, the back of one hand pressed against his mouth.

'Your hand is empty,' Dark said coldly and moved towards the stairs. The Splendifers did not follow him.

Lorca went outside and gazed down at Lake Anterity. Rushes moved slowly in the morning breeze and swans called sadly. A quest had begun here and another ended. The wind sang a song of ancient times. Lorca heard nothing else.

CHAPTER THIRTY-SIX

Lords of the Empire

The Malagashes had been dead for two weeks, but because of the various tasks that had needed attention in the wake of their demise, the cabal responsible for their deaths had been unable to meet in private. This was the first time they'd had the opportunity. It was late in the afternoon and mellow sunlight flooded the archimage's private office, high in the cathedral administrative building. Three men sat beneath a stained-glass window that depicted Madragore and his angels of fire, who all wielded bloody swords. Ruby light fell over the hands of the men as they each took a glass from a tray proffered by the archimage's servant. The glasses contained a ruby liquor, as red as blood, as red as the filtered sunlight.

'To us,' said Mordryn raising his glass. He puckered his lips to sip. 'Ah, fire of the heart!'

The other two men did likewise.

Mordryn leaned back in his chair. 'Well, gentlemen, I think events have resolved as much to our liking as we could possibly demand.'

Lord Senefex nodded thoughtfully. 'There were some tense moments, but on the whole . . . ' He smiled and took another sip of his drink.

'What are your thoughts, Darris?' Mordryn asked.

Darris Maycarpe placed his glass carefully on the desk before him, onto a tiny mat fashioned of coiled strings of beads. He ran a finger round the rim of the glass. 'There will always be shadowy areas into which we cannot pry. Coincidence aligned in our favour, that is all.'

'But you are a master of coincidence,' Senefex said. 'In fact, I do not believe it exists in your world.'

Maycarpe smiled to himself. 'It is an image I have created. Presentation is all. I learned this long ago.'

'When you were stealing artefacts from museums and replacing them with copies?' Senefex enquired, grinning.

'Oh, long before that!'

'When you acted so well for Almorante? You played the part of outraged captive magnificently, my friend.'

Maycarpe shrugged expressively. 'I did what needed to be done, that's all.'

Mordryn expelled a long, satisfied sigh. 'Whatever you say, Darris, without you none of this could have happened. None has played their part as well as you. You are a master of intrigue and manipulation! Now we have our king, his Crown and his men of power. We have our new world. And the Malagash princes are no more.'

Maycarpe grimaced distastefully. 'An ugly business, but expedient. Master Dark is an essential man.'

'His family have served our order for many generations,' Mordryn said. 'He has known since he was a boy that one day he would be required to spill Malagash blood for us.'

'How do the people regard the operation?' Maycarpe enquired. 'What will Lord Palindrake have to say about it, do you think?'

Mordryn made a dismissive gesture. 'We have our scapegoat. Dark's orders came from Alguin, who, as we all know, is widely believed to be an unstable fanatic. Fortunately, his fanatical loyalty is easily manipulated. He will not betray any connection with us. It is a religious matter with him.' Mordryn sighed deeply. 'Still, despite the security of our position, and the necessity of the action we took, it was not a good day for the Church.'

Inwardly Maycarpe shuddered, although he did not allow it to register either in his body posture or on his face. On that night of blood, when Master Dark had marched like a vengeful ghost through the corridors of the palace, Maycarpe had drunk himself into oblivion. He believed that if he'd remained sober, he would have heard every cry, every slice of the blade, even from as far away as Recolletine.

Maycarpe was a man of will and power, and he knew that sometimes murder was necessary for the greater good, but he often wished it wasn't.

His companions were also silent for a few moments, perhaps each reliving that night in their own memories. Maycarpe did not know their inner thoughts. Even though they comprised the heart of the innermost level of many layers of power, some things remained unspoken between them. It took more than a strong stomach to order the death of a child, and some images, even though never witnessed in reality, would haunt them to their graves, perhaps beyond.

Again Mordryn raised his glass, his expression sombre. 'Let us drink to Leonid. May his soul rest for ever in the sweet realms of the many heavens.'

Senefex and Maycarpe raised their glasses also. 'To Leonid.'

A lighter atmosphere descended over the company.

'Will you return to Mewt now, Darris?' Senefex asked.

'After the coronation, yes. I miss it. I'd go tomorrow if I didn't want to wait and see Valraven Palindrake wear the Crown of Silence.' He leaned back in his chair. 'Ah, Akahana, wait for me! I yearn for your perfumed delights!'

Senefex laughed. 'One day I really must come and sample them with you.'

Mordryn opened a drawer of his desk and rummaged through the papers within. 'Ah, here it is,' he said, withdrawing a slim folded document. He handed it to Maycarpe. 'Your public pardon, Darris. A mere formality, I know, but you should keep it safe. In case anyone should ask.'

'Indeed,' said Maycarpe, slipping the waxed paper into an inner pocket of his jacket. 'In case anyone should ask.'

At that moment, even before Maycarpe had readjusted the immaculate folds of his jacket, one of Mordryn's aides knocked upon the door and entered the room. He bowed. 'Your high reverence, Lord Palindrake is here to see you.'

Mordryn raised his bushy brows and glanced at his companions. Maycarpe could tell it was on the archimage's mind to send him from the room, but it was too late, because Valraven Palindrake had already pushed past the aide. His face, when he saw the tableau before him, registered a kind of resigned contempt.

'Valraven,' Mordryn said, rising from his chair. 'An unexpected pleasure. You were not due to arrive until next week.'

Maycarpe smiled to himself. Palindrake was no fool. They should have known he'd arrive early.

Valraven inclined his head. 'Gentlemen, you would think less of me surely if I did not display an eagerness to be in Magrast at this precarious time.'

Mordryn gestured expansively. 'Actually, we were quite at ease with the plan for you to spend time with your family. These have been a harrowing few months.'

Valraven turned his attention to Maycarpe. 'Are you here for my benefit, Darris?'

Maycarpe merely raised his hands languidly.

'Certain people expected to find Lord Maycarpe rotting in

Cawmonel,' Valraven said, 'but now here he is, drinking the archimage's liquor and grinning from ear to ear.'

Maycarpe was not grinning at all.

'Val,' Senefex said, 'we have to go with the wishes of the people, and the people want you. There is no point in imprisoning your allies.'

'Oh, is that what you are?' Valraven enquired sternly, still glaring at Maycarpe.

'It is what we all are,' Senefex said.

Valraven spoke coldly. 'I remember the time after Leonid's death, and all that was said that day. Somehow, I do not think this was what you had in mind, but then . . . ' His smile did not reach his eyes. 'Perhaps it was.'

'We upheld Gastern, but Gastern fell,' Mordryn said. 'It was not in anyone's interest to have another Malagash upon the throne. You know that, otherwise you wouldn't be here now. You wouldn't have killed Bayard.'

Valraven raised a hand and pointed directly at Mordryn. 'Do not think me your puppet,' he said in a low, firm voice, 'nor presume to take the credit for all that's taken place. You can tell yourselves you had a hand in it, but ultimately it was beyond your control. It was you who were the puppets of the universe.'

There was a short silence. Maycarpe stared at his hands, which were folded upon his lap. Let him think that if he wanted to. It made no difference.

'Come, Val,' Senefex said in a coaxing tone. 'We are not enemies. There is much to be done and we are here to support you.'

'Do I want the support of murderers?' Valraven said. 'I know you were behind what happened to the princes, no matter how much Alguin is willing to take the blame.'

Maycarpe was impressed. Valraven must have done some investigating of his own before coming here. He would be a wise king.

'You will no doubt call the atrocities acts of war,' Valraven said, 'but it was not that. You were merely ensuring your own futures.'

Maycarpe shifted upon his seat and cleared his throat. 'Val, listen to me. Senefex, Mordryn and I, we can never be men of light. We will never shine upon the stage of the world and be adored. We will never have the comforts of home and family. That is not our function: it is yours. But however much you despise the darkness where our spirits thrive, know that light cannot exist without it. The sun needs the contrast of the night for its shine to have meaning.'

'That is a glib justification,' Valraven said.

Maycarpe gestured with one hand. 'We exist upon a fragile web and our power is tenuous. If the world should wish it, she could flex her bones and turn herself into a hell where nothing could survive. Humanity would be no more than a bitter memory in her mind. In the face of that, our schemes are nothing more than the games of children. If we succeed at anything, it is because we have won one battle, and the battles between men are trivial. Humanity is made up of a mass of trivia, tiny flies upon the web of wyrd. We here are different only in that we understand that to shake the web with desperate wings only summons the spider. We are very still and gently pluck the threads to make changes happen. We are very still. That is all.'

'Your analogy is muddled,' Valraven said coldly. 'Just words. In your stillness, you want power and will do anything to acquire it. *That* is all.'

'You are not a saint now, Valraven,' Maycarpe said. 'What lies within us lies within all men.'

'Where did your scheme begin?' Valraven said. 'Just answer me that. When?'

Maycarpe glanced up at him. 'With Merlan Leckery,' he said. 'Just with words.'

'I don't believe you,' Valraven said. 'I think that if I delved deep enough – shook enough strands of your web – I'd discover you had an influence, however small, on firing Bayard's interest in my heritage. Am I right? Are you man enough to admit it?'

Maycarpe laughed delicately. 'You flatter me,' he said.

Valraven shook his head. 'You are beyond credibility. So many lives ruined and twisted. So much darkness. Are you satisfied now?'

'People act according to their will,' Maycarpe replied. 'I cannot influence that.'

'Your *words*, as you put it, were a slow poison,' Valraven said. 'A drop here, a drop there. You knew how it would spread.'

'If I truly influenced people to that extent, it was because they were stupid,' Maycarpe said. 'Never did I coerce anyone against their will.'

'Without Darris, there would be no Crown of Silence,' Mordryn said. 'There would be no King of Light. Do not judge us, Dragon Heir. You could be dead now and Bayard could be emperor. You cannot wash your hands of blood, no matter how much, in your new piety, you seek to erase the past.'

Valraven drew himself upright. 'You are correct,' he said. 'No one can walk the way of light without casting a shadow.'

'Then may we put aside this bickering and celebrate your victory?' Senefex said.

Valraven sucked in his breath, rubbed a hand through his hair. 'I know I cannot be free of you,' he said, 'because if I cut your throats now,

I have no doubt there would be others who'd slide invisibly into your places. At least I know who and what you are, but it is in my heart to make your path a little difficult. I cannot sit here and smugly toast the murder of the Malagashes. If I acted according to my will, so did they. Now they are all dead, innocent and culpable alike. That is a bitter victory, gentlemen, and I will not permit its celebration. You can haul their bodies out of whatever lime pit you've thrown them into and organise state funerals. The people must be made to see that I will not tolerate war crimes. I know it is not in my best interests to incarcerate or execute your scheming cabal, but at the very least you should pay a hefty fine for your part in the murder of the princes.'

'If they were still alive, your position would never be secure,' Senefex said. 'You know that.'

'I do,' Valraven said shortly, 'but we should begin as we intend to continue. Let the people see mercy and compassion.'

'And hide the cruelty and indifference?' Senefex smiled. 'You can leave that to us, great king. Keep your hands lily-white. But know that there is not a kingdom on earth that can thrive without those undesirable qualities. To think otherwise is to share the dream of the people, who are all asleep.'

Valraven fixed Mordryn with a penetrating stare. 'Did Leonid ever suspect the truth? Was he ever a part of what you were?'

'You are the first king to know,' Mordryn replied. 'Leonid saw what he wanted to see, a world shining with the light of Madragore. He was concerned about what would happen beyond his death, and in his last moments, indicated to me that I should take whatever action was necessary to uphold the empire.'

'Perhaps he did suspect,' Senefex said thoughtfully.

'Did you kill him?' Valraven demanded. 'Or was his doting wife responsible?'

'To the best of our knowledge,' Senefex said, 'Leonid's illness and death were entirely due to natural causes.'

'Yet Tatrini is the only member of the Malagash conspirators not to die,' Valraven said. 'You have spared her, and she was perhaps the most dangerous. That is a puzzle to me. I do not, for one moment, believe you think she is "only a woman".'

'Tatrini was dangerous only through her sons,' Senefex said. 'The people love her, and we will allow them to maintain their illusion. Her back is broken now. She is not a threat.'

'So it seems that you have mercy and compassion after all,' Valraven said dryly.

'Their blood continues through your son, but in a purer form,'

Maycarpe said. 'In some ways, your ascension has immortalised the Malagashes for eternity. Will you not drink to that?'

Mordryn poured out a glass of the ruby liquor and held it out across the desk. 'Drink with us, Valraven.'

Maycarpe watched the Dragon Heir from the corner of his eye. Would he take the cup or not? The act was symbolic and Maycarpe knew Valraven was aware of its significance. Take it, he urged in his mind. If you know what's good for you, take it.

The moment stretched on and then Valraven stepped forward and took the glass. He drained it in one gulp.

'You should savour it,' Mordryn said. 'It is not rough ale to be guzzled. Sip it. Be aware of its many subtle flavours.'

'It is all one to me,' Valraven said. 'I do not wish to be a connoisseur of such things.'

'Perhaps you're afraid you'll acquire a taste for it,' Senefex said.

Valraven smiled bitterly. 'Oh, I know its taste, believe me. It is the tang of the blood that has soaked into every battlefield I've created.'

'No more battlefields for you, my lord,' Maycarpe said softly. 'Be grateful at least for that.'

'There are many forms of battle,' Valraven snapped. 'I will never be complacent.' He put down his glass upon Mordryn's desk. 'I have said all I want to say for now, so I'll leave you to your conversation. No doubt you have much you wish to discuss.'

He turned for the door, then paused. 'Darris, you have proved yourself a man of wits and cunning. I will create a new post for you in Senefex's office, so that you can continue to advise and support me as you have – secretly – in the past. I expect you are delighted to be able to remain with your staunch friends, here in Magrast.'

Maycarpe could not prevent the shock showing on his face. 'Val, I intend to return to Mewt. It is my home.'

'If I remember correctly, you said your position denied you the comforts of a home,' Valraven said. 'You will stay here with me, Darris. It is non-negotiable. Merlan Leckery can take your place as governor of Mewt. It will be a post of only short duration in any case, since Mewt will soon receive her independence. Perhaps Merlan will want to remain there as ambassador.'

Maycarpe's mouth had gone dry, like the sands of a Mewtish desert. He saw his home in Akahana, the shady rooms, the exquisite light. He smelled the incense perfume of the temples, heard the whisper of their magic. A dark fist closed over these beautiful sensations and snatched them away. They were gone. He swallowed with difficulty. 'This is rather more than a fine, Val.'

'If you wish to view it as punishment,' Valraven said, 'then do so. It was not my intention.' He bowed. 'Good day to you, gentlemen.'

Maycarpe watched him leave the room, unable to speak.

Once the door had closed, Mordryn sighed and poured out more liquor. 'He is a fine man, is Palindrake. Sharp as a viper's tooth. He'll keep us on our toes, that's for sure.'

'It's what we wanted,' Senefex said. 'We knew what to expect.' He gestured towards Maycarpe with his glass. 'You have my sympathy, Darris. I know what Mewt means to you.'

Maycarpe shook his head. 'This I did not foresee.' He exhaled slowly and lifted his glass. 'I feel as if I've been beaten to within an inch of my life.'

'I am quite sure our great king will devise similar torments for Senefex and myself,' Mordryn said. 'We must look upon them as part of the price. We always knew there would be something to pay, and if it's only this, then be thankful. We must let Palindrake believe he has the upper hand. I'm sorry, Darris. You have to go along with this.'

'I realise that,' Maycarpe said. He glanced at the door. 'Sweet child. He stamps his foot and we find it endearing. We curb our temper and spare him the rod. What gentle parents we are.'

'We are indeed,' Mordryn said. 'We are indeed.'

Two months later, Darris Maycarpe rode as a state dignitary to the coronation of King Valraven I of Magravandias and Caradore. To public eyes, he was an esteemed and trusted servant of the new king, who had voluntarily sacrificed his life in Mewt to remain in court attendance in Magrast.

How different this day was to Gastern's coronation. The joy of the vast crowds was genuine, without shadow, and as many wept as they smiled. The people could not believe that Valraven Palindrake rode amongst them as king. Some would think they were dreaming, that such an event was not possible in the grim world of reality.

But it was. Valraven rode with Varencienne, his queen-to-be, to the cathedral, Tatrini riding in a carriage just behind with Valraven's children and sisters. Even Tatrini shone for the day, a faded representation of the woman she'd once been, looking a little tired and ill, but lapping up the adoration of the crowds. To the common people she was still an intrinsic part of all the positive changes. They knew little of all that had happened behind the shuttered doors of the palace, but those amongst them who suspected the truth regarded her with a kind of bewildered curiosity.

The Brotherhood of the True King – Shan, Khaster and Tayven – wore ceremonial armour that was far too impractical ever to be taken near a battlefield, but made them look like mythical heroes, astride their high-stepping thoroughbred horses. They rode just behind the first two carriages, Shan bearing a standard with the crest of the Brotherhood, recently designed, emblazoned upon it. Maycarpe had noticed Tayven's family amongst the guests in the palace courtyard and wondered whether Tayven had yet reconciled with them. He was certainly no longer a son to be disowned, even by the hardest patrician heart.

The kings and queens of many countries were present, all radiant in the knowledge that soon the government of their lands would lie once more in their own hands. Queen Neferishu had accosted Maycarpe in the courtyard and berated him for abandoning her. He had smiled tensely, privately gritting his teeth. If she knew the grief in his heart, perhaps she would temper her words, but it was not in Maycarpe to share it with others.

King Alofel was present, along with a rather subdued Princess Helayna, who at least had put her resentment aside enough to attend the coronation. She must be furious she would soon have no reason to hate Valraven Palindrake. Maycarpe smiled to himself. He would spend many pleasant evenings writing up his observations of this day.

At the cathedral, banners fluttered from the high spires bearing representations of all the elemental dragons. In the future, Madragore would be seen simply as an avatar of fire, as all other deities of the world were avatars of the elements. There would be no one god, but only an appreciation of the life force of the universe and its many masks and names. Mordryn's scribes were already composing ceremonies for the new belief system. The archimage would perform them with as much gusto and panache as he'd invested into the rites of Madragore. He was a good performer.

As he took his seat within the cathedral, Maycarpe found himself next to Merlan Leckery and his family. He imagined that Valraven might have had a hand in this seating arrangement and smiled mordantly to himself. Merlan appeared discomforted and nervous, so Maycarpe did nothing to soothe his concerns. He could not help feeling a little hostile towards Merlan, even though he knew it was not Merlan's fault that he had lost his beloved home.

'I'm sorry, Darris,' Merlan whispered, as the crowd around them shuffled along the rows of pews. 'I want you to know I did not suggest to Val that I should take your job.'

Maycarpe raised a hand. 'Think nothing of it, dear boy. You will perform your duties admirably and I can think of no one better to take my place.'

'But . . .'

'I have work here now,' Maycarpe said. 'I always knew that might be a possibility. Please don't concern yourself with it.'

Merlan looked somewhat mollified by Maycarpe's words, but a furrow was still etched between his brows.

When the Dragon Lord and his wife entered the cathedral, musicians lining the upper galleries began to blow a fanfare upon long golden trumpets. A deluge of petals fell down from the high vaults. It was like springtime, the season of birth in a magical world where the air was filled with flowers.

The entire congregation came to their feet. Maycarpe was aware that his eyes had become wet. He had worked so hard for this, risking his life and his sanity, yet he would always be part of the shadows. Not for him the long gracious walk to the altar where the prize of all prizes, the crown of divine kingship, would be placed upon his head. Not for him the joyous tears and laughter of an entire nation. He was one of the spiders on the web of wyrd. He could devour what became enmeshed in his deadly silk, or he could choose to release those bright beautiful dragonflies that were too precious to die. But no one knew that. The people outside today wouldn't look twice at him. To them, he was nothing more than an administrative clerk of the government who, when the coronation party was over, would go home alone to his modest apartment in the palace.

Mordryn's theatrical voice boomed out, echoing from the vaulted ceiling, as he recited the recently rewritten words of the coronation ceremony. Then Sinaclara of Bree appeared from a side chapel, flanked by dozens of priests dressed in ceremonial regalia. She carried a purple velvet pillow and upon it lay the Crown of Silence.

Maycarpe blinked away tears. He had to reach for a handkerchief as Sinaclara walked slowly towards the thrones before the altar, where Valraven and Varencienne sat, unrecognisable in splendid robes, their faces strangely expressionless.

A priest took the pillow from Sinaclara and she lifted the Crown in her hands. She held it high above her head and her strong voice rang out through the cathedral. 'Valraven Palindrake, in the name of all that is true, in the name of enlightenment, honesty and compassion, I crown you with this Crown of Silence as king of Magravandias and Caradore. Walk always upon the Way of Light.'

Valraven did not move. He was like a statue as Sinaclara placed the Crown on his head, but the moment it was done, the congregation erupted with cheers and clapped their hands. It was a cacophony and unprecedented at what would normally be a sombre, serious occasion.

Nothing could contain the relief and pleasure in every heart. Even the most dignified of noble ladies cried out blessings.

Merlan clapped a hand impulsively against Maycarpe's shoulder. 'We did it,' he said, his face shining with a free, unrestrained grin.

Maycarpe's resentment against Merlan evaporated. He remembered the hundreds of nights when they'd sat up late into the night together in Akahana, daring to dream about all that could be. He embraced Merlan. 'We did,' he said.

The bells of Magrast all began to toll and from outside could be heard the maddened cheers of the crowd. Today, everyone would live in a magical world. The streets would run with wine, not blood. Tomorrow, when the forlorn remnants of all the banners and bunting blew along the alleys and people emerged from their homes clutching their heads and regretting the reckless abandon of the previous nights' festivities, life would carry on as it always had. The day of the coronation would be remembered forever, but it was just the blink of an eye, a happy afternoon in the sun.

Valraven and Varencienne were walking down the violet-carpeted aisle now, the queen's left hand through her husband's right elbow. Her hair was a bright golden banner over her breast and down her back, a queen of light to the raven beauty of the new king. But Maycarpe could see beneath their smiles. If he had lost Mewt, then perhaps Valraven and Varencienne had lost Caradore, for they would remain in Magrast as he would. Everyone had had to make sacrifices so that the unimagined could become possible. As Valraven had said a few months before, everyone who walked the way of light cast a shadow.

Still enclosed by milling people within the cathedral, Maycarpe heard the roar of the crowd when the king and queen emerged from its towering doorway. Their guests would now return to the palace for the dancing and feasting that would continue until dawn. Maycarpe considered slinking away to find a quiet place, where he could mull over the events that had led to this point, but then Merlan's mother had grabbed hold of his arm, insisting he should ride with them in their carriage. 'Merlan speaks so *highly* of you, Lord Maycarpe,' she said. 'You *must* tell me what he gets up to in Akahana.'

Maycarpe smiled. Saska Leckery was a handsome creature and he might as well take pleasure in her attention. Life goes on.

'Have you ever visited Caradore?' Saska asked him as they walked to the Leckery carriage. She had linked her arm through his.

'No, but perhaps I should.'

'Absolutely,' Saska said. 'We must arrange something very soon.'

Maycarpe patted her hand. There might be compensations for his losses. If that was to happen for him, then perhaps it would happen for the Palindrakes too. 'Suddenly, the day seems so much brighter!' he said, and Saska laughed delightedly.

This is the Way of Light, Maycarpe thought. Clouds moving across the sun, then the brightness bursts through. He was glad to be alive.

CHAPTER THIRTY-SEVEN

Sea Dragon Queens

Varencienne alighted from her carriage in the driveway before the House of Foy, the retreat that the Sisterhood had set up in the wake of Caradore's independence. Here priestesses of Foy were trained and it functioned also as a hospice and retreat for those who needed sanctuary. Varencienne had come here with her lady-in-waiting, Oltefney, to visit a resident.

The Merante of the establishment came to the door to greet her even before one of the queen's guards could knock upon it. Behind her was a cluster of curious priestesses, whose bright eyes shone in the dim entrance hall.

'Your majesty,' said the Merante, sinking to the floor in a deep curtsey. 'I welcome you to our House with the greatest pleasure.'

'Thank you,' Varencienne said. 'I am glad to be here.' She took off her gloves. 'How is she?'

The Merante rose from her curtsey. 'Very well, your majesty. She seems to think we exist solely for her benefit.'

Varencienne laughed. 'I can believe it. Please take me to her at once.'

The Merante inclined her head. 'Of course. Please come this way.'

Varencienne was taken to a garden at the rear of the house which was still in the process of construction. Landscapers were hard at work on the ornamental ponds, and all the flowerbeds were filled with new plants that had not yet bloomed. On the lawn, a woman sat on a bench beneath an ancient yew; a book lay unopened on her lap. Her eyes were closed and her head was tilted back as if to bathe in the diluted beams of sunlight that came down through the thick branches. She was dappled in light that was like golden coins.

Varencienne approached her softly while Oltefney went back into the house with the Merante.

'Mother,' Varencienne said.

Tatrini opened her eyes and Varencienne saw how the skin had become papery around them. In little under a year, her mother seemed to have aged a decade. 'Ren, how lovely!' Tatrini said. 'I didn't know you were coming.'

Varencienne did not respond to this. She had written to the Merante over a month ago and her impending visit would not have been kept a secret. 'May I sit beside you?'

Tatrini moved along the bench. 'Of course. Are the children with you?'

'No,' said Varencienne, sitting down. 'Rav is in Magrast with his father, and Ellony is visiting Everna. Leo is also in Magrast with his nurse.'

'Leo?' Tatrini said querulously. 'Leo is dead, isn't he?'

'My new baby,' Varencienne said, taking her mother's hand. 'He's very much alive, believe me! He has an extremely healthy set of lungs.'

'He takes after his father?' Tatrini said.

Varencienne sucked in her upper lip for a moment. 'Mmm. I hope so.'

Tatrini made a sound of irritation and glanced towards the house. 'Where are our refreshments? These people are terribly slow, Ren. In Magrast, a tray would have been here by now for a guest.' She frowned. 'I should change the staff, I really should.'

'They're fine,' Varencienne said. 'You've done a wonderful job with them.'

'Now I've retired, I don't have as much energy as I used to,' Tatrini said. 'I am sorry, Ren. I should be with you in Magrast, helping you.'

'You enjoy your retirement,' Varencienne said. 'I envy you.'

'The coronation was lovely, wasn't it? Did you see how the people put their hands together for me?' She laughed. 'They think I'm a goddess! Silly, really.'

'I saw,' Varencienne said. 'Everyone loves you.'

Tatrini nodded, smiling privately. For some moments, she drifted away from reality, perhaps reliving precious memories.

Varencienne's heart turned over. These visits were painful. Every time Tatrini said the same things. She wanted to cry, but knew she must keep the tears inside.

'I thought I saw Almorante the other day,' Tatrini said, 'but it was only a gardener.' She laughed sadly. 'What a mistake to make!'

'Easily done,' said Varencienne. She squeezed her mother's hand and only when she glanced up did she notice Tatrini was weeping. Silent tears poured down her face in a deluge. It was almost unnatural.

'Oh Mother,' Varencienne said. 'Mother, don't.'

'Mother,' said Tatrini leaving the tears unwiped. 'I've always been "Mother", haven't I? Never Mama.' She closed her eyes. 'By Madragore, Ren, I never knew it could happen. Not this, after all these years.'

'What?' Ren murmured. She stroked her mother's hair, which was still gold, though threaded with platinum.

'The *love*,' Tatrini said, her eyes screwed up, shut tight. 'It is terrible. The love for them. Mante, Bay, all of them. I dream about them all the time.'

Varencienne made a sound of distress and put her arms round Tatrini's stiff body. 'I'll ask the sisters to make you up a potion,' she said. 'I'll make sure your sleep is your own, with no dreams to haunt it.'

Tatrini patted Ren's arm, which was pressed hard against her bony chest. 'No, my dear. The dreams are theirs. I can't take them away. It's all they have now.' She gently pushed her daughter from her and took a handkerchief from a pocket of her gown to wipe her face. 'Silly me,' she said. 'I must be getting old.'

'Not you,' said Varencienne.

'So,' Tatrini said. 'Tell me your news. How are things in Magrast? Do you like living there again?'

'I miss Caradore,' Ren said, 'but we go home as often as we can. Pharinet is with us, so I have a little bit of home with me.'

Tatrini raised an eyebrow.

'Mother!' Varencienne said darkly. 'I am perfectly happy.'

'You are a liar,' Tatrini said. 'Your heart is broken. I can see it, but somehow I don't think it's anything to do with your husband.'

'You're wrong.'

'Do you know,' Tatrini said, 'that often when people are taken captive, they come to love their captors? It's when they spend so much time together. They become like family. Have you heard that?'

'I'm quite sure than can happen, yes.'

'You have to be hard, Ren. Women in our position are rarely blessed with love. It can be . . . difficult.'

'Did you never love?' Varencienne asked.

Tatrini laughed. 'I had my share of delights, but love? I don't think so. I never let it happen, because as a queen, even when your husband is far from your heart, he's very close to your body, and jealousy can make a man do terrible things. It's all to do with appearances. I never wanted to lose a love like that. I was allowed certain things, but I knew the limit. Always.' She fixed Varencienne with a stare. 'As you do too, of course.'

'Oh yes,' said Varencienne softly. 'Can I ask you something?'

'You can.'

'Is it possible a woman can kill a man who holds the keys to her life?'

'My dear, what are you suggesting? Does Valraven gall you that much?'

'Not Val. Not me. You. Is it possible?'

Tatrini was silent for a moment, then said, 'People thought I killed him and I have never denied it. I like them to think that. But no, it wasn't possible. At the end, when he was dying, I held his hand and we talked of the past. In those moments, I came the closest to loving him that I ever did. I was glad to be with him. As he closed his eyes for the last time, he smiled. His hand became limp in mine and I knew he went to a better place. He was a good man, your father, despite everything. There are far worse.'

'Thank you,' Varencienne said.

'I never *knew*,' Tatrini said. 'That was the strange thing. I thought I was in control, but I wasn't. It was a game, and it wasn't mine.'

'I know,' Varencienne said.

Tatrini made a visible effort to pull herself together. 'Well now, enough of this glum talk. Let's go into the house and find the lazy priestesses. We grow magnificent strawberries in the kitchen garden here. You simply must have some.'

She got to her feet and, for a few moments, Varencienne remained sitting down.

'Come along, Ren,' Tatrini said. 'There's been enough sorrow. I don't want to see that miserable face. You have a new baby and you are a queen of two countries. Now you are about to sample the delights of my kitchen. What more could you ask for?'

Varencienne looked up at her mother and thought about Tatrini's life, how she had been married to a stranger when she was little more than a girl, how she had borne so many children, how all but one of them were now dead. Tatrini had fought against immeasurable odds to create a place for herself in Magrast, and other women had benefited from her efforts. She had closed off her heart at a very young age, because she'd had to.

'I really admire you, Mama,' Varencienne said.

'Tush!' said Tatrini, clearly delighted. 'I am an evil old witch. Anyone will tell you that.'

'That's part of the attraction,' Varencienne said. She stood up and took her mother's arm. 'A certain evil old witch I know awoke the Dragon Heir to his heritage. She was a dreadful creature, who manipulated everyone she knew. She believed in divine kingship, but got a bit muddled about who the divine king was. She was such a meddlesome creature, who created all sorts of trouble, yet strangely enough her

407

actions precipitated the most marvellous changes. She didn't intend that to happen, of course. She just wanted to conjure up demons in the cellar of her house. Have you heard of her?'

'Overrated,' said Tatrini, grinning. 'Don't believe everything you hear.'

Varencienne kissed her mother's cheek and together they walked into the House of Foy.